Shakespeare
Conspiracy of Silence

ISBN: 978-0-578-30476-2

Printed in U.S.A. by Goulet Printery, Barkhamsted, CT

Cover by Michael Corvin

Photo by Chia Messina – New York, NY

Follow the Author on Instagram: @raf_lindia
www.raflindia.com

"I learn in this letter that Don Pedro of Aragon comes this
night to Messina . . .
He hath an uncle here in Messina will be very much glad of
it."
—*Much Ado About Nothing*

4

Chapter 1

When Michelangelo arrived at the door of the sacristy, Father Franco was engrossed in counting the hosts left over after the last mass.

"Did you call for me, Father?" the well-mannered boy asked, giving the priest a start.

Father Franco spun around, his expression harried. "Yes, yes, Michelangelo. Thank you for coming."

Michelangelo knew that tense, contrite expression well. His mentor had something important to tell him. Michelangelo's mother, Signora Guglielma, was a wealthy aristocrat of the city, and despite her dismissive approach to the Catholic Church, she had always let her son maintain his friendship with the old parish priest of the neighboring church. Over the fourteen years he'd been alive, Michelangelo had come to know Father Franco well.

With a soft "Michelangelo, come with me," the priest led the boy out of the sacristy to the now-deserted south aisle of the cathedral.

The church was in semi-darkness; the late afternoon sunlight could hardly penetrate the thick, opaque windows. Not for the first time, Michelangelo was captured by the peace exuding from this majestic, silent place.

Father Franco sat down at the second desk, facing the small altar dedicated to the Black Madonna, and the young man took a seat beside him. "I have some important news," said Franco with an uncharacteristic tremor in his growling voice, "and before the irreversible happens, you must listen to me and do as I tell you."

Michelangelo could tell by the priest's tone that what he had to say would worry him too.

The priest leaned closer, bending his head at an almost prayerful angle to keep his voice from carrying. "You and your family are in grave danger. I have already talked to your mother and she refuses to leave town, but *you* must heed my warning. The Vatican is using hard methods toward Calvin's followers throughout the peninsula, and there is a big risk that you may be . . ."

"Persecuted," Michelangelo offered, seeing that Father Franco found it hard to say that word.

Franco nodded. The aged priest was heavily built and generally stoic. People in the village said that before he'd been called to the service of the Church, he had been a mercenary wrestler. Some even said he had killed many people, but the well-known discretion of the priest left those stories shrouded in the mist of legend.

But he seemed truly fearful now. His hand shook as it clasped Michelangelo's. "Michelangelo, my dear boy, I have made arrangements for you to flee to England, with the help of one of my dearest brothers, who has booked safe passage for you to the port of Sangatte, in France. From there, you will sail to Dover. When you arrive, you will be taken in by a family, former parishioners of mine. They will help you reach London and find accommodation to start a new life."

Fear seized Michelangelo's heart, squeezing it in his chest as he struggled to memorize the details of the plan. His mother would be devastated by his leaving, yet the thought of the journey also thrilled him. His mind raced at the possibility of new inspiration and plots for his beloved diaries and tales. This journey was an adventure that surely, one day, he would commit to ink.

The woman's body lay splayed on the bed. Naked. Cold. Lifeless.

By 10:00 a.m., the forensic team had already recorded every detail of the room—the bed, the body, the bedside tables, the carpet, the folded clothes on the chair under the window. When Detective Carlo Torchia entered the room, the coroner was intently examining the corpse from the foot of the bed.

"What do you think, doctor?" the detective asked.

"A single shot to the forehead, at close range," said the coroner without turning around. He'd recognized Torchia's unmistakable gait when he'd entered. The short, heavy fifty-two-year-old detective had suffered a leg injury a few months prior in a shootout that had claimed the lives of two cops and affronted an entire neighborhood already resentful of the police.

"While she was already lying in the bed?" Torchia asked, sounding perturbed.

"No, sir. The woman was probably standing in front of the bed." The coroner looked at him now. "The shot must have thrown her back on it. And there she remained."

The worry lines spiderwebbing out from the corners of Torchia's eyes deepened. "How can you tell that?"

The coroner pointed at the body. "Can you see?" he said patiently. "Look at her hair—some locks on her face, others on the pillow. This shows that the body fell back on the bed. Moreover, there are no obvious traces of gunpowder on the pillow that might suggest she had been lying down when she was shot."

Torchia circled the bed, placing each step gingerly to avoid disturbing the scene. "What about the estimated time of death?"

"I'm not sure yet, but about ten hours ago, give or take."

"At around midnight, then," Torchia concluded, checking his scratched Rolex. He turned his attention back to the lifeless body. Blond hair, a fair complexion, a pleasant face, and a lithe model's body. "What was the victim's name?"

The coroner moved to the opposite side of the bed. "Based on the documents in her purse, it's Eugenia Massari. From Rome. At the reception desk, they say she rented the apartment three days ago. They don't remember ever having seen her leave during her stay until eight in the evening. And they can't tell us if she received someone after that time."

"Does anyone know what she was doing in Messina?"

The coroner shot him an irritated glance. "That's your job, Detective. Ask your men."

Torchia flinched inwardly; he had hastily asked the coroner a question he should have addressed to his deputy, who was currently interrogating the neighbors. Truth be told, he had much preferred the role of deputy and wished, not for the first time, that things were as they once were, with Marchese in the lead. He offered the coroner a quick apology and added, "I don't like this story at all."

"Why is that?" the coroner asked, though he had already turned his attention back to his work.

Torchia ran his hand through his short graying hair. "My gut tells me this murder does not have a clear and simple motive." He said it more to the body of the young woman than to the coroner.

Deputy Detective Davide Ricci cleared his throat as he strode into the room, and Torchia tore his eyes away from the grim scene. Ricci's disheveled dark hair sharply counterpointed the careful tidiness of his superior's slicked back gray hair.

"Has the doctor finished examining the body?" the deputy asked.

Torchia gave him a scrutinizing look. "Almost. And you? What can you tell me?"

Ricci opened his notebook and, like a TV detective, read from his notes, confirming what the coroner had reported. "The victim is Eugenia Massari. Thirty-nine years old, born in Rome. She had been in Messina for three days and arrived at this apartment on August fourth at precisely ten in the morning. Just a suitcase, only a few belongings, the necessary items for a trip of up to seven days, maybe a vacation. Nobody knew her. No one has seen her enter or leave during these days, and no one has heard anything unusual. Like a ghost, sir."

"What about her relatives?" Torchia pressed. "Has anyone heard from them? About why she was in Messina?"

Ricci's grimace told Torchia it couldn't be anything good. "We've only been able to locate her sister. As far as she knew, Eugenia left work three days ago, without communicating her destination."

"What kind of work?"

"She worked in a municipal library in the Capitol," the deputy replied. "But her colleagues said that six days ago she had taken a week off for a vacation. Nothing else."

Torchia turned half-lidded eyes to the floor. "I figured it wouldn't be an easy case." Little had been easy for him since Marchese had taken his leave of the police force.

The detective moved around the bed once again in thoughtful silence, while the forensic team prepared the body for transport to the morgue.

"Let's briefly summarize, Ricci," said Torchia at last. As the detective spoke, Ricci scribbled in his notebook like a dutiful university student. "The woman tells the family she is leaving for work, without saying where she is going. At work, she tells them she is taking off for a week just three days before her arrival in Messina. Is there any trace—airline tickets or anything else—that can tell us if she went somewhere else before getting here?"

"No, sir," said Ricci reluctantly. "And surprisingly she didn't have a cell phone, so we can't even analyze cell towers."

Torchia frowned. "Any friends or a boyfriend or someone who knew her well? Someone she talked to about it?"

"We're working on it," Ricci assured him. "But I can tell you that she hasn't had a boyfriend in the past three years. That's what her sister told us."

The conversation stalled as the victim's body was gingerly placed in a body bag and taken away on a gurney.

"How is it possible that nobody knows more?" Torchia demanded.

"We're working on it, sir."

Torchia paced around the now empty bed. Only a spot of blood on the pillow and some long strands of blond hair hinted at the grim display that had occupied the bed minutes before. "She leaves from Rome, telling fibs to her relatives and at work, then arrives in Messina. Alone. She locks herself in this studio apartment, and after three days, someone kills her. And how were we informed about it?"

"The cleaning service. They come in once every three days to clean the residence."

"Every three days," Torchia repeated. "So we have no other clues that can help us understand and track her movements. Any cameras in the residence?"

Ricci shook his head.

"I could have guessed that, too."

"What do you mean, sir?" the deputy asked with a frown.

"I mean this murder was planned in detail."

Ricci's eyes widened. "How do you know for certain?"

"When the murderer entered this place, he was certain not to leave a trace. Not to be seen or noted. Maybe they were having an affair. Probably she was already naked when he arrived, as her clothes were purposely folded on the chair. Nobody does that in the heat of the moment."

Torchia paced around the room, stopping only to reflect upon his preliminary theory before summarizing it for his deputy. "It is clear that she had a different idea than her killer had. The murder must have been swift. He came in. She was already undressed and led him to the bed. He pulled out the gun, shot her, probably with a silencer, then left."

"But why?" Ricci replied, looking mildly flustered. "Why kill her . . . without, um, taking advantage of the situation?"

Torchia stopped at the foot of the bed, fixing his gaze on the area where the body had been. "I don't know, Ricci. Yet. I believe this was a premeditated, well-organized murder—not a crime of passion. The killer was no imbecile and knew the same was true of his victim. This was cold-blooded and accurate. Everything done cleanly. This behavior is not typical of a jealous lover. And there's not so much as a bullet casing or a trace of gunpowder. I'll bet a search won't uncover any fingerprints either."

Torchia scanned the room, noting the numbered placards that marked the position of evidence—very few numbers marking very few objects. The forensic agents had found little. All was in order. The suitcase was intact, and a book on the bedside table suggested the victim had been reading. Other than a toothbrush and toothpaste, the bathroom was almost immaculate.

Little blood. Just one shot, straight to the forehead. Torchia knew it was too early to draw a cut-and-dried conclusion. Something new from the investigation could still emerge. Still, he felt almost certain this wasn't a run-of-the-mill murder. This was Messina after all, where people kill for drugs, theft, revenge, the mafia, or passion. And almost always, those crime scenes were full of clues. Which made the case he was now facing an anomaly.

None of the victim's acquaintances had known where she was —except one. It was clear that she and her killer had been acquainted. It was clear that something tender or sexual had existed between them, or perhaps she'd wished to establish such a relationship during that meeting. And it was clear that the mystery of her departure had something to do with her death, a secret that, if kept to herself, would make it difficult —if not impossible—to find her killer. And as his luck would have it, finding her killer was his god-awful job.

His deputy looked at him expectantly, but Torchia only raised a hand in farewell. "See you at the police station . . . try to bring something, *anything,* we can use with you."

MORTELLE BEACH (MESSINA)

Shortly before noon, Francesco Marchese tossed a last pair of socks into his suitcase.

As he turned to close the dresser drawer, he caught sight of his own reflection in the mirror above it. Somber green eyes gazed back at him, recent worry lines creasing the space between his dark brows, his black hair uncharacteristically unkempt over an otherwise clean face. Forty-one years old, he had taken an open-ended leave of absence from the department and handed his position over to his reluctant deputy, ten years his senior, nearly two years prior. After those nightmarish days spent chasing after his girlfriend's murderer, he had chosen to live in relative isolation in a small cottage by the sea of Mortelle, just outside Messina.

But he needed a break from his seclusion.

He had just zipped up his suitcase and toted it into the kitchen when the doorbell rang.

"Who's there?!" he shouted.

"Torchia," a muffled voice replied. "You there?"

Marchese cracked a smile and then sighed as he crossed the room to open the door. "Would you believe me if I told you I'm not home?"

Torchia stepped in, no invitation needed. "Are you leaving?"

"You're becoming a real detective," Marchese groused, leading Torchia through the house to the back porch overlooking the beach. "If you're referring to my suitcase, yes. I'm going to take a short trip. Just for a few days."

Torchia rubbed his injured knee as he took a seat in a wicker armchair and gazed out over the sea. The exquisite Aeolian Islands were visible on the horizon.

"To what do I owe the honor of this visit?" Marchese asked.

Torchia sagged in his chair. "Damn, Francesco, I'm tired. I'm tired of this job. The station hasn't been the same since you left. I was actually happy as your deputy. But now, the responsibility of dealing with all this shit—dead people, thieves, mobsters—has worn me out. But what's tiring me the most is this State. I'm fed up with them using us as a shield and thwarting us at every turn."

Marchese took a seat in the armchair next to his friend. For a long moment, they both stared silently out over the water.

"Do you want a beer?" Marchese finally asked.

The detective sighed. "Yeah, why not."

Marchese made quick work of retrieving two ice-cold bottles of Peroni from the kitchen. "So, you mean to tell me you want to give up?" he asked upon his return. He handed his guest one of the bottles before sitting back down and sipping from his own.

"I guess so," Torchia said wearily. "This morning I got a new case."

"What's it about?"

"Murder," Torchia said flatly, his eyes still gazing out to sea. "A Roman woman found dead. A single gunshot to the forehead. No clues at all. A perfect crime."

Marchese nodded. "What are you thinking?"

Torchia sighed and examined his bottle as if the answer could be found there. "I don't know. I'm sure it's not a crime of passion. Several details make me think it's something more complicated."

Marchese emptied half his bottle. "Tell me more."

Torchia placed his own bottle on the small table between him and his former superior. "No sign of a break-in or a struggle. The woman was naked. She was probably standing at the foot of the bed. A single shot was fired to her forehead at close range. The apartment was fully intact with no trace of the murderer."

"It would seem to be a perfect crime," Marchese offered ruefully.

"Maybe a professional killer," the detective muttered. "Who probably knew his victim well."

The men fell silent for several minutes, staring out at the scenery.

"Where are you going on holiday?" Torchia asked at last.

"To the mountains, in Calabria," Marchese replied. "For a bit of fresh air."

Torchia gave him sympathetic nod, indicating that he understood his friend's particular demons. Moments later, he rose and stretched. "Okay, I've put it off long enough. They're likely all at the station waiting on me for the briefing."

Marchese stood as well, and Torchia added, "Hey, if I need some advice, can I call on you?"

"No," Marchese replied, eliciting a raised eyebrow from his friend. "Don't count on me."

Torchia gave him a tired, pleading look, and Marchese gave in. "I'll think about your case, and if something occurs to me, I'll let you know."

Marchese saw Torchia to the door, worried for the detective's future. His friend clearly hated his job. Almost as much as he had hated it. Or maybe it wasn't the job he hated. Maybe it was that he had a hard time reconciling what the job had become with what he had hoped it would be when he joined the force. When he'd joined the police department, he'd never imagined he'd find himself here, well before retirement age, living on little more than beer and bitter memories in an empty house overlooking the sea . . . a sea he was sick of staring at.

Marchese packed a few more items in his backpack, and within an hour, he left the beach house behind. The case Torchia had told him about swirled in his head unbidden. A woman, naked, in a bedroom, with a bullet in her forehead. Nothing else. It could be a premeditated murder. But why? What was she doing away from home, in secret? These thoughts preoccupied Marchese on the drive to the ferry that would take him to the other side of the Strait of Messina to Calabria.

Chapter 2

MESSINA

When Torchia arrived at the station at 12:35 p.m., as expected, he found the team waiting for him—the coroner,

Deputy Ricci, an officer from the forensics department, and another from digital investigations.

"Are we all here?"

"Yes, sir," Ricci answered for all.

"So, what do we know?"

Ricci stood up and, holding his notebook, got close to the digital screen showing the photos of the crime scene. He summarized the late Eugenia Massari's details again and reminded the gathering they had no witnesses. Everybody nodded at each step of Ricci's summary.

"The killer used a small-caliber weapon," Ricci went on. "We are waiting for the bullet extracted from the victim's skull to be analyzed. We determined she was not sexually violated. We do not have witnesses. Her family didn't know about her trip or her destination, nor did her colleagues or superiors whom she had left two days prior."

The scrolling onscreen gallery stopped on a panoramic view of the crime scene.

"In the last two hours, we have begun to investigate on several fronts," Ricci said, gesturing to the screen as he spoke. "First of all, the laptop we found in her suitcase is being examined by IT experts, but it will take time to get answers. We've begun to check cameras, both in Rome and in Messina, to verify her movements. We're checking the phone records from her house and workplace. The autopsy is not yet complete, but we believe it will reveal nothing new. We can only say that she had some snacks for dinner, perhaps taken from the hotel vending machine. We are at a standstill. But there is a murderer. If he or she made mistakes, hopefully they will surface, but for now, we are shooting in the dark."

"What about the woman's past?" Torchia asked wearily.

"We're investigating," Ricci replied. "Her family says she'd always had her head on straight. She'd had a few relationships with some colleagues at work, but nothing serious. She lived alone. She'd had no particular vices or hobbies. Our colleagues in Rome are about to inspect her home. We will soon know if any details from there could be useful."

Ricci returned to his seat. After a few moments, Torchia stood up. It was time to organize the investigation. As he approached the screen, he wondered if Ricci had overlooked anything. Nothing came to mind.

"So, it's fairly obvious that we are facing a premeditated murder," Torchia began. "We're not dealing with a jealous boyfriend who killed in a fit of rage. We have a single shot. No struggle. No mess. Nothing. You all know very well that killers *always* leave some clues. In this case, the killer seems to have been especially careful. The perpetrator here is no rookie."

The phone on the credenza began ringing, and Torchia nodded at Ricci to take the call. The deputy listened intently for a moment, and then his eyes went wide and his notebook clattered to the floor. "When?"

The team members came to full alert.

"OK. We're coming." Ricci hung up. "There's been another murder," he informed the rest.

Torchia scowled. "Where?"

"In the Falcata area," said Ricci, sounding dazed. "Near the gates of the State Railway Ferries. A woman's body . . . at the wheel of a car parked on the side of a quiet road. The agents of the nearby Harbormaster's Office found her."

"Did they tell you anything else?" Torchia asked as he crossed the room and picked up the fallen notebook, his gait more unsteady than usual.

Ricci nodded. "It seems she was killed by a single shot in the head."

Any doubts about the first murder that had nagged at Torchia were immediately replaced by a sure and sinking feeling: a serial killer. Within minutes, Torchia and his team were headed to the scene of the second crime.

MESSINA—AUGUST 7, 1943

Bishop Casale knelt alone in the chapel, his rosary beads clacking softly through his thin fingers. The Americans had just warned an invasion and the bombings of the town would start again, just a month after the last wave of violence had swept Messina. It was expected this time that the damage would be worse than before.

And that meant more victims. More dead bodies, military and civilian, littering the streets until they were collected and given a worthy burial.

Traumatized by what he had seen during these last years of this terrible war, the bishop supplicated bitterly at the feet of the statue of the Madonna.

The heaviness of his prayers resounded in his mind, but his thoughts drifted to all the souls snatched away by the war—this hateful war that was nothing less than the symbol of Satan on earth. He offered up those souls to God, those souls that had been and would continue to be sacrificed for who knew how long.

Casale had been appointed bishop at the start of the war, and for five years he had tried, in every possible way, to help relieve the people from the suffering and hunger the fighting had caused. He had organized food distribution for those in greatest need and designated an area in the church for medical treatment. But too many people needed to be treated, and it was impossible to help them all.

Casale's fatigue was catching up with him; he was getting old and his health was failing as well. He prayed for the physical strength and fortitude that bearing this burden would again require.

At the door of the chapel, his secretary appeared—the trusted Father Gabriele. "Your Excellency, you'd better eat something."

Casale barely raised his head from the altar. "At the moment, dear Gabriele, my body is simply hungry for forgiveness and mercy."

There was pain in Gabriele's voice. "Your Excellency, you are doing everything possible for your Church. And the Lord will help us heal the wounds inflicted by the Devil."

The altar stone scraped Casale's brow as he shook his head. "This time, the rage of man will be horrific. Messina will have to face appalling suffering. And we will be devastated once again."

"We can count on the omnipotence of God," said Gabriele, a resolute certainty in his tone that Casale had felt slipping away from his own heart in the past few years.

"You're always right, Gabriele." Casale stood up with difficulty from his kneeler. "I'm grateful for your support. One day, you will be a fair and honest bishop who will guide this Church toward vigor and prosperity."

"Thank you, Your Excellency," Gabriele said, sounding humbly gratified.

"Now, however, I must ask you for yet another sacrifice. A delicate issue. Something I've put off for a long time, but now, given the danger we're facing, we can no longer delay."

Casale walked past Father Gabriele and headed to the ancient sacristy of the Cathedral. He could feel Father Gabriele's disquiet as the younger man followed.

"There is something," said Casale, "that must be safeguarded as, if it remains here, there is a risk that it may fall into the wrong hands. Handed down by all the bishops of this diocese, there is one thing that has always been safeguarded over the centuries. And that every bishop, obeying this tradition, has preserved."

"Are you talking about a relic, Your Excellency?"

Casale turned to his secretary with a cold, heavy stare. "It's not a relic, dear Gabriele. But a secret. A secret that the Holy Church has decided it must keep forever."

Gabriele still did not understand; Casale himself had not understood at first. But by Gabriele's deepening scowl, Casale knew the Father already recognized the importance of what Casale would reveal. The secrets of the Church, the most important ones, were usually kept in Rome. In the Vatican Grottoes. Where no one had access. Inside, it was said, lay secrets that could shake the Faith—secrets that could destroy the Catholic Church itself.

"What is it then, Your Excellency?"

As they reached the sacristy, Casale approached a small, carved wooden niche, a simple ornament to the unaware. He slid off the crucifix he wore around his neck and inserted it into a small hollow in the wood, and the frame opened. Inside, hidden by the ornaments of the sacristy, was a secret casket. He could feel Gabriele's eyes following him.

"It's an old box," Casale breathed, feeling the invisible weight of old ritual on his shoulders. "Which keeps an ancient secret. A secret kept over hundreds of years, entrusted to the Bishops of this church. One after another. With the burden of that responsibility."

"Why, Your Excellency," asked Gabriele slowly, "is this secret, this little box, kept here and not among the Vatican treasures?"

Casale placed the small wooden box on a shelf in the sacristy. "It seems, dear Gabriele, that this box contains one of the most important secrets of Messina. Originally, this small casket only held significance for its owner, but time has changed that significance, and now its contents could shock the world. And so it has remained hidden here."

Casale opened the small dusty box and observed it for a moment with the eyes of one who had already seen it several times. Then he moved it to show the contents to Father Gabriele.

The stern face of the young parish priest filled with disbelief and amazement. "But . . ." That was all Father Gabriele managed to utter. Casale knew what he was thinking, for he'd had the same thought many years before: All those years at the service of his Bishop, without knowing.

MESSINA—AUGUST 7, 2012

When Torchia and his team arrived at the crime scene at 2:00 p.m., a group of journalists had already begun flocking to take photos. The car, a brand-new black Mini Cooper, stood parked on the left side of the road next to the dock. The forensic team, which had arrived only a few minutes earlier, was just getting started.

One of the sailors from the Harbormaster's Office approached Torchia and welcomed him with a salute. "I'm Lieutenant Nicotra, the one who found the body."

Torchia headed to the open door of the Mini Cooper with the lieutenant hurrying at his heels. "What can you tell me?"

"I had gone out for a walk around noon, as I often do," the young sailor replied, "and arriving near the car, I saw the woman with her head bent over the steering wheel. I thought she was sick, so I knocked on the window. But she didn't move. Then I tried the door and found it unlocked. When I saw the blood, I immediately called the police."

Torchia looked at the woman. Brown, curly hair. Young, probably around twenty-five. "Did you notice anything strange before your discovery, Lieutenant?"

The young man seemed to be gathering his thoughts. "No, sir. This is an isolated road. It ends right in front of the entrance to the military area of the Harbormaster's Office. Sometimes, in the evening, couples come here for . . . um, privacy . . . but nothing more. On my way from the barracks to here, I don't think—actually, I'm sure I didn't meet anyone and didn't see any cars pass by."

"Did you hear anything?"

"No, sir. The body has probably been here for many hours."

Torchia pulled on latex gloves and pushed the woman's hair off her brow. What he saw confirmed his expectations: A single shot. To the forehead. At close range.

The same killer. Torchia was sure of it.

"Can anyone tell me about the victim?" Torchia called out as he peeled off his gloves.

Ricci quickly approached his superior. "I'm working on it, sir. At the moment, I can tell you that the victim's name is Barbara Scassi, from Messina. Twenty-six years old. We are contacting her family. I'll know more shortly."

"Find out if there is any connection between the two women," Torchia instructed.

"I'm on it, sir," Ricci replied.

Torchia nodded and stepped away from the crowd of agents around the car. He watched the scene from afar, as Marchese used to do. *To understand, To study the place,* Marchese had told him.

A deserted road, just a few steps from the Harbormaster's Office. A place where couples seeking privacy would hook up. Used condoms and tissue dotted the roadside.

The earlier crime scene was only a few miles away. Who had been murdered first? Eugenia or Barbara? Torchia's gut suggested Eugenia had died first, but he would have to wait for the coroner's report.

CAMIGLIATELLO SILANO
AUGUST 7, 2012

Marchese had been standing at the reception desk of the small hotel filling out the registration form for his 2:30 pm check-in, when the small TV on the counter behind the concierge flashed a breaking news alert. Before Marchese could brace himself, scrolling images of Detective Torchia near a car cordoned off by the forensic team flooded the monitor. "Can you turn up the volume, please?" he asked the receptionist.

"This is the second murder victim found this morning in Messina," the reporter stated. *"Two murders have taken place only a few kilometers apart. It could be the work of the same killer. Possibly a serial killer . . ."*

The reporter continued with the story, but Marchese had heard all he needed to hear. Torchia had been right about the first murder. As reluctant a lead detective as he was, Torchia's instinct had not been wrong. Marchese was impressed. The serial killer theory had yet to be confirmed, but clearly the two murders fit the same profile: a single shot to the head.

With a furrowed brow, Marchese finished his paperwork and retired to his second-floor room. Out his window stood a breathtaking view of the endless expanse of the age-old pines of the Sila mountains, yet he could not divert his thoughts from the Messina murders. This could very well be Torchia's most difficult case since his promotion, and he hoped his friend could handle it, especially since Marchese feared these two murders would not be the last.

He stretched his six-foot-two frame diagonally across the king-sized mattress and reached for the telephone. He dialed Torchia's cell number from memory. "You were right," he said when Torchia picked up.

"Francesco? Where are you calling from?"

"Camigliatello."

Torchia chuckled. "When are you going to start using your cell phone?"

Marchese caught the honk of a car horn on the other end of the line. Torchia was likely driving back to the precinct. "I saw the news."

Torchia sounded weary. "A tough nut to crack. Really tough."

"Is it the work of the same killer?" Marchese asked, though it seemed elementary.

"I need the coroner's report to confirm it, but I'm sure of it," Torchia replied. "Same method, and, I think we'll find, the same weapon, on the same night and with the same lack of evidence left behind."

Marchese frowned. "What's the connection between the two victims?"

"I don't know yet. This one was twenty-six, she was from Messina and studied literature at the university. As to the other, you already know."

"Do you have any leads?"

"None." There was an edge of frustration in Torchia's voice. "None. I'm going back to the station. I'll let you know if anything new comes up. Meanwhile, just enjoy your vacation from your vacation."

"Thanks," Marchese sighed, and despite his earlier claim to be unavailable, added, "If you need me, call me here, at the hotel."

As Marchese hung up, the images of his beloved Renata's death flooded his mind. The terrible scene, indelible in his mind, of his love lying on that couch, cold and lifeless, still burned fresh and clear in his mind despite the time that had passed. He had gone to the mountains to get rid of his ghosts. He'd left his job, his home—everything. Nothing had worked. He had to try to free his mind. But now new thoughts and worries were filling it again, and all he could do was stare, blankly and dry-eyed, at the wall.

MESSINA

The same group from earlier regathered in the same meeting room. Now there were two murders to contend with —most likely connected.

Once again, Torchia yielded the floor to Ricci. The deputy moved in front of the screen. "The second victim's name is Barbara Scassi, twenty-six years old. She lived with her family in Messina and was studying literature at the University of Messina. Her family informed us that she left home at ten o'clock last night without saying where she was going or whom she was going to meet. She was very studious but also liked to have fun—many boyfriends, short relationships, many friends. Among those we have contacted so far, none has been able to tell us anything about last night. She didn't meet any of them and she informed no one about her movements. She had her phone on her, and it appears she had called her ex-boyfriend, with whom she had been in a big fight—this is according to him. But he has more than one alibi for that night."

An ominous feeling of déjà vu hung over the silent group. Torchia felt his skin crawl.

"As far as we know at the moment," Ricci continued, "she was shot in her forehead at close range with a single shot. Small caliber. Potentially the same weapon used for the first murder. No sign of violence, no sign of a struggle. She probably opened the door to her murderer, because the driver's side window was closed and intact. This suggests she knew the killer. We're ninety-nine percent sure that the murder took place right where we found the body."

"Any links with the Roman woman?" Torchia interjected.

"No, sir. Or rather, we haven't found any yet. Their families claim they didn't know each other. Nor did their acquaintances. No apparent connection."

"Hmmm," Torchia mused, "the only connection between the two victims appears to be the killer." And that was the crux of the problem. Torchia knew they'd have to find a link between the victims if they had any hope of solving their murders.

***

As usual, Bar Progresso was crowded. The murders were the topic of the evening. Each patron had their own theory. Each had their own ideas. Everyone had something to say about the incidents. Two murders in a matter of hours in Messina represented an extraordinary case—and it imbued a mounting sense of fear into the town.

In one corner of the bar, a lone man listened silently and with indifference to the various conversations. Young and handsome but grizzled. Thin but muscular. A stranger with an English accent. He sipped his Campari slowly. The bartender tuned the TV over the bar to the local channel. The evening news had just begun and the images mirrored the conversation in the bar.

The stranger stared at the screen.

The television footage showed the entrance to the residence where the first body had been found and the car in which the body of the woman from Messina had been discovered. A journalist reported that the killer of the two women was potentially the same person but that no statements from the police had confirmed this theory. As the report dragged on, the footage cycled again and again, showing the places where the bodies had been found. Reporters rounded out the scenarios with interviews and speculation from commentators. Only the police officers maintained the utmost reserve on the matter and refrained from comment.

The young man reached for the bag that sat on the chair beside him and pulled out a tablet. He turned it on and, settling in with his drink, began to surf the internet.

***

It was nearing midnight. The photos of the crime scenes, the reports drawn up by the forensic team, the medical report, and Ricci's notes lay spread across Torchia's desk. The forensic reports confirmed that the same weapon had been used in both killings. There was no sign of struggle. As Torchia had surmised, the murder discovered first had also been committed first, and the second had occurred at least an hour later. The killer would potentially have had plenty of time to commit the first murder and move to the Falcata area to shoot the second victim.

Torchia now pored over the photos for clues. It was like groping in the dark and finding nothing yet to grab onto—no careless cigarette butt, no stray hair. *Nothing*. Only two small casings from a small-caliber gun that could have come from any one of hundreds of weapons.

The office television drew Torchia's weary attention. On the local media TV channel, the incorrigible journalist Luigi Capra seemed to be at it again. His daily, highly watched talk show about the events and happenings of the city had just begun, and it was no surprise to Torchia that the opportunistic journalist had raised the topic of safety in the city. Torchia had muted the TV a few moments in, but Capra's gestures and attitude conveyed his arrogance. Blue-eyed and fair-haired, Capra's movie-star looks as well as his flair for the dramatic had made him the most recognized journalist in Messina, and his lack of journalistic integrity had put him on Torchia's personal hate list. He'd built a whole separate fiction-writing career on his sensationalistic stories.

Behind Capra, photos of the two women from happy times flashed across the screen. Then came interviews with bereaved family members and friends. At intervals, passersby stopped within the cameras' view, looking for their minute of celebrity. This was Capra, a gossip journalist. A shark in shallow water.

Torchia was exhausted, physically and mentally. He longed for the days when he had still been Marchese's deputy, his number two. He missed his mentor's keen instincts and reserved confidence.

***

Maria took a last look at herself in her bathroom mirror and then glanced at her phone: 11:50 p.m.. It was late. Her meeting was set for midnight at the bar of the harbor station.

Her roommates were all home and in their rooms. She took her backpack and phone and left the apartment on Viale

Garibaldi, electing to walk to the meeting place. Despite the late hour, there were still many people hanging out enjoying the nightlife or walking along the Cortina del Porto in search of relief from the oppressive heat on that August evening.

She looked at her watch again. Midnight. She was late.

She quickened her pace toward the harbor. She had been asked to be there at midnight sharp. She had been waiting for this moment for years. She could not miss it.

So she started running.

She'd dressed for running—gray tracksuit, hair tied back in a ponytail, a T-shirt with the Sicilian Pride logo on her chest, and a backpack on her shoulder. Even if she hadn't been late, anticipation would have made her hurry.

The date had been scheduled weeks ago. Soon, she would have what she had wanted all along. She hadn't slept a full night for weeks; she'd just laid there and thought about this meeting and all it would mean.

She was a student of foreign languages and literature and in top academic standing. Excellent grades, all 30 out of 30, and only her thesis stood between her and finishing her degree. She had never engaged in excesses. But this situation was different—she had entered a vortex and had become gleefully and completely obsessed.

Breathless and panting, she reached the entrance of the harbor station bar at 12:02 a.m. and scanned the crowd, trying to pick out the man she'd come to meet among the people milling around the room. No luck. None of them met his description.

She walked into the bar. Nothing. Her anxiety rose; perhaps he had left. Punctuality, it had been expressed, was imperative. She went back outside to wait exactly where they were supposed to meet. She hoped he was just late. She stopped in front of the docks as she had been instructed and leaned against one of the barriers, facing the door of the bar. Waiting.

She had only been two minutes late. Weeks of anticipation were making her unduly nervous, she reasoned. She took a deep breath to calm herself. He would come. He would give her what had been promised to her. *That's the way it's supposed to be,* she assured herself.

Chapter 3

Torchia's phone vibrated. The detective raised his head from the pillow and recognized the number. He fumbled for the phone. "Torchia here."

"Detective?"

"Who's speaking?" Torchia growled.

"Ricci, sir."

Of course. "Tell me. What's up? Any news?"

A few seconds of silence followed—too many. Torchia knew before Ricci finally spoke what he was going to say.

"Another body was found this morning."

The news settled in Torchia's chest like a lead weight.

"Sir? Are you there?"

Ricci's voice sounded muffled to Torchia's sleep-deprived mind. Though it was 8:00 a.m., he had slept only three hours and was still in that mental haze between waking and sleeping. He pulled himself to sitting position and then rose, the phone still pressed to his ear. "Where are you?"

"The tracks of the State Railways Harbor Station," Ricci replied. "Near the dock where railcars are loaded on to the ferry."

Torchia's pulse quickened. That was right in the center of town, at the port. "I'm on my way."

"Okay, sir," said Ricci uneasily. "But hurry up. The news crews have already arrived."

Torchia stifled an infuriated snarl. "I'm not surprised to hear it."

Within minutes, Torchia drove in pensive silence toward the third crime scene. When he came within a quarter of a mile of the dock, he could see the satellite dishes of the TV vans overhead. Once on foot, he passed the checkpoint into the area cordoned off for the police officers and investigators. As he approached the crime scene, he realized that this spot, seldom frequented at night, had no security cameras. It was one of the critical issues of the infrastructure of that area. Daily from that port, hundreds of railcars were loaded on ferries bound for the mainland and an equal number docked there. At night, the port was still busy, albeit there were longer intervals of quiet.

A woman's body lay between two tracks of the ferry dock. She was dressed in a tracksuit and a T-shirt, the Sicilian pride logo now soaked with blood. Nothing else lay in her vicinity.

Deputy Ricci had not seen him coming as he had been intently watching the coroner examine the victim as Torchia approached. "What do we know, Ricci?"

Ricci walked a few feet from the crime scene and launched into the details. "The victim's name is Maria Cicco, a university student. Born in Catania, but she lived here, in an apartment located on a side street of Viale Garibaldi. Her roommates called the precinct about an hour or so ago, worried about her absence. She had no identification on her, but she matches their description perfectly. She was a student of foreign languages and literature, a senior preparing her thesis. According to her friends, she spent most of her time doing research at the library. She was a quiet girl, living the typical life of a non-resident student."

"How was she killed?" Torchia asked grimly.

Ricci heard the suspicion in his voice and replied, "Not with a firearm. She was stabbed. But that doesn't mean that it's not the same murderer. He, or she, could have decided to use a different weapon to mislead us."

"Or maybe," Torchia countered, though he himself didn't believe it, "it's a different killer."

"Maybe, sir," Ricci conceded. "Maybe someone took advantage of yesterday's bustle to get rid of the victim. Hoping to make us believe that the killer was the one who everyone now calls the Monster of Messina."

Torchia opened his mouth to ask the obvious question, but Ricci cut him off. "No connection, apparently. As far as her friends and relatives know, the victim didn't know the other two women. She did not attend the same faculty as Barbara, had no relationship with Eugenia, and it appears she hadn't been in Rome during the last year. It's hard to know what to say. The coroner's report will tell us more. Apart from the weapon, everything seems to match the dynamics of the other two murders."

Torchia stared at the young woman's body on the tracks. Another life coldly and mercilessly ripped away, a ruthless killing, the reason or logic for which had yet to be determined. Torchia's instinct told him that it was undoubtedly the work of the same killer. He knew the murderer had carefully chosen that place and had been patiently planning these killings and who knows how many others with meticulous premeditation. Everything had been thoughtfully worked out. Each victim had a meeting with the murderer in a place of his or her choosing where he or she knew they would not be seen on camera.

How many more will there be? What am I missing? These questions haunted Torchia as he gazed motionless at the corpse. A sense of uselessness, of futility, rooted him to the spot, unable to move.

"Sir?" Ricci's voice snapped Torchia back to reality. "The journalists are requesting a statement for their reports," he said with a wince. "What do you want to do?"

Torchia glanced up at the crowd of onlookers and journalists leaning against the barriers, trying to catch some glimpse through the policemen watching over the area.

"Let the prefect or the chief of police take care of this," Torchia said shortly. "We have other things to do. Let's head back to the station."

CAMIGLIATELLO

For the first time in a while, Marchese woke up past 7:00 in the morning. In fact, he had slept until 9:00 am. The theory that the mountain air would relax him was proving to be true. He'd had no nightmares.

He actually felt rested—a bizarre sensation rendered even stranger by the fact that his mind had been fixed on the violence in Messina up to the instant he'd fallen asleep. It was becoming harder for him to shake the sensation that he'd left Torchia at the wrong time. Two women dead, killed within hours, maybe minutes, of each other, executed with the cold calculation of the kind of trained killer often written about in crime dramas. There had to be something that linked them together, outside of the dispassionate manner of their deaths. These thoughts had tossed and turned him in his bed, but not for long. He felt almost guilty that they hadn't kept him up all night.

He decided to stay a few more minutes under the cozy sheets. He grabbed the TV remote to flip through the news channels. The first image he saw on the screen was from a special report about the "Monster of Messina." The number of victims had risen to three.

He stiffened and immediately sat up in bed in disbelief. During the night a third body had been found near the

Messina harbor railway station. The footage appearing on the screen recapped the events of the three crimes. A heinous monster was killing in cold blood, again and again.

Marchese's anger rose as he thought about how detrimental the media could be to the work of the investigators and for the psyche of those, like Torchia, who were trying to make headway into a case. He grabbed the phone and dialed up his old deputy.

"Hello, Francesco?" Torchia sounded wrung out. "Did you hear the latest?"

"Yeah. How are you holding up?"

"An impossible case," Torchia responded. The noise of the busy police precinct in the background nearly drowned him out, and then came the sound of a closing door and Torchia's voice came clearer down the line. "And it's getting worse by the hour."

"Haven't you found *anything*?" Marchese asked.

"Nothing. But it's got to be the work of the same person. It's just that, this time, he used a military knife. The blade sliced her throat. No sign of a fight."

Marchese felt his own throat tighten. "Any connections?"

Torchia sounded more frustrated than Marchese had ever heard him. "Not that we've found. But there has to be one. And that's what I'm working on. I'm going to examine the last victim's apartment to see if we can find anything leading us back to the other murders."

"That's a good place to start," Marchese replied.

Torchia's voice sounded calmer when he spoke again. "And you? Are you resting?"

"Yeah. But I'm concerned for you. I know the pressure you'll have on you."

Torchia sighed deeply. "You're right. I've already been called by the prefect, the chief of police, and the mayor. They want the killer. You know how it is. They want 'em *now*."

"I know," Marchese said sympathetically. "I know."

"Thanks for the moral support, Francesco," Torchia said and ended the call.

The note of discomfort in Marchese's former deputy's words still rang in his ear after he hung up. He knew *exactly* how Torchia felt. He knew very well what it was like not to have any useful lead to follow. He wished he could convince himself this wasn't his problem to take on, but he still felt responsible. With nothing else to do, Marchese headed to the shower.

MESSINA

Maria's room was typical of a nonresident student. All in one. Bed, wardrobe, and desk. When Torchia and Ricci entered at 9:45 a.m., they noted that everything had probably been left hastily the night before. Dirty clothes were strewn across the unmade bed, and the bath towel, still damp, hung tossed on a chair. A number of books and a couple of notepads were stacked on the desk. Maria's roommate, her eyes red from crying, gave them the tour.

"Were these all Maria's books?" Torchia spoke to the girl without looking at her, intent on taking in every detail of the room.

"Yes," she replied with a sniffle. "Maria was working on her thesis about the life of Shakespeare."

Ricci began to leaf through the books on the desk and looked at Torchia with a bit of a smile. "You know, sir, some say Shakespeare was actually from Messina, not actually English at all."

Torchia didn't respond. He was focused on combing through old photos, souvenirs of concert and theater tickets, lost in trying to find something useful in Maria's room.

"Her graduation ceremony was supposed to be next month," said the roommate, and she broke down sobbing.

Ricci put down the books he was holding and placed his hand on her shoulder. "We will do our best to find her killer."

In the same instant, Torchia's phone rang. He stepped out into the hallway. "Torchia here."

"This is Officer DeSantis, sir."

Ricci poked his head out into the hallway, and Torchia waved for him to follow as he paced further away from the door to avoid the young woman eavesdropping. "What is it?"

"We've just received a call from the San Paolo district," said DeSantis. "It seems that the superintendent of a building broke down the door of an apartment because the owner had not answered her mother's calls for days, and they found the body of the owner, a woman, in advanced stages of decomposition."

It took Torchia a few seconds to parse out the officer's words. "You're telling me *another* body was found?"

"Yes, sir. Shall we send some agents?"

Torchia swallowed his fury. *That's four, then.* "No, DeSantis. I'm going personally. Ricci is with me. Tell me where."

Ricci looked up as Torchia turned to him, and his face went white. "Another body?" the deputy whispered.

Torchia nodded sharply. "A woman. It seems she's been dead for days. The cause of death is still unknown. The coroner is on his way over there right now. We'd better go, too. I have a bad feeling."

***

A disdainful crowd of onlookers had gathered around the entrance to the apartment building by the time Torchia and Ricci arrived at 11:00 a.m. It was one of those neighborhoods where the presence of law enforcement was unwelcome. Four police officers stood guard at the front door. Their presence baffled Torchia, but the high-ranking military officer who strode out of the building to welcome them immediately clarified the matter.

"Detective Torchia?" At Torchia's nod, the officer offered his hand for a shake. "Sergio Selva, Lieutenant Colonel of the RIS. Could you give me just a few minutes?"

Torchia raised an eyebrow. Selva was a tall, bald man with a strong physique that made him look more like a Special Forces officer than a member of the Italian Forensic Science Department of Messina. "Of course, Lieutenant."

They withdrew behind one of the police cars. Selva wasted no time. "It seems that the case of the Monster of Messina has become of national interest. Especially from an institutional point of view."

Torchia frowned. His agency and Selva's didn't always see eye to eye, so professionalism was imperative, even if Selva had the distinct air of a man used to getting his way. "I don't understand, Lieutenant."

Selva clarified, "The head of the Ministry of the Interior are calling for a collaboration between law enforcement to capture this monster quickly and save lives."

Torchia put his hands in his pockets and bowed his head, as if to think it over. "Do you mean, Lieutenant, that we, as policemen, are supposed to work with the Carabinieri, the Military Police, and who knows who else in the investigation of this hypothetical serial killer?"

Selva seemed taken aback. "Why do you say *hypothetical*?"

"Because to date three bodies have been found—"

"You mean four," Selva corrected.

Torchia bit back a snide reply. "Yes, four. I suppose. But we are not yet sure the killer is the same person. We don't know what is really behind this, and we don't want the media to lead us toward hypotheses that are not yet confirmed, even if our superiors have communicated those hypotheses. We have to let the facts lead us. And, at this point, we don't have proof that it is a single perpetrator or if it's a gang—maybe from Eastern Europe."

Torchia didn't really believe the latter was possible. He knew well—or at least his gut told him—that they were dealing with only one killer. Most likely it was a man, and the motive was not robbery or sexual abuse. But he couldn't bear the thought of a collaboration, imposed from above, on a case that was firmly in his jurisdiction.

Selva raised a placating hand. "Torchia, you were Francesco Marchese's deputy. And it shows. I understand your hesitance and the difficulty in facing interference from above. I feel the same way. But in this moment, we are asked to make an effort. Let's try to be practical, and instead of butting heads, let's try to solve this puzzle. We are talking about human lives, too many in just two days."

Torchia bowed his head again. The lieutenant had a point. It was a huge case. And either way, he also knew these matters were over his head.

Seeing the detective had no further argument left in him, Selva stepped aside and gestured deferentially toward the building entrance. "Shall we go in and see the scene of the fourth crime?"

"Of course."

As they climbed the stairs, Torchia voiced a concern that had been nagging at him. "Lieutenant, what makes you think *this* crime is related to the others?"

Selva cast a frown over his shoulder. "Haven't they told you anything about it?"

A knot of unease rose in Torchia's throat. "No."

As they arrived at the entrance to the cramped apartment, Selva's face grew grim. "Then follow me, and you will understand."

***

Luigi Capra stood behind the barriers that separated journalists and ordinary citizens from the area outside the building, peeking glances into the sideview mirror of his TV van. The cameras weren't on him right now, so he took a moment to twist one of his short chestnut brown curls over the middle of his forehead. He thought the "wayward" curl gave him that rakish look his female viewers found irresistible. He smirked at himself with full pink lips and winked. Even while he did this, he kept an eye on Torchia and the lieutenant as they met and presumably discussed the newest murder. He watched them disappear into the building, wishing he could be a fly on the wall.

He missed the time when Marchese had been in charge of investigations. Marchese had had an unassuming way about him, a lack of puffed-up ego that made the TV viewers trust him. Ratings had always gone up when Marchese was involved. Marchese had been particularly loved by the people of Messina. When Mayor Caruso's wife had been tragically murdered, Marchese had been the one to track the killer down. Marchese had a mysterious and magic aura around him. Sometimes that aura had worked in his favor, other times less so.

Torchia was another matter entirely. Watching the scene in front of him, Capra realized with little enthusiasm that the media coverage was really going to be a circus.

This case should have been a massive ratings boost. A serial killer, four murders in twenty-four hours, all apparently unconnected. This detail made the news even more interesting. The facts were malleable for journalistic purposes and left ample room for colorful interpretation.

National and international journalists already crowded the barriers like flies, ready to make their report for Quarto Grado, Quinta Colonna, Porta a Porta, and various TV programs from elsewhere in Europe and beyond. Messina was living through one of its worst moments, and this horrific atmosphere was exposed by the media for all to see. And Capra planned to take full advantage of it.

***

The victim had been there for more than two days; Torchia knew by the stench of death and decay that hit him the instant he limped across the threshold. The apartment comprised a kitchen, bathroom, and bedroom, all squeezed in a cramped forty square meters and overlooking the gloomy condominium complex. Followed by Lieutenant Selva, Torchia made his way among the dozen or so agents, Carabinieri, and coroners and headed toward the bedroom where a scene much more gruesome than the previous three awaited.

In the middle of the room, on a bare and dirty bed, lay the rotting body of a woman, her pajamaed legs dangling off one side of the bed. A single bullet hole pierced her forehead.

Around the bed, pages of notes scattered the room like dead leaves.

"What did she do for living?" Torchia asked the lieutenant.

"She was a theater director," Selva replied.

"And are these notes hers?"

"We think so, sir."

Ricci came rushing in, grimacing at the stench as he entered and covering his mouth and nose with a handkerchief. From his labored breath, it was clear he had run up the stairs.

Torchia greeted him with a nod. "Ricci, what did you learn?"

The young deputy hesitated. He obviously had something delicate to communicate. Torchia left Selva and followed Ricci to the landing. Police and Carabinieri were shuttling up and down the stairs, so Torchia took Ricci by the elbow and steered him to a corner out of the flow of traffic.

"Tell me everything."

Still breathless, the deputy responded, "The woman's name was Alessandra Catona, thirty-eight years old. She worked as a theater director for various companies performing at the Sala Laudamo in Messina."

"Lieutenant Selva already told me as much."

"She had a boyfriend," Ricci went on, bracing his hands on his knees. "They are taking him to the station right now. We'll be able to question him soon. His name is Vittorio Vetro."

Torchia heaved a sigh, wrinkling his nose at the stench that had already made its way to the landing. "So, that's it?"

Ricci's face darkened. "No, sir. It seems that the victim and her boyfriend had a violent fight three days ago and he left the apartment screaming and threatening to kill her."

"That means everything and nothing," Torchia huffed.

"In what sense, sir?" asked Ricci, frowning.

"If we follow our theory," Torchia answered patiently, "that the victim was murdered by the same person who killed the others, then I can't explain the boyfriend's involvement, unless he is the same one who then killed the others. And given the state of decay, this must have been the first victim."

Ricci seemed satisfied with the answer. "Indeed, sir. The boyfriend could have killed his girlfriend first and then, gripped by exaltation, struck again for some strange reason. And even if there were no connections among the victims, perhaps he knew them all."

Torchia raised a skeptical eyebrow. "That's a stretch, isn't it? But we'll know more only after questioning him."

"So, shall we go, then?"

Torchia turned to the front door of the apartment. "You go ahead. Warm him up a little. I'll come when I'm done with the Carabinieri."

CAMIGLIATELLO

Marchese took a noon stroll through the wood just outside the mountain village. He walked for a few miles, admiring the trees, basking in the sounds of birds and the cool breeze that made the leaves rustle. His thoughts wandered everywhere, from his beloved Renata to his former work, to his future, and to Torchia's alarming investigation.

Sooner or later, he would have to make a decision: Rejoin the force or do something else. But what else?

He could only be a cop. At Torchia's suggestion, he had often thought of writing a book, taming his thoughts and getting lost in the pages of a story. It was one of the many ideas he was turning over in his mind. He'd thought about moving away from Messina, maybe getting a small-time police gig in some rural town that had never heard of him. He'd even thought of taking up fishing. But nothing quite gave him the surge of energy that the thought of returning to his job gave him, even with the ache of Renata's death still in his chest.

He came upon a small farmhouse where a family of vacationers was setting up an outdoor picnic. He felt a certain envy in seeing the father play soccer with his son, laughing and joking, while his wife watched them adoringly as she laid out the lunch.

Marchese had missed out on a family. That possibility had been denied him.

He wondered if he would ever have another chance. If he would ever meet a woman who could fill the gaping void left by the loss of his love. He wasn't sure such a person existed. How he'd even found Renata had been a miracle he'd never been able to comprehend, and the chances of someone like her ever entering his life again seemed impossible.

Marchese turned back to return to his hotel to go in search of lunch.

Chapter 4

Messina

Torchia continued his perusal of the apartment while the body was removed and carried out. By half past noon, the RIS team had finished photographing every detail, not disturbing anything as they worked. Lieutenant Selva was giving orders to his men. Out of the lieutenant's hovering attention at last, Torchia noticed a small, torn piece of paper at the foot of the bed. He leaned down, unobserved, and picked it up.

"Michelangelo, I love you so much!"

A short sentence written in pen, probably by the victim, and surrounded by small hearts.

Torchia slipped the piece of paper into his pocket, unnoticed, and left the room.

"Detective!" Selva's voice stopped Torchia just outside the doorway.

"What is it, Lieutenant?"

"We have a joint meeting with the prefect tonight," Selva replied, striding up to the detective, "to review the situation and update each other on our work and findings to date. Through close collaboration, we should be able to get ahead of this killer."

Torchia stifled his irritation. There was no point in worrying about it now; he had the interrogation waiting for him at the police station. "OK, I'll be there."

Torchia ignored the flurry of reporters as he stepped out into the street. As he took his car key out of his pocket to open the door, a microphone shoved its way into his face. Torchia raised a glare and found Luigi Capra on the other end.

"Detective! Tell us something about the status of these murders! Can you confirm we're facing a serial killer? How many more victims will there be?!"

Torchia seethed, but he remained silent, letting Capra finish his questions, and then looked straight into the seedy journalist's eyes. "No comment."

He got into his car, leaving the journalist standing impotently in the road, and peeled out toward the police station. As he drove, he sifted through the puzzle in his mind. The note in his pocket might not mean anything. But Alessandra had a boyfriend named Vittorio. That small piece of paper bore the name of another man. The note might not even be hers. But it might also be a memory of one of her past love affairs. Or maybe that name referred to a current lover. If this last hypothesis was correct, it would be necessary to search for him.

As always, the traffic seemed to conspire against him. It seemed like every last car in Messina had piled out onto the roads at once, even flooding the bus and emergency lanes in flagrant disregard for their function. Torchia wondered with a certain gallows humor how anyone who might call an ambulance or law enforcement at this hour could possibly expect help out of this ridiculous gridlock.

In any one of these cars or on a sidewalk somewhere could be the killer. He could be the mustached gentleman in the Fiat Panda driving alongside Torchia's own Yaris, or perhaps he was the young man with the shoulder bag bustling down the sidewalk. Or maybe the distinguished, elegant gentleman trying to cross the street against the traffic light. Heck, *he* could even be a *she*.

The murderer could be anyone, for all they knew. Which was nothing.

***

When he arrived at the police station, Torchia went directly to the interrogation room. An agent was on guard at the entrance.

"Any news?"

"No, sir," the guard replied. "Deputy Detective Ricci is inside."

"OK, open the door."

Torchia steeled himself and marched in. He sat down right in front of the suspect, who had been sitting there for over an hour, weeping. Torchia's first task was to make it crystal-clear those tears would not deter him.

Ricci stood and moved behind his superior.

"Are you Vittorio Vetro?" Torchia demanded.

The man bowed his head and nodded.

"Answer," said Torchia sharply.

Vittorio risked an upward glance. "Yes, sir. That's me."

"Then, why don't you tell us what happened? So we can get this over with quickly."

Torchia knew he was just wasting time. He was certain that Vittorio was not involved, but he needed something to work with. He hoped the young man would unconsciously offer up something useful.

"I don't know, Detective," Vittorio sniffled. "I do not know. Someone killed my girlfriend. And I don't know why I'm here."

"You are here," Torchia replied briskly, "because we know you had a fight with her just before she was killed. And no one else, as far as we know, saw her after you. And she did not leave her apartment."

Vittorio's face crumpled. "I didn't do it. I loved her!"

Torchia laughed theatrically. "I've heard that at least a hundred times. And in ninety percent of the cases, the killer is the one who says it."

Only then did the man look into Torchia's eyes. "Detective, I swear I didn't do it! Alessandra and I argued over nothing. It was stupid. We took a break from each other because we couldn't stop bickering over nothing."

"Yes, but as you were leaving, you threatened to kill her," Torchia hurled back. "You came back later and maybe you did it."

"No!"

"So where were you that night, then?" Torchia snapped. "Do you have an alibi?"

The young man bowed his head again. "Not really."

"Vittorio," said Ricci gently, "you're in a lot of trouble if you don't tell us something that can convince us you are innocent."

"What do you want me to say?" Vittorio cried.

"Start with the reason you two argued," Ricci replied.

The young man took a deep breath. He looked at Ricci first, then at Torchia. "I went to her place," he said, more softly. "As I often did. And, as often happened, we were eating something on the bed after we had sex. The fight started when she told me she had to work that night and she couldn't go out with me."

"What was her job?" Ricci interjected.

"She wrote plays," Vittorio replied. "But not only that. She was a researcher of old, unknown works that she readapted for the stage. It was a real obsession."

"Did she work alone?" Ricci asked.

"Yeah. She worked at home. Always huddled over a mountain of notes or at the computer. When she wasn't writing, she did research."

Torchia heard Ricci's pen scribbling away. "And how did the argument end?"

"Nothing in particular," Vittorio answered. "We had a heated discussion. We were arguing. I just wanted to get some air, go for a walk. She'd been acting differently for some time now, obsessive about her research."

"What kind of research?" Torchia asked.

"I couldn't tell you. The more she dove into work, the more I lost interest in what she did. It had become the thing that was destroying our relationship."

Torchia reached into his pocket and took out the note, placing it on the white table in front of the young man. "Is this Alessandra's writing?"

Vittorio looked curiously at the slightly torn note. "Yeah. It's hers. But . . . who is Michelangelo?"

"We were hoping you would tell us," said Torchia with scornful derision. "You must know who it is! Haven't you ever suspected that Alessandra could have another guy?"

Vittorio sprang to his feet, beet-red and glaring. "Alessandra had nobody else but me! Don't you even dare think that!"

"Calm down, Vittorio," Ricci said, rounding the table and placing a hand on the man's shoulder, inviting him to sit down again.

"If this Michelangelo is no one, explain the hearts and the phrasing," Torchia pressed. He picked up the note and read it patronizingly slowly. "'Michelangelo, I love you so much.'"

Vittorio looked around as if to search the walls for the answer to a question that was obviously going to haunt him, too.

"So? Vittorio!"

Torchia could see the man's mind racing and knew what he was thinking: Alessandra had not betrayed him. It couldn't be true. There was no Michelangelo at all in her life. How could that be possible?

"I don't know, sir," he said at last, his voice hollow. "That's definitely her handwriting. But I can't explain it. I don't know any Michelangelo, and if he is someone she dated, then I'm even more baffled and confused."

Torchia knew the fellow was telling the truth; he could see it in his gaze. There were things in life that were impossible to lie about.

Dammit.

But then, who was this mysterious Michelangelo? What could he have to do with the death of Alessandra? And, above all, what connection was there between her and the other three victims?

***

Late in the afternoon, in Viale San Martino, a tall man stood admiring a suit in a shop window. It was the embodiment of Italian-tailored elegance, although he usually preferred the style of his motherland. He saw his reflection then and ran his hand through his short reddish-blond hair. Just as he was about to enter the shop door, his phone chimed.

"Hello?"

"It's David Graham."

At the sound of his boss's smooth voice, the man turned and walked away from the shop entrance. "Yes, Mr. Graham."

"I have read that your work is progressing well." Graham sounded almost pleased. "Have you been able to recover all the Origins?"

"Almost, Mr. Graham," said the fellow uneasily. "Two of them are still outstanding."

"And when are you planning to finish?"

The dispassion in Graham's voice was chilling. The man looked around. On a nearby street corner, a couple of policemen were checking the documents of a non-EU citizen.

"Within two days," he said with certainty. "And as soon as I recover the last two Origins, I'll fly back to London."

"I hope you haven't left any traces," said Graham coolly.

Though he bristled at the implication, he kept his voice even. "No, Mr. Graham. Absolutely not."

"Good. We cannot risk that even a single Origin ends up in the wrong hands. Get them, and then get back to London immediately."

The two policemen finished their check and left.

"I will complete the work as ordered. Don't worry."

"I don't doubt it," said Graham almost jovially. "I will see you in London for your full report. Until then, you won't hear from me."

"All right, Mr. Graham."

The call ended without any other pleasantries. The man returned his phone to his pocket and entered the shop.

"I'm looking for a dark suit," he said to the solicitous saleswoman who greeted him.

"Certainly, sir," said the woman brightly. "If you follow me, I'll show you our collection. Are you looking for a particular designer?"

"No. But I wouldn't mind trying something by Dolce & Gabbana."

The well-clad woman led him into the room reserved for men's clothing and began to go through the rack. After carefully scrolling through the options, she produced a dark gray suit. "There we go. This Dolce & Gabbana will fit you perfectly. It is roomy enough to accommodate your muscular physique."

She led her customer to the dressing room, where he disappeared behind the curtain.

CAMIGLIATELLO

Marchese finished his lunch on the hotel terrace. Mushroom risotto and veal shank. The last time he had eaten this well was when his mother, a mountain woman, used to cook for him.

An attractive older woman sitting at the table opposite him had stared at him all through lunch. He'd kept his eyes averted and could still feel her gaze on him as he left the terrace. Renata had often teased him for being oblivious to such inspections, so that he had taken notice of her scrutiny unnerved him; she certainly wasn't subtle. And there was something calculating in that stare, fleeting as his glimpse of it had been, rather than lascivious, which would have been unnerving enough. Every time he glanced her way, Renata's face loomed up in his mind.

When he returned to his room, he stretched out on the bed and dialed Torchia. He knew he should be enjoying his time away, but he felt the pull of the mystery in the air.

"How are you doing?" Marchese asked once he'd reached his friend.

Torchia's voice was harried. "I suppose you heard about the fourth victim."

Marchese's blood ran cold. "Fourth? What? No, I didn't hear anything about it."

"Well, there was a fourth victim, and potentially the same killer. Firearm and a hole in her forehead. No mistakes."

"So, three were shot," Marchese recounted, "and one was stabbed. You sure it's the same killer for all four?"

"It's probable," Torchia said. "He must have changed his choice of weapon for a reason."

"Any clues?"

"One, maybe."

That's good news, Marchese thought. "What about witnesses?"

"Nobody," Torchia replied. "We have just finished questioning the boyfriend of the last victim. This last victim seems to be the first one killed, based on the state of decomposition."

"Did you get anything out of him?"

Torchia sighed. "No. The guy is squeaky-clean. He has no alibi, but I have no doubt. And he has no motives to kill the others."

"Anything else? You said maybe you have a clue."

"Let's say I'm following a lead."

Marchese's ears perked up.

"Small," Torchia clarified immediately. "My instinct tells me what's in my hand is a clue. It's a note. A love note. With the name of a man. Found in the room of the last victim."

Marchese sat up. "Who is he?"

"Don't know. He's called Michelangelo. But we don't have anything else."

Marchese felt his blood heating and his resolve sharpened. Renata, he realized, should have been the last straw for him, but the body count in Messina had risen to four while he'd been dawdling. And the killer was still at large. "I see. I'm heading back to town tomorrow. I'm bored here . . . and maybe I could help you."

Torchia's voice held unconcealed shock and more than a glimmer of hope. "Really, Francesco? Are you coming back? Will you—"

"Hold on there," Marchese cut in, "I'm just coming to *maybe* help you."

***

Mark Connell stepped in front of the mirror for the third time. He raked a hand through his thick blond hair, then tugged the jacket lapels so the garment sat a little straighter on his broad-shouldered, six-foot-four frame, and grimaced. Yet another suit that didn't convince him. He was looking for something really singular. Elegant. The day he would meet with Graham, holding "The Origins," he wanted to be perfect.

He had been given a delicate task, a once-in-a-lifetime opportunity to change history. And the reward he had been promised was mind-boggling. He had been working for months on this operation. And now the day of fruition was coming. It wouldn't do to look like a culchie arsehole when the time came. He discarded the suit and lifted the next one off its hanger.

Only two copies of the Origin remained. Two more copies, and one of the most important secrets in history would be in the hands of one man, David Graham. A man who could have this vision. And he could afford it and thus play a role in history.

This secret would change the world's understanding of literature.

"This will do. I'll take it. And I will also take those two ties."

Connell looked in the mirror one last time before he undressed and handed the suit through the curtain to the saleswoman to have it packed.

"Do you want to see anything else, sir?" she asked as he exited the dressing room in his own clothes.

"No," he replied briskly. "That's fine."

"We have some samples of the autumn collection, if you want," she persisted. "I'll show you a preview of it."

"I said it's okay," he replied sharply. Another reason to wrap up his work and return home. He hated the pushy attitude of everyone in this town.

"Very well," she replied, visibly deflated. "Please come to the sales counter."

He paid, took the package containing his 2,000-Euro Dolce & Gabbana suit, and left the store. He gave her a large tip to make up for his rudeness, and he could tell by her smile that she immediately forgave him. He smirked to himself as he exited the store.

Everything had a price in this world. And he knew it too well. Six lives were a small price to protect one of the most important historical finds in the world.

As he left the shop, he looked at his watch: 3:30.

It was time to get back to work.

The streets were crowded with people walking around the avenues and shops. He liked Messina itself, but he hated the superficiality and chaos typical of the Italians. Cars parked everywhere, crazy drivers honking horns, dirt all over the streets—it reminded him of those Turkish towns he had frequently visited during his paid missions.

His role as mercenary had placed Connell in situations even more delicate than this one. Murders of important politicians committed on behalf of unscrupulous businessmen from London were his most frequently entrusted commissions.

Political murders always had an economic motive. If the interests of large international business groups were hindered by overly loyal activists or politicians, an intervention was required. And Connell was one of the best in this field.

But this was the first time he'd had to kill otherwise innocent people. The first four murders had practically been unnecessary. Without purpose. Four stolen lives, only as a precaution. A price to be paid to avoid future complications.

It was more than half the job completed, and within two days, he would finish his job.

As he arrived in front of his hotel, he checked the time again. It was 4:00 p.m. sharp. He still had five hours left. Enough time to get ready, grab a bite to eat, and arrive in time for that evening's appointment.

***

Torchia leaned back in his desk chair, the monitor of his computer flooded with photos of the most recent crime scene. He'd put Ricci to the task of finding Michelangelo, but his optimism was low.

Not even a small clue. The body analysis had led nowhere. Not even one hair had been found. All very clean. A professional job.

There was still no connection among them. And Torchia's agitation was mounting.

His gut told him that none of this was over. There *would be* other victims. And the lack of connection made it impossible to predict who would be targeted next. The only link that seemed to bind these women was their quick and certain death.

Ricci arrived, out of breath and running as always, waving his inseparable notebook. "I'm here!"

Torchia raised his head from the monitor, hoping for good news. "Anything?"

Ricci's shoulders slumped. "Nothing. I questioned the victims' friends. No one remembers anyone having a relationship with a man named Michelangelo. Nobody can tell us anything useful. None of them can confirm or deny that the victims knew each other."

"I figured. And I'm afraid that this Michelangelo will lead to nothing. Even if my instinct tells me the name means something."

"What are you going to do?"

Torchia rolled his eyes. "I'll be going to my infuriating meeting with the prefect and the chief of police—empty handed. Let's see if the Carabinieri have found anything more concrete than we have."

"There's no way," Ricci scoffed.

Torchia looked at his deputy reproachfully, but he inwardly agreed with him. They were the best. The police of Messina were the pride of the city. They always solved the cases before anybody else. But this time, Torchia knew he was facing perhaps his biggest and greatest test of his career. And, truthfully, he didn't feel completely up to the task. Fortunately, Marchese was on his way.

* * *

The prefect's office was crowded with NCOs and men in uniform. As he came in, Torchia realized he was the last of the group to arrive.

The prefect gave him a disapproving glance. "Detective. Please, take a seat. We've been waiting for you."

The prefect, like many others, still missed Marchese. And Torchia knew this. Marchese's charisma was too memorable. It was impossible for anyone, even Torchia, to replace him.

Marchese's quiet but commanding edge and his courage, genius, and self-sacrifice had made him a legend.

Now, however, a cunning killer had to be found. And they were all on it—the Carabinieri, RIS and the Special Branch, the chief of police, and the prefect. All had gathered to coordinate the search.

The prefect chewed nervously on his lower lip. Torchia suppressed a smirk; the prefect obviously had politicians breathing down his neck. "Can anyone share something new about the case?" When no one spoke up immediately, he turned with visible reluctance to Torchia. "Detective, you were the first on the case, and you've been at all the crime scenes. What can you tell us?"

Torchia cleared his throat, as if he had been caught by his teacher drawing circles on his desk. "That's true, sir, we found the first three bodies. Several aspects make us believe the same person has committed the murders. It is also true that nothing else new can be added to what you have read in our reports. Four victims and no apparent connection among them. No clue, no trace, no interesting piece of physical evidence to be chemically examined, nor something to look for in our databases. Nothing."

Torchia stopped just to catch his breath. Every eye in the room was fixed on him.

"This leads us to believe that these crimes are the job of an experienced, professional killer. I think it's something very sophisticated. We should expand our search, beyond our region. The victim who arrived from Rome widens the scope and makes me think that this is something beyond Messina. Something that could cross not only the Sicilian canal, but also the Italian borders."

Hearing these last words, the prefect cocked his head and stared at him. The rest of the gathering looked shocked.

"Detective." There was no respect in the prefect's voice now. "Am I to believe that you want to sell the story of a psychopath who kills women, maybe simply at random, as an international intrigue? Be careful with your statements, or we risk having INTERPOL knocking at our door. Your judgment is misguided, and if your statements leak, they could create alarmism and unpleasant consequences for all those who are working on this case. We have image problems enough without such histrionics."

Torchia felt as if the prefect had slapped him across the face, and fury bubbled up in his gut even as humiliation made him want to sink into the floor, if only to escape the gazes of servile disapproval that all present were turning on him. The prefect had dressed him down in front of all the heads of law enforcement of the city.

Torchia was furious.

The prefect turned dismissively away. "Lieutenant Selva. And you? Can you tell me something less . . . let's say imaginative?"

Selva crossed his legs, as if he were in a TV studio posing before the cameras. "Let's say, sir, that Detective Torchia's hypothesis of an experienced professional is possible. Examining all the elements, I'd say that we are facing a serial killer. He acts according to a logic unknown to us at the moment, and certainly according to a precise and well-defined plan. If we find the common denominator, we'll be able to outline the profile of the next victim. We could also search our databases to analyze murders committed by serial killers with similar characteristics and maybe get a clearer picture of the man we're dealing with."

He sounds like a TV crime psychologist, Torchia thought bitterly.

"This kind of approach," Selva continued, "has gotten results in other cities all over the world and it is worth trying. Furthermore, given the lack of available evidence collected by the police first, and by us in this latest case, we have little material to go on with this investigation."

The prefect's mouth puckered in a peevish frown. "So, what do you suggest?"

Selva's gaze darted fleetingly to Torchia, and the detective swore he saw a sudden and malicious triumph in the lieutenant's eye. "Unfortunately, although it may seem heinous, I think we should wait for his next move. In the meantime, we should investigate deeper into the lives of the targets chosen by the murderer."

The prefect looked stunned, and then he pressed thumb and forefinger into the corners of his eyes as if to rub away a headache. "You're telling me you think we should wait for this maniac to claim other victims?"

No one spoke. Torchia's silent seething had given way to crawling anxiety. He tucked his hand in his pocket and felt the note he'd taken from Alessandra's apartment crinkle between his fingers.

The prefect's tone of voice rose in anger. "I urge you all, in close collaboration, bring me this bloody maniac as soon as possible! I don't want more victims in this city! I want grid searches, interceptions—every resource and effort to find this murderer!"

The meeting ended without any great illumination as to a direction to take to find the killer. Torchia returned to the precinct and stalked to his desk, his mind fixed on the crime scene photos, the reports, the interrogation with Alessandra's boyfriend—and on Michelangelo and the note and name he had not mentioned during the meeting. If he'd understood Selva's look correctly, the lieutenant was more concerned with one-upping the police than he was with stopping the killings, and Torchia refused to sit back and wait for the killer to strike again.

He hoped Marchese would see this all differently somehow. But Torchia had to admit to himself that not even his former superior could perform miracles without a precise lead to follow. He knew it was going to be another sleepless night.

Chapter 5

Father Franco's letter opener broke the waxen seal that held the letter shut. It was from Michelangelo and dated more than two months earlier, having come all the way from Verona. The parish priest heaved a sigh of relief that the boy was now away from the danger of the Vatican's influence.

The first part of the letter told of Michelangelo's passing through Rome, his sojourn to Milan, and then his longer stay in Verona.

Verona is an enchanting city. It makes me forget the loss of my home by the sea, the waves and the spectacle of the Strait of Messina. I am staying at the home of some merchants, living in a room above a horse stable. I spend my evenings writing and often composing letters for you and my beloved mother. From my window, I can see the stars.

Father Franco smiled as Michelangelo's words turned to something unexpected.

Out the opposite window of my room, I see a dwelling where a girl named Giulia lives with her family. Her beauty enchants me, and I spend the nights watching her through that small portal. It is then in my imagination that I feel close to her. My hosting family and hers are not on good terms. And an ancient hatred exists between them. My host family has urged me not even to look at any member of that family. It is frustrating to see her and not have the chance to hear her voice, look her in the eye, or see the shape of her face when she smiles.

She looks like a sad girl. She lives a reclusive life, as if in a fortified castle and I, her knight, am forced to look at her without being able to give her freedom.

I'm leaving for England in a few days, and this regret will dwell in my heart forever.

The sentiment in young Michelangelo's words smote Father Franco, but moving on, he knew, would be the safest course for the boy. He felt heartened to know his young friend was safe.

MESSINA—AUGUST 8, 2012

At 7:00 p.m., Marchese maneuvered to exit the ferry by car. The ship was full of tourists and the air was muggy. He regretted having to leave Camigliatello, but only because the weather in the mountains was markedly cooler there. Staring at the mountains for days had never soothed his mind, which needed always to be busy. The city of the Strait had welcomed him with a temperature approaching 95 degrees Fahrenheit and a humidity rate of over 70 percent.

The traffic was heavy, and it took almost an hour to return to his house in Mortelle. As he drove, he looked around. Messina was a beautiful city, but it could be loved and hated at the same time. The different administrations that had bickered with one another since long before he'd lived there had crushed and impoverished it. Its natural and architectural beauties were a unique heritage, violated by the presence of men who did everything to vilify and degrade it. And sometimes he had the feeling that even the local people, over time, had been brutalized. Messina seemed to be in a downward spiral and even its inhabitants were trapped in the current.

Marchese felt contempt for the system that victimized them. Those who had not bent to the politicians in office in the last twenty years had been abandoned, left to feel useless and wasted. If they had not accepted the crumbs, they had remained hungry. Messina was the reflection of the new social policy.

Marchese wanted to stay out of this trap. He didn't want to get too caught up in matters concerning the State, groping for the sense of belonging and patriotism that had vanished after the last real postwar political battles.

He had seen the State before these changes. Renata had seen it, together with Leo Marino and all those who had fallen, innocent, sucked into the system of management of power against their will. Marino had been a young freelance journalist. Too young. Luigi Capra had caught Leo in his unscrupulous web, promised his subordinate fame in keeping with Leo's ego and ambition, and it had gotten Leo killed. Marchese's stomach turned over at the thought the same thing could happen again.

When he arrived home, he was relieved to see it was just as he had left it. The door was locked. The porch had not been invaded by snails or insects, and in the fridge, two beers were still waiting for him, ready to be drunk.

His recent effort to relax had been somewhat restorative. But now he planned to dive back into the muddy world of detective work to help his friend and bring a killer to justice. When he decided to take an extended leave from the force to make a plan for the rest of his life, he had requested that his deputy take his place. Though Torchia had been reluctant, he had accepted the role with grace. But now Marchese wasn't sure he had done his friend or the force a favor. His former deputy was not making headway with this ugly matter, and Marchese wanted to stop this killer. But more than that, he wanted to unmask whatever was behind this bizarre killing spree. His former deputy was right about one thing: Something strange and macabre hid behind those deaths.

* * *

Mark Connell hopped in the shower at 7:30 p.m. with an hour and a half left to go. He was a punctual person, and he demanded punctuality of others.

The cold water slid down his back, washing away the sweat of that sultry day. He hated the heat and longed for the cold, wet climate of his native England with mild summers and no excesses. His mind went to what he had done in those last few days.

To the faces of his victims who, caught by surprise, had found themselves exhaling their left breath.

To blood.

To Eugenia, naked, who'd wished to indulge in their long-awaited lovers' meeting.

All had easily fallen into his trap, a trap well laid in all its details and now yielding its expected results. Now only two more marks and two more copies of the Origin to have in hand. He would be meeting up with the first shortly in an old cinema outside the city. No cameras, no lights and a movie whose screening, when he got there, would be close to its end. She had been instructed to sit in the last row at the right end of the hall and wait.

Connell had done two trips to check the location thoroughly. Everything would go as planned. As always.

He stepped out of the shower and dried himself in front of the window from which he could see a large part of Messina. What a stupid city. For five hundred years, its inhabitants had squandered the opportunity and resources to transform the little unknown area into an important and international city. For the second time, they were missing out on a chance to take the city to a different level.

It was said that Messina was called "babba," which in the city's own dialect meant *stupid* and *naive*, and he felt it was an appropriate nickname.

Connell dressed and looked at his watch. It was ten past eight —time to go. He had to drive several miles before arriving at his appointment, and he didn't want to keep his young admirer waiting. Before leaving, he looked in the mirror one last time, smirked at his reflection, and closed the door behind him.

In the lobby, there was only the concierge. At this hour, the hotel guests were still enjoying their evening in the city. Soon Connell's rental car sped toward the cinema of Alì Terme, a few miles away from Messina. The streets were empty; in August, half of the population moved to vacation homes along the Tyrrhenian or Ionic coasts.

At each traffic light, the killer touched his gun out of habit. That evening, however, he wouldn't be using it. He had a different plan for this appointment.

* * *

Patrizia decided to show up looking her best to that evening's date. So she chose a very short black dress that showed off her long, lean legs.

She turned off her computer and took the envelope lying on the keyboard that she was to bring to her appointment. The awaited day had come.

"Where are you going?"

Patrizia turned her gaze to heaven, annoyed by the interference of her mother in her private life.

"I'm afraid," her mother pleaded. "I don't like what's happening. There's a murderer lurking around the city!"

"Mama!" Patrizia groaned, slipping the envelope into her handbag. "I'm going to the cinema with an old friend!"

"Can't you postpone it?" her mother begged, one hand gripping the doorframe. "Is it so necessary to go there tonight? I'd feel better if you stayed home."

Patrizia sidestepped her mother, hurrying out the bedroom toward the entrance of the house. "I have been organizing this evening for a long time. Please leave me alone."

"Don't talk to me like that! I'm worried. If you must go, then go. But be careful. Don't park in isolated places and try not to be alone."

"Okay!" Patrizia snapped impatiently, turning to face her mother. She immediately regretted her tone when she saw the genuine concern on her mother's face. "You know, I'm not a careless person."

Patrizia's mother kissed her on her forehead, saying nothing, and went back to the kitchen. Patrizia had already turned away, taking a last glance in the mirror near the entrance as she left. This evening was too important for her. For no maniac in the world would she have missed this appointment.

As she reached the street, Patrizia looked at her cell phone. "Shit! I'm late! The movie is about to start, and I must be the first to get there to get my spot."

She hurried to her car and sped off toward her blind date, convinced she'd be contributing to one of the most important discoveries in literature. She had studied for years and was in possession, by chance, of a letter that would reveal one of the most accepted untruths of the last twenty years.

When her grandfather, an elderly notary, had given her the letter, she had been immediately intrigued. She had done endless research, until she had found her way to membership in a secret group that had been trying to shed some light on the theory for years.

Now the long-awaited moment had arrived. She would meet the leader of this group and share her piece of the discovery.

* * *

Connell parked in front of the cinema and sat in his car, waiting for his fifth victim to enter the cinema, buy a ticket, and take the seat he had told her to take.

He would join her soon after. He looked at his watch and sneered in displeasure. "These Italians have no concept of punctuality."

Connell despised each victim—or tried to. His deliberate cold indifference allowed him to do his job without running the risk of any entanglements or mistakes. He had wisely decided to never go beyond his mission. This had been a steadfast focus to his approach in the two years he had spent trying to obtain the letters.

All the victims had believed in him and in this project. All of them had succumbed, trusting in him and their group purpose —in the purpose Graham had set and had asked him to help fulfill.

And the victims had fallen, one after another, without any glitches.

But it was five past eight now. And no sign of Patrizia yet.

He felt his skin growing hot with frustration. He had stressed punctuality. Had she had a setback? If so, his plan would be blown. He would have to reorganize everything, to move to a different plan. But his contingency plan would certainly be more dangerous. The bustle caused by the first four murders had the police on high alert.

"You fucking bitch, where the hell are you?"

Just then, a small car stopped almost right in front of his own. A young woman got out of it. Dressed in black.

It was Patrizia.

"Good," Connell whispered venomously. "Now go, get the ticket and sit where I told you."

And the young woman did just that. She entered the cinema, and he watched through the glass doors, paid for the ticket, had it punched by the usher at the entrance to the hall, and disappeared behind the dark curtain.

He surveyed himself in the rearview mirror, giving his fake mustache and dark-haired wig a final preening. The mustache itched abominably, but it was certainly better than having to grow and dye a real one that would clash with his golden locks. Only then did he get out of the car. He knew soon after the discovery of the body, the police would ask the identity of all those who had entered the cinema. His disguise was top notch.

He entered the cinema and purchased his ticket, following the path Patrizia had taken moments before. The film, a movie by Scorsese that had been having little success, was beginning, and the lights were dim. Connell scanned the theater. He counted eleven people, ten of whom were coupled up. Patrizia sat in the last row, in the most extreme far seat, as previously arranged. The seats surrounding her were empty, just as he believed they would be. She spied him and waved eagerly. He suppressed a ruthless smile and maneuvered his way into the row of seats.

* * *

Torchia threw down the television remote in disgust. Just after dinner, he'd tuned into the local news and promptly wished he hadn't eaten.

The Rai Television news raved about a serial killer who lured women, all of them possibly involved with a satanic sect, and then killed them for some strange ritual. Trying to follow their wild theories and strange calculations and maps made his head spin, so he'd changed the channel.

The next station had strung together a whole series of conjectures that had tarnished the memory of the victims. Sordid environments, sexual deviations, orgies and couple exchanges were some of the speculations—a theory that, besides being more unfounded than the first one, was especially degrading.

Torchia couldn't finish listening to the news and clicked to the local TV, only to find it was being hosted by the equally offensive Luigi Capra.

Whenever he saw Luigi, the terrible moments that had changed his life and Marchese's invaded his head. A flood of images flashed across his memory like movie stills, the phases of that frenzied chase in the mountains of Aspromonte, followed by the investigations into the death of the mayor's wife.

Among all those who lived through these events, directly and indirectly, Capra was the only one making profit from them. In the intervening years, Capra had grown up a bit, professionally speaking, but it was his bank account and fame that had grown dramatically. All the others involved had lost something, in terms of career and affection. Like Marchese, who had lost his beloved partner in life.

Torchia retrieved the remote just as Capra launched into speculating about the killings—and just as his doorbell rang.

He looked at his watch. A quarter to nine, he noted uneasily. Who could it be at that hour?

Francesco Marchese peered past him as Torchia opened the door, caught sight of Luigi Capra's face on the screen, and smirked. "Haven't you learned to stop watching trash TV yet?"

Torchia grinned. "Tired of the mountains, then?"

Marchese stepped in and headed to the kitchen, opened the fridge, and grabbed for a bottle of beer. "Don't you have anything less cheap?"

Torchia followed him with his eyes, proud and heartened by his presence. "You know, Francesco, I'm not a connoisseur like you. But I always have one in the fridge, hoping you will visit."

Marchese scoffed. "Since you buy cheap beers, I think that hope's about to die."

For a moment, neither said a word, then they both laughed heartily.

"C'mon, Francesco," Torchia chuckled, "take a seat."

Marchese took his bottle with him. On a small table at the foot of the sofa, several photos of the crime scenes of the recent days lay scattered. The merry atmosphere fled at the sight of the victims, their expressions glassy and lifeless.

Torchia knew it had been a while since Marchese had faced images like these and that seeing such things again was like revisiting hell.

"Terrible, aren't they?" Torchia ventured, probing for Marchese's thoughts, wondering if what his former superior was seeing would convince Marchese to help and engage, or whether it would deflect him before he even started—move him to leave the house and the investigation and further his resolve to remain detached.

"He is not going to make a mistake, and you know it."

Torchia released the breath he'd been holding. "I know. I'm sure. Only an idiot might think so."

"Like Selva."

Torchia's mouth fell open. "How did you know?"

"I called him, just to say hello," Marchese replied, shrugging. "But you know what he's like. He poured his heart out and told me everything. You know he doesn't like you?"

Torchia dropped into the armchair next to Marchese's. "I know, I know. He misses his collaborations with you. He has never thought me good enough to replace you."

Marchese looked up from the photos and stared at him. "You make such a big deal out of it. It's not like you to show self-pity. What's wrong with you?"

Torchia sighed and ran a hand wearily over his creased face. "Well, I just think Selva is right. I'm not like you. I'm not supposed to be the leader. I might be a good right-hand man, by the side of someone like you, but I'm aware of my limits."

"Don't talk shit," Marchese growled. "To be a good leader, one must know, first of all, how to work well with others. On that note, you know what I am like. I want to do everything by myself. I'm not ideally built for this job, either."

Torchia went silent. His eyes stared at the toothpaste advertisement dancing across the muted TV.

Marchese got down to business. "Now, do you want to tell me something about this case? Otherwise, how am I to help you if we waste time talking about Selva and your skills? Let's get to it. I didn't leave behind an attractice woman who was doing everything to attract my attention to sit here talking philosophy."

Torchia looked at him with surprise. He hadn't seen that light in Marchese's eyes for years. His old friend had been escaping and getting out, or so Torchia had thought, but now the drill detective he knew was coming back.

* * *

At the end of the first act, the lights of the hall turned on. The usher pulled the curtain to let out those who wished to use the bar and the toilets. Some people stood up to go out and smoke and stretch their legs. A gentleman noticed a woman in the last row leaning forward against the seat in front of her. *Maybe she's sleeping,* he thought. The movie was a bit slow, and he wondered if he would make it through the second half. After a few minutes more, the lights dimmed and the movie resumed.

A few miles up the road, Connell pulled the car over to a parking area. He took out of his pocket the envelope the woman had shown him in the theater. He withdrew the letter inside with a wax seal bearing two initials: MF. The sealing wax had been broken. Who knew how many times that letter had been read in the last centuries? Who knew how many hands it had passed through? Despite his natural insensitivity, Connell felt a bit intrigued that he held such an ancient and important document. He shook that feeling away. One letter was still outstanding. A last copy of the Origin to acquire and he could finally return to England.

He'd just returned the letter to his pocket when a Carabinieri patrol car pulled up next to him, lights flashing. The murderer nearly leapt out of his skin. His mind raced: If he had to shoot them point blank, it might get him out of that situation. He didn't want to have to kill these two men in uniform. It would have been risky and detrimental to him and the entire project. He had only a few seconds to decide.

The two men, an agent and a marshal, got out of their car and aimed a flashlight straight in Connell's face. His heart raced so frantically that he could hear it in his eardrums. He lowered the window and flashed his best smile.

"Are you having problems, sir?" the marshal asked.

Connell immediately relaxed. "Yes, sir," he said brightly in deliberately shaky Italian, speaking up so his accent would be obvious. "I am a tourist."

The marshal looked nervously at his colleague.

"Do you speak English?" Connell asked the agent.

"Just a little." The agent approached the driver's window. "Do you have a problem?"

What an idiot. "Yes, sir." He made a show of asking the rest in Italian, noting the agent's wince as he butchered the pronunciation. "I am looking for . . . road to get to the boat."

The agent turned toward the marshal. "He's a tourist," the agent explained in Italian. "He got lost. He's trying to reach the ferry boarding, I think."

Connell reached for a map of Sicily he'd seen earlier in the glove compartment, looking to play his part the best he could.

"And what does he want from me?" the marshal responded, clearly annoyed. "Give him directions."

The marshal walked back to his car, while the agent leaned close to Connell's window trying, through a few words and gestures, to give him the directions. "You have to go, always straight, as they say, on this way, and when you see a *cartello* —"

Connell was painfully close to laughing in his face.

"—with write *Boccetta*, take that way and at the end of the road go left. Five hundred meters on the right side, you will see the ferryboat."

Connell warmly thanked him with a few words in Italian while the agent wiped the sweat of effort from his forehead. The two nodded good-bye, and Connell slowly merged back onto the road and drove in the direction the agent had indicated.

He glanced several times in the rearview mirror. No more sign of the patrol car with the two Carabinieri. He considered the horrible risk he'd taken and just narrowly avoided, and he burst into loud, almost hysterical laughter.

After the first four murders, the police checks had intensified. He promised himself to be more careful going forward. Only one more letter was missing.

"Come on, Mark," he assured himself aloud, "you're almost there."

Chapter 6

The sun was coming up as Father Gabriele exited the church and stepped onto the street. The city was starting to wake up. In every corner of Piazza del Duomo, there were people intent on arranging their carts for the market that was to open that day. At this point in the war, everything was sold there, from food to every kind of junk. People were scraping together anything they could to support their families. Only a few could still afford to spend money casually.

Gabriele, hitching up his shoulder bag, headed to the port. There, he could find someone ready to take him to Taormina in exchange for some lira. The object he was carrying was of inestimable value, and he had no time to waste.

As he arrived at the port, he found a gentleman intent on saddling a mule. Father Gabriele approached him. "Sir, do you know someone who can take me to Taormina?"

The man turned, his expression surprised at the sight of the young priest. "If you have to leave immediately, I am going there to do some work. How much can you give me?"

The priest took some coins from his pocket and displayed them to the man, who suddenly seemed to regret his inquiry. "Leave it, Father. I have to go there anyway. I'll take you in exchange for some bread to be shared on the way."

Father Gabriele smiled. "Thank you, my good man. I will be happy to share my lunch with you."

The journey was uncomfortable and psychologically tortuous. The war had killed more civilians than soldiers, and those who had survived lived in abject hunger and despair. And if starvation did not kill them, the war would scar these people forever. Too many war-torn years had passed, even for those who lived off their own crops, and especially for all the women whose husbands and sons were in trenches by order of the military machine.

Gabriele spent most of his trip praying the rosary, his gut clenching at the misery he observed. As he did every day, he prayed for the suffering and troubled people and for himself, so that God would give him the strength to go on, to support his bishop and all those who needed his comfort.

As they arrived on a promontory from which they could see the beauty of Taormina, Gabriele took his shoulder bag. He was nearing his destination, where he would deliver the casket containing the secret of the Messina Church to Father Carlo.

Don Carlo Parisi was one of the men closest to the bishop. On behalf of his superior, Father Gabriele had asked Parisi to keep the precious treasure, waiting for the war to free Messina from the unceasing bombings and enemy raids.

It had now become too dangerous to keep the important casket hidden in the Duomo. News came from all over the world about how the Germans were plundering works of art and treasures in every city they invaded. Taormina was a less significant place and the casket would be safer. And, after all, it was said that Carlo Parisi would sooner or later become the new bishop of Messina.

Before starting the ascent to Taormina, the priest and his companion stopped at a corner of the road to have some lunch. Father Gabriele pulled out from his bag a bundle containing two slices of hard bread and a piece of goat cheese.

The man licked his mustache. Gabriele realized the poor man probably hadn't eaten for days, so he decided to renounce his portion and leave it to him for the return journey. The man thanked him warmly and, with tears in his eyes, asked him if he needed to be taken back to Messina after his duty.

Gabriele thought it over. "I'll take a few hours. We could meet at sunset at the arched door."

They parted ways just inside the gates of the town, agreeing to rendezvous in the evening. The Cathedral of Taormina was a few hundred meters away. It did not take Gabriele long to reach the front door.

Inside, Father Carlo was celebrating Mass, so Gabriele sat down in the last pew and waited, listening to the parish priest's words.

"God is within each of us," Parisi said reverently, his gaze drifting slowly over the crowd. "Don't go looking for him among material goods, money, and human weakness. There is only one God. It is enough to know how to look for Him within our soul and, when you find Him, you will recognize Him because He will give you serenity."

Hearing his charismatic voice, his reassuring strength, Gabriele understood why everyone in Messina believed Parisi would be the next bishop, designated by the pope to lead the church of the city.

Parisi smiled as he went on, "Let peace be with you and let the world know what God speaks to you. If you come here every day and you can't keep within you what you feel when you are here when you are outside, in the street, in your daily life, then you are distracted. But if you listen carefully, it is much easier to reach and hear the Lord our God. It's hard not to be tempted by the Evil One. The Church, this sacred place, must keep alive for you the memory of the sacrifice He made for us and of the reward for having served Him, which is Eternity."

Father Gabriele looked around. Everyone seemed intent on the priest's words. The church was almost full. Not even in the Cathedral of Messina were there were so many faithful followers during Sunday Mass.

At the end of the service, Gabriele left the cathedral and sat down at the feet of the Minotaur Fountain, waiting to be called by one of the servers and received by Father Carlo.

He opened his shoulder bag and looked around him before he took the casket out. He was guarding a piece of history, an important secret. A revelation.

He was holding something of immeasurable value, he thought. The thought made him close his eyes. It pierced his soul—his faith.

He shuddered and tried to repent for the sinful thought that had just passed through his mind. He prayed to God, asked the Lord to ward off the Evil One. And his momentary temptation.

MESSINA—AUGUST 8, 2012

By 10:00 p.m., Marchese was on his second beer, listening intently as Torchia ran through all the case details.

"Clearly there's not a single clue linking them all together," Torchia concluded.

Marchese reflected in silence for a moment. "And yet there must be *something*," he said at last. "I don't want to say that you missed it, but we must focus on something to go forward."

Torchia nodded. "I believe the same. But we only found books and papers and work notes. And that note bearing the words *Michelangelo, I love you so much!* which may mean nothing."

"And we didn't get any matches," Marchese intoned.

"No. No one, as I told you. Ricci is working on it. But still nothing."

Marchese frowned, rubbing his stubbled chin thoughtfully. "You talk about books. What kind of books?"

Torchia thought it over. Days of poor sleep were catching up to him. "I don't remember. But they were pertinent to the studies of each of them. Three of them were students. Ricci knows more about this if you want further details."

Marchese continued to peruse the reports. Not the slightest clue, not even among all the reports made by the forensics. "It was such a clean job. The killer somehow gets in touch with the victims, they agree to meet with him, and when he shows up, he kills them immediately. No struggle. Nothing. There is certainly a well-formulated plan behind these killings."

"What do you suggest we do?"

"We need to look even more closely for clues," Marchese replied firmly. "Uncover every stone in these people's lives, search the web, go way back on Facebook and their other social-media accounts; they may all share a common connection that's yet to be discovered. Let's forget for a moment the killer's motive. Let's try to figure out how he communicated with them."

"We are searching everything," Torchia replied despondently. "We checked out their Facebook pages, LinkedIn, Instagram, Twitter, too. There is nothing out of the ordinary. No shared connections. Nothing particularly interesting."

Marchese shrugged. "So, they're connected by some other thread. We need to search into each of the victim's last actions."

"That's what I have Ricci doing," said Torchia sourly.

"Let's meet with your deputy tomorrow morning, but away from the police station. Too risky. If someone sees me working with you on this case, it would become the top news of the week."

Marchese was serious, but the thought still made Torchia chuckle. "You're right," he conceded.

"On the other hand," Marchese said, his face clearing and his finger wagging, "maybe it would be better that way, so they can stop all their idiotic reporting of these last few days."

Torchia's phone rang before he could reply, and he snatched it up. "Torchia here."

"It's Ricci."

"Tell me," he said, though he had a sinking feeling what his deputy was about to say.

Ricci sounded more agitated than before. "Someone called us from the cinema of Ali Terme saying that, at the end of a movie, they found a dead woman against one of the seats."

Torchia put his hand to his forehead and stared at Marchese. "How?"

"Probably a heart attack."

Torchia's temper flared. "Then why are you calling me?"

"I said *probably*."

The ominous note in Ricci's voice sent a shiver up Torchia's back. "And what does *probably* mean? Don't be cryptic."

"From the information we have, we know that the woman went alone into the cinema, but an usher remembers seeing a man with her."

Torchia's annoyance evaporated. "Where are you now?"

"I'm going to the cinema. I'm almost there."

Torchia stared again at Marchese. A fierce glint had entered his mentor's eye.

"Okay," Torchia said, "we're coming."

"We?" Ricci repeated. "Who?"

"Me and Francesco Marchese."

* * *

Having made sure he wasn't being watched, Mark Connell tossed the wig and mustache into a sewer drain, knowing the recent rains would carry it far from the crime scene and wash away any trace of DNA that might have clung to them. Then he took a leisurely stroll back to his hotel.

Once in his room, he flopped down on the bed and turned on the TV, flipping through national and local channels. None of them were covering it yet, although the movie was certainly finished and it was likely the body had already been found. Connell left the television tuned to the local station that, up till now, had been the promptest one to give the news of the other murders.

He took a small bottle of whiskey from the minibar and uncorked it. He only needed one gulp to empty it. Connell never drank when he had an important job to do, but now he was in the last stretch to the finish line.

Only one piece of the puzzle was missing. Just one meeting. The last one. The sixth person.

The channel was in the middle of airing an old movie starring the beautiful Virna Lisi when "Breaking News" appeared on the screen.

Connell felt a thrill of anticipation. *Here we go.*

Luigi Capra stood in the foreground. Behind him loomed the entrance to the Cinema Vittoria of Alì Terme.

"Dear viewers," said Capra somberly, "we are forced to interrupt our programs to give you a terrible update on the Monster of Messina. A few minutes ago, another murder victim was found right here, behind me, inside the Cinema Vittoria in Alì Terme. The information we have collected suggests that the victim died of a heart attack, but this hypothesis leads to serious doubts. In fact, halfway through the movie, there's evidence that a man was seen leaving the hall. That's still to be verified. The Carabinieri of RIS have just arrived on the scene. We will give you more updates soon. Stay tuned."

A smile flitted across Connell's pale face. *A man with a mustache and black hair,* he thought. And he smiled again.

Now he only had to wait for the statements of those incompetent officers of the police and the Carabinieri departments.

* * *

Torchia's car pulled directly in front of the entrance of the cinema at 10:35 p.m. Marchese wrinkled his nose at the sight of the TV news teams already surrounding the theater. When the car doors opened and Marchese emerged from the passenger's side, it was as if everything froze for a moment and then turned into a frenzy soon after.

The first to run, jumping over microphone wires and ducking under cameras, was Luigi Capra, his giddy smile a tasteless counterpoint to the story he was there to report. Marchese could already see Capra stringing together the announcement: The great detective had returned. There, at the crime scene. At the right moment.

Three policemen tried in vain to stop the journalists' race toward Torchia's car. Capra's microphone was just one of a bouquet shoved under the nose of the former drill detective.

After years, Capra's eyes met those of Marchese again. Like old times.

"Detective Marchese, it's a relief to see you. Can you tell us the reason for your return?"

Marchese remained impassive, but a familiar and terrible feeling of disgust and anger burned in his stomach. On the way, he had thought about what he would face here. How he would feel deep inside. "I'm here only as an outside police consultant," he said blandly, hoping that would be sufficient to shoo the journalists away.

But Capra didn't let him go.

Marchese stopped in front of the entrance of the cinema, steeling himself. He turned a flinty gaze to the crowd again and saw a few of the journalists recoil. "Ladies and gentlemen," he said in a diplomatic tone, "I understand the right to report events, but if you don't let us work, you risk obstructing the investigation and, unwittingly, becoming accomplices to a probable murder. What we can tell you— and that's a promise—is that the Messina police will catch this criminal. We will give you all possible news quite soon, so as to satisfy you, your viewers, and the population of Messina."

Marchese turned back and disappeared behind the front door of the cinema, followed by Torchia, Ricci, and two other policemen. As he stalked off, Marchese could hear Capra already breaking the news in a hasty and breathless voice: "Dear viewers, we have just witnessed the return of the great Detective Marchese! The legend! The one who, for years, has been the face of the law in Messina. We remember him . . ."

The detested voice faded as they passed through the theater curtain.

* * *

In a hotel several kilometers away, Connell stared baffled at the TV screen. Who was this man and what was so special about him that he drew the journalists' attention so raptly?

For a moment, Connell felt challenged. He had glimpsed a confidence in that man's eyes that annoyed him. Until then, he had defined the investigators who appeared on TV as complete idiots who tried their best to make an impression in front of the camera. Not this man; he had avoided it. Then, as a challenge, he had stared directly into the camera.

A new excitement entered Connell's heart. This new sheriff would be disappointed and dismayed in a short while. He rose from the bed and crossed to the table to turn on his laptop. He had to confirm the last appointment for the next day.

* * *

As they walked into the theater, Marchese and Torchia found themselves facing a sea of officers. For an instant, every eye in the room seemed to turn their way, and Marchese caught a muttered "holy shit" from somewhere to their left that rang out too loud in the fleeting quiet that followed.

Everyone either knew him or about him. Everyone knew his reputation. They also knew of his pain and his leave of absence. But Marchese was here now. On the latest scene of a probable murder, one of now five mysterious murders in the city of Messina.

Marchese didn't so much as acknowledge their stares.

A uniformed officer escorted them to where the body was still sitting, unnaturally, in the last row. He recognized Ricci, Torchia's deputy, standing behind the theater seat alongside Lieutenant Selva, who looked up as they approached and smiled at seeing his old and esteemed friend. He stopped examining the victim, took off his latex gloves, and shook Marchese's hand.

"Dear Francesco," he said warmly, "you really can't stay away from trouble, can you?"

Marchese smiled, but his main interest was the victim. The young woman's face wore a pained expression that twisted Marchese's heart.

"What can you tell us, Sergio?"

Selva turned his gaze to the body. "The witnesses were right about one thing. She didn't die from a heart attack."

Marchese frowned. "What do you mean?"

"That she did have a heart attack, but it was induced."

"By what?" Torchia chimed in.

"Poison," Selva replied, shooting Torchia a petulant look.

Marchese ran his hands through his black hair. What he had hoped was the unthinkable had turned out to be true. Another murder, a female, a different dynamic. "Poison?" he repeated.

Selva visibly swelled with pride at Marchese's amazement. "Yeah. A very strong and deadly poison."

"And how could the killer have given it to the victim?" asked Torchia, sounding awestruck himself.

"Maybe a poisoned candy," Selva answered. "The killer probably offered it to her. It took only a few seconds. I'm almost completely certain it was cyanide salt. See the foam around the mouth there? This type of poison enters the bloodstream immediately. Death was painful, but immediate."

Marchese examined the body from all angles. He wondered if the woman had time to realize her trust had been betrayed. "Did they enter together?"

Ricci chimed in then, as if he felt he was expected to answer this question. "No, sir. Apparently, the woman entered alone, just a few minutes before the movie had opened, followed by the man after the movie started. He left before the end of the first act, and that's what made the usher suspicious."

"What about the man's description?"

"About six foot or so," Ricci replied, reading off his notebook, "athletic build, mustache, and straight black hair."

Marchese's mind raced to process and incorporate the new information as he parsed out what he already knew. "Ricci, go to the victim's house. Make an inspection. Make note of everything you find. Question her family. Try to determine if she knew the other four victims and we will see you at—" Marchese stopped abruptly. He knew he couldn't show up at the police station so suddenly without hurting Torchia's reputation. "At Torchia's house," he finished. "In a couple of hours."

Torchia had remained silent, watching, willingly allowing his former superior to make the decisions. Marchese knew with certainty then that Torchia wanted him to assume investigative leadership of the case, so Marchese obliged, rattling off his orders like a general marching into war. Everyone very naturally obeyed.

"Torchia, we'll need to look into the identity of that man, but it's very likely he was in disguise. If he's the same one who killed the other women, he's too smart to show his real face. Order some identikits without a mustache and with wavy hair. Set up checkpoints everywhere, and tight control. The man arrived here by car, I'm sure, so appoint someone to check private and public cameras from here to Messina."

He turned to Selva. "Sergio, what about fingerprints and DNA? Is there any evidence to work with that might lead us to the killer?"

Sergio gave a sharp nod. "We've collected some samples, but we'll have to wait until tomorrow for results."

"Too late," Marchese said sharply, and he paused to reflect. "Who can tell me something about the victim?"

Though Ricci stepped forward to speak, a policeman who had arrived on the scene earlier took the floor. "The victim's name was Patrizia Darra, a graduate in classical literature. She was a city employee who dealt with the preservation of ancient literary works. Apparently, she went out to meet an old friend, according to her mother's first statements."

"Anything else?" Marchese asked.

The officer shook his head. "No, sir. That's all for the moment. The forensic team is checking the victim's car parked nearby."

Torchia remained silent. Marchese stared at him. "You understand it's not over yet?"

"Yeah, I know," replied Torchia ruefully. "What shall we do, then?"

Marchese glanced one last time at the body and his resolve hardened. "We *will* find him."

With that, the two detectives left the cinema.

The journalist's cameras and lights were still hovering outside on vigilant standby. A wry smile crossed Marchese's face. He descended the steps and strode toward Capra, who, seeing him approach, reached eagerly for the microphone tucked in the back pocket of his jeans. Seeing the movement, the other journalists jostled for position behind the makeshift barriers the traffic wardens had placed to protect the area.

"Are you ready for a statement, Luigi?" Marchese asked loudly.

Every microphone jabbed toward Marchese, and every spotlight and camera swung to focus on him as every journalist in the crowd waited breathlessly for his words.

"We can say with some certainty," Marchese began, "that this is the work of the same person who murdered the other four victims in the last few days. However, this time he left more evidence than he had at previous crime scenes. We are already analyzing it and comparing it with the few other clues previously uncovered. We do have a strong lead at this point in the case but cannot say more. Now, please, let us work."

Marchese turned around without paying attention to the onslaught of questions. He and Torchia stepped into the car and drove off, maneuvering slowly to avoid mowing over any overeager journalists and picking up speed as they reached the main thoroughfare.

For several minutes, Torchia said nothing. He simply kept his eyes on the lamplit street ahead. But Marchese could see he had something on his mind.

"Why did you do it, Francesco?" Torchia ventured at last.

"Because we have no clues," Marchese replied shortly, "and there will be other victims. Therefore, I hoped to rattle the killer and put pressure on him. Or at least hurt his pride."

Torchia's mouth twitched in an incredulous smile. "But for what?"

Marchese glared out the windshield. "Nervousness and pride mess up even the most confident ones."

* * *

Deputy Ricci went alone to Patrizia's home not long after Marchese and Torchia left the cinema. He wasn't quite sure of how he felt about Marchese's sudden appearance on the case. Marchese's leave of absence had left a hole in the department, but Torchia, Ricci thought, had stepped up to fill the space well. He couldn't ignore the feeling of having been knocked down a rung again, just when he'd become accustomed to the increase in scrutiny. He wasn't even sure what role he filled now. Was he even really a deputy detective anymore?

Patrizia's parents remained in the kitchen as he headed down the hall to her room. Tears and screams of despair broke the silence.

This was not the first time the young deputy detective had had to face such a situation. His heart had hardened over the years. It was his job, he often reminded himself, to concentrate on the case without allowing the emotional atmosphere around him to cloud his judgment.

He pulled out his notebook. He rarely needed to review it once he'd taken anything down, but he always kept it close to hand. Having the facts there, in writing, made it easier to detach himself from the anguish he frequently encountered. Or at least they made it easier to pretend he could. Flipping through his notes was the closest thing he could get to meditation. Certainly it was better than the memory of the look on Patrizia's mother's face when he'd first visited to break the news—a look that said she knew what he was going to say before he said it.

He began to take notes on what he saw: the titles of books left where they'd have been frequently picked up again, photographs taped to the vanity, notes she'd posted around her computer.

Another victim who read a lot, he thought. *Always books.* He had seen so many in the last few days. He was something of a bookworm himself; he loved novels and literary works. Going by the titles he scribbled down, Patrizia had been fond of great writers of English literature and theater.

He snapped a few photos of the room, collected a few of the notes Patrizia had left around, and left the apartment, his notebook tucked in his left breast pocket.

Chapter 7

Mark Connell grabbed for his second bottle of minibar whiskey that evening, his eyes riveted on the newscast covering his latest job—the fourth masterwork of the "Monster of Messina."

He felt annoyed. Nervous even. Marchese's statement was false. He was sure of it. That damned smug detective had challenged him.

A nervous laugh slipped from his lips, and he stifled it with a swig of the questionable liquor. He had left no clues, neither on this last occasion nor during his previous meetings. This was a bluff. There was no reason to doubt it, surely.

He rose from the bed and paced the floor, his mind whirling. It was not possible. Connell knew he never left a trace. He was fast. Accurate. Careful. The arrogant detective had certainly lied, he told himself again.

He stripped down completely, his clothes suddenly too tight, and got into bed. It only took a few minutes for him to fall into a deep sleep. A sleep full of nightmares.

It was this way every night. The ghosts of his victims always tormented his sleep, and there were many of them. But the newest, Patrizia's specter, came in sharper and more persistent, almost violently so, than any other ever had.

She had smiled at him as he was sitting down next to her. Her face clean, carefree.

And he had ended her life.

For the letter, the *Origin*.

For the dirty work for which he was paid.

But suddenly a new face reared up in his dreams, not a victim but a foe—the detective whose arrogance had caused Connell to mistrust himself for the first time in his heinous career. He jerked awake in a cold sweat, his terror transmuting to rage. How dare that arrogant face follow him into his nightmares. Connell would make him pay for his impudence, and he'd do so with ease. A sneer curled his lip as he pictured the shock that would burn the smug grin right off that detective's face as the life seeped out of his body.

By this hour the next day, he'd have not one but two victims disposed of, and then he'd disappear into thin air, along with his sizable paycheck.

* * *

Neither Torchia nor Marchese spoke again the rest of the drive to the detective's house. They entered and worked in silence, organizing everything—reports, photos, and evidence—and waited for Ricci to arrive. Torchia circled the table while Marchese sat at its head.

Torchia had hoped having his old superior back on the job would lift the weight off of him. But despite that Marchese may have taken charge on the scene, as far as the police department was officially concerned, Torchia was still in charge. That pressure weighed heavier now, with everything laid out before them on the table.

This was everything and still they had nothing. And the killer was working fast.

Without the shuffling of papers, true silence fell. Both scoured that material for every bit of detail, any ephemeral thread of information the women might have had in common. When Ricci knocked at last three hours later, bearing new photos and his usual notebook, they'd made no headway.

"Tell us, Ricci," Torchia urged as he ushered his deputy into the house. "What can you share with us?"

Ricci sat down at the table, looking wrung out. "Minor stuff, as always. A few things from her room and a few photos. Many books and no obvious clues as to why she would be hated to the point of someone wanting to kill her. According to her family and friends, she didn't know the other victims, and apparently, she has nothing in common with them. And no boyfriend, no suitor—nothing. She's a recent graduate, down to earth. Her relatives say she was supposed to meet an old friend at the cinema, or at least that's what she told her mother before she went out."

Marchese had leveled a scrutinizing stare at Ricci of a kind that used to nail Torchia to the spot. But Ricci's report just sounded redundant. All these victims really seemed to have had in common were mundane lives.

"You know what?" said Marchese suddenly. "Let's make a summary of what happened. C'mon, Ricci, explain everything. Walk me through every single detail, without leaving anything out. Let's see if we can hit on even a small detail, something useful to start."

Ricci straightened in his chair. "OK, sir, where do I begin?"

Torchia suppressed a smile.

"With the first victim," Marchese replied.

"OK." Ricci placed his notebook on the table but made no move to open it. "The receptionist of the Residence Garibaldi called us yesterday morning. They'd found a lifeless woman in one of their rooms. We arrived after twenty minutes and found the victim, Eugenia Massari, thirty-nine years of age, born in Rome, employed in a municipal library of the capital. She'd flown into Catania Airport to spend her holidays here in Messina. Her family told us she had neither boyfriends nor hobbies in particular. We found her lying on the bed, naked, with only one, deadly wound, a gunshot point-blank to the forehead. The room was tidy and nothing was missing, apparently. Clothes were arranged neatly in their place, a book on the bedside table, a laptop in her suitcase, and the usual personal stuff necessary for a trip of a few days. From the available evidence, she had never left the room, at least during the hours when the reception desk was supervised, and she rarely went out during the three days following her arrival in Messina, that she reached through a flight from Rome to Catania airport."

Marchese nodded. Torchia's eyes fixed on his old mentor, waiting for a flicker of clarity.

"As to the second victim," Ricci went on, "we found her a few hours later, in her car by the side of a little used road in the Falcata area. As with the first victim, she bore a single gunshot wound to the forehead—same weapon, confirmed by the forensic team."

Out of the corner of his eye, Torchia saw Ricci's head swivel in his direction, so he nodded to confirm he understood.

Ricci continued, "The victim's name was Barbara Scassi, twenty-six years old, a literature student from Messina. We found nothing in her car—no evidence. And, as in the case of the first victim, no sign of struggle or violence. There was nothing questionable at her home, just books, notes, and a computer. The family didn't know the identity of the person she was supposed to meet.

"The third victim was found on the rails of the harbor station —no gunshot wound this time, she was slaughtered with a knife. The killer assumed to be the same, and again there's no sign of struggle. Her name was Maria Cicco, from Catania. She studied foreign languages and literature in Messina. In her home, which she shared with other students, we found nothing. She had a backpack with the usual things and inside her room we found nothing important. Just a bunch of textbooks."

Marchese looked back at a photo among those scattered on the table. "Isn't this the victim right here, wearing the *Tantu scrusciu pi nenti* sweatshirt?"

Ricci nodded. "From what we've determined, she didn't know the other victims, either. We checked her social-media profiles. Nothing interesting. Just chats with some friends from afar. For sure, she hadn't made an appointment with any of them."

Torchia began tapping his pen agitatedly on the table, his gaze now skimming over the grim photos between them.

"As to the fourth victim, she actually seems to have been the first killed," Ricci said wearily. "However, the autopsy is still in progress. Her name was Alessandra Catona. She was thirty-eight and worked as a theater director. She was killed by a single shot to the forehead, too. Like the others, she knew her killer. She opened the door for him. Like the others, she probably trusted him. And she was killed immediately as well. But there's one little difference with the others."

Marchese's chair scraped the floor as he straightened up.

"Indeed, more than one." At last, Ricci flipped open his notebook. "First of all, the killer apparently turned her room upside down, tearing through notes and rummaging through them. And unlike the others, she had a boyfriend, whom she had quarreled with a few nights before. And Detective Torchia found a note among the scattered sheets by the bed written by the victim, in which she declared her love for a man named Michelangelo. This name does not correspond to her boyfriend's name. She also had only books related to her job at the scene, and nothing else. There was no shouting heard, no struggle, and no sexual assault."

As Ricci continued, Marchese began shuffling through the photos of the victims and arranging them in order of occurrence.

"As to the fifth victim," Ricci resumed, "the dynamic was certainly different, but we are almost sure that the killer was the same for several reasons, which I'm sure you're already aware of. We know that a powerful poison killed her, although the body has just been taken for autopsy. It was a professional killer, same as the other cases. The victim's name was Patrizia Darra, employed at the Palacultura of Messina. She also was irreproachable personally. No excesses, no romantic attachments. She was a bookworm. As her mother told us, she had to meet an old friend at the cinema. We found nothing in her room, just books, a computer, a few photos, and some posters of old movies and plays."

Torchia glanced up from the photos at Marchese, who was now scribbling away on a piece of paper, listing what looked to be a series of words, names, and numbers.

"Coming back to sexual assault," Ricci said, "as I told you, none of them appear to be touched or otherwise wounded by the killer. And even if Eugenia was to have been found naked and the others were willing to meet him in very isolated places, the killer did not take sexual advantage of these situations. He killed without any involvement, cleanly, without drawing attention to himself. American-mafia style. Just a clean shot and walk out. This reinforces the theory of a professional killer."

Silence fell, punctured only by the scratching of Marchese's pen and Torchia tapping on the table. Ricci stared at the detective in silence; Torchia stared at the table.

After several agonizing minutes, Marchese stopped scribbling.

"Okay, so from what you've told me and based on your official reports, I've extracted a series of words. Names, times, details. Nothing overly compelling, but there is a common thread among the victims."

Torchia leaned forward in his chair.

"One, indeed," Marchese reiterated. "Books. All were avid readers. You've repeated the word *book* several times. It was the most used in your account."

"And that means we have very little in our hands!" Torchia exclaimed, exasperated, throwing his pen down on the table. It rolled away among the photographs.

"Maybe," Marchese allowed. "But it's better than nothing, and it could mean something. It's small, but it's something useful, in my opinion."

Torchia gaped at him. "Are you serious? What's that got to do with their deaths? The fact that the victims were avid readers?"

Marchese remained thoughtfully silent, but Torchia could tell by the set of his jaw that the former detective was serious. He glanced at Ricci and found his deputy staring back, puzzled and pensive.

Marchese looked up at the ceiling as if hoping to find an answer there. "I'm just saying there's a connection. Maybe —"

Ricci leapt to his feet so abruptly that even Marchese jumped. The young deputy began shuffling frantically through the photos, his eyes wild, his notebook clutched in his hand.

Torchia rose apprehensively from his seat. "Ricci, what is —?"

"Fuck, fuck, fuck!" Ricci exclaimed. "We had it near at hand. Totally."

Torchia froze, casting a side-eyed glance at Marchese. A slow smile began to spread on Marchese's face.

"They all loved plays," Ricci blurted. He dropped his notebook on the table, its normally smooth pages now rumpled from his frenzied search, and kept hunting. "And actually, being passionate myself about this author . . ."

Ricci trailed off, but a grin spread over his face. Torchia held his breath as his deputy slid their carefully arranged evidence out of the way in by-victim piles, clearing a space in the middle of the table. He shuffled through the crime scene photos as if he were possessed, singled out a photo, moved it, then set a few aside and chose another, laying them in the cleared space as he went.

"Oh my God, sir," Ricci breathed.

Then his voice dropped to a rhythmic mutter that seemed almost familiar, so much so that Torchia felt a shiver pass through him. He looked at the photos Ricci had already laid out: Maria Cicco lying on the rails. The note found on Alessandra Catona's floor. Eugenia Massari's room.

"Ricci, what are you doing? What's going through your head?"

Ricci muttered and moaned, but he didn't reply. Torchia's patience evaporated, but as he opened his mouth to speak, Marchese glared at him as if to say, "Back off."

That look, more than anything, assured him that Ricci was really on to something. The rosebud. And maybe something more.

"Sir," Ricci said, laying down three more photos, "we had it near at hand since the first day. Since the first day. But we couldn't know. Now we know. Now at last." His eyes were almost crazed as he looked at Marchese and Torchia. "It is here. Among the photos." He jabbed his finger at the photos one after the other as he said, "The key is here, here, here, here, and in these two here."

The first, of Eugenia, showed a small bottle of water standing beside an antique-looking book on her bedside table— Hamlet. The second showed Barbara's bookshelf. The third depicted Mary's *Tantu scrusciu pi nenti* sweatshirt, soaked with blood. The fourth was an enlarged photo of the note found on Alessandra's floor. The fifth showed the beautiful leather-bound collection of books next to the computer on Patrizia's desk. The sixth showed the skull-shaped key ring of Barbara's car.

Torchia followed Ricci's gesturing, fumbling to grasp what Ricci was seeing in these images. He passed the photos to Marchese, feeling like an underachieving schoolboy.

But Marchese smiled. He understood. "The author," the former detective concluded.

"Exactly, Detective," Ricci crowed. "It's always the same."

Marchese leaned over the table to clap the deputy on the shoulder. "Brilliant, Ricci. Brilliant."

Torchia dropped the photos and sat down. "I don't follow," he confessed sourly.

"Ricci, answer that, please." Marchese went to the fridge for a beer.

"All the victims are connected by the same author," Ricci clarified obligingly. "Shakespeare. All of them."

"You're kidding me. *Shakespeare*?"

"Yes, sir, Shakespeare! Do you remember?"

A rush of anxiety flooded Torchia's mind. "What's the deal with this picture of the note, then?"

Ricci's triumphant look told him his deputy had expected that question; clearly it was the one he most wanted to answer, a flex of his knowledge. "Detective, in that photo the victim swears love to somebody called Michelangelo. And we couldn't find him. Because he's dead."

This only served to make Torchia more nervous. "In what sense is he dead?"

"In the sense," Ricci replied airily, "that the Michelangelo to whom Alessandra refers is Michelangelo Florio."

Torchia rolled his eyes to the ceiling as Marchese had done moments before. "And who is that?"

Ricci's voice took on a confidence Torchia had never previously heard. "According to the theory of some scholars, Shakespeare was born in Messina. His true name would be Michelangelo Florio, a Calvinist who fled first to Milan and then to London to escape the Inquisition. It looks like he took his mother's English name, Guglielma Crollalanza, which in English is translated into William Shakespeare."

Torchia's eyebrows shot up.

"And in Messina," Ricci went on, "there is a school of thought that supports this revelation with conviction. In fact, the third victim's sweatshirt—" Ricci picked up the photo of Maria. "—is by Sicilian Pride, a brand that shows, on its clothing, the most popular sentence in relation to Shakespeare and Sicily: *Much Ado About Nothing*. Which is a play set right here in Messina."

Marchese dropped onto the sofa. Torchia stared at him for a long moment. "What do you think, Francesco?"

Ricci turned to the former drill detective, waiting.

"I think he's right," Marchese announced. "In fact, I am sure that this is significant, their all having something to do with Shakespeare. Also because nothing else links the victims. Nothing. And there are no other reasons for these murders. Rarely in my career have I seen something more nebulous. This could be the key."

That was good enough for Torchia. "How shall we go on, then?"

Ricci sagged in visible relief and collapsed into his chair.

"We need to understand why," Marchese replied. "I don't know why he kills them. What drives him to kill these women passionate about the famous playwright, whether he's English or from Messina? And above all, why only women? But we must stop him, and quickly, given how fast our killer acts. We need to figure out the identity of the next victim."

Ricci piped up, "We should look for those who study and firmly believe in the theory on Shakespeare's Messina origins." He paused, grimacing. "But we don't know when he'll strike again. Maybe he's already killing someone right now."

The hopeful atmosphere in the room seemed to thin. Marchese was silent, clearly thinking, staring at his half-empty beer bottle, which rested in his hand on the arm of the chair.

Once again, Torchia found himself waiting with bated breath.

Marchese nodded to himself. "Yeah. It might work. Maybe."

Torchia's pulse raced. "What?"

"It might work." Marchese stood up and walked to the door. "Come with me. I might have a way to stop this trail of blood. Let's go, I'll explain everything on the way."

MESSINA—AUGUST 8, 1943

Father Carlo invited Gabriele to sit in the armchair in front of his desk. "So, the bishop sent you to me. Why, Father Gabriele?"

Gabriele's hand fell to the shoulder bag in his lap. "Father, the bishop has entrusted me with a very delicate task. And he chose you for another one, even more important."

Father Carlo raised a graying eyebrow. "And how is my dear friend, the bishop? We haven't seen each other for months. Tell me."

Father Carlo's lighthearted tone soothed Gabriele's frayed nerves. He sensed an eagerness to help in the would-be bishop that lacked any self-serving air.

"His Excellency is very tired," Gabriele confessed. "He's suffering a lot because of the war and the decay and death spreading in the city." Horrid memories rose in Gabriele's mind, and he found himself faltering a bit. "But he is a strong man and trusts in God. Prayer strengthens him and makes him do great works to help poor people who are suffering and need the comfort of the Church."

Father Carlo sighed, his expression becoming a little despondent. "I can imagine. And I hope you'll also understand the greatness of our Lord. Our bishop is a saint, and you're lucky to be with him."

There was nothing disingenuous in the priest's voice, and Gabriele smiled. "That's true, Father."

"So, let's talk about the reason for your visit," Carlo said brightly. "What can I do for the bishop that's so important?"

Without hesitation, Gabriele took out the wooden box he had kept until then in his shoulder bag. He laid it gently on the desk between them. "The bishop put me in charge of bringing this to you so you can keep it safe, as he wishes. According to him, quite shortly, there will be a serious attack, even fiercer than the one of July twelfth, and he is afraid this casket may fall into the wrong hands."

Father Carlo looked at the small wooden box, but he did not touch it. "Michelangelo's famous letters."

Gabriele's eyes widened in surprise. "How could you know the content of the casket, Father?"

Carlo smiled fondly. "I am a great friend of the bishop. And you may have heard, he wishes, when he becomes a cardinal, that I take his place. So he entrusted this secret to me as well."

A flicker of disquiet passed through Gabriele's mind. It seemed, among the men closest to the bishop, he was the only one who'd been kept in the dark.

"So, the bishop wants me to keep the casket here, waiting for the war to end?"

"Yes, Father."

Carlo sat upright in his chair, reached over the desk, and brushed his fingers across the lid of the wooden box. But he did not open it.

"Aren't you curious, Father?"

Carlo sat back, steepling his fingers in front of his chin. "No, I'm not. Curiosity is an original sin. An instinct to be repressed."

Mortified, Gabriele held his tongue.

Carlo studied the box a moment more before he nodded. "You can tell the bishop that being entrusted with this task is a great honor for me. And that I will protect with my life this ancient and precious treasure of the Church."

* * *

Gabriele left the cathedral at dusk. As he strode toward his rendezvous, he thought about what Father Carlo had told him. About his kindness and his charisma.

He understood now why Father Carlo would be the next designated bishop of Messina.

Guilt twisted in Gabriele's chest so strongly it made him wince. And it wasn't the shame of Carlo's gentle admonishment that plucked at him.

Gabriele put his hand in the pocket of his habit and thumbed the six letters he had taken away from the stack in the casket. Those letters were of immeasurable value, unique and illuminating documents that could affect the history of literature.

He had given in to temptation.

At the meeting place, waiting for him, was the silent man who was feeding his mule. Gabriele pulled his hand from his pocket and greeted him affectionately. He shoved aside the guilt of his misdeed as he and his fellow traveler set out on the road to Messina.

The return journey seemed longer and more tiring. The sun had been down for a while, and the darkness depressed their spirits, and the discomfort of the means of transport was debilitating.

As they reached the crest of a small hill only a few miles from the outskirts of the city, the sky suddenly lit up, and a thunderous roar echoed in in the air. As during a patronal feast, the sky blazed momentarily and then quickly darkened again.

"What is it?" asked the man driving the mule.

Gabriele was so stunned, he almost couldn't reply. "They are bombing the city."

Unmoving, on the hill, Gabriele and his companion watched for what felt like endless hours as a massive evilness poured down onto the city. Helpless tears streamed down their cheeks as they watched the city and its people—its families—annihilated.

On that August 8, Messina went up in flames, victimized by the satanic war machine.

As dawn broke over the smoking horizon, Gabriele put his hands in his pockets again. His guilt, his shame for his weakness, the sin he had committed doing this despicable action, had made him unable to pray to God. The letters seemed suddenly pointless and not. What were they against the tragedy of death, which, at that moment, was everywhere in his town? In taking them, he'd betrayed his bishop and his city. His faith.

Father Gabriele felt truly lost.

Marchese took the wheel of Torchia's car, while Torchia rode shotgun and Ricci took the back seat. Marchese veered toward the city's center.

Torchia's house was located on the coast road in the Pace district. The traffic, at midnight, was nonexistent, and the city revealed its full splendor. Marchese loved Messina, its streets, its enchanting view over one of the most beautiful glimpses of sea in the world—everything was unique. He regretted deeply when its people mistreated it. The history of the city, lost in the millennia and in the history books, had been ruined by politics, hypocrisy, and malpractice. The local administrations alternated and survived by means of electoral appeals, careless handling of economic resources, and a patronage system, leaving neighborhoods in decay and neglecting all measures aimed at preserving the beauties of the historical center.

Anger gave Marchese a lead foot, and he drove like a madman toward a destination still unknown to his passengers.

"Francesco!" Torchia cried as Marchese wove through the scanty traffic. "Do you want to fill us in and possibly slow down?"

"I had an idea," Marchese barked, addressing the first question and ignoring the second. "We have a way, although unorthodox, to try to find the next victim before the killer does."

"Unless he is killing her right now," said Ricci grimly, his hand white-knuckling Torchia's headrest.

"True," Marchese snapped, "but we must try anyway."

"Would you like to explain your idea to us—at least before you drive into a tree with *my* car," Torchia quipped, his eyes glued to the road.

"I'm taking you to see one of our old colleagues. Hopefully, he can help us warn the next victim."

"And who's that?" Torchia replied skeptically.

"You are about to find out."

A few silent minutes later, they stopped in front of a building in Viale della Libertà, one of those residences for the bourgeois of Messina who loved to live in the center of the city and getting to face the sea. All the buildings on that avenue overlooked breathtaking views of the strait and the port of Messina; it seemed like one could reach out of the apartment windows above and touch the immense cruise ships that docked in the port below.

Marchese led his companions into the building. They crossed the elegant lobby to the elevator and rode it to the sixth, topmost top floor. They stepped out into an entryway and were greeted by a frosted-glass door, locked, with a panel of labelled doorbells on the left side.

"This is it!" Marchese declared.

As he pressed the appropriate doorbell, Torchia grabbed his elbow, his eyes wide with disbelief. "Are you crazy?"

* * *

Rosella Lecci drew her knees up under the covers and rested her notebook against them, tapping her pen against the page of notes she'd just completed. She was thinking about what the next day would hold.

At fifty-two years old, Rossella's once-blond hair had darkened and lines had formed in places she preferred them not to be. But her looks had never mattered to her. Her clever mind was her greatest gift. From age sixteen onward, she had developed a great passion, and now, finally, she was about to experience a culminating moment to all her research. She'd taken a sabbatical from the university where she'd taught literature for almost twenty-five years to pursue this unbelievable opportunity.

She'd always felt her path was predestined. That path had clarified just five years earlier, when her beloved uncle, a former Catholic priest, had passed away, leaving her with an inheritance far more valuable than money.

Grief and affection squeezed Rossella's heart as she slipped her hand into the top drawer of the bedside table and reached for the letter. She opened it and read it again, for the umpteenth time.

My dear Rossella,

By the time you read these few lines, the Lord will have summoned me home. I hope that, once before Him, I will receive forgiveness for my human weakness, just as I have asked all through my life. Now I leave you this precious gift that is the result of one of my weaknesses.

I have watched you grow in your passion for literature and for the author I too, have loved so much, to the point of tormenting nights, which have led me to leave you with this evidence that will illuminate your studies and one day give you the chance to become part of history.

This is only one of the six letters in my possession that I managed to preserve these long years. The other five were lost, perhaps burned in a fire that destroyed my rectory years ago, soon after the war.

But many others are in the hands of the Church, I'm sure, for I have seen and touched them. For reasons that are far reaching, that treasure is kept by the Church and not to be revealed to the world. Don't reveal it, until it's clear it's the right time! You will know that time when it arrives; it will be obvious to you.

Always remember, my dear Rossella, that God is great and will accompany you in this mission. Be patient. And always put your heart into what you do. I have loved you as a daughter. And I thank God for His giving me your smiles and your affection.
Your beloved uncle,
Gabriele

Rossella tucked the letter back in the drawer and lay down, staring at the ceiling.

She could not sleep. She would become part of history, proving it to the city that had always mocked her for her theories. She would restore to Messina its history, its pride. She, Rossella Lecci, would make Messina one of the most famous towns in the world.

Midnight had just struck. The new day had arrived, and, in a few hours, she would finally meet the person who would take this to the next step.

Chapter 8

Messina—August 9, 2012

When Capra's doorbell rang shortly after midnight, the last face he expected to see was that of Francesco Marchese. He didn't know whether to smile or worry, but he suddenly felt faint. The Detective of Steel stood before him at the door to his home. Fear and excitement mingled in his veins.

Capra was bare chested. In his living room, overlooking the breathtaking view of the strait, a casually dressed young woman, one of the latest interns on his editorial staff, sat on the sofa. Seeing Marchese enter with his two companions, she quickly got up and disappeared into the next room, shutting the door behind her.

"To what do I owe this visit, gentlemen?" Capra crowed, determined not to seem flustered even in the awkward situation.

"We need a favor," said Marchese, quietly stern.

A thrill ran up Capra's spine, and he stifled a grin as he gestured to the sofa. Marchese wanting a favor was better than anything that intern might have offered him that evening. "Sit down. Can I offer you something? A beer?"

The three men followed his gesture to the center of the huge living room, muttering "no thank you" as they went.

Capra perched himself in his leather armchair, facing the three men on the couch as if he were hosting an official interview. "So tell me. What's the favor?"

"We need you to release some news," Marchese replied. "Repeatedly. I'd daresay incessantly."

Capra's eyes narrowed. "What news?"

Marchese's brows lowered in a scowl. "First, you must guarantee us, however, that what we're telling you will not be used incorrectly. It might undermine the whole investigation."

Capra stifled a gleeful giggle, twisting his mouth into a frown. "Spit it out, Marchese."

The former detective looked at Torchia and Ricci, and Capra caught surprise on their faces. *Interesting*.

"We suspect that the murderer chooses his victims on the basis of an interest that links them," Marchese said at last. "It's just a suspicion, but we are attempting to warn other possible victims about it."

Capra's mind was already stringing together an opening monologue to break the news. "What interest are you talking about?"

"It is a passion shared by all the victims, a real obsession for a writer."

Capra's eyes widened. "That's very interesting," he agreed eagerly. "The stuff of crime novels. That's crazy. And who is the writer?"

The three detectives exchanged glances, nervous ones that got Capra's blood racing even faster. This time, the youngest of them—Capra could never remember his name—answered: "Shakespeare."

Capra almost slipped from his leather chair, momentarily speechless. But Marchese's grim face told him it wasn't a joke.

"As I told you before, it's just a theory."

Capra shook his head in disbelief. "You mean the Monster of Messina murders people who are fond of . . . Shakespeare?"

Torchia's face hardened. "It is a hypothesis we've formulated based on the few pieces of evidence in our possession. But we think we may be on the right track, so we must be careful."

"It seems a banal story, unless . . ." Capra trailed off, stood up, and crossed to the windows.

"Unless?" Marchese repeated. "What?"

"Unless," Capra replied, "it is related to the theory of its alleged Messina origins."

"That's what we believe, too," blurted the deputy.

Capra turned just in time to see a chilling glance from Torchia withering the deputy in his seat.

"Shit." Capra stared off over the strait, at the flickering lights of the city reflecting on the water. "That's crazy."

"It's just a theory," Marchese insisted.

"And how can I help you?" Capra returned to his place, this time taking a less defiant pose. His eagerness to know won out over his desire to have one over on the former detective.

"We would like you to release the news," Marchese replied. "But it will have to be true to the format I'm giving you. Without adding any personal opinion or comment."

Capra cocked an eyebrow. "Do you guarantee exclusivity?"

"Yes, provided you do what we tell you," Marchese replied firmly.

Capra could live with that. "Tell me, then. When should this news come out?"

"Immediately. Call your editorial office. Every hour, on every newscast. And a continuous scroll during all the scheduled programs. Always."

Capra wrinkled his nose at Marchese's commanding tone, but exclusivity like this was too good to pass up in the territorial world of journalism. "What should we say?"

"That according to rumors," Marchese said slowly, "the murderer lures and kills women who have a passion for the playwright. Say nothing about the theory of its origins. We just need to alert the possible future victims who may already be in contact with the killer."

"In what way are they in contact with him?" Capra asked.

"Don't know. We aren't certain of the theory's validity, but my gut tells me we've got it nailed down."

"Rarely have your instincts failed, Marchese," Capra said with deference.

He well knew that if the former detective had gone this far, there had to be something to it. Capra trusted the famous "Detective of Steel," even if he had dropped off the map these past two years.

"Call your editorial office," Marchese ordered. "Please, don't do other than what I have asked you. And, obviously, we were never here."

Capra didn't bother to hide his self-satisfied grin. "Don't worry, detective, this won't be the first time I've provided pivotal assistance. I won't disappoint."

It was true. Capra's effort had led to decisive success in several cases. But the hard look on Marchese's face assured him that he had not forgotten the death of Leo Marino in the Aspromonte mountains. Capra had been instrumental in that, too, and his mood soured as he realized that Marchese still didn't trust him.

No matter, he thought, ushering them out and giving Torchia a simpering smile that Marchese's former underling met with a blatant sneer. By this time tomorrow, he, Luigi Capra, would be making headlines again.

* * *

It was 9:00 a.m., and Rossella had not slept all night.

In a few hours she would meet her mysterious friend, a colleague in her research, who in the last two years had been a reference point for the group on the blog called "The Millennium Secret."

114

She had never met him in person, but for two years, they had exchanged opinions on her blog about her research. She knew by the comments section that other people were in communication with him on the same subject.

Then, one day, he had contacted her on her private chat. And it all started, a professional relationship that had become more and more involved. They began chatting every day. They exchanged their views on the research they were doing and the information they were compiling. And when she confided in him about the letter, he shared with her that he had one, too.

This incredible shared secret created a bond between them. She had never before met another mind so curious and excited for the playwright whose work had so enthralled her. They agreed that the two letters had to be compared, to verify that both had been written by the same famous and legendary hand.

Rossella took a shower and then, still in her bathrobe, sat in the kitchen to have breakfast in front of the television. She was alone that morning; her sister was out on a leisure trip and she had the apartment to herself.

It had been difficult, not being able to tell anyone of how her passion for her work on Shakespeare, her obsessive vocation —her destiny—had brought her to the meeting she was so eagerly looking forward to. She hadn't even told Martina, and she told her older sister everything. But it seemed too good to be true, and she didn't want to jinx it. Her sister would have laughed at her superstition.

While she soaked some biscotti in milk, she started to flip through the TV channels, pausing occasionally on the local ones. She had been following the news about the recent murders. Being home alone now only made her more anxious. Her sister had called her frequently in the past few days, reminding her to be careful and to not go out at night and to keep the doors locked.

She had opted not to go out at all. Except, of course, for this important appointment, which had been set many weeks before.

She paused on Luigi Capra's talk show, the first of the stations to address the local news every morning. The normally animated journalist seemed particularly keyed up today. He flattened his hand on the desk in front of him and stared piercingly into the camera.

"Good morning, dear citizens. We open this newscast with breaking news on the so-called Monster of Messina. He has already killed five women, and it seems he may have no intention of stopping. However today, we've had what may very well be a break in the case, a connection that could explain how this horrible massacre—"

Rossella's cell phone began to ring. She muted the TV and picked up the call. "Hello?"

"Rossella, it's me!"

Rossella smiled. Caller ID had already given that away. "What's up, Martina?"

"How are you?" her sister replied brightly. "I'm surprised you're even out of bed! Shouldn't you be lazing around? Isn't that what sabbaticals are for?"

On the TV screen, Capra's yammering face was replaced by scrolling images of the crime scenes. Rossella grimaced. "I'm doing well, Marti. What is Scotland like?"

"Beautiful, and above all, fresh," Martina replied. Rossella could hear a brisk wind in the background. "What's the weather like over there?"

Rossella began to clear the table with her phone stuck between ear and shoulder. "Warm. Actually, very hot."

"You're not going out, are you?"

"No, hush! You're such an old mother hen!" She smiled as Martina laughed on the far end of the line. "How's Antonio?"

Antonio was Martina's boyfriend, and if the plan he'd confided in Rossella before they left went well, he'd come home her future brother-in-law. That possibility had been the perfect excuse to stay home. Capra's agitated expression drew her eye again, so she turned away to focus on the call.

"He's fine. And you, be careful." Her sister's voice grew shaky. "Even here the newscasts don't talk about anything else but what's happening in Messina. We are worried about you."

"Don't worry, Marti," Rossella soothed, placing her dishes in the sink. "I didn't go out. The only reason I didn't go on vacation with you was that I know you and Tony need some time to yourselves. I will not go out. And if so, I won't leave home after sunset."

"OK, my love. I won't pester you. And if you're afraid, call me back."

Rossella smiled affectionately as she turned back toward the screen. "OK, Marti. Have fun, and don't think of anything else."

A painting of William Shakespeare appeared on the TV screen.

Rossella said good-bye to her sister and put down the phone with one hand, fumbling for the remote with the other.

Capra's voice blared again. "—just a development, however the source is very reliable. And we from Media TV would not fail to advise you of any possible way to keep you safe."

Rossella had missed what the journalist had said about Shakespeare, and it left her baffled. She started flipping through other local channels, but no other newscasters mentioned any development. Just the usual reports about the monster and the city. Nothing about the playwright, Shakespeare. Her passion.

She flipped back to Media TV and tossed the remote aside, spying the time on the wall clock. "Damn it!" she exclaimed, realizing she had fewer than two hours to prepare herself for her appointment. She left the television playing but paid it no mind as she went to her bedroom to get ready.

* * *

Marchese had not slept a wink, either. Now he sat riveted by Luigi Capra's news channel.

As he requested, the news had been released. Just the way he wanted it to be. And the channel had begun to scroll the information. Now there was nothing to do but to wait and to hope.

The night before, nothing had happened. The killer, as far as he knew, hadn't struck again—or at least nobody had reported the news.

Satisfied with Capra's performance, he shut the TV off and headed to the shower. Relaxing under the jet of water, he mulled over the theory they had developed the night before.

It's possible, he thought. *It is.*

He vaguely recalled having heard the theory that Shakespeare had supposedly been born in Messina and had fled to England to avoid the Inquisition. He had heard of people who were looking for evidence and studying theories about it. He did not understand, however, why the murderer had killed those women because of it, if that was truly his motive. What did he want from them? What was his problem with their interest in this?

Marchese knew anything was possible. The motives for murder he had encountered during his career were the craziest, the most disparate, the most meticulously and diabolically calculated ones. Therefore, even this hypothetical reason could be plausible. It might not turn out to be a waste of time.

Even if it was, he couldn't afford to sit idly by any more. He hadn't realized it until he'd faced off with Capra again, but the work he'd initially gone to the mountains to escape from turned out to be the only thing that kept the gnawing guilt away. Maybe helping bring this murderer to justice would help him lay Renata's memory to rest.

* * *

Rossella wore a pair of Levis and a black T-shirt that read "Don't Worry, Futtitinni." She brushed her hair and surveyed herself in the hallway mirror. It felt strange, going out in casual dress on a day when she knew classes would be in session. She knew one thing for sure, her sabbatical would be temporary. She never thought she'd miss teaching so much.

But she was ready. Even if she almost had two hours to go.

Luigi Capra's voice sounded again from the kitchen and, with time to kill, she purposely tuned in to hear what he was saying. *The Monster of Messina . . . Shakespeare.* Rossella bolted to the kitchen, gaping at the TV.

"Many people have defined this theory as a publicity stunt aimed at increasing the audience, but I assure you that our source is more than reliable. Furthermore, the police are already doing a thorough search for anyone who, for various reasons, are involved with anything to do with the famous playwright's work. We feel it is our duty to warn these people who seek only to cultivate their innocent passion for Shakespeare . . ."

Rossella's hairbrush fell from her nerveless hand and clattered to the tile floor.

Capra went on, his brows knitted in a scowl, *"It is not yet clear why the murderer chooses his victims among the fans of the famous English writer, and it isn't clear to the police either, but from the evidence gathered by the investigators, there seems to be a shared connection among the women murdered. And it is exactly their shared passion for Shakespeare that has made them a target. If you have any news related to this, or something to share with us, you can contact us in our offices . . ."*

Rossella was so stunned that, for a moment, she was almost certain she'd heard wrong.

The Monster of Messina killed women passionate about Shakespeare?

Her hands shook violently as two years passed before her eyes. The blog, her English friend. The coincidences. Her appointment.

Everything.

She began to tremble. She couldn't stop, and the trembling grew nearly to convulsions.

She threw up, on the floor of her kitchen, right in front of the television.

***

Marchese could have killed Capra with his bare hands.

The hotline number scrolling across the TV screen went to Capra's editorial office, an attempt to poach information that would deter people from calling in to the police station.

It was a bad deal that could cost someone's life.

Marchese's phone rang. He knew who it was even before answering. "If you're calling me about Capra, I just heard."

"He's completely screwed up the plan," Torchia said, audibly seething.

"I know," he replied, glaring at the screen. But suddenly a grin spread across his face. "I've got an idea. See you in twenty minutes. But not at the police station."

"Where, then?"

"At the editorial office of Media TV."

Moments later, Marchese stormed to his car and sped off toward the news station, pulling into the parking lot at the same moment Torchia and Deputy Ricci, the latter of whom was red-faced in visible fury, parked their police cruiser and stepped out.

When the disgruntled detectives entered Capra's office at 9:40 a.m., the smirk Capra had been wearing vanished.

"You're committing a crime, don't you know?" said the journalist.

Marchese focused his bloodshot eyes on Capra. "If you don't want me to commit a bigger one, move aside and let us do our job. We made a deal, and you violated it. But I expected as much. Your ambition has always taken precedence over the lives of the victims."

Capra sat back in his chair, the picture of indifference.

"You have no blood in your veins, Luigi Capra," Marchese accused, jabbing a finger at him. "Not even Leo Marino's death could trigger guilt in your miserable excuse for a heart."

It was true. And Capra knew it. He was a calculating, self-invested man, and an absolute bloodhound when there was a story to be had, to the point that he knew some of his younger staff thought him devoid of empathy. He had lived his life with only one focus: his own success. He had no regrets. He did not allow Leo Marino's memory to touch him. Capra was willing to do anything for a news story, and if that meant accidentally pushing the young journalist toward his own death, so be it. He would not take any responsibility for that. And he felt the same way about the death of Marchese's beloved partner. *Not* responsible.

He stood impotently by while the bumbling detective Torchia and Deputy What's-His-Name took positions at the telephones the station had designated for the hotline. The Detective of Steel made himself comfortable in Capra's cushy office chair.

Already they'd had a number of calls from mythomaniacs and good Samaritans wishing to make their contribution or offer tips. Careful screening of the information was necessary. But one thing was for certain: If the detectives' theory was accurate, any possible victims seeing the report would be sufficiently alarmed. Perhaps this would stop the Monster of Messina from carrying out additional murders. Even Capra wanted this to be the case. He had enough as it was to milk this new story for a while. He was also aware that the murderer himself might hear the news about Shakespeare's theory and would vanish into thin air, making his capture quite impossible. It was a risk the detectives were taking.

* * *

Rossella staggered to the bathroom and splashed cold water on her face, the taste of bile still on her tongue. She turned over her shaking hand and looked at her watch. In under two hours, she was supposed to meet her English friend. Mind whirling, she considered where that meeting was supposed to take place—an isolated spot. All too secret.

Everything started to fit together in her mind.

He was the Monster of Messina—her English friend who was so intent in verifying the authenticity of the document in her possession. But it also meant that, perhaps, she didn't have the only copy of the Origin. She remembered the words written in uncle Gabriele's letter: *The other five letters had been lost.*

Until that day, five women had been murdered in Messina.

Five women. Five lost letters, if Gabriele's letter had been truthful.

She could have been the sixth woman to be killed.

She understood almost everything: That man was looking for the copies of Michelangelo Florio's letters. The proof of Shakespeare's Messina origins.

But why? That, Rossella didn't understand. Why kill her? Why kill her, just to get those documents, that proof? Maybe for their value. Or to hide the truth. Or maybe just for madness.

Rossella returned to the kitchen. She jotted down hotline number scrolling on the screen and grabbed the phone.

* * *

Marchese sat with his feet propped up on Capra's desk.

Capra passed in front of him, heading to the newscast set. "Your shoes have mud on them," the journalist commented. "And that desk is *oak*."

Marchese made as if to move his feet off the desk but simply shifted his position and gave Capra a hard stare. The journalist's jaw tightened, and he left.

Torchia hung up the phone from a caller with a supposed tip. Though he'd taken notes, he knew they were worthless. "The chief of police and the prefect have called me three times this morning, Francesco," he told his friend with worry in his voice. "They want to know more. They want to know what we're doing, where I am. I don't know how much longer I can put them off. This is huge risk."

Now Marchese placed both feet on the floor and leaned toward his former deputy. "I know, but we have nothing but this. Not even the Carabinieri came up with any leads. This is the best shot we've got right now."

The phone rang again. Ricci answered with "Deputy Detective Ricci of the State Police." He stated the caller's name aloud: "Rossella Lecci." He listened a moment and said, "What's that you say?" He gave the other officers a look that suggested this call might be the real deal.

* * *

Mark Connell stepped out of the shower and glanced at his watch on the hotel desk. He had to get ready. A pair of jeans and a white T-shirt awaited him on the hotel bed. He sneered at the cheap, plasticky comforter as he stepped into his shoes. He wouldn't miss this room, with its cheap carpeting and scratchy sheets, and he certainly wouldn't miss the bored indifference of everyone on staff here, either. And he was sick of the sensationalist Italian news, even when it was about him.

His final meeting would be held at Capo Peloro, far from the hotel, in an abandoned behemoth of a steel building situated on the beach—a safe place for a murder. Only at night did some romantic couples go there, seeking privacy in the shadows sprawling between the magnificent Scilla and the useless electricity pylons.

One more victim, the last. And then it would be over. Along with the heat, Italy and especially Sicily and its coarse inhabitants would be behind him.

The last letter of the Origin. The last bit of evidence.

The amount he would be paid sprang to mind again, and as always, it made his hands shake with excitement. Graham had been generous for this mission. Two years' work, six victims, a long, delicate and sophisticated job. But one million pounds was a lot of money. Connell turned on the TV and tuned into the RTL music channel. Queen's "Bohemian Rhapsody" music video filled the screen, making him feel at home. He turned up the volume and sang along as he got dressed.

He had saved his most interesting contact for last. The one whose uncle was the priest who had found the six copies of the Origin.

There were six. And he had recovered almost all of them.

David Graham had entrusted him with this delicate task. How the English tycoon had discovered the existence of the letters was a mystery to him, but he was not really interested in that. He only cared about getting paid by this rich man once the job was done. Nothing else.

Once dressed, he donned a gray linen jacket, turned off the TV, and headed out.

* * *

Ricci sat forward in his chair, brandishing a pen over his open notepad. "I'm going to place you on speaker, Ms. Lecci, and I'd like you to repeat we you just told me."

The woman's voice was shaky. "I have an appointment in one hour with a man who I've been corresponding with for two years about Shakespeare's Messina origins. We're planning to compare our letters."

"What kind of letters?" Ricci asked.

"A few years ago I inherited from my uncle who was a priest one of six letters proving that William Shakespeare's real name was Michelangelo Florio."

Hearing the number of the existing letters, more than any other detail, convinced them all that Marchese's hunch had been correct. Releasing the news according to the plan had led to the desired result and perhaps Capra had helped them once more.

"Where are you now?" Ricci asked.

"I'm at home, on the Coast Road," the caller replied. "Not far from Capo Peloro. Where, as I said, I have the appointment in an hour."

Marchese leaned over the phone and said firmly, "Don't move. We are coming. Please give us your exact address."

Moments later, the three men charged out of the office and leapt into the waiting police car parked out front. Torchia took the wheel and, he was maneuvering, Marchese's eyes met those of the woman whose car was parked on the other side of the road. He had seen that face, those eyes before. Though he never forgot a face, sometimes he had difficulty placing them in his memory. It nagged at him for only a moment as he had other problems to solve presently. He ordered Torchia to hurry, and then instructed Ricci to call the police station.

If they wanted the killer to bite the hook, they would need bait.

* * *

The longer Mark Connell sat in traffic on Viale della Libertà, the more he seethed. He hated the city and its people more and more. He had been there for just over a week and already he couldn't take it anymore. The rudeness of local drivers enraged him. He wanted to kill them all.

Arriving in front of the now-decaying Fiera Campionaria, he heard a police siren in the distance. He stiffened. All the sirens worried him. The siren was getting closer and closer to his location, until he saw beside him in the tramway lane, a police car moving at high speed.

He'd been worrying for nothing. In his moves and plans, he had left no traces. He was used to executing clean jobs. And these simpleminded Sicilian policemen would not succeed in catching him. He was overcautious and highly professional, while they were bumbling idiots who still hadn't figured out if there was more than one murderer at large.

Chapter 9

Rossella gave a start upon hearing the bell ring. Heart pounding, she tiptoed to the door, grasped the knob, and asked who was there.

"Detective Torchia," came a male voice from the other side. "I'm with Deputy Detective Ricci and Detective Marchese of the State Police. May we come in?"

Rossella unlocked the door and faced the three men.

"Are you Rossella Lecci?" asked Torchia.

Rossella nodded. "Yes, sir. That's me."

"Tell us everything," he urged, "as quickly as possible. We have no time to waste."

Rossella led them to the small living room, where she flopped down in the armchair while her visitors sat on the sofa. "A few years ago, I inherited a very important document—a letter, which could prove William Shakespeare was born in Messina birth and his real name was Michelangelo Florio. This thrilled me, since Shakespeare's works are a passion of mine. Two years ago, I joined a blog where people discussed and exchanged information on the Messina origin theory."

The three policemen listened in silence. Rossella shifted nervously in her seat.

"The blog manager, a man named Mark, began chatting with me privately. Eventually I told him about the letter, written by Michelangelo Florio while he was in England to an old friend of his, a pro-Calvinist priest in his native Messina. That's how we became friendly, so to speak. We talked about undertaking a possible research project together."

"What kind of research, given that the letter was already hard evidence?" asked Ricci eagerly. Rossella sensed a common interest on the subject that hours ago would have thrilled her. Now it just made her stomach flip again.

"It's not like that," she replied. "I know the letter was written by Florio. Proving it is a whole other matter. And to prove it's not a fake will take a handwriting analyst. That's the only way to affirm with certainty that Michelangelo Florio of Messina and William Shakespeare are one and the same."

"So?" Torchia replied, wheeling his hands in front of him. "What happened next?"

"Mark told me that he has a letter written by Florio," Rossella answered, her hands beginning to shake again, "different from mine, and probably written soon afterwards, given the close dates. Therefore, we decided to meet and compare the documents."

Marchese scowled. "And he probably used the same strategy with the other five victims."

"I think so," Rossella confirmed, "but I didn't know about any other copies. My uncle's letter mentioned five other letters that had been his possession, but he wrote they had been lost and perhaps destroyed. But now I suspect that's not true."

"So this Mark met all five victims, stole their documents, and then killed them," Marchese summed up.

"How long did they say before Officer Caracciolo arrives?" Torchia asked Ricci, looking at his watch.

"She'll be here soon," Ricci said though a little uncertainty laced his voice.

Rossella glanced at the clock on the wall. Only a half an hour remained before her appointment with the Monster of Messina. She wrung her hands in her lap to hide their trembling.

* * *

Connell arrived at Capo Peloro at 10:45 a.m. The appointment was set for eleven sharp, so he had plenty of time to inspect the area. Different from the others, it was the first time he was to meet one of his victims daylight. It was very dangerous. Someone might see them and interfere with his plan. Unlike a few of the others, she clearly had no romantic interest in him and had insisted on a daytime meeting. So he'd chosen this place. In fact, the old steel structure had housed a shipyard some decades before but was now deserted, though there were plenty of swimmers on the beach. Connell chose the most hidden corner to await his victim as he climbed onto a low wall and waited in silence.

His task about to come to an end. He was already thinking of returning home and enjoying his reward.

* * *

When the female officer arrived at 10:50, there was little time to explain the plan. Officer Giovanna Caracciolo was the only female officer on duty who resembled Rossella even a little bit. They hoped the resemblance would be close enough to prevent the killer from immediately becoming suspicious. The agent who had accompanied her remained behind with Rossella.

Giovanna put on her bulletproof vest. Within five minutes, she was ready, but nobody knew for what exactly. Only Torchia, Ricci, Marchese, and Caracciolo were involved in the operation, as there was no time to orchestrate something more elaborate.

Rossella's house was about a half mile away from Capo Peloro. Torchia drove, and Ricci took the passenger seat. Marchese, seated in the back beside Officer Caracciolo, coached her on what to expect. "We are potentially dealing with a ruthless murderer. He just wants a document. And having ascertained that you have it and that it is what he is looking for, he *will* try to kill you. You *must* stall him."

Marchese's skin crawled at the idea of potentially feeding a fellow cop to a monster. He felt responsible for Caracciolo's life, but he had no choice but to put her in danger. If something went wrong, he would live forever in guilt, and certainly, Torchia's career would be over.

"Take your time," he instructed. "We will follow your every move."

The officer nodded, but he could see the fear in her eyes. Likely she had never taken on such a potentially dangerous mission.

"We'll stick close and jump in there as soon as the time is right. We want him alive—and you unharmed. So be careful. Keep your gun accessible but well hidden. The women who have met him so far were likely enthusiastic about meeting him, so try to seem as easygoing as possible."

The cars stopped under the old lighthouse, a few meters away from Capo Peloro, not far from the decaying structure of the old shipyard and a couple of two-story houses.

Marchese and the officers got out of the car.

The former detective gave Caracciolo a hard stare. "Ready? You will proceed on foot. Ricci will walk behind you nonchalantly and at a distance. Then he'll move to a barely visible place. Meanwhile, we'll position ourselves in two other corners of the structure."

Marchese turned to Torchia. "Go around to the other side. Position yourself near the old brick wall. The killer will likely try to take her behind the old ruins to avoid being seen. I will try to go around, passing by the beach, if they move toward the east wing of the structure. I will be able to control the whole area from there."

Marchese retrieved the ancient document from his pocket. He had not opened it, but he trusted its contents. He thought a bit and then turned to Officer Caracciolo again. "I'm going to hold on to this. If you take it with you, it could seal your doom."

Ricci looked at his watch. It was eleven o'clock. "We're late," he mumbled, as he watched Torchia adjusting his usual limp for a quicker gait toward the spot Marchese had indicated.

* * *

Officer Caracciolo walked toward the beach leading to the steel structure. Under the high midday sun, sweat accumulated under the bulletproof vest hidden beneath her blue linen jacket. As she drew closer, she fought for the necessary composure to keep her fear from betraying her.

She glanced around but saw none of her backup, although she knew they were close by. She trusted Torchia and knew Marchese's reputation. She didn't feel alone and, knowing she was protected, kept calm.

Only after passing among the old steel pillars that supported the decaying roof, consisting of pulleys and metal architraves, did she see at the opposite end of the concrete platform a man sitting on a low brick wall. She felt a deafening pulse hammering in her temples and stopped a moment to take a breath.

* * *

Marchese had taken off his shirt and rolled his jeans carefully up under his knees to look more natural as he crossed the dunes. Torchia had already positioned himself behind the old walls, looking for a slot that let him keep a constant line of sight on Caracciolo. Ricci walked along the dirt road skirting the edge of the beach, pretending to be engrossed in a call. He was the only one who, until then, could see and protect the undercover officer and was the first to spot a man in the distance, leaning against an old brick wall facing the sea.

Though the presumed killer had his back turned to her, he had obviously heard Caracciolo coming up behind him because he turned toward her, flashing a smile.

The pair was fewer than twenty yards from Marchese, who was having difficulty making his way through the reeds that separated him from the old shipyard's platform. After an exchange of pleasantries that was difficult to hear but easy to see, the alleged killer and his prey began moving in the direction of the ruins—toward Torchia's post.

* * *

Only minutes before, Connell had been congratulating himself on the straightforwardness of his plan. He and the woman would meet in that scenic spot, and he would guide his unsuspecting victim to the narrow and isolated area of the ruins as they chatted. It would take no more than five minutes, and then, within ten minutes, he'd be headed the hotel.

However, Connell knew that wasn't Rossella. Though her presence on the internet was scant, he had uncovered photos of her from her family's social-media profiles. He knew it was a trap. Now he had to figure a way out. He decided to buy some time and take her to a shady area. Connell smiled at the imposter, but, feeling hunted, tension grew quickly inside him.

As they talked, he looked around for whoever was lurking, waiting to attack him. His mind raced. It was clear the imposter, whoever she was, thought he'd fallen for the trap. She talked about Messina and asked him his impression of it, and if it was his first time there and so on. He wondered how long she would try to continue carrying on the charade.

* * *

Torchia slipped into one of the passages of the decaying structure. Caracciolo and the suspect were now just ten feet from him. He positioned himself and rubbed his aching leg, cursing how it had interfered with his agility. From his vantage point, he could see everything—even Marchese, in the distance, who was approaching from the beach.

Meanwhile, Ricci had lost sight of the suspect and the undercover officer, as well as Torchia, but he could see Marchese moving in closer. If the suspect were to turn, he would see the former detective approaching in the distance. The situation was coming to a head. Ricci drew his gun from his shoulder holster.

Connell and Caracciolo arrived in front of the wall dividing the open area from the ruins of the structure. She seemed to be growing worried now, her eyes darting around. Out of the corner of his eye, Connell saw someone, a gray-haired man, hiding in the passage directly in front of him.

"Rossella," he said. "It's time to compare our letters." He reached into the inner pocket of his linen jacket as if to retrieve the letter. "Do you have yours?"

Instead of a letter, he withdrew his gun, fitted with a silencer, and the imposter's eyes widened. She fumbled in her purse, but he had already pulled the trigger. She wasn't his target. Instead, he'd shot past her toward the passage at the gray-haired man and saw that he had made his mark. The woman stumbled back, and then Connell turned the gun on her.

From behind him, he heard, "Police! Drop the weapon!"

He shot anyway. The bullet landed in the imposter's chest and her knees buckled. Connell spun around and fired at the bare-chested brute who'd come up off the beach but was still too far away for an accurate shot. The tall man returned fire, grazing Connell's arm. He felt searing pain, a pain he'd never experienced before and it enraged him, giving him a much-needed shot of adrenaline.

Like a bolt of lightning, Connell zigzagged his way into the passageway, hopping over the lifeless man he'd just shot, as another armed man was hurriedly approaching through the passages. Clearly, the downed comrade had caught the other's attention, giving Connell the opportunity to knock him out of his way.

He knew the man from the beach was hot on his trail, so he ran as fast as his legs would carry him, his feet hurling up sand behind him as he scrambled toward the street, his mind raging at his failure and wondering how they'd managed to discover his plan. His thoughts flashed to Graham's disappointment and the payment he wouldn't receive. When he reached the parking lot, he risked a glance over his shoulder. He'd managed to put quite a bit of distance between himself and his pursuer.

At his car, a pair of sloppily dressed young men were chatting by the driver's side door. He aimed his gun at them. "Move away! Get out of my way!" he screamed.

They moved a few steps from the car door, which Connell hurriedly opened. As he slid into the seat, one of the pair entered the car by the rear door and the other slid into the passenger's seat. The one beside him made quick work of relieving Connell of his gun.

"What the fuck?!" Connell shouted. Then he felt the barrel of a gun on the back of his neck.

The man beside him, who at second glance wasn't so young, smiled thinly. "Hello, Mr. Connell. Start the car. Your pursuer is getting close. We'll answer your question as soon as you start driving."

* * *

The ambulance arrived on the scene within ten minutes, escorted by three police cars. Though shaken, Officer Caracciolo was relatively unharmed thanks to the bullet-proof vest. Ricci orchestrated the search for the killer's car, which Marchese had described in detail, setting up checkpoints on all the roads leading to the city center or the highway.

Marchese kneeled at Torchia's side as his friend clung to life by a thread. He'd been shot in his chest and had lost lot of blood. "Hang on, buddy," he urged, as the paramedics worked on him. Then he watched helplessly as they loaded the detective into the ambulance. Sure, they had prevented another murder but possibly at the expense of Torchia's life. Worse yet, the killer was still on the loose. Failure.

* * *

Connell stopped the car on a narrow street, just outside the village of Torre Faro, as instructed by the man in the passenger seat. They hadn't answered his question as promised. Waiting for them was a black sedan with a male driver and a female passenger.

"Get out," the man in the back demanded. "Don't try anything."

Connell obeyed. The woman in the sedan also got out and approached them. She was dressed smartly in a svelte navy suit, and in a different situation, Connell might have admired her look.

"Mark Connell, you are a difficult man to locate."

"Who are you?" Connell demanded. "And what do you want from me?"

The elegant woman smiled blandly. "I'm with MI5."

Connell paled. The UK's Security Service. Not only did he fail at his mission, but he was also as good as dead. If MI5 agents had come to Sicily to find him, it meant this case was particularly relevant and that what he had was extremely important to the English. He understood why. "What do you want from me?" he asked anyway.

The woman came closer, standing toe to toe. Though many inches shorter, she had a demanding presence. "Let's say you *found* something we need. We would want you to hand it over and we would also want to know who ordered you to find it."

They wanted the letters. Whether by the hands of M15 or Graham, Connell knew he had come to the end of the road. All his years of meticulous planning foiled in a single afternoon. Grasping at straws, he replied coldly, "They are hidden in my hotel room, but I want some guarantees."

The woman gave him a dismissive once-over. "Who hired you? Was it David Graham?"

"No, nobody," he fumbled.

Her smile grew. "Don't lie to me. I can make it so that you won't ever see the light of day again."

Connell felt himself sinking. "At least I'd still be breathing."

She cocked an eyebrow. "That's not for sure. Let's go and get those documents. Then we'll talk about who paid for your trip to Italy."

All four climbed into the black sedan, and the driver headed downtown, abandoning Connell's rental car.

* * *

Marchese grabbed a cold beer and sat down under the porch facing the sea. The sun was about to disappear beneath the horizon. His chest constricted with despair.

Torchia had died en route to the hospital. The bullet had severed a pulmonary artery. With an appropriate display of grief, Luigi Capra reported the news of the detective's death, attributing it to a firefight with the newly dubbed "Shakespeare Slayer." He also reported that the killer had escaped capture and that the car he'd fled in had been abandoned not far from Capo Peloro.

The former detective felt responsible. It was his plan after all. What's more, even though he had never admitted it to himself before, Torchia had been one of his best friends, maybe his only friend. Without Renata and now without Torchia, his life felt empty. He downed his beer and headed to the kitchen for another. Halfway to the fridge, he heard an insistent knock at his door. He had no interest in seeing anyone.

"Who is it?"

"Mr. Marchese," came a woman's voice, "I am a friend of yours."

Marchese opened the door, revealing the attractive woman he had seen several times in the past few days in front of the Media TV offices and also in Camigliatello. Marchese was baffled. "But you . . ."

She smiled. "Yes. It's no coincidence our paths have crossed." She walked inside, brushing past Marchese. "May I sit down?"

Seeing no reason to ask her to leave, he left her standing in the entryway while he retrieved two bottles of Peroni.

"Beer?" he asked when he rejoined her.

She nodded. "With pleasure."

He handed her the bottle, then led her through the house and out to the porch in silence.

When they sat, he said, "So, you're a friend of mine, you say? Sorry I don't know you. I just know that you've been trailing me."

"I know you very well by now, Mr. Marchese, but I have you at a disadvantage. Allow me to introduce myself. I'm Agent Paola Valton with M15."

Marchese gave no sign of surprise. He took a swig of his beer, further drowning his sorrow. "What do you want from me, Agent Valton?" he asked.

"Let's just say I wanted to meet you because I needed you to do me a favor. But then I didn't need it after all."

The cryptic answer stirred Marchese's curiosity. "And now?"

"Now I need you to do me a different favor."

Marchese finished his beer and placed it on the ground next to a small collection of others. "I don't understand."

She shifted in her seat and took a small sip from her bottle. She placed the bottle in the indentation in the armrest and wiped her wet hand across her pant leg. "Let's start from the beginning, so it will be clearer."

"Right. That's better."

She crossed her legs and admired the last light of the sunset for a moment before she began to speak. "At MI5 we discovered that a ruthless mercenary had left for Sicily to retrieve some documents that are extremely important to England. We failed to intercept him. We knew what he was looking for but didn't know how he planned to obtain them. We don't have much leeway here. Each day we're here, we risk creating a diplomatic incident that would reveal information our superiors don't want disclosed."

Marchese scowled. "Namely that, in reality, Shakespeare is no Englishman."

Agent Valton nodded. "More or less."

"So?"

"So, we asked a couple Italian Security Service agents with whom we work for the name of a contact person in the territory."

"You mean spies who snitch," Marchese snapped.

She gave him a thin smile. "Something very common among agents from all over the world," she replied diplomatically.

"Yes, I know. It's a shitty world."

"However, one of those agents advised us to approach you for help."

"And how can *I* help you?"

"Well, we hoped you would help us find the killer before he acted. Maybe involving your contacts at the police station."

The irony almost made Marchese laugh. "Then, without your needing to ask me, I rushed into the search for that bastard and now you don't need to ask me anymore."

The agent winced. "That's right."

"OK, then, but I haven't captured him. The bastard had accomplices, and he got away."

"It's not like that, Mr. Marchese."

Marchese didn't even flinch. He had already guessed it: The M15 had already caught him. "You have him."

"Yes, but we could deliver him to you—if you want."

"In exchange for the favor you are about to ask me, I imagine." He looked down at his collection of bottles and noticed one was still half full.

"Yes. You should do us a little favor."

Marchese downed the warm beer. He could feel the effects of the alcohol calm his nervous system. He planned to drink for the rest of night and maybe for the undetermined future until the world and all its problems shrunk down into an imperceptible itch. "Tell me, what's the favor?"

The agent had another sip of the bitter liquid and turned to Marchese. "You have a very important letter in your possession."

Rossella's letter. With the death of his friend, he'd forgotten it was still in his jacket. "It doesn't belong to me," he countered.

"Yes, I know," Agent Valton replied easily. "I'm sure she doesn't want it back when having it in one's possession carries the risk of death. She told me so herself."

Marchese's eyes narrowed and his grip tightened on the empty bottle. "In return, you'll give me the bastard who killed my friend?"

"Yes."

"Do I have a choice."

The agent offered a sad smile. "Don't make me answer no."

"It wasn't a question," Marchese scoffed.

He stood up to retrieve his jacket from the coat rack. When he returned to the porch, his jacket was slung over his arm and he held two more beers. He didn't offer her one. He sat back down and placed the jacket across his knee while he nearly emptied one of the beers. He wiped the condensation off his hands and retrieved the letter from his jacket. He placed in her outstretched hand.

"Did you open it?"

"No."

The agent raised a shapely eyebrow. "Aren't you curious to know its content?"

"No."

"They told me that you are a pragmatic and direct man."

Marchese snorted and took a swig. "Do you believe everything people say?"

"No, but in this case, they weren't wrong."

Marchese found himself suddenly furious. "Why were you even bothering to look for a letter that simply proves a writer was born in Messina rather than a small town outside London?"

"That village is called Stratford-Upon-Avon," the agent corrected. "And that village, like most of the south of the Kingdom, relies on tourism and mainly on that attraction."

"It's just a tourist problem, then."

"No. Rather, it's a matter of English pride. If it turns out that William Shakespeare was really your Michelangelo Florio, this would require embarrassing explanations from the Crown. Imagine what people would say. A fake birth certificate, displayed in the church of Stratford, and that would only be the tip of the iceberg: numerous works and documents, having been analyzed in recent years by experts of the queen, would come under scrutiny, and those experts would be accused of hiding obvious proof in favor of the theory that many of your fellow citizens have claimed for years. The pillar of English culture turns out to be Italian? You don't think that would be a controversy worth covering up?"

Marchese looked at her puzzled, still trying to understand what all of this meant. "But why would MI5 be involved?"

"MI5 is the domestic counterintelligence and security agency that is in charge of matters of critical domestic importance," Paola explained. "And the Crown can direct MI5 to handle its sensitive missions, like this one."

By now, Marchese had lost patience with this conversation. His mind was on Torchia and the damn monster who'd killed him and the others. He thought of Renata and all the people who had died for political reasons. He was tired. He stood up and indicated with a wave of his hand that the agent should do the same.

He stalked back to the foyer, placing his hand on the doorknob in an obvious gesture of dismissal. "I understand your concerns, Agent Valton. But I don't share them. For me, human lives come before these matters. Spare me the political lessons, issues of security, and the national image." He opened the door.

The agent tucked the letter in her suit pocket. "Tomorrow you'll have what I've promised."

He closed the door behind her and returned to the porch. The lights of the strait gradually dimmed, just like his mind, heavy with alcohol. Moments later, he fell asleep.

* * *

A 9:00 a.m. newscast opened with the report that a body had been discovered. Marchese grabbed the remote and turned up the volume.

This morning the body of a man was found on the beach of Capo Peloro, where only two days ago, Detective Carlo Torchia was killed during a shootout. The identity of the victim is unknown and cannot be determined due to the state of the body. The coroner has determined that the victim has been dead for about twelve hours. This is not believed to be the work of the Shakespeare Slayer. Anyone who may have information is urged to call the Messina police.

Marchese's face sagged. Sure, they handed over the killer as promised, but only for his personal satisfaction. Nothing could link the dead guy to the recent murders or much less to

Florio's letters. There would be no justice for the victims' families. Agent Valton had tricked him.

Marchese turned off the TV, and he soon found himself striding along the shoreline, red-hot anger slowly giving over to numbness. He'd had enough. He would leave Messina once and for all.

Messina—August 12, 2012

The bishop of Messina, Alessandro Perri, dialed his driver's number on his new iPhone. "Michele, get the car ready."

The young driver had parked in the shadows, under the trees of the narrow street that ran along the Cathedral of Messina. "Yes, Your Excellency. Where shall we go?"

The bishop sighed before answering. "To the airport. I'm leaving for Rome."

"Certainly, Your Excellency. I'll be right there." The young driver started the black Mercedes and drove toward the side door of the cathedral.

The bishop was very close to the new pope. He knew that the day when everything had to be taken back and guarded by the secret and secure walls of the Vatican would sooner or later arrive. From the small secret niche, hidden in the wall of the sacristy of the cathedral, he took out the small and ancient casket, a wooden box whose grime-darkened patina clearly showed its age.

Inside, the most important part of the greatest secret in recent years was still preserved. And the latest events that had occurred in the city had led the bishop to finally decide to secure the truth, inconvenient for many, but ardently desired by unscrupulous people. He knew it wasn't over. He knew they would be back again and that the one who had been behind so much death in those last days was still bloodthirsty. Paradoxically, as in great *Hamlet*, the risk was that too many people would do anything to be in possession of it—to the point of death.

The bishop tucked the box into his luggage and left the sacristy.

The car took him just to the foot of the stairs of the Vatican aircraft that had been readied for takeoff for hours now. The bishop never left his suitcase, not for a second. Shortly before boarding, he turned to his driver one last time and said, "You will come back tomorrow morning. I'll be back then. I'll let you know the exact time."

The driver nodded before disappearing behind the tinted windows of his Mercedes.

Minutes later, the plane left the runway of Catania airport on its way to Rome, carrying one of the best kept secrets in history.

Chapter 10

A black sedan with a Vatican City license plate greeted Bishop Alessandro Perri of Messina at precisely 1:00 p.m. in front of the Fiumicino airport terminal in Rome.

The driver opened the rear door. It was a hot day; the temperature had reached 107 degrees Fahrenheit.

"Welcome to Rome, Your Excellency," said the driver, bowing clumsily.

The bishop nodded politely before sliding into the right rear seat. The driver put the small luggage cart in the trunk, got behind the wheel, and then left for St. Peter's.

Traffic proved to be as slow as he'd expected; the ride would last no less than one hour. the bishop held the small suitcase on his knees and, as he caressed it, his thoughts returned, once again, to the death and despair that had overshadowed the beautiful city of Messina. How was it possible that six of the letters from the casket had been stolen? How powerful was this secret that it could unleash the devil inside one who was willing to fall for his wickedness and cause so much death and pain? Five innocent lives had been taken by evil to take possession of that inestimable proof, a secret so well guarded for over five hundred years.

After the tragic events, it was time to rely on those who would prevent this from happening again. Only one place would be adequate to keep in darkness the casket that, once opened, could unleash such evil. Only the secret rooms of the Vatican, where it had been safe for so long, could protect it from the devil's hands and guarantee the balance between the Roman Church and the English Crown. After the recent events, the elderly prelate had to surrender. He could no longer risk that the dark greed of man might bring more suffering.

As the car moved slowly through the traffic of the GRA ring road, headed toward the Eternal City, the bishop stared at the treasure in his lap and whispered the "Our Father."

MESSINA—AUGUST 12, 2012

Marchese had hardly slept these past forty-eight hours. He looked at his watch: 1:05 p.m., nearing time for Torchia's funeral. Over the years, the lives of far too many innocent people had been cut short by mobsters, Masons, security services, and other low lives. He'd lost his beloved Renata. And now Torchia.

Lying on his bed in a snug suit and tie, Marchese had no desire to get up. The funeral would be held in the cathedral of Messina at 3:00 p.m., attended by the press, curious citizens, his former colleagues, and, worst of all, the hypocritical politicians who had abandoned him, the police, and the city by surrendering it to the hands of evil in exchange for power and money throughout the years.

Marchese had often looked back on the past three years and thought he had seen it all in his job until the M15 had used him to take possession of the sixth letter and snuffed out any chance of true justice. He looked at his watch again; time to go. He stood up and caught his reflection in the mirror. Though he'd fought against it, the creases across his face revealed the sorrow and death that blackened all his days.

He knew he had to find a way out. This vortex would kill him if he didn't find an escape and give meaning to his life. He needed purpose, something that freed him without devaluing what he had lost, sacrificed, and destroyed. He needed a new life.

* * *

The bishop looked out the window of the Mercedes. They'd been driving for almost a half hour. He recognized the roads that still breathed the history of mankind and the foundations of the Church, his gaze lost among the ruins that reminded one of the greatness of Rome and its history, the history of emperors and early Christians, of sacrifice and wars.

As the car took the Lungotevere, the dome of St. Peter's appeared before him. Along the river, hundreds of tourists photographed this spectacular view. The greatness of the Catholic Church, its history, its secrets were all represented, guarded, and protected by that immense masterpiece of architecture. The bishop caressed the case containing his precious casket again.

"You will stop being the cause of tragedies very soon," he whispered.

They arrived in front of the Vittorio Emanuele bridge, but the driver, instead of crossing it, continued a little further on, turning onto Via Paola.

"I don't understand. Why didn't you take the bridge?" demanded the prelate.

"We must first make a stop, Your Excellency," replied the driver without a backward glance. "It'll only take a minute."

The bishop's heart raced. "A stop? What do you mean? I am expected at the Vatican, and I cannot stop. I have to take care of very important matters. The pope himself is waiting for me!"

At that moment, the car slipped into a small garage on the corner of Via dell'Arco dei Bianchi. "I'll be back in a moment, Your Excellency," said the driver, unbuckling his seat belt and opening the door. "Do not worry."

The driver turned off the car's lights and the garage door closed automatically behind him. The bishop looked around, baffled. The car's engine switched off and darkness fell around him.

* * *

Wrapped in the tricolor flag, the coffin entered from the main portal of the Messina cathedral, where Marchese sat in the last row. He watched as coffin passed, carried by six uniformed State Police officers. Immediately behind came Carlo Torchia's elderly mother, supported in her sorrow by her sister. *What a torment for a mother to have lost her son,* he thought bitterly. *How can she keep living, knowing that her child, her own flesh and blood, is lying in a cemetery?*

The procession following the coffin arrived at the foot of the altar. The cathedral was overflowing. Marchese saw many familiar faces but also some less recognized ones he'd encountered in the corridors of the police headquarters. Grief hung heavy in the air. Somehow this only served to anger him more.

Ricci stared steadfastly and proudly toward the altar, though his eyes were bloodshot.

We are the good guys, Marchese thought. *Even in death, we will always be on the right side of the world.*

Strangely enough, the rite was not performed by the bishop of the city but simply by the pastor of the police. The absence of the high prelate was unusual for a state funeral of this kind. Marchese registered this dimly; his eyes kept traveling to the casket, to the flag so tidily arranged on its lid. Torchia had died protecting that flag. It seemed almost obscene to see it draped over the box that would hold his friend's remains.

At the end of the Mass, Marchese decided not to queue up to pay his respects to the family. He had never understood that excruciating procession and the demand of sacrifice imposed on the deceased's relatives at the end of a funeral. In those moments, especially for a mother, he knew from experience that every hug would only exacerbate the pain and sorrow.

He left the cathedral, waiting on the parvis for the solemn salute by the police. Feeling parched by the scorching heat of the day in mid-August, Marchese found shelter under one of the trees lining the square and loosened his tie.

"I knew you'd be here, Marchese."

He immediately recognized the voice, and its heavy accent, coming from behind him. "What do you still want from me?" he demanded, turning to face Agent Valton. "Today's not the day. Leave me alone. You got what you were looking for. Now let me mourn my friend in peace." He turned his back on her and stared again at the main portal of the cathedral.

"I understand, Mr. Marchese, that you are a little angry with me," she said softly. She stepped forward to stand beside him, looming in the corner of his vision. "But one way or another, I kept my promise. I gave you Mark Connell, but it was naive of you to think I could give him to you alive. Too many people have learned of the secret my country has guarded for hundreds of years. You have taken a terrible risk. We can't afford to jeopardize the safety of others who might think of spreading this information."

"What can I do with a dead man?" Marchese spat. "A man I can't bring to justice for a fair sentence? Look at this square. In that church, my best friend is lying in a coffin. His mother is mourning a son without knowing *why* he died and, above all, without being able to see the perpetrator of all this suffering brought to justice."

Agent Valton winced. "Mark Connell paid with his life for what he did."

"Justice doesn't work that way," Marchese snapped, jerking his head around to shoot her a withering glare. "Not for me. Not even when I found myself in front of my murdered partner did I betray justice. And, believe me, I had a great desire to blow the bastard's head off more than anything else in the world."

Paola Valton stared at him. He didn't need her validation; he knew what he was talking about. For a year he had chased Renata's murderer, and when he'd found him, he had not had the strength to pull the trigger and kill that man, and it had nearly cost him his own life. That man was dead now, but at the hands of someone else, and he drew comfort from that. But Connell's death didn't seem to soothe him the same way.

"I respect you very much, Mr. Marchese," the agent replied, "and I admire your sense of justice. I'm sorry that things had to go this way. But, in life, things don't always go as they are described in the manual we were given when we joined up."

At that moment, the coffin in which Carlo Torchia lay, left the cathedral, and the six officers of the State Police placed it before the hearse. Marchese stared at them. "You're right, Agent Valton. Things do not go according to the manual, and I'm trying to live with that. But I prefer to do my best so that I don't have to go against the rules. Otherwise, you risk going around and around forever without finding a way out."

The M15 agent remained silent for a few minutes, as if letting Marchese bid farewell to his friend. In the square, the rifles of law enforcement shot blanks into the air, while Torchia's coffin was loaded onto the hearse that would take him to the city cemetery.

Her silence said more than what sympathy she'd verbalized. He sensed a shared history between them, of too many friends lost in action to protect the interests of the government, dead on a battlefield nobody talked about, victims of a silent war that swallowed, like fog, men and women guilty for having ideas not always understandable and shareable. And silence was the only way to mourn those victims, without ever losing the sense of responsibility for and confidence in what needed to be done to protect the majority.

Marchese had fallen into a spiral that had taken him away from that world. That sense of responsibility had evaporated for good the moment of Torchia's last breath. But without it, Marchese had become a disoriented man with no point of reference. He had lost faith in institutions and needed to find new meaning in his life.

And from the question he felt building in Valton, she was about to offer him one.

Marchese turned to her. "Now, if you don't mind, I have to go."

Agent Valton cleared her throat. "I have another favor to ask."

I knew it. Marchese looked skyward before settling his gaze on her angular features. "What else could you want from me?"

She beckoned to young man driving a black Jeep parked nearby with the engine running. "Come with me. It will take a bit and we'd better move away from prying eyes."

* * *

Outside the church, journalist Luigi Capra watched Torchia's final send-off with a contrite expression. He had never grown to respect Torchia, but he felt moved in such a solemn circumstance, despite his customary coldness. Deep down he knew Marchese was right. Human life was the most precious of commodities, and it had to be protected. Individual daily choices could affect other people's lives, and, sometimes, those actions could lead to death.

Capra had realized that, too often, his ambition made him forget the importance of the lives of others. For the first time in a long while, his thoughts went to Leo Marino, the young man who had lost his life for having listened to him. Capra had always pushed Marino to go beyond the possible to get the news first, and now he had finally admitted to himself that he had caused the poor fellow's death.

He looked away from the coffin and turned around. His eyes fell upon Marchese getting into a black SUV from afar.

"What the hell are you up to now, my friend?" he whispered. His reporter's instinct told him that this scene preluded something interesting, something breaking. "What's brewing?"

FIUMICINO AIRPORT, ROME

A man in black sat in the second row reserved for first-class passengers.

"Can I bring you something to drink, sir?" asked the flight attendant.

He looked at her without smiling. "Nothing for the moment, thanks."

"Shall I put your briefcase in the overhead compartment?" she asked, and he saw her glance down at the dark briefcase resting on his knees.

"No thanks," he replied impassively, turning his eyes to the window. "I have to read during the flight."

"No problem, sir, just please put it under your seat before take-off."

The flight attendant moved on, leaving the man staring out at the tarmac.

It was going to be a long flight, he thought, but he couldn't allow himself a nap, although he knew he could sleep for all nine hours of the trip after the brutality of the day's heat.

He fastened his seat belt without ever letting go the leather handle of his briefcase. He looked around, his face deliberately bland. In a few minutes, his 3:45 p.m. flight would be in the air, and everything would have gone according to plan, without delays or hitches. He was prepared to deliver the seemingly insignificant and incalculably precious relic as soon as he landed. Only forty-eight hours earlier, the plan had been falling apart. But suddenly there had come a fortuitous turnaround. Everything was back on track and proceeding correctly.

The boss would be proud of him and his team.

They finally had what they had worked for for years, diligently and without pause. In less than ten hours, this matter would be concluded with a victorious ending. He smiled.

As the plane taxied on the runway, the man looked around again and smiled at the woman sitting in the next row separated by the aisle. She replied by looking away, back toward the magazine she had been reading.

He looked out of the window again and closed his eyes, still clasping the briefcase.

MESSINA—AUGUST 12, 1943

Father Gabriele knelt at the foot of his bed, made the sign of the cross, and began to pray.

Messina had been bombed and almost burned to the ground, leaving in its wake hundreds of victims. He had spent

155

uncountable days helping wounded, distributing food to those who had lost everything, and celebrating mass. Exhaustion was the least of his problems; his conscience was devouring him.

Father Gabriele slid his hand under his thin mattress and took out the six letters. Why had he taken them? He couldn't understand it himself.

The devil did it, he had continuously repeated. *The devil did it.* And what he had done caused Gabriele a horrible feeling. He had to return them; he had to leave for Taormina and put the letters back in the exact place they had been hidden for centuries. His conscience wouldn't rest until he'd done so.

Father Gabriele dropped his head toward his hands and began to pray the rosary.

Chapter 11

The black Jeep carrying Marchese and Agent Valton stopped in front of the gate of a villa situated on the scenic road north of the city of the Strait. The automatic gate opened, and the Jeep continued its ride along a tree-lined avenue.

In front of the villa stood two security personnel guarding the entrance. Marchese and Valton got out of the car and the two men escorted them through the main door.

The villa looked like a museum. Works of art hung in every corner and statues and paintings adorned the length of the corridor. As they came to the end of it, the security guard invited them into the office. The huge window across from them opened onto a breathtaking panorama of the Strait of Messina.

The agent offered Marchese one of the chairs in front of a majestic desk. She sat opposite him, put her elbows on the desk, and stared across at him.

"First, can I get you something?" she asked, glancing at the guard still lingering in the doorway. "A glass of wine, a beer?"

"Thanks, just a glass of water."

Agent Valton nodded to the guard, who disappeared out the door, and turned her attention back to the former detective. "Let's get back to why I invited you here."

"Indeed," Marchese fired back. "Tell me what I'm doing here, what kind of favor do you want me to do, and then let me get back to my life."

The guard reappeared with two glasses of water. He put them on the desk and exited again, leaving the pair in privacy.

The agent made no move to take her glass. "I want to offer you a job, Mr. Marchese."

Marchese scoffed. "A job? And who told you I'm looking for a job?"

She smiled knowingly. "Let me explain to you first what it is and then you can decide, OK?"

Marchese nodded as he took a sip of water.

"Mark Connell was a contract killer," Agent Valton began, spreading her hands as if this went without saying. "Behind him there is a very powerful man, a large English organization that for years has been trying to take possession of the various treasures of the English Crown. Those who hired him to work here in Messina will not stop. The proof of William Shakespeare's true origins is worth a fortune. Let's say that each letter has an estimated value higher than a work by Picasso."

Marchese cocked an eyebrow. "But now you have recovered all the letters, I think."

Paola Valton's gaze drifted, and she stared at the glass in front of her. "It is not really so. According to our intel, there are fourteen more letters written by Shakespeare."

"You mean by Michelangelo Florio," Marchese corrected airily.

The agent half-smiled. "As you like. There are fourteen other letters written by Michelangelo Florio, and many others, of lesser value, by the priest with whom the young man had this epistolary relationship."

"And where are the letters kept?" Marchese asked, not particularly concerned with the answer.

The agent's eyes locked onto his. "We don't know. Or rather, we knew it up until three hours ago."

Marchese's eyes narrowed. "What do you mean *until three hours ago?*"

For the first time since he'd met her, the M15 agent showed something less than confidence. She drummed her pen on the desktop, her eyes shifting around the room as if to find the right words to explain.

"Until four days ago," she began slowly, "all the letters, or so we thought, were kept in the cathedral of Messina. Passed from bishop to bishop, the letters have been protected and hidden in a secret niche of the cathedral for more than five hundred years. No one in the last few years had ever suspected that a few decades ago, during the war, six of them had been removed. We are still working on how they ended up in the hands of the five victims and the last potential victim. These letters have always been one of the pillars of the relationship between the Catholic Church and the English Crown. We do not divulge the truth about the true origins of William Shakespeare, and Italy does not divulge your secrets about many ambiguous events that happened during the Anglican schism, when the English Crown broke from the Catholic Church."

"And here I thought it was only about Henry VIII wanting to hop from bed to bed," Marchese said with a touch of irony.

The agent gave him a reproachful look. "It was not only that —we have proof that during the schism, the Pope ordered the retrieval of all the gold from the Catholic Churches in England. And, to this day, we continue to have leverage over the Church. British intelligence has been gathering evidence for the last two hundred years that directly implicates every pope in the coverup of systemic sexual abuse in the Catholic Church. So there you have your quid pro quo—if we don't tell the story, you don't tell the story."

Paola paused to let this new information sink in before continuing. "The fact is that this perfectly balanced situation has been gradually compromised by very ambitious people, all driven by different interests that boil down to power and money. The letters disappeared this morning."

"I'm listening," Marchese said, genuinely intrigued now.

Agent Valton sighed. "The twenty letters written by Shakespeare, or Florio, were kept inside a sixteenth-century wooden casket. Locked up in a secret niche in the cathedral, as I have already told you. After much research, my agency discovered its exact location."

Marchese's tone became accusatory. "And why didn't you take them?"

She steepled her fingers and pointed them at him. "Because we have always wanted to let the Vatican believe the situation was under its control and that it was a step ahead of us. After so many years, our relationship is very peaceful one. Religious wars belong to history by now. We have other interests. However, we wanted to protect ourselves."

"In what way?"

Looking down again, she replied, "A few years ago we replaced the original casket with an identical one . . ."

"Equipped with a GPS tracker," Marchese finished.

The agent nodded. "Exactly. A way to keep the letters under control. It is quite well known that you can't really trust the security systems of the Vatican in your country."

Marchese stood up from his chair and crossed to the window, staring down at the Strait. "Then how did you lose track?" he asked a moment later.

"After the recent events that occurred in Messina," she said carefully, "it seems that the bishop of the city left this morning for Rome. He finally decided to take the letters to the Vatican's secret archive."

Marchese snorted. "So you mean you can no longer track the casket over there?"

The agent's expression darkened. "It's not really like that. The bishop of Messina never arrived in San Pietro's."

Marchese stared hard at Paola Valton, his stoic expression hiding a racing mind. He now understood the reason the bishop had not attended Torchia's funeral. Probably someone had intercepted the prelate during his journey to the Vatican and then kidnapped or killed him to take possession of the letters.

"Explain to me clearly," he said coolly. "You mean that the bishop never arrived in Rome and that you lost both him and the casket?"

"Not exactly," Agent Valton replied uneasily. "We found them both."

Marchese sat down again, his gaze still riveted on the agent. "What do you mean by that?"

"Our agents found the bishop in a pool of his own blood, in the back seat of a black sedan inside a garage a few hundred meters from the Vatican. He was still alive when they found him but, unfortunately, there was nothing left to do for him."

Marchese's eyes narrowed. "And what about the casket?"

"It was found in the briefcase he had with him, and it was empty."

Marchese leaned back and glared at the ceiling, running his hands exasperatedly through his black hair. Once again, someone had died, in another city nevertheless linked to Messina, his city that now he hated so much. He realized bitterly that he wasn't surprised to find Torchia had not been the last victim of this intrigue. And in light of the latest developments, the former detective felt there would be many others.

"And what do you want from me?" he asked in a near whisper, still looking up at the ceiling.

Paola Valton, in turn, stood up and looked out the window, her back to Marchese. "We want you to go to New York and get the letters back."

No surprise there, either. He'd suspected as much as soon as she'd offered him a job, by all the flattery she'd heaped on him. "How? And why me? You have the best agents in the world, unlimited resources, connections in every country. Why me?"

"We need someone to analyze this matter through a different point of view," she answered immediately. "Someone who is still hungry for justice and has a specific acumen. You are a very interesting person, Mr. Marchese. But you've lived in limbo for years, losing your enthusiasm for what you are best at, which is letting justice prevail over evil. I understand what you have experienced these years—pain, frustration, abandonment by the Italian institutions. Your involvement would help us a lot, of course, but it would be helpful for you, too."

Marchese listened carefully. He knew what she was saying was true. He had lost enthusiasm for what he was best at, for what he had loved for years, for his passion.

And perhaps she was right. He balked at the thought.

"I wouldn't even know where to begin!" he countered.

"It's always like that at the beginning of an investigation, isn't it?" she said with a shrug. "You never know where to begin. But then you always find the key to the problem. I've read many reports about you. In the end, you always succeed in piecing together the puzzle and closing the case."

"Yes, that's true." Marchese paused. "Although it often happens when it's too late. That's cold comfort, and New York is a new place, completely foreign to me."

The agent turned to face him again, a soft smile on her face. "You know what? Right now my staff is booking a flight to New York for you. It leaves in the morning. Take the evening to think it over. If you accept, I'll see you tomorrow at seven o'clock at the airport in Catania, where I'll explain fully. And, of course, if you accept, I will make sure you have all the resources you need in New York."

Marchese thought about the current state of his life and could see no reason to disagree, so he nodded.

NEW YORK CITY

David Graham recognized the caller ID and answered. "Paul, any news?" he said without greeting. He leaned contentedly back in his leather armchair. His hireling wouldn't be calling unless it was good news; his employees knew better than to do otherwise.

"We have all fourteen letters. They are already on their way to New York."

A surge of triumph coursed through Graham's body. "No problems, I take it?"

"No, boss," Paul assured him firmly. "Frank Larsen is in the air right now. It was a clean and quick job."

"And the casket?"

There was a smile in Paul's voice as he replied, "We left it as a souvenir for our MI5 friends."

The call ended shortly thereafter, and Graham gazed out the widow of his Manhattan office at the breathtaking view of Central Park. He sat comfortably, his hands behind his head, enjoying the spectacle of the park on that hot August morning. The tycoon was fifty-two years old but looked closer to sixty. The last thirty years spent building his empire had taken their toll.

But now, it was all over at last. "Plan B" had worked. He had known that if Connell were caught, the Catholic Church would move the casket for security reasons. If he couldn't take possession of the six letters, he'd reasoned, he could obtain the other fourteen.

It had been a gamble, and Graham loved betting. A few hours from now, he would have them in his hands.

The queen should have battened down the hatches to keep that secret intact, Graham thought smugly. After five hundred years, he, David Graham, had succeeded in taking possession of what many before him had sought in vain.

He had decided to keep the treasure in New York, rather than London. His new vault, located on the twentieth floor of his building, together with the security systems he had installed, would be inaccessible to MI5 or any mercenary they hired for that dirty work.

Graham called his secretary by Intercom. "Kathrine, convene the board of directors tomorrow at three p.m. I have important matters to communicate."

"Certainly, Mr. Graham."

STRATFORD-UPON-AVON—AUGUST 12, 1592

Michelangelo opened the letter with as much care as his shaking hands would allow. Several months had passed since he'd received a letter from Father Franco, and the thrill of this letter's arrival set his heart racing.

My dearest Michelangelo,
Thank you for your letters. Epidemics and wars have made our lives here in Sicily particularly difficult in the last few months. But I'm fine, now. The Church is strong and unshakable faith pervades my soul. I also had news of your

successes through a dear missionary friend of mine, who told me about the fame you are acquiring in London. I smiled when I read that, in England, everyone knows you as William. I imagine, what with missing your family, your beloved mother, and our city, that you are suffering a lot. And reading your letters, I perceived the deep sense of loneliness you are feeling right now. But at the same time, I also sensed the great fervor of your theatrical success.

The words of his beloved friend—the thought of his beloved mother and of the pain that Messina was experiencing—were so moving that a tear slid down Michelangelo's face.

My dear Michelangelo, I miss seeing you running through the aisles of this great church. I miss all our talks and our long strolls. Everything seems empty now. I jealously treasure all your letters as a precious gift, here in your church. May the Lord always accompany you on your journey and never let you lose that bright smile that is always in my mind. You were still a boy, but your path was already enlightened by that special light around you . . ."

The young man smiled at the memory of his childhood and the beautiful days spent together with his beloved mentor. Everything came back to his mind, even the hidden nooks of the great cathedral where he used to hide and daydream of battle and love stories—all that he had lived, dreamed of, and was now reviving in his plays.

He put the letter down and looked through the small window overlooking his backyard. He smiled. It was time to dedicate a theatrical work to his beloved city, he thought. A grandiose work that would remain in people's memory for centuries.

Messina—August 12, 2012

Marchese usually didn't sleep much, but this night was different from the others. His thoughts kept drifting to Paola Valton's words. She was right; this was the chance he needed to get rid of the ghosts that had accompanied him for too long. Where else would he start from? He certainly needed to leave Messina; he had tried so many times without success. He had missed the adrenaline of chasing criminals. But above all, he needed to know who was in charge of the organization that had killed his friend.

It was not an easy choice; it meant leaving everything and going away. But what did "everything" amount to? There was almost nothing left here—no Renata, no friends, no work. He no longer had anything that could keep him in Messina, not even the memories that still lived in those streets or on that beach. The time had come to break the thread that still kept him there. He would make a new life. For how long, he was not sure. It would mean risking facing new monsters in a new, unknown city, like a naked warrior thrown in a new arena. Marchese felt more disoriented than scared at the thought.

Wending in through the window, the sound of the sea that had lived with him in the last years was clear and imposing. The waves beat hard against the rocks. He would miss this house, the sea, and the beach of Messina. He would miss the climate, even the scorching heat that oppressed the city in the summertime. He would miss his porch and his beer.

It would be a long, sleepless night.

Messina—August 13, 1943

At 9:00 a.m., Father Gabriele entered the cathedral that had been partially destroyed by the bombings of the days before. The roof had been destroyed down to the stone beams, leaving the interior open to the sky, and the charred remains of the once-breathtaking ceiling had been reduced to a heap of rubble that filled the nave floor. The white-washed walls were scarred and blackened. Looking around, Gabriele had the sinking feeling that the evil one was winning this earthly battle. In every country across Europe, the people had been suffering for years from starvation, death, and epidemics. His Jewish brothers and sisters had been deported, reportedly detained in concentration camps and murdered. Even the children had not been spared this deadly project.

In every corner of the church, people were camped out in the aisles to find shelter and sleep. Outside, in the great square, a crowd of people had queued up for food and any other useful items for their sick, wounded, and hungry children. Upon returning to the church, Gabriele had devoted himself to assisting and helping these suffering human beings, a silent atonement for the sin he'd committed in taking the letters. He shuffled quietly from family to family, stepping over chunks of the ruined ceiling as he went, offering aid and solace where he could. But the weight of his guilt bowed his back and made his legs heavy.

He paused in the doorway of the church, gazing wearily over the crowd, and heard the bishop stepping up beside him. Gabriele knew it was him by the whisper of the hem of his cassock brushing across the splintered floor.

"You should rest, my son," the bishop insisted. "You look tired."

Father Gabriele turned to the bishop. "Your Excellency, there are still those in need of our help. There is no time to rest."

The bishop was silent for a moment. "I received a letter from Father Carlo."

Gabriele braced his hand on the doorpost as his knees threatened to buckle. Had someone discovered him, or maybe noticed that the six letters had disappeared? For a moment, Gabriele saw his whole world crashing down, reduced to rubble like the ceiling of the church.

"He wrote me that the casket is safe," the bishop went on. "Fortunately, fate was not so cruel to Taormina, so someone will come to help us soon."

Relieved, Gabriele sighed inwardly. The bishop had not mentioned the disappearance of the letters, so Father Carlo probably had not opened the casket. Perhaps he didn't even know exactly how many letters were meant to be in the casket. "Perfect, Your Excellency," said Gabriele calmly. "We really need help in this moment."

"Yes. And quite soon the casket will return safely to its place, here, where it has been kept for centuries."

This eased Gabriele's mind even more. As soon as the casket had returned to Messina, far from prying eyes, he would open the niche and put the important missives back in their place. No one would have noticed that six letters had been stolen that week. This would wipe his conscience clean and alleviate his guilt. Atonement would triumph over temptation.

CATANIA AIRPORT—AUGUST 13, 2012

As Marchese crossed the automatic door of the airport terminal, he found Paola Valton and two British intelligence agents awaiting him.

"I was certain you would accept my proposal," Agent Valton said with a genuine smile.

Marchese grimaced. "I haven't even gotten on the flight yet. Don't be so sure. I still need to understand many things, and I expect a proper explanation before the plane takes off."

Valton beckoned Marchese to follow her into the small terminal bar. "Everything will be clarified. Meanwhile, let's have a good coffee. This is the only thing that I will really miss in this country."

They sat, ordered, and drank in silence. Presently, the agent set her half-empty coffee cup down on its saucer. "Mr. Marchese, my colleague, Olivia Fischer, will be waiting for you in New York. She will be at your disposal for everything. She will give you all the information you need to get up to speed on what and who we are looking for, and she can direct you to people you can count on. We have a team working on this operation led by a Dean Zona. You'll like him—he's a good agent. You will stay in one of our apartments in the SoHo district in Manhattan. It's very comfortable. I've stayed there several times myself."

Marchese nodded over the rim of his own cup, but he held his tongue.

The agent reached into her briefcase, took out a white envelope, and handed it to him. "In here is cash. It's just something for the beginning. You will find more money in the apartment safe. I recommend sticking to cash only for your transactions."

Marchese nodded again.

"I can't tell you much about what you're supposed to do," the agent admitted. "Agent Fisher will be responsible for that. I can tell you that the letters have reportedly come into the possession of David Graham, a rich and unscrupulous English businessman. We know he lives between London and New York, and currently he is in New York City, where he spends most of his time. Graham is the head of an international organization that imports and exports works of art all over the world, both legally and illegally."

Marchese scowled. "Why don't you just arrest him?"

She sighed. "We don't have solid evidence on him. He is also a very powerful figure in England. More than four members of Parliament are his men, and my superior risks his head and the future of the investigation if we stumble."

Marchese raised his eyes to the ceiling. "And there's the political hitch I love so much!"

The agent let out a wincing laugh. "I know, Mr. Marchese. I don't like it either. But we're called to do the work that we chose to ensure democracy in the world. The work that you also chose to bring criminals to justice, with or without the help of politicians and with or without being hindered by politics."

Marchese's eye drifted to a family of three standing nearby, surrounded by a platoon of suitcases. The little boy was playing with a toy airplane. How many unsuspecting people traveled around the world and lived their lives, unaware of the fact that there was someone fighting for their safety and their freedom? He knew this was his destiny. Blessed or cursed by fate, he had the responsibility to play his role in the world. People like him had to accept they would never be free in order to guarantee freedom to others. He had made a choice years ago and he had been reneging on it for too long. Maybe he had already given up.

It was time for him to get back up, to keep fighting and play his role, as dictated by his destiny.

* * *

Luigi Capra strode into the airport terminal just in time to see Marchese walk away with three people. One of them was the woman he had seen with the detective the day before. Capra had followed the Detective of Steel from his home to the airport. He had lurked the night before not far from the cottage on the beach and had seen him leave at dawn with a suitcase.

Marchese was leaving. But for where? If he had taken a non-European flight, Capra couldn't have followed him; he had not brought his passport with him. He had to wait and see where he was going to check-in. So he sat near the entrance just in front of the bar and dialed his assistant's phone number, just in case.

Marchese and his associates left the bar and headed for the check-in area at the Alitalia counter just as Capra's assistant breathlessly crossed the terminal door. Decked out in a cap and sunglasses, the young assistant had apparently felt the need to come in disguise. In two short years, he had become Capra's trusted right-hand man. He asked few questions and was always ready to intervene to make up for all journalistic extravagances of the eccentric anchorman.

"Nice, Eugenio, bravo! You're just in time!"

Eugenio had clearly run all the way from the parking lot; he bent forward, bracing his hands on his knees as he tried to catch his breath. "I got here as quickly as possible, Luigi."

"Did you find everything?"

The young man righted himself and retrieved Capra's passport from his pocket and passed him the handle of a small roller suitcase. "I grabbed whatever clothes were in your closet and undergarments from your drawers. What's going on? Where are you going?"

Capra checked the validity of the passport and put it in his pocket. "I don't know yet. I'm just following my instincts. Marchese is readying to depart. Something's up, and I plan to find out what."

Capra followed Eugenio's gaze as he turned to the check-in area. He saw Marchese and his three companions were queueing at the Alitalia gate. The monitor above them reported destination and flight number: Flight AZ 610 for New York.

"Eugenio, give me your cap and sunglasses."

The young man peered at him, sighed, and handed him what he had asked for.

Chapter 12

New York—August 14, 2012

Frank Larsen exited JFK into the bustling pickup area at 9:00 a.m. and immediately felt breathless. At 95 degrees Fahrenheit, it was the hottest day of the year in New York. The humidity exceeded 90 percent.

There was no comparison between this and Rome's balmy climate. But he hated the Italians, their arrogance, disorganization, and superficiality in so many things. He was finally home, and in a few hours, he would meet Graham.

Customs had gone smoothly. The security systems would not detect "some old papers," he had been told, and it was true. The letters had traveled from Rome to New York without a hitch.

Paul Morelli, his trusted colleague, awaited him outside the terminal, and squeezed him in a triumphant hug as he exited. It was all over, and they had won. The two climbed into the back seat of the waiting limousine.

"How was your flight, my friend?"

Frank's heavy figure slumped in his seat. "Great, even though I haven't slept."

Paul's pockmarked face became sympathetic. "Some turbulence?"

"No, I kept an eye on the briefcase throughout the flight. I won't feel peaceful until I've delivered it to Mr. Graham."

Paul nodded gravely. "I understand. After that asshole Connell's failure, we can't take any chances."

The limo finally escaped the snarl of airport traffic and headed toward Manhattan. In the distance, the New York skyline stood out in a clear blue sky that August day. It was one of those spectacular views loved all over the world, one Frank never tired of admiring.

"That's true," Frank replied with an inward shudder. "Those MI5 bastards had no mercy for him. The coroner's report I got my hands on said his teeth had been ripped out and his toes and fingers burned so that his prints couldn't be identified." Frank's voice shook, and noticed Paul's worried glance.

"Even if Connell didn't go softly," Paul replied, referring their associate's victims. He clapped Frank on the shoulder. "Don't worry. It's over. Soon you'll hand those damn things off to Graham. It won't be your problem anymore, and starting tomorrow, Graham will be one of the most powerful men in the world. And you, Frank, you played a part of history. You'll see, we'll be properly rewarded!"

Frank smiled. Finally, he would be able to afford the little apartment in the Village he had always dreamed of.

ROME

The pope listened in silence to Emanuel Tertón, the tall, muscular Commander of the Swiss Guard, who sat before him. Tertón's elbows rested on the arms of the plush leather armchair, his fingers interlaced before him.

"Your Holiness, Bishop Alessandro Perri was found dead in one of our cars." Despite the grimness of the news, Tertón's face bore his usual practiced impassivity. "Our driver is still missing."

The pontiff made the sign of the cross and sighed. "What happened to the casket?"

"Vanished," said Tertón mildly. "Together with its contents. We are in contact with the AISE who claim to be totally in the dark. They assured us that they would go to work immediately to find out what happened."

The pope sat back in his chair, resisting the urge to run a hand exhaustedly over his face. "Who do you think did this?"

His security guard looked down at the thin manila folder resting on his knees. "We know that, for years, the M15 has been trying to take possession of the letters, and I think they would do anything to have them. We know that they intercepted the killer in Messina and recovered some of the letters that had somehow been stolen from the casket years ago. And maybe, I'm not sure, they thought it was time to recover them all. Bishop Perri had finally decided to bring the remaining ones here, in a safe place, but someone knew it and intercepted him before he arrived."

The pope clutched his golden crucifix tightly to his chest, as if he could wring an answer from it. He had been dealing with various problems for years—mysteries, bombings and attacks, priests and bishops involved in cases of pedophilia inside and outside the walls of the Vatican. But now even his trusted Tertón seemed uncertain, despite his bland demeanor. *This is not good,* he thought. "Convene with the English ambassador as soon as possible. Maybe it's time to resolve this case which has been pending for too many centuries."

"Certainly, Your Excellency."

The Commander of the Swiss Guard took his leave and left the elderly pontiff alone in his office. As Tertón strolled through the sumptuous corridors of the Vatican, he took out his phone, opened the message app, and typed: "The old man took the bait."

He waited for an answer, staring at the screen.

Almost immediately, he received the thumbs up emoji. He smiled and put his phone back in his jacket.

NEW YORK

David Graham sat at the head of a long table, his gaze drifting casually across the faces of the assembled Board of Directors of the Graham International Art Company. Behind him, a screen dominated the wall, and Kathrine was busily queueing up a series of images on her laptop to deliver the news.

Most of those present were English members that Graham trusted, in particular his manager responsible for relations with China, the purchasing manager for the United States and England, his business partner, Claude Fanz, and other delegates of the organization. These were the only ten people who knew all the illicit activities the company carried out in addition to their normal import-export activity of works of art around the world.

And then there was Kathrine. For ten years, she had been privy to meetings like this, as well as private talks in Graham's office. He had the utmost confidence in her abilities and loyalty. There were few things, albeit big things, he did not disclose to her. On the rare occasion that he was in London for an extended time, Kathrine had full autonomous control of the company's affairs here in New York, and she'd never steered wrong.

Kathrine didn't appear to have a private life. She was forty years old with blond hair and a tall, thin runner's body. Her day consisted of administrative duties like arranging meetings and booking flights as well as making sure his "secrets" were kept. She enjoyed the esteem and respect of all those present, who had collectively dubbed her "iron woman." When everything was ready, Kathrine nodded to Graham. All eyes turned to him with rapt attention.

"My friends," Graham began, spreading his hands in welcome, "today is a historic day for our company—one of those days that you will mark on the calendar, and in the future, write about in your autobiography."

Kathrine dimmed the lights, and the screen lit up, haloing Graham briefly in light before he stepped aside to allow everyone a full view of the spectacle he was about to present to them.

"Two hours ago, I finally held in my hands the most important documents in English history, the answer to a question much speculated about for five centuries—the end of research, unsuccessfully conducted by many illustrious figures of our history. Research there has led us to discover the truth about one of the most beloved writers in the history of England."

David Graham turned his gaze to Kathrine, who stood beside the screen. She tapped her keyboard and a video began to play.

One of the fourteen letters written by Michelangelo Florio to Father Franco appeared on the screen. Beside it, a typed translation revealed its contents. It told the story of how he had decided to change his name by translating his mother's into English, effectively marking the moment Michelangelo had become known in England as William Shakespeare.

A buzz arose in the room, the sense of amazement among his colleagues palpable, and a look of satisfaction appeared on Graham's face. "Yes, that's right," he said brightly. "Just read a few lines of this letter, written in the sixteenth century, to understand what I'm talking about."

All the board members began to whisper, leaning into one another, and by turns pointing at the screen. They all understood the value of what Graham had displayed on the screen.

"Dear friends, thanks to this letter, and the thirteen others in my possession," Graham continued as the letters in question one by one appeared on the screen, "we can finally declare that the debate on the true origins of William Shakespeare is over. This theory has been widely discussed in Italy, although never supported by proof. And even if there has been any, the queen of my own beloved England has cleverly kept it hidden from us and the whole world."

He glanced at Kathrine and found her sharp green eyes scrutinizing all those present. She smiled in obvious satisfaction. Graham understood; there was nothing quite like seeing these powerful men excited like children in front of a chocolate cake.

"Many years ago," Graham went on as the whispering diminished to silence, "I came into possession of a letter written by a Sicilian priest to a young man in England. Its content clearly showed that the priest was writing to a man we know as William Shakespeare, but he called him *Michelangelo*. In this letter—" He gestured to the screen, and the image in question appeared right on cue. "—the priest, this Father Franco, referred to works written by the playwright. I became convinced that, if there were letters written by this priest, then there might be others written by the young man himself. I have privately funded this research for years and today, my friends, finally we can acknowledge that the man we have always considered as a pillar of English culture was actually a young Sicilian who escaped the Vatican's inquisition, to become the greatest playwright in English history."

Almost all those present began to speak at once. They all wanted to understand one thing: How this evidence could be turned into gold.

Marchese stood in line to pass through security, one of hundreds of people waiting to be questioned. After 9-11, U.S. customs had become obsessive. Fingerprint scanning, detectors, and searches were mandatory for almost all passengers from abroad.

Throughout the vast area, Marchese took note of countless permutations of the majestic stars and stripes of which all Americans were proud—on hats, pins, badges, T-shirts. The United States had no roots in Roman culture, European battles, or great philosophers. Their flag represented independence from the European countries that had discovered them. It represented their union and the unity of the fifty states that had gathered together under a single allegiance. And it was everywhere, impossible to overlook or ignore.

When his turn came, he approached the custom agent officer, a stiff-postured man in a black uniform. "What's the reason for your visit?" he asked flatly.

"Just a short vacation," Marchese replied.

"Where are you staying?"

"At a friend's apartment," Marchese answered calmly. "In Manhattan."

The officer glanced quickly at the passport and turned his attention to Marchese. He stared at him for a few seconds, closed the passport, and handed it back across the counter. "Have a good time in New York, sir," he said in a tone that said he didn't care one way or another if his suggestion was taken or not.

As he left the terminal, Marchese looked around. Agent Fischer was supposed to be waiting for him, but he didn't know how to recognize her. And then he wondered for the first time, exasperated, how she would recognize him.

He dragged his heavy suitcase to the edge of the sidewalk and was immediately accosted by the hectic bustle of horns from the yellow taxis and beckoning drivers offering transfer services.

"Welcome to New York, Francesco," he whispered to himself.

"Welcome to New York, Mr. Marchese."

Surprised, the former detective turned, clumsy and embarrassed and fumbling his luggage. A sunny smile welcomed him. A striking woman in her mid-thirties with short black hair, dressed in tight jeans, black heels, and a blouse that would draw any man's attention, stuck out her hand in greeting.

"I'm Agent Olivia Fischer," she said brightly, her English accent more apparent as she spoke again. "I've been waiting for you."

Marchese put down his suitcase and shook her hand. Her grip was firm. "Nice to meet you."

She smiled again, glancing down at his ponderous luggage. "First time in New York?"

"No, I was here in 2000," he told her, suddenly very conscious of his Italian accent. "Before the terrorist attack on the Twin Towers."

The woman sighed, her smile visibly dimming. The 9-11 topic always roused grief. "Many things have changed since then," she replied optimistically. "The city has rebuilt and healed some, but you can still find signs of the tragedy, especially downtown. If you'd like, I can take you to visit Ground Zero. But we'd better move along now. After three o'clock, the traffic toward the city is absolutely atrocious."

* * *

The taxi Luigi Capra had hailed pulled up in front of him, a few feet from where Marchese was talking an intriguing-looking woman.

"Where you headed?" the driver asked as Capra slid into the back seat.

"Wait for a moment," Capra replied, craning his neck to peer at Marchese in the rearview mirror. "I don't know yet."

The taxi driver scowled. "The meter's running. What do you mean?"

Capra gave the man an annoyed look. "I know. Don't worry, let it run. Just stay here until I tell you what to do, we will move in a moment."

As he watched Marchese, Capra realized he had done something crazy. He had flown to New York just to follow an instinct, oblivious of what Eugenio had packed for him, having nowhere lined up to stay and no assurances that his instinct was even valid. For all he knew, Marchese was here for a vacation or a consultation of some kind.

But something told him that Marchese was in New York for significant reasons. Three days after the death of his friend, the former drill detective boards an intercontinental flight and was escorted to the gate by three people who certainly seemed to be Security Services agents? There was no way this was a mundane trip.

Capra knew that Marchese's movements always meant "action," and for every action, there was a scoop for Capra himself. *Always.*

As soon as the taxi carrying Marchese and the woman left, Capra instructed the taxi driver to follow them at a safe distance. A couple of taxis stood between the two cars, and the journalist felt certain that with all these yellow cabs, Marchese would not notice the one that was following them.

"Where do you think they're heading, sir?" asked the cabby.

"I am not sure," Capra replied absently. "Follow them wherever they go. When they stop, you stop a few car lengths away."

In the rearview mirror, Capra saw the driver eye him uncomfortably. "Okay."

Marchese and the woman were barely visible from where Capra peered at them from between the driver and passenger side front seats of the cab. Whoever the woman was, Marchese had known her, or at least known to get into a cab with her. *What business does he have with a woman like that?*

"What's going on?" asked the taxi driver, breaking the silence. "Are you a policeman tailing or what?"

"No, nothing strange like that," said Capra lightly. "I am an Italian journalist following a personality from my country for a scoop."

The driver seemed satisfied by that answer, then asked, "A famous person, huh? Who is he?"

For a moment Capra felt caught off guard and scrambled come up with something without arousing suspicion. "He's a character from a police TV series," he said quickly. "Popular in my country."

The driver pulled an impressed face. "Wow, what show?"

Nosy bastard. "I can't really tell you anything more. It is very important we do not lose him."

"No problem," the driver replied wryly. "The traffic here makes it impossible to lose someone you are following."

***

"Mr. Marchese, I am sure you have already been told that your apartment is in SoHo. It's very comfortable. And I live nearby. A great area to live in New York."

Marchese gazed out the window. Next to him he could see the houses of Queens facing the skyscrapers of Manhattan on the opposite side. The opposing skylines, whether they meant to or not, clearly symbolized the American social system. The imposing Manhattan skyline conveyed the type of real money and power it took to live and work there, the steel and concrete kingdom contrasting with weather-worn wooden houses.

"Yes, thanks, Agent Fischer," he said, realizing he'd been staring out in silence too long. "Agent Valton told me about this, but I expect you will get to the more important details."

"Please call me, Olivia, and yes," she replied. "Once you've had a chance to settle in, I will pick you up for dinner and give you all the details and updates on the investigation."

The cab took the tunnel between Queens and Manhattan, passing under the East River and emerging on the intersection with 2nd Avenue and 36th Street.

* * *

The board members departed at 4:30 p.m. Kathrine remained to straighten the paperwork that had been distributed during the meeting. She glanced at Graham, who sat in his armchair, looking tired yet satisfied. "They were very pleased by your news, Mr. Graham," Kathrine commented as she stacked the papers.

Graham smiled at her, his blue eyes dancing with merriment. "Money and power would please anyone. If all goes according to plan, this will be worth their while."

"It will go according to plan, sir," Kathrine said simply, as if it already had.

Graham looked at his watch. "I'm in a very good mood today. Please book me a massage—the usual treatment. And take the rest of the day off."

"Of course," she said, unimpressed by the early dismissal, and returned to her desk and dialed the number from memory. The recipient of the call answered with, "Good evening, Kathrine. The usual massage?"

"Yes, please."

"Time?"

"Within the hour," Kathrine replied mildly.

"As always."

"Thank you."

She informed Graham that his appointment was set, grabbed her Gucci bag, and left the office.

She took the subway at Lexington and 59th Street, electing to stroll around SoHo and browse the luxury shops and find something to wear for the upcoming annual charity gala organized by the Graham International Art Company. It was an important benefit for cancer patients and only a week away, an evening like so many others during which millionaires donated crumbs for tax deductions, rather than for altruistic reason. The evening would be the usual theater of hypocrisy. Kathrine despised this aspect of her job. She knew the cancer foundation well and appreciated that at least the money did go to good use.

She seethed at the thought that all these evenings, hosted in New York by various organizations for that purpose, raised money of which only a portion went to fund any research. The luxury of the night itself cost half of what was collected and, in the end, research centers received less than ten percent of what was taken in. This thought burned in her mind as she alighted at her stop and ascended the subway station stairs to the street above.

* * *

David Graham was now alone on the office floor. On the upper floor of the same building was his residence, overlooking Central Park, facing the zoo. Sometimes Graham would pause to watch people walk in the park twenty floors below. It relaxed him. His life was hectic, but it was the kind of life he had chosen. He never stopped and was hungry for more money, power, and influence.

David Graham had not taken a real vacation in twenty years. He allowed himself only a few vices, one of which he was about to enjoy shortly. He closed his office door, entered the alarm security code, and left.

While in the elevator, he thought again of the letters he had put for safe-keeping in the vault of his office. In addition to the codes for the alarms placed on the floor and at the entrance of the building, the vault itself was coded and alarmed. The codes were changed by a software system every twenty-four hours, according to a pattern only Graham knew.

The letters are safe, he thought.

His driver was waiting for him in the street. "Where shall I take you, sir?"

Graham slid into the spacious backseat and took up the newspaper. "233 Broadway, thank you."

"OK, sir."

In a matter of minutes, the car pulled up in front of the Broadway building, just a few steps from Ground Zero. Back in the car, his driver picked up a magazine, knowing that he would wait a while before his boss returned. It was not the first time he had taken him to this address.

The doorman let him pass without asking any questions. They all knew what was going on and that when Graham arrived in the black BMW, it was clear to which floor he was headed.

Graham entered the elevator and hit PH, the top floor. Once there, he walked down the long corridor to the single apartment entrance on that floor.

A man who called himself George welcomed David Graham at the door. "They're expecting you in the bedroom, sir."

"Thanks, George." Graham took off his jacket, handed it to George, and walked toward the door of the room he knew very well.

When Graham entered the room, he found two naked young men waiting for him. He was familiar with one of them; the other was new, and Graham acknowledged his presence. The two men approached him and, in unison, began to undress him.

"What are you up for today, David?" asked the one he had met previously.

Graham studied at them both. Two statuesque bodies. "Today I want to have an especially great time with you. I have to celebrate!"

The two men smiled at each other knowingly. One grabbed Graham by his hair, causing him to fall back on the waiting bed. "Then today we will give you the full service."

Chapter 13

The car carrying Marchese and Olivia Fischer stopped at the corner of Prince Street and Mercer Street at 5:30 p.m. Olivia paid the driver and they got out of the car.

The pair entered the building next to the Fanelli Cafe. "That's one of the oldest bars in the city," Olivia said, nodding toward its entrance. "It opened in 1847. Many famous personalities and artists used to meet up here, like Rocky Marciano and his friends and Bob Dylan. People also say that Silvester Stallone was inspired to write his first movie while drinking at the bar."

Marchese raised a skeptical eyebrow. "And how is the food?"

Olivia smiled. "Not bad. I like the cheese ravioli. But since you live in Sicily, I guess you are used to enjoying *authentic* Italian food."

Marchese smiled in turn. "Maybe one of these days I'll cook my ravioli for you." He chided himself as the words left his mouth; Olivia was already too friendly, and he wasn't in New York to make friends.

Olivia's smile widened to a grin. "Sounds good, Mr. Marchese."

"Francesco, please," he said as they entered the apartment.

The place appeared to be quite comfortable. Olivia showed him around. The kitchen was small but the bedroom had a private bathroom, while another room adjacent to the small living room housed a sofa, a widescreen TV, and a small bar stocked with whiskey and vodka. The windows faced both Prince Street and Mercer.

"I hope you like it," she concluded with a grin.

Marchese stared down at the street below from the window of the living room. "It's not the Strait of Messina," he said, not unkindly, "but I'll get used to it. In any event, I'm not here for the view."

* * *

Kathrine had stopped in front of Miu Miu's window on Prince Street, when a man with a roller suitcase approached her. "Excuse me, madam!"
The woman turned with a questioning look. "Can I help you?"
"Could you please tell me where the nearest hotel is?" The man had an Italian accent and charismatic smile, but there was something disingenuous about him. "Possibly with a view here, of Prince Street."
Kathrine thought for a moment, then turned toward the corner of Mercer Street. "There you go. I suggest the Mercer Hotel and its fabulous restaurant. The entrance is on the side there, but I think many of their rooms face right here, above us. Can you see?" She pointed up at the building.
The gentleman smiled. "Perfect. Thanks for the help."
Kathrine smiled and returned her gaze to the window before entering the shop.

* * *

Exactly an hour after Olivia left Marchese's apartment so he could take unpack and shower, she strode back down Prince Street toward his apartment. As she arrived in front of Louis Vuitton she saw, two shops up ahead, a woman carrying two Miu Miu shopping bags. Their eyes met.

She recognized her immediately. It was Kathrine Leed, David Graham's secretary.

That's a shocking coincidence, she thought, shaken. She had only seen the woman from photos until now. From the nonchalant way in which Kathrine averted her eyes, Olivia couldn't even be sure if the recognition was mutual. Her colleagues had been following her for years, but she had never seen her in person. Olivia nonchalantly stopped in front of one of the windows. As soon as she saw Kathrine entering another store, she went on toward the apartment.

When Marchese answered her knock, the ever-present pensive look on his face gave way briefly to surprise. Olivia knew why; her face was slightly more made up and she had changed from her jeans to a short black dress and flat shoes. She didn't consider herself knockout, but she wasn't oblivious to what her looks did to even the most stoic men she encountered.

She smiled at him. "Ready for dinner, Francesco?"

"Yes, I just need to grab a jacket," he replied. He half-raised his arm as if to check his watch and dropped it again. "I don't want to look bad beside your elegance."

She laughed. "I had forgotten about that typical Italian charm."

"Where are we going?" he asked as he adjusted a black blazer over his white shirt and jeans.

"To the Mercer Kitchen, right here in front," Olivia replied. "You'll like it. Their wine list is to die for."

Marchese seemed relieved. After a long day of travel, Olivia had figured a nearby dinner would suit him. "Excellent. I'm ready!"

* * *

Capra had been lucky. There had been only one room left in the Mercer Hotel overlooking Prince Street. His window faced the building where Marchese had entered.

The room was on the fifth floor, and the windows of the small building in front of him did not go above the fourth floor. His man had to be in one of those four floors in front.

He put down his suitcase and began peering into every window. Years of journalistic nosiness meant he didn't feel even a hint of embarrassment at peeking in on people.

A few minutes later, he spied Marchese on the fourth floor almost directly across the street, staring down at the road below him.

"I got you, my friend," the reporter whispered, taking a step back to avoid falling into Marchese's sights. "Now let's find out what you are doing here in New York."

From his room, Capra could see almost everything happening in the apartment below him. He saw Marchese receive the woman—the same one who'd met him at the airport—put on his jacket and leave with her.

It looked sort of like a date, maybe for dinner or a drink. Capra was almost disappointed. He would not follow them; he knew Marchese would return eventually. He'd be better off waiting and trying to figure out his next move.

He hadn't yet planned how to organize the tailing and did not want to think about what would happen if he were discovered. He had to be careful. But if he knew Marchese at all, Capra knew the risk was well worth the reward if his journalistic intuition was right.

* * *

Graham's driver had been instructed not to move in the two hours during which the businessman had let himself run the gamut of being pampered, beaten, and subdued by the two young men from George's massage service. This was Graham's little secret. Not even Kathrine knew what went on during his massage sessions. Aside from George and his employees, no one knew about his occasional need to be possessed and dominated.

He was always in a dominant position over others, mainly his employees, collaborators, associates, and the people with whom he did business. He had fallen into this a few years earlier and often felt the need to escape, to let his adrenaline to find an outlet. The women he had encountered rarely had satisfied him; they did not know how to handle his desires, not even when two or three of them let themselves be used.

Ultimately, he realized he wanted to be used. To feel pain.

He had started with homosexual relationships. But it was not enough; he needed more. After carefully looking into it, he had found this place. George's services were the answer to his perverse needs. George was private and confidential and serviced an exclusive Wall Street crowd. It was an expensive but worth it.

He was particularly perturbed when Kathrine called him shortly afterward, killing his buzz. She rattled on about how she'd run into MI5's Olivia Fisher, out with some man Kathrine hadn't recognized. Fisher wasn't a threat, and he assured Kathrine of this; the little tart had been so easy to identify as British Security, it almost felt like she wanted people to know. Their hiring must have gotten lax of late. He buttered Kathrine up with the usual platitudes and hung up, his mood soured. He was grateful for such a conscientious assistant, but sometimes the woman did tend to get a little hysterical.

* * *

Olivia had booked a table in the basement of the restaurant. It looked like an old Roman *trattoria*, with brick arches and soft lighting. The restaurant was surprisingly quiet for such a popular spot, and a stream of soft piano music floated in through discreet speakers hidden around the room. Olivia had picked this place for a reason; even if the Italian fellow just wanted to be friends, she preferred getting to know someone in a place that didn't necessitate shouting across the table.

They requested a bottle of Cabernet Sauvignon, then perused the menu. Olivia ordered the herb-roasted chicken, and Francesco settled on the roasted black bass.

"So, Francesco," the agent said, holding her glass and staring at the wine inside, "where do I start?"

"From the beginning," Marchese suggested with a note of sarcasm.

"Sure." She cleared her throat. "Agent Valton told you about David Graham—his international organization, his power and reach, and his long obsessive intent to take possession of William Shakespeare's letters."

Marchese shrugged. "In broad terms."

Olivia nodded. "Here in New York, David Graham owns several floors of 825 Fifth Avenue, which faces Central Park. Some days ago, he arrived in New York after a lengthy stay at his London residence. Which is a strange coincidence given the letters went missing yesterday. This makes us think that the letters arrived in New York rather than London. This would have been a smart move to avoid having Scotland Yard on his tail."

"Or maybe he wants to mislead you by coming here while the letters are on their way to London," Marchese replied, as he poured them each a second glass of wine. "Or better yet, they never left Italy."

"That's possible," Olivia conceded with a shrug. "But Graham, who is both clever and evil, would never leave the letters too far away from his personal control. He has been obsessively on this and it's a personal matter for him. We all believe that the letters are on their way to New York, or that they have already arrived here."

Marchese raised a skeptical eyebrow. "And how do you think we can retrieve them?"

"You mean how *you* can recover them," Olivia corrected with a wink.

Marchese suppressed an eye roll. "How do you think I can retrieve the letters, and why don't you give this task to one of your agents?"

"We can't because, just as we have our own agents, Graham has his," Olivia replied, setting her wine glass down and folding her hands on the table in front of her. "All our agents have probably been profiled by Graham's security. And, given the quickening pace of the events here, we don't have enough time to train someone or find someone with the right skillset. While we were discussing this problem, Agent Valton came up with the brilliant idea to bring on board the famous Francesco Marchese. Who more than you, right now, would want to catch this criminal? Given your detective skills and the lack of a better alternative, we decided to rely on Agent Valton's winning intuition."

That seemed to close the subject for the moment. He mulled it over for the rest of the meal, which they both agreed was fabulous. They ordered a second bottle of the Cabernet when their meals were complete and a chocolate marshmallow cake to share.

"I had a strange encounter today," Olivia said as she stuck her fork in the marshmallow cream.

Marchese took a sip of his wine. It felt odd, sitting across the table from a beautiful woman in a foreign country, enjoying an expensive meal and more wine than he'd consumed in a year in one sitting. He wondered briefly what Torchia would think of him, and the sting of Torchia's recent loss took the edge off his buzz.

"Kathrine Leed, Graham's personal assistant. Right out front." She gestured vaguely toward the entrance. "She was coming out of a shop near us."

"Do you think it was coincidence?"

Olivia looked pensive. "Maybe. Kathrine Leed has been David Graham's personal assistant for a decade. We have a whole file dedicated to her. She's the closest person to Graham and has his full confidence, it seems. But she is also a bit of a sphinx. No relationships, except for a few short or occasional affairs, no vices or excesses, except shopping as I witnessed today." Olivia's grimace betrayed her envy. "There's no pretext to reproach her on. We believe she has very little to do with her boss's dirty business and that she is primarily the person who organizes his work and life here in New York."

"But, as you said," Marchese countered, "she is the only one with full access within his office."

"Yes, I believe so. But it could be risky approaching her. She's not the type of person who lets herself be corrupted, and she would certainly report anything out of the ordinary to Graham. We probably have to find other in-roads to him."

Marchese scowled. "What can you tell me about the security systems in his offices?"

"Everything and nothing. His offices are protected by a fairly sophisticated security system, but the most interesting part is a safe that makes us think the letters are potentially hidden in there. It's equipped with an alarm created by an Arab company that even we, at MI5, could not intercept. It's a system known only to Graham. Without his presence, it is impossible to access it. We don't know whether it is a fingerprint or retina recognition system, although we are still working on this."

Marchese had only a few bites of the cake, while Olivia made quick work of it. If that was any indication of how she usually ate, he wondered how she managed to keep her figure. Marchese, on the other hand, had more than his fair share of the second bottle of wine, and poured her what was left of the second bottle once only crumbs of the cake remained.

She nodded to the waiter for the check. "Maybe we could finish our conversation over a glass of Hibiki," she suggested. "Your personal bar the apartment has a fine assortment of whiskey. What do you think?"

Marchese looked down at his empty glass. "Sure. If it is part of the MI5 benefits, why not?"

* * *

Capra had been on the lookout for over two hours. He had ordered dinner to his room and ate while staring down at the main door of Marchese's building.

The jet lag was getting to him, and by the time Marchese finally returned with the woman from earlier, Capra was peeved.

They went inside together. A few moments later, the lights came on in the apartment, and Capra had a clear view of the living room. He saw Marchese approach the window while his companion made herself comfortable on the sofa. Then

Marchese disappeared again, returning shortly after holding two glasses.

"Compliments to our Italian lover!" Capra said aloud.

It was as if Marchese had heard him; he crossed the room and deliberately lowered the blinds. Capra heaved a sigh.

"This chapter is over," he groused. "I'd better get some rest. The bastard has always been a morning person."

* * *

Marchese felt Olivia's eyes scrutinizing him over the rim of her whiskey glass. "I read your personal file and know that you just lost a close associate. I'm really sorry."

Marchese winced. "Yes, I've lost many people in that city in recent years. It's been difficult."

"Is that why you were giving up?"

Marchese cocked an eyebrow at her. "Giving up?"

"I-I didn't mean. . ." she stammered. Her eyes darted to her glass as if she'd just realized the nightcap might have been a bad idea. "I meant why you took a leave of absence from the force."

The correction wasn't reassuring. "I think we all come to a point eventually where we can no longer take it. That's why I accepted this job. To start again, in a new city, and rediscover my sense of enthusiasm for bringing criminals to justice."

"Agent Valton told me that you are a special person," Olivia said after a long silence. "A pragmatist, but an intuitive and experienced detective. I know you've solved many impossible cases in your career, many where you simply followed your gut. 'Something genial about him and steely'—those were her exact words."

Marchese smiled. "Maybe. But don't believe everything you hear."

A few minutes of silence passed. They finished their second and then third glass of whiskey. Olivia emptied her third glass with a single swig, set it down on the glass coffee table, and propped her chin up on her hand. After a moment, she closed her eyes.

Marchese went to the bedroom and grabbed a blanket. By the time he returned to the living room, Olivia had curled up on the sofa and was snoring softly. He draped the blanket over her, smiling paternally as she snuggled under it in her sleep. She was an attractive woman, but there was a certain mature quality he'd always found appealing in women that she clearly lacked. *Perhaps if MI5 didn't give its agents an unlimited liquor budget,* he chuckled inwardly, *they'd have caught Graham by now.*

He tiptoed back to the bedroom and collapsed onto the bed.

* * *

Marchese woke to the sound of a police siren passing the building. It was still early; the sunlight coming in through the blinds was still a little early-morning gray.

He rose and went to the living room to check on Olivia. She was still sleeping soundly, tucked under the blanket and hugging a throw pillow.

Marchese sat on the couch next to her, and she stirred, blinking owlishly. "Good morning, Francesco," she said thickly, sitting up and stretching her arms above her head.

"Good morning," he replied. "Did you sleep well?"

Olivia yawned, then winced. "Yes. And you? Jet-lagged?"

"Not really," Marchese replied, surprised to find he wasn't. "I slept very well actually, as I haven't slept for a long time. Do you want coffee?"

Olivia sat up a little straighter. "Sure! An espresso?"

"Let's see what's inside the MI5 cupboard."

Unlike the bar, the cupboard left quite a bit to be desired. Marchese managed to eke out a pot of coffee from the countertop pot, but the smell wasn't encouraging as he poured two cups. Olivia seemed unfazed; she spooned in sugar and powdered cream as she spoke.

"I had an idea last night. I don't know if it will work. But it might be a way in to the mystery around the letters that Graham has in his hands."

Something in her tone made Marchese uneasy. "What is it?"

"You said it yourself, Kathrine Leed knows more about Graham's operations than anyone else."

Marchese nodded, frowning.

Olivia gave him a cheeky wink. "Well, I suspect your irresistible charm might be just what we need to make Ms. Leed's impenetrable heart melt."

Marchese gaped at her in with amazement. "What are you suggesting?"

Olivia stared at him for few seconds. "I'm trying to say that every woman in this city would fall at the feet of a handsome and charming Italian like you. Your air of mystery makes you irresistible. I know it might sound weird but if you charmed the *iron lady,* maybe you could find a way in and we could find out more about those letters."

Marchese eyed his coffee but left it where it was. "Do you really think these spy-story methods can work?"

Olivia scoffed. "Believe me, they work! They definitely work!

Marchese studied the woman. She had answered as if she were speaking from personal experience.

"It's just an idea," Olivia said with a wave of her hand. "If you're not sure, today we have a meeting in our New York office. We could ask the others on the team for their opinion."

"Sounds good," he replied, grimacing in disappointment as the flat American coffee touched his tongue.

Olivia finished her coffee; Marchese tossed his down the sink drain. After a quick shower, he returned to the kitchen. Olivia was still sitting on the kitchen stool in the clothes she'd worn the night before.

"Where is your office?" Marchese asked as he buttoned his shirt.

Olivia hopped down from the stool. "If I tell you, you wouldn't believe it."

Marchese raised his eyes to the ceiling. "In Graham's same building?"

The woman laughed. "No, that'd be too easy, but we are practically opposite of it. On the west side of Central Park, in the building next to the Dakota."

"Where John Lennon was murdered?"

"Yes. In the building next door, actually."

Marchese snorted. "So you, what? Peek at him with binoculars?"

"We have an agents assigned to do that, actually," Olivia laughed. "Which isn't easy, since more often than not, the calculating Graham closes the blinds."

* * *

Despite having had hours to burn the night before, Capra had not yet decided how to organize his tailing of Marchese. He had to come up with a strategy and quickly. Marchese and his new girlfriend were getting ready to go out, and soon they would be out on the street. He had to try not to lose sight of them.

Just as this thought percolated, Marchese and the woman made for the apartment door.

Capra dressed hastily and put on Eugenio's cap and sunglasses as he went out the door.

His hurrying was wasted; a few minutes later, he watched the pair hop into an Uber before he could flag down a taxi. The car carrying Francesco Marchese and his intriguing companion sped off, and the journalist swore in frustration.

Chapter 14

David Graham made his way down to the office floor at 9:30 a.m. and greeted Kathrine, who had had been at her desk since seven. "Good morning, Kathrine. Please call Paul Morelli and Frank Larsen right away and tell them to come to the office."

"Yes, Mr. Graham."

He thanked her and disappeared behind his office door. He gazed out of his office window. Since early morning, the day had promised to be particularly sultry. In the park below his office, people were strolling and the tourists were taking pictures on the pathways, while the habitual residents jogged by, no longer impressed by the scenery.

He stared at the horizon above the trees. Across the park, he knew there were MI5 agents spying on him, so he smiled the brightest smile he could muster. He hoped it made their skin crawl, knowing he'd won the battle. Nothing could stop him revealing hundreds of years of lies by the English crown, unless the Queen yielded to his compromise and took his deal.

* * *

The Uber carrying Marchese and Olivia first took West Broadway and then turned right onto 6th Avenue.

"The team on Graham's case is eager to meet you, Francesco," Olivia said, laying her hand on Marchese's forearm.

He looked down at her hand and raised an eyebrow at her.

"You're not my type," she assured him.

He shrugged and looked out the window at the sidewalks teaming with people rushing to work as well as tourists and hobos. Along Sixth, children played at the Minetta Playground in the Village, and the chaotic Herald Square contrasted with the ever-peaceful Bryant Park.

New York is a whole world enclosed in a few square kilometers, he thought. The scenery of the city changed block by block, each revealing a different continent and another social, cultural, and economic environment. This could be experienced by simply moving from the Village to Midtown, which were shaped by completely different mentalities and lifestyles.

As they arrived at 57th, the driver turned left and then right onto 8th.

Columbus Circle was jammed with taxis and police cars. At the entrance to Central Park, people were lined up for horse-drawn carriage rides, waiting to take a tour of the most famous green rectangle in the world. The car pulled over at the curb before MI5's base, right next door to the famous Dakota.

As he got out of the car, Marchese glimpsed the side entrance of the building where, thirty years before, a man had shot the controversial Beatles singer. He mentioned it aloud.

"Do you remember that day?" Olivia asked.

"Vaguely. I was still a kid at that time, but I remember my mother crying in front of the television."

Olivia gave him a sympathetic look and said, "Here we are. They are waiting for us."

The pair entered the main door of the building, guarded by a stiff fellow in a classic doorman's uniform.

* * *

The ten agents working on the Graham case gathered around the table in the MI5 conference room. Dean Zona, with a full head of white hair, headed up the team and began the meeting in a somber tone. He introduced Marchese and left a few moments for the exchange of niceties. Thereafter, he dove into the initial plan. Marchese would become acquainted with Kathrine in an effort to get her to confirm that the letters were definitely in New York. Ideally, their relationship would develop to point that Kathrine would agree to help the Italian man retrieve the letters.

Marchese listened in silence. He knew Olivia had briefed Zona over the phone on the way there, but Zona had it so neatly laid out that Marchese suspected he'd had the Kathrine option in his head all along. Marchese also knew the plan was fanciful and far-fetched.

Kathrine's photo appeared on the screen, catching his undivided intention. A striking blond with a pixie cut, soft features, and a pleasingly toned figure. Olivia gave Marchese a sly look that seemed to suggest he'd enjoy this job, but he returned a disappointed frown. He wasn't overly fond of her cavalier attitude toward deceiving this woman, even if it did mean foiling Graham.

"Miss Leed," Zona was saying, "goes to the gym every night around seven p.m.—Remorca Fitness at 171 East 74th Street, two blocks from her apartment on Madison Avenue. Then, she usually stops for a drink at Caffè dei Fiori alone, takes out her iPad, and reads."

As he spoke, Dean Zona stared Marchese down; all this information about Kathrine's daily routine was of no real use to anyone else in the room but him. It was up to Marchese to nail down the right moment within this routine to make contact with her. And he had to make it work, as there were few, if any, alternatives.

"She often dines at home," Zona continued, "ordering from the various restaurants in the area. But when she wants to go out, she stops for a meal at her favorite restaurant, the East Pole at 133 East 65th Street, usually between 8:30 and 9:00 pm. You must be determined and act quickly, Mr. Marchese."

Marchese clenched his teeth at Zona's directness. He hadn't so much as flirted with a woman in years, yet everything hinged on his success. Again, he mused over the ridiculousness of the plan and wondered why these agents couldn't come up with anything better. However, there wasn't much else anyone at the table could do to move toward possession of those damned letters. He knew that Graham wouldn't even flinch at a plan like this. He'd killed five innocent people, seven if he counted Torchia and the bishop of Messina, through a hired gun without ever once dirtying his own hands. Deceiving a woman would probably seem like child's play to Graham. Marchese realized this was the way it had to be. Kathrine Leed was the only key to Graham's office.

* * *

Graham was flipping idly through the photos he had received from Messina when Frank Larsen and Paul Morelli entered his spacious office. Connell, failure though he was, had been thorough; the photos proved he'd spied on the victims for more than a year before making a move. There were also photos of the letters Connell had later delivered to MI5, as well as of the dead bishop of Messina and various policemen involved in the investigation.

"Well, gentlemen," Graham said, beaming as he looked up, "I must say you lived up to your brief. If that asshole Connell had not been caught, we would never have had almost all the letters in our hands. His stupidity has been our gain."

"Thank you, Mr. Graham," Frank said.

Graham turned aside and activated the intercom. "Kathrine, please bring in the envelopes." Graham returned his attention to his hirelings. "I have something for you, gentlemen," he announced brightly. "A reward for the risks you have run for my cause."

Kathrine appeared in the room carrying two bulky yellow envelopes. Graham gestured for her to distribute them, smiling at his henchmen. "For you."

Paul peered inside his envelope and grinned; however, the thickness of the envelope alone indicated the sum inside was enormous. Frank simply tucked his envelope under his arm.

Kathrine approached the table and fingered one of the photos. Until that moment, Graham had entirely forgotten she'd never seen them before. Striking a casual tone, he asked, "Is something wrong?"

Kathrine had blanched, staring down at the desk. She paused a moment before tapping her finger several times on a photo, a headshot of a man. "This is him. The man I saw on Prince Street with Olivia Fischer."

Frank moved closer. His brows immediately knitted in a scowl. "When?"

"Yesterday," she replied.

Frank's expression grew confused. He picked up the photograph and handed it to Graham. "This is one of the Messina detectives. I think he's with the Italian police. What's he doing in New York with an MI5 agent?"

The tycoon sat back in his chair and drummed his fingers languidly on the table. The answer he came up with was almost too funny. "He's obviously here to help them get their hands on my letters." Graham snorted. "An Italian policeman!"

* * *

After further discussion and directions, Kathrine returned to her desk and the two men who had been paid handsomely for their services left. Mr. Graham had been clear: He would meet with the UK ambassador in New York to send a very direct message to the queen. If the Crown wanted to keep Shakespeare's origins a secret, the sovereign would have to accept the deal Graham was putting on the table. Mr. Graham held a treasure of inestimable value to England and the entire world. One of the most buried secrets in history, and if the queen decided to keep it that way, she would need to agree to his demands. Kathrine didn't feel that Graham was being entirely underhanded. Rather, she considered him a Robin Hood type of character who had uncovered a startling truth but had enough respect to keep it quiet for the right price. At least this is what she kept telling herself.

Kathrine called the office of the British Consulate General in New York to schedule the meeting. Her mind kept drifting to the face of the man in the photo. With regard to the more gruesome images she'd seen scattered around Graham's desk, she intentionally pushed them from of her mind.

* * *

Capra had been idling in the Fanelli Café for hours, listening to a regular drone on about the historical significance of the place, when Marchese and his companion stepped out of a cab just outside. He watched the woman shake Marchese's hand goodbye before she turned westward along Prince Street.

That's it!

The journalist made his hasty goodbyes to the old man and left the bar. Marchese had just entered the main door of his building when Capra caught sight of the woman in the distance. When she arrived at the corner of Prince Street and West Broadway, she turned right. Capra crossed onto the other side and continued to follow her.

Mercifully, she stopped to peer into the window of the Coach store.

Perfect, Capra thought. He bolted across the street and reached her side just as she turned to move on. She gave him a quick once-over and smiled.

"Excuse me, miss," he said in broken English and nodded a lock of curly hair off his forehead. "Can I ask information of you?"

The woman ran her hand through her hair in embarrassment. "Sure. Ask me."

"I'm new to the area. The place I am staying is nearby." He gestured vaguely up the street. "I moved here recently. Could you kindly recommend a couple of places to eat. You know —" He winked and watched her coffee-colored eyes dart to his blue ones. "—I am Italian and finding good food in New York is not easy."

The woman smiled. "Italian? What a coincidence."

"Coincidence?" Capra asked, feigning a questioning look.

"Nothing. So, let me think . . ." She looked around, her cheeks reddening. "You could try Piccola Cucina. The Italian food is excellent. I know of many Italians loyal to the place. They have homemade pasta and great seafood."

Capra looked where she'd pointed and flashed a TV-worthy grin. "Sounds interesting. Do you have a plan for tonight by any chance? I don't know many people here."

The woman drew a sharp, surprised breath.

"Oh, sorry, I know this is a bit rude," Capra said hastily, doing his best to look embarrassed. "I understand. You don't know me. But . . ." Capra put his hand on his chest. "I'm a good guy. Don't take my invitation as anything but a way to get to know someone. Do you live in this area?"

The woman looked down, but Capra knew he'd won. His disarming charm had helped warm his bed more than once. The fact she was considering it told him her relationship to Marchese wasn't romantic, at least not in any serious way.

"I guess I could," she said at last, gazing at him. "I have no plans for tonight. Why not? Maybe we'll have some laughs and you'll tell me what an Italian is doing in SoHo."

Capra smiled. "What time?" he asked, taking note of her flushed cheeks and widening pupils.

"Six-thirty sharp. I'm Olivia, by the way."

The reporter shook her hand, his mind racing. He couldn't risk her telling Marchese she'd met a Luigi. "I am Pietro."

"Nice to meet you, Pietro. See you tonight, then."

"I look forward to it."

Capra followed Olivia with his eyes as she walked on and entered a building a few steps ahead.

"That's a step forward," the reporter whispered to himself.

* * *

Marchese entered Modell's Sporting Goods at the corner of Broadway and Chambers Street. Make a good impression on Kathrine at the gym required appropriate fitness attire.

He made quick work of choosing a comfortable pair of Nikes, a few pairs of gym shorts and muscle shirts, and a sports bag. He left the shop and hailed the first yellow taxi that approached.

"Where you headed, sir?" asked the driver as Marchese slid into the backseat.

"171 and 74th on the Upper East Side."

The taxi pulled away, and Marchese made himself comfortable. He took out his MI5-issued phone and called Olivia. She picked up immediately. After they exchanged greetings, he told her he'd be signing up at the gym and would let her know how his first encounter with the target went.

"I have a date," she said, "but I'll have my phone with me. Don't hesitate to call."

Marchese hung up, briefly wondering why the agent felt the need to mention she had a date. The taxi traveled North on the FDR, and he gazed out the window, enjoying the view of the midday sun sparkling on the East River. They passed near the Williamsburg Bridge and the Queensboro Bridge before the car turned in the direction of Central Park.

ROME—AUGUST 14, 2012

The British Ambassador in Rome, Tomas McFee, arrived at the Vatican at 8:00 a.m. to avoid the prying eyes of the paparazzi. Over the past ten years in this role, he had met the pontiff three times, but this present appointment made him feel as if the collar of his shirt was suddenly too tight.

The pope was in his office when the ambassador was announced.

"Your Holiness. It is a great pleasure and honor to meet with you again." McFee kissed the pope's ring, waiting to be invited to sit down.

"Thank you, Ambassador." The pope gestured to the plush leather armchair before his desk. "Please, take a seat."

The two found themselves facing each other, separated by the Holy Father's desk. The Commander of the Swiss Guard, Emanuel Tertón, stood nearby, and he approached to shake the ambassador's hand before stationing himself on the left side of the imposing, inlaid table.

The pope spread his hand inquiringly. "I don't know if you know why I have asked you to come."

McFee smiled sadly. "I am not entirely certain, but I have an idea, Your Excellency."

"The letters." The pope's face fell. "And above all, poor Bishop Perri."

This confirmed the ambassador's worries. The pontiff asked for explanations about what happened two days prior, why his bishop had been murdered and, maybe most important, where the letters had ended up.

McFee knew about the Graham case, but he was not authorized to disclose this information. Not even to the pope. So he was forced to dissemble. "Your Holiness, we also are trying to figure out where they ended up and who committed this brutal act toward a member of your Church. We believe a criminal organization whose purpose will be an improper use of the letters is responsible for this, but that is all I can say for certain."

The pope nodded sadly. But Tertón's expression of disappointment caught the ambassador's attention, and it rankled him. "Don't you believe me, Commander Tertón?"

Tertón's half-hidden sneer was answer enough. "We know that your secret service agents took possession of the six lost letters. And this makes us suspect that they may have also decided to seize the remaining ones, the ones kept inside the casket."

The ambassador stared at the pontiff, seeking support after the insinuations of the Vatican security chief. But the pope's expression was carefully neutral. McFee drew himself up. "This is a very serious allegation that, without the right support of evidence, is dangerous for the relationship between the Crown and the Vatican."

"An allegation if—"

The pope raised his hand to interrupt Tertón. When silence fell again, the pontiff looked down again at his desk. "Dear Ambassador, would you please forgive my security chief? We are all still shaken by what has happened and by the loss of a person very close to me, a fellow son of God. But you also must understand our skepticism regarding the alleged and strange coincidence of everything following the tragic events in Messina."

The ambassador nodded in agreement. "At this moment, according to the information in my possession, our MI5 agents are searching for the letters that were stolen from you. And I promise you that I'll keep you informed about any updates of this situation. As for your doubts, I hope to clear them up as soon as possible."

* * *

Everything is going as planned, Tertón thought, watching the ambassador duck into his car not long after. Closing the meeting with doubt and keeping the pontiff's attention focused on the English Crown would give his boss needed time and the advantage of a Vatican distracted and still in the dark.

At that delicate moment, Tertón could not afford siding against even the pope. The involvement of the Vatican, in synergy with the English Crown, in the hunt for the letters would have meant involving the Americans and the secret services of all the countries in the world close to the Holy See. Better to keep the Crown and the Church suspicious of one another.

What Graham had asked of him was happening.

NEW YORK

Dean Zona was working through his third cup of coffee when an agent burst into his office without so much as a knock. "Graham has requested an appointment with the ambassador."

Zona set his cup down. "I beg your pardon?"

"His admin, Kathrine Leed, phoned the consulate," the agent replied, leaning breathlessly on the doorframe. "They took a message and immediately contacted us for instructions."

Zona planted his elbows on the desk and lowered his head into his hands, pondering for a moment. "It's likely Graham wishes to meet with the ambassador to send a message to the queen."

"Do you think he intends to demand a ransom from her for the letters?" the agent asked.

Zona smiled. "If it's about blackmail, we're talking about an enormous sum. Those letters are worth a king's ransom." He smirked at his own pun. "If Graham wants to bargain with the Crown, he's up to something very ambitious."

The agent straightened up. "What are you suggesting, then?"

"We have to bide our time," Zona replied. "We need to give the Italian the necessary time to get closer to Leed and ultimately to the letters. Get me through to the ambassador. I have an idea."

"Yes, sir," the agent replied, already rushing from the room.

As Zona stood, his knees cracked, and he thought of the day of his retirement. Already past retirement age, he wondered if such a day would ever come. He looked out the window, gazing into the distance toward the building where he felt certain Graham, at that moment, was surely gazing out over Central Park like a pompous emperor. Moments later, his phone rang.

Settling back in his office chair, he answered. Ambassador Grang was on the other end. He instructed the ambassador to agree to the appointment with Graham but to schedule it for ten days in the future.

"Graham's influence is far-reaching," the ambassador argued. "Such a postponement will *not* be met favorably."

Zona clenched his fist. How had David Graham managed to put the fear of God in those in power? "I understand, ambassador. Just have your admin tell Graham's admin that you are leaving for London and won't be back any sooner."

"Surely Graham will be suspicious," Grang countered. "Also, I am expected at the gala next Saturday evening. A failure to attend goes against the usual protocol. You *do* understand this, don't you?"

"Yes, ambassador," Zona replied, rolling his tired eyes. "Meet with Graham any sooner and you won't like what he will expect from you. I wouldn't want to be in your position. Just potstone the meeting so we can do our job."

* * *

Marchese signed up for a monthly membership at Kathrine's gym. He patted his belly and decided he could certainly lose the few pounds he'd recently put on due to all his beer drinking. It would be a few hours before the "target" was scheduled to show up, so he went for a walk in Central Park. He figured the fresh air would help him prepare psychologically for his mission.

As he strolled along the narrow pathways, he thought about his work. He had always been a frontline detective. When a murder occurred, he was the first to investigate and often the first to solve the case. He questioned witnesses and suspects and hunted criminals. He was good at those things—*very* good. He was not a secret service agent who was used dealing with traps and covert operations, and he was unsure if he would succeed at the task he'd been assigned. On the surface, he feared failure, but deeper down, he felt invigorated. Yes, he was intrigued by his mission.

The thought gave him pause. He'd never been good with women, no matter what Olivia assumed, and Renata had been an exceptional one. It would have been overwhelming enough trying to chat up Kathrine under normal circumstances. He wondered if he'd catch himself finding a little of Renata in Kathrine's face, and the idea terrified him. Attachment always seemed to lead to loss in his life.

Marchese found himself in the Mall Literary Walk inside Central Park and paused under the statue of William Shakespeare. As he'd learned from his recent internet research, notable academics had been suggesting the crazy hypothesis about Shakespeare's alleged Italian origin for years. Martino Iuvarà, a Sicilian university professor, had even written essays on the subject, all regularly ignored by the European intelligentsia.

As Marchese stood beneath the imposing sculpture, his phone rang. It was Olivia. She quickly filled him in: Graham had contacted the British ambassador to demand an in-person meeting. The ambassador had managed to stall, but only for two weeks.

Marchese groaned inwardly. "And this means I have until then to complete the operation."

Olivia's voice oozed genuine sympathy. "That's right. You have all of two weeks."

Marchese ran his hand through his hair, dampened by sweat. "You mean *just* two weeks."

"I know," Olivia said airily. "But you've got this. At least we know nothing will happen between now and then. Graham won't make any other moves prior to his meeting. So, are you ready to make a good impression on our Ms. Leed?"

The former detective narrowed his eyes at Shakespeare's statue. "I suppose."

Olivia laughed. "We have faith in you, you handsome Italian."

Marchese bristled at the sexist compliment, briefly considered its inappropriateness, and hung up. He shoved the phone back in his pocket and trudged on along the path that led to The Pond.

Chapter 15

Capra tipped his head back and enjoyed the stream of water massaging his face. He allowed himself the luxury of a long shower now that he had a partial plan in place. He had not relaxed since he had seen Marchese in Piazza del Duomo in Messina, during Carlo Torchia's funeral. In half an hour, at precisely 6:30 p.m., he would be sitting across from the mysterious woman who had been Marchese's consort for the past two days. Through her, he planned to find out what the Detective of Steel was doing in the Big Apple.

This Olivia was quite beautiful, he thought, and he found her British accent alluring. He'd have to proceed carefully. He wasn't entirely certain of her relationship with Marchese yet, and he didn't want to put himself in Marchese's line of fire again. She had quickly accepted his invitation, which suggested nothing too serious was going on between her and the former detective. Perhaps it had only been a one-night stand. Or maybe she had simply slept with him for some other reason. He would figure it out over the course of their dinner date. The challenge made him smile. He stepped out of the shower and headed to the sink for a shave, which he hadn't done in three days.

* * *

Kathrine entered her apartment on the fourteenth floor of 955 Madison Avenue. From the window next to the entrance, she could see the trees of Central Park. She hurried to the bedroom to get ready to go to the gym, eager to release the tension of the day on the treadmill. Things had taken an odd turn and made her feel a bit agitated. The letters had become her boss's obsession, through all these years of tracking them. And now everything was culminating.

She put on her workout clothes, trotted to the kitchen for a bottle of water from the fridge, and organized her gym bag. On her way out, she stopped in front of the entrance mirror to apply some lip balm. Her hands froze in place as her eyes locked with their reflection in the mirror. She sensed then how quickly the years were going by and how alone she was. Work had overtaken everything, robbing her of her desire for a more balanced life.

* * *

Marchese paced the sidewalk on 74th Street, between 3rd Avenue and Lexington Avenue. Kathrine would have to pass by there to get to the gym. He wanted her to walk in first so he could gauge how to get close. He hadn't figured out yet what tack to take, so he would have to improvise.

At the corner of Lexington Avenue, he paused before the window of a cheesy souvenir shop boasting shelves line with hundreds of miniature Statues of Liberty, that famous symbol of the many who had left everything meaningful behind them to travel thousands of miles in search of freedom. Had they traded all of that to end up enslaved to a new system that was all about working to get ahead? All this, simply to buy a little suburban house with a garden and enjoy a barbecue every July fourth?

The world is a treadmill, he thought.

His reflection in the shop's window showed a different man from the one he had been a few days before. Something was changing inside him. That night spent talking to with Olivia had made him feel alive. Soon this new Marchese would break out of his own prison.

He looked at his watch. Six thirty. Shortly thereafter, Kathrine would appear, and his heart began to beat faster at the thought.

Sure enough, fifteen minutes later, Kathrine appeared at the corner dressed in leggings and sneakers. Her hair was pulled back by a colorful fabric headband.

The photos hadn't done her justice; she was much more stunning in person. Every move showed her height and athletic build to riveting effect. As she walked briskly down the sidewalk of 74th toward the gym, Marchese headed in the same direction on the opposite side of the street. He watched her greet a woman she apparently knew and pass through the glass doors of the stylish gym.

Marchese sighed deeply. It was time, and his pulse began to race.

* * *

Arriving at Piccola Cucina, Capra requested a table for two by the open window facing onto the street. *Quite the intimate setting,* he mused. Actually, everything was small here; the place had only about a dozen tables. But the aroma coming from the open kitchen was a reassuring omen of great food.

He looked at his watch. Six-thirty. Olivia would show up soon. *American women are punctual.*

Just then, Olivia entered the small restaurant, smiled at him from the doorway, and approached.

"Hello," Capra greeted her, rising to shake her hand.

She looked embarrassed. "Sorry, Pietro."

Capra grinned as he pulled out her chair and then took his own. "If one minute means being late to you, then what they say about American women and punctuality is true."

218

Olivia smiled and made herself comfortable. "Technically, I'm Argentinian and Jewish. I was born in Argentina, but I've been here most of my life, living in the most fascinating city in the world. What about you?"

Capra took a sip of water as he thought about the role he had decided to play. "I am Italian," said the reporter, raising both his hands.

Olivia laughed. "Yes I know, but what else?"

"I'm a writer. I moved to New York to write a new novel."

She raised one shapely eyebrow. "Interesting. What kind of novel?" Her hand shot up to stop his reply. "Wait! Don't tell me. As a proper Italian, you are writing a love story."

It was Capra who laughed this time. "You got it! Yes. It is a love story."

At that moment, the waiter appeared at Capra's elbow, and he realized neither of them had even glanced at the menus. They took a few minutes in silence to consider their orders and to give the waiter a moment to return with a bottle of rosé.

Capra noticed Olivia glancing discreetly at her watch as he told her his life story, in which he had more than partially embellished the details. "Are you in a hurry?" he asked amicably.

Olivia startled. "Why do you ask?" she replied, clearly flustered.

Capra gestured to her wrist. "It's the third time in less than twenty minutes you have looked at your watch. Maybe you're bored by me?"

"No, definitely not," Olivia assured him swiftly. "I'm expecting a business call and I'm a bit anxious. But don't worry, your story is actually very interesting, so don't read anything into that."

The waiter returned to refill their glasses. As he poured, Capra felt Olivia watching him. *Comparing me to Marchese?*

he wondered, smirking inwardly at the thought. He wondered how they measured up in her eyes, Marchese's dark detective with a troubled soul against his own fascinating traveler aspect. Capra had lived a wild and passionate life, and it showed. He knew from experience that he was the sort of man who could entice a woman into a dangerous and intriguing relationship.

And by Olivia's smile, she wanted to get to know him better, this mysterious brunette Italian with the ever-gesturing hands. He'd be happy to oblige.

* * *

Marchese entered the gym, stowed his gear in a locker and headed for the first workout room. Dozens of people already crowded the room, and many of the treadmills and exercise bikes were occupied.

Down the room he saw Kathrine running—not jogging, full-on running—on one of the treadmills. Fortuitously, one of the machines beside hers was unoccupied. Marchese smiled at his luck.

The moment had arrived for his grand entrance.

He approached and moved to step onto the treadmill, pressing the unfamiliar buttons to get it going. Kathrine didn't seem to notice his presence; she had her Bluetooth earbuds in and didn't even glance in his direction.

The former detective ran, feigning concentration, too.

A few minutes later, Kathrine stopped her treadmill and grabbed her gym towel to dry her neck and forehead. Only then did she look at the man running beside her.

Nothing for it, thought Marchese grimly—and he deliberately stumbled, allowing the treadmill to hurl him off.

"Oh my goodness!" Kathrine gasped. "Did you get hurt?"

"Well, my pride is hurt, but otherwise I am fine," replied Marchese, trying to steady himself with the woman's help.

Kathrine burst out laughing, but that laugh choked off as she looked him in the eyes. Her expression shifted briefly to horror, then to stony seriousness so swiftly Marchese wondered if he'd imagined the fear he'd seen there. She turned as if she were going to leave the room.

"This is my first night at this gym," he said hastily, "and I guess I am making a fool of myself!"

Kathrine, her back turned on him, fumbled with her gear and didn't answer.

"Have you been coming here long?" asked Marchese.

After a second's pause, she turned and smiled with a warmth that didn't reach her eyes. "Yes. I've been a member here for a long time," she replied in a shaky voice.

Marchese's heart pounded in earnest, and he gave her a questioning look. "Did I say or do something wrong? You seem upset."

Kathrine's eyes darted away. Toward the door . "No, not at all, Mister . . . ?"

"Francesco. My name is Francesco."

Kathrine let her breath out without introducing herself. "Hah, I am sorry, it's nothing. I just suddenly have a splitting headache. I think I'd better call it a day."

"I'm sorry," said Marchese with an embarrassed smile. "I hope I have not put you off, a clumsy man like me falling in front of you?"

The woman allowed an amused expression. "Don't worry. I really just have to go."

Marchese forced himself not to slump in defeat. "Alright. See you again, I hope."

This was the wrong thing to say; the now-undisguised fear on Kathrine's face told him so. She bolted for the door and vanished into the dark New York City night.

Damn it.

* * *

Capra cleaned his plate of the pappardelle with wild boar sauce. "I thought I'd never eat this well in New York," he confessed with surprise. "What a great plate of pasta!"

"I told you it'd be worthwhile," replied Olivia triumphantly. "I often frequent this restaurant."

"A great choice," Capra declared. "And I'm thankful you agreed to join me. I know it will not be easy to make friends in this chaotic city. I am among so many people, yet there is little opportunity to meet and make eye contact with anyone. Or to open up with someone you can potentially call a real friend."

Olivia's eyes sparkled with interest. "That's true, Pietro. Living here and trusting people isn't easy. It's difficult here to make that happen. I could tell you several absurd stories that I've been through meeting people."

Capra placed his elbows on the table, laced his fingers together, and propped his chin on them, peering at her. "Then why did you accept my invitation for dinner?"

Olivia smiled straight into his eyes. "Because you are Italian. You Italians, you are gentlemen. Maybe a little crafty, but not dangerous."

Capra laughed. "Crafty? What do you mean?"

Olivia shrugged. "You like to flirt. You know . . . you love and leave, amuse and lose. You are certainly not faithful."

A thrill went up Capra's spine. The journalist tried to put on his most serious and sincere expression. "I understand what you mean. But I'm really trying to make some friends in this city. I like it so much that I might not necessarily go back to Italy after finishing my novel."

Olivia smiled. She clearly liked him, as he'd intended. He had not been vulgar, and he came across as entirely authentic. Years on TV had taught him how to convey a genuineness he didn't necessarily possess.

At that moment he looked at his watch. "Oh my gosh, it's very late. I have to finish an email for my publisher back in Italy by tomorrow. You know, he always wants reassurance that I'm working and that my book will be ready in time for its promotion."

Olivia seemed surprised, as if she'd been expecting him to suggest they finish off the evening with a nightcap at another bar—or to go back to one of their respective apartments. He hadn't even tried, and by the mixture of half-hidden disappointment and delight on her face, it had worked to his advantage. She was hooked. She wanted to see him again.

The fascinating Italian writer persona whose look could melt even the most reticent of women. Pietro. He'd have to keep this one in his back pocket for the future.

Capra asked for the bill and then turned to her. "What about trying another place tomorrow night?"

Olivia's face lit up. "That would be nice. I like the idea. But we have to go easy on Italian restaurants and pasta; otherwise, you'll become a recipe writer and I'll ruin my figure."

The two laughed and exchanged smiles.

Struck by Cupid's arrow! Capra said to himself.

Capra paid—Olivia offered, but he insisted—and they rose together to leave. Just as they were about to exit the restaurant, a woman sitting at the table near the entrance leapt up and blocked their way. She seemed particularly excited and surprised.

"Sorry to stop you," she gushed, utterly ignoring Olivia, "but I wanted to ask if you could take a picture with me. I am Sicilian and I have read all your books! I adored *La moglie del Sindaco* and, oh! *Il Ponte di Fango* made me cry at the end. I'm so excited to actually meet you, here in New York!"

Capra's blood froze in his veins for an instant before he realized the woman had been speaking Italian. Those were his books, all right. His false identity had almost been blown by a zealous fan. "Sure. What's your name?"

"Antonella," replied the girl as she moved next to the journalist for a selfie. He gave Olivia a "sorry" wince and she smiled, stepping outside to wait for him.

The girl pulled him toward her, and Capra felt her breast pressing against his ribs. Her mischievous eyes flashed as she shifted her hips suggestively against him. He stared at her for a moment.

"If you don't move, I'll be back in ten minutes," he whispered as she posed for a second photo.

Her eyes darted first to him and then at the woman waiting for him right outside the restaurant door. She smiled. "Sure. Oh my God. Of course I will wait for you!"

Olivia linked arms with the man she knew as Pietro as he stepped out of the restaurant. "Wow, that girl stopped you in the restaurant to take a picture with you?"

Capra smiled. "Yeah. An Italian girl. She recognized me and said she had read some of my books."

Olivia looked at him with surprise. "So, I had dinner tonight with a *famous* Italian writer?"

"*Famous* is a strong word," said Capra, just as they arrived at the corner of Prince Street and West Broadway. "It was just a coincidence. And anyway, you'll still have dinner tomorrow night with me, I hope?"

Olivia smiled, flattered. "Sure! Let me think of another little place that you might like and I'll let you know. Meanwhile, here's my number."

She watched him add her number to his contacts. "I have an Italian number," he said presently, "so I'll contact you on WhatsApp."

"Of course, I don't want to spend a fortune on a few calls!"

They both laughed. Silence fell between them as they crossed the street, and they paused together on the corner.

"See you tomorrow, then?" he asked.

Olivia flushed with excitement already. "See you tomorrow, and . . . well, anyway . . ."

The Italian tilted his head and gave her a slow smile. "'Anyway' what?"

Olivia lowered her head shyly. "I enjoyed this, and I'm sorry you have to end the evening so soon."

His smile broadened. "I promise that tomorrow night my schedule will be more freed up," he said with palpable sincerity.

Inexplicably, Marchese popped into Olivia's mind. She had been a little attracted by the mystery behind his intense gaze and had felt a profound respect. But that was all—respect. Pietro's eyes, on the other hand, held something more.

Olivia grinned. "Sounds good. See you tomorrow, then."

* * *

Kathrine arrived home utterly agitated. She palmed her phone to call David Graham and tell him what had happened but, at the same time, didn't want to disturb him. Surely, he would tell her this was her imagination and that nothing at this point could affect his plans.

She was scared nonetheless. She set the phone on the foyer table and went into the kitchen, took a bottle of rosé wine from the fridge, uncorked it, and filled a glass. Then she headed for the couch, taking the bottle with her, and mulled over what had transpired.

She couldn't get that man's face out of her mind. Behind his charm and intense gaze was an intent—a man who wanted something from her or, probably more accurately, from David Graham. He wanted the letters, most likely, or at least information about them. And her mind began to race to something worse. The letters were a serious obsession of Graham's—maybe serious enough that this stranger might be willing to kill her or her boss.

Her hands began to shake. She emptied her glass and rose, trying to shake off this train of thought by pacing the room.

An hour later, she had finished the bottle of rosé and had settled back onto the couch. Alcohol had melted away her fears and replaced them with a curiosity about the attractive man who had approached her at the gym. He had a sense of humor, although she wasn't sure whether it was artificial and meant to manipulate her.

There was something about him nonetheless, even in the way he had awkwardly approached her. If she hadn't seen him with Olivia Fischer in the photos on Graham's table, she would have liked him.

She placed the glass on the coffee table next to her and turned on the TV.

* * *

Marchese was still furious with himself when he reached the MI5 apartment. His first approach had utterly failed with Kathrine. He shed his gym clothes and trudged to the shower.

He could not get the woman's reaction out of his mind. It was as if she had recognized him—as if she was visibly surprised to see him. Maybe Graham had a file on him already, or she wasn't used to the fact that a man, a stranger, had approached her like that. Something hadn't gone right. But it was only his first attempt; The next day he would do better. If she didn't show up at the gym, it meant the plan had blown up. But if she did, then it might take a different turn. At least he had broken the ice, but what had initially felt like a straightforward task was becoming a chess game.

After the shower, he called Olivia.

"How did it go with Kathrine Leed?" she asked cheerily.

At least her evening's going well. "Not very well. There was even a moment when I felt like she knew who I was."

"What do you mean?"

Marchese held the towel around his waist with one hand and clutched the phone in the other as he walked to the living room. "I don't know how to explain it. She seemed surprised, even shocked, when she saw me."

"Don't start getting paranoid, Francesco," Olivia said soothingly. "The woman can't know who you are. I don't think Graham has been profiling police officers around the world. And I don't think Ms. Leed can memorize every one of those faces in the files. That's not her job. You'll make better headway tomorrow."

"And you? Did you rest a while?" he asked her.

There was a lengthy pause on the other end of the line.

"Yes I did," she replied, and he could swear she sounded coy. "I'm watching TV at home. I'm going to sleep soon. I'll see you at the meeting in the morning."

"OK. Good night."

Marchese poured himself a glass of Hibiki, alternating sips with bites of a pizza he had picked up on his way back from the gym. He crossed the room to gaze out the window. Across the street, just barely visible by streetlight, he noticed a couple making love, leaning against the window of the building opposite. He smiled, lowered the curtain, and sat down on the couch, lost in his thoughts.

Chapter 16

Kathrine walked briskly through the office door at 9:00 a.m. Graham was at his desk, engaged in a phone conversation, which carried to her desk through his open door.

"So, it *is* true the ambassador had to return to London. What time did his flight leave?" Seeing Kathrine, he waved at her to enter. "OK. I need to know if he visits the palace and meets with the queen. I'm sure they were alarmed by my request for a meeting."

Kathrine stood in front of his desk, and he motioned for her to sit down.

"Keep me posted." He closed the conversation and stared at Kathrine, who was still standing.

"Good morning, Mr. Graham," she said flatly.

He gestured again for her to sit, and this time she did so.

"Good morning. I need your updated report on the gala preparations. I don't need to remind you that I want *everything* to be perfect."

She nodded in agreement, but with little enthusiasm.

Graham's brows furrowed. "Is there something wrong?"

Kathrine weighed her words carefully before she spoke. "Last night I had a strange encounter at the gym."

Graham raised an eyebrow. "Strange? What do you mean?"

She folded her hands in her lap to keep them from shaking. "I saw the Italian officer in that picture at the gym. He tried to strike up a conversation with me."

Graham relaxed in his chair, apparently deep in thought. "Very well. This means MI5 is working with the Italians to retrieve the letters."

"Maybe. But why approach *me*?"

The man gave her a smug smile. "Because they believe they can get useful information out of you about the letters. Or maybe they are thinking about forcing you to collaborate with them. Clearly they are desperate if they are resorting to these methods."

Graham laughed, but Kathrine squirmed.

"I ordered a profile on Francesco Marchese," Graham continued, taking a yellow folder from his desk drawer. He opened and showed it to Kathrine.

She lifted the photo of Marchese out of the file.

"Former Messina homicide detective. He is a sort of legend in the city and is revered as a superhero rather than just a good cop. His steely character, the tragic killing of his beloved companion by the Italian gangland, and the high-profile cases he has solved have made him quite a notable figure. However, after avenging his wife's death, he left the department on an open-ended leave."

"So why is he here?" Kathrine asked.

Graham's casual shrug did little to ease her mind. "Probably a series of coincidences. He may have helped stop the crazy murderer hired to recover the letters in Messina. Why is he here? We are going to find out." Graham paused for a second and smiled. "Or rather, you will find out!" He laughed again.

"*Me*? What do you mean?" she asked warily.

Graham rose from his chair and came to stand by her side, leaning against the desk. "Since the Italian approached you, we should make MI5 believe they've found a breach in my organization. We have two weeks until I meet with the ambassador. I ask you, Kathrine, for two weeks of sacrifice. Date him. Let him take you to dinner. Talk about irrelevant aspects of your job. Make those desperate MI5 agents believe we've fallen into their trap. Just for two weeks."

Kathrine listened in silence, still staring at Marchese's photo. She was to let him approach her? Talk to him, show interest in his conversations, and pretend to be interested in him? She was shaking her head when Graham returned to his plush chair.

"Kathrine," Graham said placatingly, "I know I'm asking you for something difficult. But this way, we'll learn about their strategy. If the MI5 agents realize that we have discovered their trap, they will use other methods we aren't privy to. We have an advantage over them and they don't know it. They believe we do not know who Francesco Marchese is. And we must let them believe it. Just for two weeks."

Kathrine nodded this time. The idea was upsetting, but she understood what Graham was asking of her. She got up and headed for the door to leave the office, but she paused in the doorway and turned again to her boss. "Can I ask you a question, Mr. Graham?"

"Of course."

Her heart pounded as she spoke aloud the question that had sprung into her mind in the middle of the previous night. "Did any of the men you hired have anything to do with the Messina murders?"

Graham's face grew instantly appalled. "Certainly not, Kathrine!" He stood up. "I'll forget you asked me that. After ten years, you should know me better."

Kathrine swayed on her feet in palpable relief. "I apologize. I'll go get the gala dossier."

* * *

Capra gazed at the naked woman slumbering in his bed. It had been a long night and the two had fallen asleep at dawn, and it was already approaching 10;00 a.m. The

231

champagne bottle stood empty on the table. Capra picked up his phone and found a text message from Olivia.

He read it and smiled.

He smiled as he read it and decided to reply immediately.

"Good morning, dear Olivia. Sorry it took me so long to get back to you. I fell asleep before I could even finish my e-mail. You made me drink too much, I think. LOL I can't wait to see you tonight."

As he pressed send, Antonella opened her eyes and smiled at him. The sheets fell away as she approached and embraced him. "Good morning!"

Capra smiled. "I'm sorry to rush you, but I have important business to complete this morning."

She broke off, visibly disappointed. "I see. Just time for a shower and then I'll go." She turned toward the bathroom, but she only made it to the doorway before she turned to him again. "Shall we see each other again?"

The man stared at her. "Who knows? Maybe?"

Once she had departed, Capra took a quick shower and decided to spend the rest of the day exploring the streets of Manhattan. The dinner with Olivia had been set for seven o'clock that evening, but she had not yet told him where to meet her.

Capra had a coffee at Starbucks around breakfast time, then he ate a pizza at Eataly in Madison Square for lunch. It was a sunny day, and hot, but the humidity was mercifully low.

Capra left Broadway and continued on 5th, gazing up at the Empire State Building in the distance. Its massive size made it seem very close, even though it was still ten blocks away. He turned South to admire the Flatiron. Being a big Spiderman fan, Capra found it fascinating to admire, with his own eyes, the building he had seen so many times in his favorite comics. Since he started his career as a journalist, he had been dreaming of having an editorial office like the *Daily Bugle's*.

It took him more than an hour to walk all the way up to Rockefeller Center. The square was full of tourists. It was almost impossible to walk and even more difficult to stop amidst that huge crowd that jostled him here and there.

Crossing the street, Capra headed toward St. Patrick's Cathedral, hoping to cool off a little inside.

Walking through the aisles, the reporter pondered the evening ahead. Their second date. If all went to plan, she would want to have sex with him. He had to earn her trust to find out why Marchese was in New York. He had an idea about how to bring their conversation around to this matter and smiled at the thought.

Capra lit a candle, looked toward the large crucifix hanging above the altar, awkwardly made the sign of the cross, and left.

* * *

When the MI5 meeting ended nearly two hours after it had begun, Marchese felt somewhat reassured. Olivia had pointed out in her own cavalier way that expecting Kathrine to "get on her back" just because he'd flirted a bit wouldn't work; Kathrine's personal history had shown she wasn't much of a romantic. It might take a little work, but he felt suddenly invigorated to try again—at least while MI5 still had faith in him.

He caught up with Olivia in the hall. She was smiling down at her phone.

"Good news?"

She jumped and pressed the phone to her chest. "Well, I don't know if it's good news or if it spells problems," she said sheepishly.

"Life will tell, someone once said," Marchese replied. "Anyway, I have to thank you. I appreciate having a woman's perspective on this, and I think you're right. I'll do better with Kathrine tonight—assuming she shows up at the gym."

Olivia smiled and placed a hand on his arm. "I'm sure you will. And I'm sure she'll be there."

Though he wasn't certain how Olivia could be so sure, her confidence reassured him.

Dean Zona approached when Oliva took her leave. "Do you have a minute for me in my office?" he asked.

"Sure," Marchese said and followed Zona into his office.

They both took seats.

"Look, Marchese, I'm sure you will do whatever you can to reach Ms. Leed and get the intel we need in time. However, I want you to be aware that there's a plan B a few of my agents are on. Agent Fisher is unaware of it, and I'm only telling you so that the burden of pressure doesn't get to your head and cause you to screw up. Please keep this alternate operation strictly confidential."

"The fact that I know nothing about it won't make that difficult, sir," Marchese said with only a hint of sarcasm. That Olivia wasn't in on this "plan B" made Marchese inexplicably nervous.

The MI5 lead of the Graham operation stood up and reached for Marchese's hand as the Italian detective rose, giving it a firm shake. "I admire your work as a detective, and I am impressed by how you are adapting in this situation."

Marchese merely nodded his thanks and left the office.

A parallel operation. A sort of parachute, he thought. But Zona, in an attempt to be gentle, had not put it that way.

Marchese knew that the risk of failure with his task was high. And he understood the need for an alternate strategy. The common goal was to get the letters before they disappeared or before David Graham's shady plan went into motion—all to preserve the English Crown's centuries-old lie.

* * *

Kathrine Leed sat at her desk, poring over Marchese's file. His story was fascinating. Full of success, pain, loss, and accolades. He was certainly celebrated in his country. He had lost the woman he loved in a tragic way and had avenged her. And, just a few days earlier, he had lost his former deputy in an attempt to catch Mark Connell, the murderer who had killed five innocent women to retrieve the letters Graham had hired him to recover. Five women Graham had sworn he hadn't hired Mark to kill. She shook off an intrusive *what-if*, but she couldn't ignore the chill that went up her spine at the thought that perhaps Graham's assurances didn't match his actions.

This intriguing man seemed so different from the powerful businessmen Kathrine dealt with every day. But something about Marchese also frightened her. Suppose that he had not approached her for the purpose of getting to the letters. In such a context, she would have been attracted to him. Unfortunately for her, he was the "enemy," one who did not care about her life and wanted to destroy her boss's. She closed the file and looked at her watch. Now it was up to her to play the role of the woman taken in by him. She would repay Francesco Marchese in kind.

* * *

David Graham met with three consultants to discuss the serious fiscal problems his organization was having in some South American countries. But Graham's thoughts weren't on the issue at hand; they went to Kathrine and what he had asked of her. He hoped the woman would be able to carry out the task he had given her. She had to keep Marchese busy for a couple of weeks, to make him believe that she trusted him. To convincingly become his friend by telling him less important secrets of the office, if not outright lies. Graham needed sufficient time to start negotiations with the Crown. If the queen wanted those letters, she would have to pay his price. So many years of research and work. He could not afford to lose them to British Security Services now. He was not a fool; he knew Kathrine could fail. And he'd have to make arrangements for just such a possibility.

* * *

Olivia rushed into her apartment. She had to be at Ribalta to meet her new "friend" Pietro in two hours, and she wanted to look particularly inviting for the occasion—sexy but, at the same time, easy to strip. The thought made her smile. Her job required a certain level of discretion that made it difficult to make friends, never mind boyfriends, so having the chance to behave like a 9-to-5 woman for a change was thrilling, especially when the company was so intriguing.
She liked Pietro quite a bit. Attractive and confident, he had been a perfect gentleman the night before, the kind of man who wasn't easy to meet in New York. He hadn't even tried to get her into bed. Indeed, he had shown no sexual interest in her. This second thought made her a bit morose. What if he wasn't attracted to her and was only looking for a friend?

This doubt bothered her, but it only made her more determined to seduce him that evening.

She grabbed a dress from her closet and held it in front of her, looking in the mirror. She pulled a face, hung the dress back up, then selected two others and repeated the process. Then she spotted it—the slinky black number she'd bought on a whim months ago and hadn't had the chance to test drive. She pressed it against herself and grinned. Even on the hanger, it hit all the right curves.

"Let's see if you can resist this, my dear Italian writer," she murmured to herself and ran to the bathroom to take a shower.

Chapter 17

This evening, Marchese planned to be at the gym before Kathrine. He didn't want her to think he was following her. He hoped she might acknowledge him first; otherwise, he knew what he had to do.

By 7:10, he was already breaking a sweat on the treadmill when Kathrine showed up. Marchese pretended to be watching the television hanging above him on the wall. The machine beside him was free, but so were several others in the room. She could take any one of them.

Kathrine pulled her gym towel out of her orange bag, walked toward Marchese, and draped the towel over the arm of the treadmill right beside him. She stepped onto the belt and started up the machine.

Marchese smiled in greeting. Nothing else. Kathrine responded in kind and began her run to nowhere. Five minutes passed during which they ignored each other.

Marchese looked at his watch, stopped the machine, and went to the bathroom. He lingered in the doorway for a few minutes, hoping to build her curiosity. When he emerged and got back on the treadmill, she smiled.

"My name is Kathrine," she said, glancing at him as she ran.

Marchese smiled.

"And I wasn't in a good mood last night," she continued, "and I was probably rude. I'm sorry."

"Don't worry," he replied brightly. "Anyone can have a bad day. Anyway, if I were in your shoes, neither would I be inclined to know such an awkward man."

Kathrine laughed, putting her hand over her mouth. "It was actually a bit comical."

Marchese pressed the stop button on the treadmill and jogged until the belt finally stopped. "Then if I fall again, on purpose this time, might you agree to have a drink with me?"

Kathrine laughed again. "Maybe. You could try, but I won't guarantee the result."

This time, they laughed together. She stopped her machine and studied him for a moment. He'd never felt so scrutinized in his life, and he hoped his intentions didn't show on his face. "We can go for a walk together after the gym," she suggested.

Marchese's hopes soared. "I would enjoy that. And I promise you I won't stumble."

She gave him a confused look.

"A joke," he said.

She stared at him blankly.

"Referring to when I fell off the machine."

"Oh, of course," she said with a forced chuckle.

He felt his face flush with embarrassment. Truly, he had no idea how to flirt and worried for the success of his mission again.

* * *

Olivia sat fidgeting at the table, trying and failing not to look at her watch. It read 7:05.

Pietro is late, she thought, just as Capra entered the pizzeria.

He rushed to the table, visibly flustered. "I'm so sorry, Olivia." He leaned down and kissed her cheek. "First I got on the wrong subway and then the wrong side street—"

"No problem. It's only five minutes. I'd have waited for two more before leaving," she joked.

The two stared at each other for a moment and burst out laughing.

"So, here we have the best pizza in New York, right?" Capra asked.

"Trust me, the pizza in this place is excellent," Olivia gushed. "The owners are from Naples. You will like it."

The journalist sighed. "I trust this of course, after last night's great dinner."

They picked up their menus.

Olivia felt Capra's eyes on her as she murmured the various names of the pizzas in Italian and resisted the urge to smile. *So far, so good,* she commended herself. He seemed more interested than he'd been on their last date. She was not as made up as the night before, and she'd styled her short, dark hair in soft, face-framing curls. The dress she had chosen had a neckline that showed off her cleavage. By the intensity of his focus, he found her even sexier than he had before.

Capra looked down at the menu again.

Olivia risked a peek at him over the top of her menu. As he went through the appetizer list, the way his lips moved made her intensely curious about how it would feel to kiss them. The pizza no longer seemed appealing; she yearned to be alone with him.

"Well, for me, a Parma pizza," said Capra finally.

"Good," she replied with a wink. "And a capricciosa for me."

They chatted idly until their orders arrived a few minutes later. Olivia stared at Capra as he tasted his pizza. "Well? What do you think?"

The man swallowed and looked at her thoughtfully. "OK. You were right for a second time. This pizza is really good, much better even than those I have in Sicily. Unbelievable! Two points for you!"

Olivia smiled and lowered her head bashfully. "How is it going with your book?"

Capra sighed. "Slowly, but that's normal at this stage."

"Will you let me read any of it?"

Capra's eyes sparkled with humor. "Can you read Italian?"

Olivia laughed. "Not really. Let's just say I understand a little bit, but you could translate some passages for me, at least the most interesting ones."

Capra took a sip from his wine glass. "I'll do it if you propose a third, excellent restaurant."

Olivia stared at him reproachfully. "That's nothing but blackmail. Yes, you really are Sicilian!"

Capra laughed. "Are you declining my invitation, then?"

A not-unpleasant shiver went up her back. "I thought you'd prefer a little negotiation first before I make a decision."

Capra cocked an eyebrow at her over the rim of his glass. "I'm a bit out of practice haggling for third dates, I'm afraid."

Olivia chuckled. "I'll cut you a break, then, just this once, and let you win."

Capra absolutely beamed at this. "When would you like to, then?"

"Well, that's better, now," she replied, smiling.

Capra asked the waiter to bring another bottle of wine.

"Are you going to get me drunk?" Olivia accused.

"Well, it's much more likely that you will get me drunk!" replied Capra, and they laughed again.

* * *

Marchese and Kathrine left the gym 8:15, and they stopped before the stairs of the building.

"Still up for a walk?" Marchese asked lightly, flashing a smile.

"Sure," she replied, as she set out along 74th toward Central Park. "So, Francesco, what are you doing in New York?"

Marchese fell into step beside her. They crossed on Lexington. "Something like a vacation, so to speak."

Kathrine cocked an eyebrow. "What do you mean?"

"I mean I don't know when I'll go back to Italy."

Now the other eyebrow rose. "Does your job allow you to have that freedom of choice, then?"

Marchese smiled. "Let's just say I've taken a hiatus for reflection. A break that has been going on for some time. Honestly, I don't know if I even want to go back to work."

"What's your job?"

"I was a policeman in Sicily."

The woman stopped and stared at Marchese. She looked genuinely surprised. "Wow. A policeman? It must be a difficult job."

"It is," Marchese confirmed, his chest tightening as painful memories rushed up. "So I decided to take this vacation, taking advantage of the kindness of a friend who lent me her apartment."

He could see Kathrine was trying to put the jigsaw together. He'd told the truth—so far. It was a technique used by undercover cops. The half-truth strategy. "And you, Kathrine? What do you do?"

She sighed. "Well, let's say that my job is less exciting than yours. I'm the private secretary to the CEO of a major corporation here in New York. He's English but he has a lot of business here, too, in the United States, and he spends most of his time here in New York."

They arrived on 5th and headed toward the side entrance to the park, at the corner of 73rd.

"You live here in this area, I guess," Marchese ventured.

There was a tiny pause, and he wondered if he'd asked too much. "Yes, very nearby. And my office is here. Ten blocks down, so very easy to get to." She gestured toward the south end of the street. "And you? Where is your friend's apartment?"

"In SoHo," Marchese answered honestly. "On Prince Street."

Kathrine brightened. "Beautiful. I love SoHo."

The two entered Central Park and headed for Conservatory Pond a few steps away.

"Yes, it's nice," Marchese agreed. "But this area is not so bad either."

They sat on a bench in front of the small artificial pond.

"But considering its cost, I don't know if it's worth it," Kathrine said a little sadly. "I always promised myself to move to Lower Manhattan, to the Village or SoHo. I would save money and maybe enjoy living there more. But I have not made the effort to do it."

* * *

Capra was eager to leave the restaurant and be alone with Olivia. Time was running short and he had not yet been able to steer the conversation toward Marchese. They talked about travels, books, and work. Olivia had told him that she worked at the British Embassy, a typically vague response from those who work as diplomats or, perhaps, in security services.

This could be a piece to the puzzle, he thought. "Can you explain further? What exactly do you do at the embassy?"

Olivia fiddled with her fork. "I deal with the preservation of ancient literary works. It's indeed a pretty boring job."

Clarity dawned in that instant. That was why Marchese was in New York—the literary works! All of this just three days after Torchia's death. The former detective was still on the trail of the secret of Shakespeare's origins. It *had* to be this. Now he had to find out what or who he was hunting.

243

"Did I say something wrong, Pietro?" Olivia asked, noticing Capra's absent expression.

"No, Olivia," he assured her, smiling. He laid his hand over hers. "I just want to get out of this place."

Olivia looked at his hand and smiled. "And *where* would you like to go?"

Capra shrugged. "I do not know. You are my guide."

"I'll come up with something," she purred. "Let's ask for the bill."

* * *

Marchese and Kathrine talked as they walked until finally they arrived in front of her apartment building.

"So," he said casually, "did I earn the right to a drink one of these nights, or not?"

She looked at her watch. "Why not now?"

He spread his arms wide to indicate his gym clothes. "I need a shower first."

She smiled. "In my living room nobody will notice your outfit. And you can take a shower at my place while I'll pour you a nice glass of wine."

Kathrine had gone too far proposing this. She had to remember that he was there for a purpose other than an attraction to her. If he'd asked her the same, she would have rejected this offer, but Marchese replied before she had the chance to change her mind. "I will only accept if you promise me you won't peek," he replied in yet another failed attempt at flirting.

For a moment, Kathrine was stunned. Then she burst out laughing. He really seemed very sweet, even if that sweetness was for show. "I can't guarantee that, Francesco," she playfully replied, leading him into the luxurious lobby.

Kathrine's living room was twice the size of Marchese's apartment in SoHo. The sunset over Central Park illuminated the whole room as if, in the distance, an immense fire had consumed everything around it in a crimson glow. The park itself was awash in late evening light.

"Beautiful, isn't it?" Kathrine said, stepping up beside him and letting the red light bathe her face.

"Yeah," Marchese replied. He was staring at her, but she felt him drag his gaze away. "Very, very much so. I haven't seen a sunset for days. In Italy, I have a veranda overlooking the sea, and every evening I sit down with a drink and enjoy the view. For a long time, that's what I did every night."

Kathrine stared at him. This man was a continual discovery. Every expression, everything he shared with her, led her to a new facet of his personality, as if he were opening new doors to his soul. Sometimes he was terribly gloomy, and suddenly he turned and emanated brilliance that softened to almost sensual sweetness. If things were different, she would have ardently wished to kiss him. This was not her task at hand.

"Here is a clean towel," she said, pulling a lush bath towel from the linen closet. "The bathroom is over to the right. Meanwhile, I will open a bottle of wine."

* * *

Capra followed Olivia out of the pizzeria, where Olivia hailed a taxi. "Let's go, writer!"

"Where are you taking me?" asked Capra as he slid into the back seat next to her.

"473 West Broadway, please," the woman said to the driver.

"And where is this?" asked the journalist, pretending not to recognize the address.

"My home."

While the taxi headed south, on 5th toward SoHo, Olivia laid her hand over Capra's. He turned and stared at her. She seemed dazed by his big blue eyes.

He leaned over and kissed her passionately.

Olivia's hand moved to Capra's pounding chest as his breathing became faster. All thought of Marchese drifted from his head. He wanted to get her home as quickly as possible.

The taxi driver turned right onto Washington Square, then left onto MacDougal Street to Houston Street, and then drove eastward to the intersection with West Broadway, pulling up at the curb in front of Olivia's building. She paid the fare and the two got out.

Capra grasped her hips between his hands as she fumbled in her bag for the keys. He could feel her quivering uncontrollably. She wanted him.

They entered Olivia's apartment, barely making it through the door before she turned and kissed him again. Capra pushed her back against the door and roughly pulled off her black dress, thrilled to discover she was wearing no underwear. She stood completely naked, staring at him and smiling.

"I wanted to make it as easy as possible," she murmured.

"I love easy things," replied Capra.

* * *

Marchese's strategy was working; Kathrine seemed far more relaxed than she had before. But now it was a delicate maneuver, he thought as he disappeared behind the bathroom door. He had yet to see how much she would open up and trust him.

Marchese undressed in the commodious bathroom. The shelves of the medicine cabinet seemed to contain every kind of beauty product, all in perfect order. He hopped in the shower and turned the hot water on, already feeling confident by his progress.

As he lathered, Kathrine's nude silhouette suddenly appeared on the other side of the now-steamy glass. She opened the glass door and slipped in to join him. The water flowed down Marchese's face and she moved close to him.

For a long moment, they just looked at each other in silence. She stretched up on her toes and kissed him gently.

He raised a hand and stroked her face, watching the water wet her hair. Kathrine closed her eyes, smiling, as she wrapped her arms around him and he felt his warm and wet skin meet hers.

Marchese's mind darkened with a thousand thoughts. The desire he felt for her was inescapably real, but Kathrine was dragging him into a vortex of passion so strong it alarmed him. And he couldn't ignore that, at least on his end, it was built on a lie.

They came out of the shower and, still wet, ended up on the wooden floor of the bedroom. They looked at each other for a moment, and he saw exhilaration and shock in her eyes. He kissed her breast and she arched her back, and they gave in to desire.

* * *

Olivia lay beside Capra, stroking his chest. "What are you thinking about?"

The reporter weighed his answer carefully. "The first day I met you and introduced myself as an Italian visiting, you said that it was a coincidence. What did you mean?"

Olivia's eyes unfocused, like she was searching the exact moment the man was referring to. "Nothing. It was nonsense."

"Tell me," he urged gently. "I want to know your nonsense, too."

Olivia hesitated a moment longer, this time as if trying to piece together an answer. "OK. That day, I met another Italian. A man I'm working with on a project. He came to New York to help my team. Nothing important, though."

Capra feigned amusement. "An Italian expert in English literature, really?"

"It's not that simple, of course," Olivia said absently. Abruptly she waved a hand. "I shouldn't even tell you about it and, honestly, I don't know why I'm talking about it now."

Capra turned his gaze to meet hers. "Sorry. I didn't mean to get into your stuff too much. Honestly."

Olivia rose and straddled him "You must not apologize, Pietro. We've known each other only briefly and I do a dangerous job. I feel like I want to open myself to you. I've felt the need to open up to someone for a long time. And it's as if you have arrived here with the right key to do it."

"Go on," said he, caressing her face.

She sighed and looked up at the ceiling. "I will just explain that England has lost some very important documents, and we're looking for them. That's it."

"And the Italian?" he pressed. "What does he have to do with it?"

"He was involved in the search, in a certain way, and we invited him here to help us recover them." She began to caress his neck. "But now I cannot say anymore."

"I do have some ideas about what I can do now."

Olivia leaned down toward him and began to kiss his chest, slowly descending to nibble him teasingly.

Capra moved his eyes to stare up at the ceiling as the woman took care of him.

It's all becoming clearer, he thought, smiling to himself. Marchese was after the origins of William Shakespeare.

* * *

Kathrine had finally gotten around to pouring the wine into two glasses when Marchese strolled into the living room. Coming up behind her, he slid his arms gently around her waist and felt her stiffen.

She caught his worried frown as he asked, "Something wrong?"

She turned and handed him a glass. "I'm afraid I have been too impulsive. And I'm embarrassed."

Marchese smiled. "I'm sorry you feel this way," he said softly, holding her briefly around the shoulders. "I'd hoped you were as happy as I am."

"I don't know if I can trust you," she said flatly. "I really don't know you well enough."

Marchese flinched guiltily. "Come here. Let's sit down. You can ask me whatever you want. I'll answer everything honestly."

She let him steer her to sit on the sofa. They both settled in, glasses in hand.

She stared at him, waiting. Surely he would tell her only lies, to try to convince her that he was someone she could trust, could open up to. And then he would ask her about Graham, dancing around until he fooled her into giving up something that would let him get to the letters. He was just using her.

And she had let him.

It was terrible mistake to experience these feelings for a stranger—and a dangerous one. Francesco Marchese was an Italian policeman, working for MI5. He wasn't romancing her; he was trying to extract information. She was foolish to believe this could lead to something else, naive in hoping that everything she was learning about might be true just a fabrication.

She had desired him from the moment she saw him fall on the ground at the foot of that treadmill, before she knew his real identity and purpose. She wanted him even after she knew he was there to harm her.

And strangely, despite that she knew the truth he hadn't admitted to her, her deepest feelings propelled her towards him like a magnetic force. She could not deny the attraction she felt, even as she was conscious that she was bound to suffer from it.

"Are you really here on vacation?"

Marchese stared at her. She knew question was odd, and she realized it would make him suspicious that perhaps she was picking up on the untruths. But she had just made love with him, so she hoped he would chalk it up to insecurity and regret.

"Not really, Kathrine," he admitted. "It's like a vacation, but I'm also here to help some colleagues solve a problem."

She held the improbable hope that the amazing feelings she was experiencing meant there was more to their connection than that he was just there using her. "What kind of problem? How can you, an Italian policeman, help them do this?"

Marchese bowed his head. The question seemed to pain him, almost as if he didn't want to lie to her. But she knew he couldn't tell her the truth. Being honest meant losing the opportunity she presented to MI5. He didn't know she knew, which made deciding what tack she'd take that much easier. If he lied, it would answer all her questions.

"I can't share much," he said at last. "I don't even know if I can help them. I got involved in this case by chance, and I'm not really happy for being asked to do what is necessary to deal with it."

This was a surprise. But he still hadn't told her the truth. Kathrine continued to stare at him as she sipped her wine. "I sense some regret in your words, Francesco."

Marchese was still looking down. "A colleague of mine lost his life for all of this. And I feel it's my duty to help. I would like to give some validation to my friend's death. It is not easy to explain. This whole situation is not my doing. I don't care about the problem itself. And I don't understand why what they are after is so important that it needs to lead to the death of innocent people." He cleared his throat and sat back, sipping from his glass. "But I don't want to bore you with my problems and frighten you by talking about these crimes."

Kathrine laid her hand on top of Marchese's. "I understand what you mean. I understand what it's like to lose a loved one. And what you just said doesn't frighten me." She paused, stunned herself at what she said next. "It's odd, I've only known you for a very short time but you inspire in me a confidence. I actually feel safe near you. And yet I don't know you at all. I'm sure this is your way. I'm usually not mistaken in my reading of people."

Marchese moved closer to her and kissed her. This kiss felt even more intense than the last ones had been—and there was something more sincere in it now.

Kathrine had a pain-filled past that still weighed her life down. By nature, she was a resilient and optimistic woman with a strong and successful outward appearance, but deep inside her soul had been bleeding for some time now.

As Marchese pulled back, she saw a change in his eyes, a self-assured confidence that had not been there before. He'd made a critical decision. Now she had to wait and see what that meant for her. For them.

Chapter 18

When Pietro woke at 8:01 a.m., Olivia made sure it was to the aroma of freshly brewed coffee. She tried not to stare as he rose from the couch and wandered into the kitchen. He moved to kissed her.

"Did you sleep well?" she asked.

Capra stroked her cheek and then her shoulder. "Except for a stiff neck, very well."

"I know," Olivia replied, wincing in sympathy. "I thought about suggesting we move to the bed, but you were sleeping so deeply that I left you in peace."

"Can I take a shower?"

Olivia kissed him. "If you promise that you will leave the door open so I can join you in five minutes, yes."

She saw him smile as he headed for the bathroom and blushed.

A few minutes later a knock sounded on her apartment door. Olivia looked at her watch with annoyance; it was too early for solicitors. She peered through the peephole.

Her heart shot into her throat. Francesco.

She opened the door, keeping it ajar, to hide her semi-nakedness. "What's happened? Something wrong?"

"No," he replied. "I didn't mean to bother you. I thought I'd come in for a coffee, chat about my success last night, and then we'd travel to the office together."

Capra's voice, singing cheerfully in Italian, reached their ears. Marchese grimaced. "Oh, sorry, I'll just see you at the briefing." He turned and headed for the stairs.

"Uhm, if you wait, I can be ready in just a minute. I'll meet you outside."

Marchese turned around and waved a forgiving hand. "No, there's no need," he said, smiling. "Really. I can find my own way to the office."

Just as Olivia closed the door behind her, Capra appeared in the living room, wearing only a towel wrapped tightly around his waist. "If I had waited for you any longer in the shower, I would have drowned!"

"Excuse me, Pietro," she replied shakily. "I just had a visitor."

Capra put a hand on her shoulder. "Is everything OK?"

"Oh yes, of course. My Italian colleague just stopped by. He picked up on the fact that I was not alone and quickly left."

Capra looked absolutely horrified for a microsecond before his expression softened. That flicker of fear gave Olivia pause, but she assumed it meant he took her alarm seriously. Her heart fluttered at the thought.

* * *

When Kathrine arrived at the office, she found all the staff arriving, along with David Graham, to make a final review of the charity gala. Everything was ready—a list of illustrious guests, a fabulous menu, wine selected, speeches arranged, and table placements set. The hall itself was fully decked out; only the floral arrangements remained to be delivered, and those wouldn't arrive until the day of the event.

She sat down next to her boss and began to leaf through the file in front of her. David Graham leaned slightly toward her and whispered, "Did you see Marchese last night?"

Kathrine nodded.

"And how did it go?"

She turned to look at Graham. "Well, casual chit-chat that led to my being able question him a bit."

Graham's brows lowered. "Then it's true that they ordered him to get to you. Did he come up with something interesting about why he's in New York?"

Kathrine forced a smile. "Yes. He explained that he's here to help some colleagues solve a problem."

Graham smiled. "I was sure of it. Good. Will you see him again?"

"I don't know."

"He will certainly want to see you," Graham replied coyly. "He believes he can get information from you about the letters. That's what these mugs are trying to do."

"OK, sir," replied Kathrine absently. Her mind was on the night spent in Marchese's arms, of their conversations and the pleasure they'd experienced on that floor.

The memories saddened her, and her thoughts fell dark at the remembrance that everything was fake and Marchese was just a spy.

They had not exchanged phone numbers. No other meeting had been set up. He had left early that morning—vanished—kissing her on the lips while he thought she still slept. Perhaps she would see him at the gym that evening, or perhaps he would disappear, realizing that he would not get anything significant out of his relationship with her in terms of information.

Kathrine didn't know what to think anymore, and that confusion unsettled her.

MESSINA—AUGUST 16, 1943

Father Gabriele saw Father Carlo arriving back. The letters had been returned safely in Messina, just over a week after the harrowing journey Father Gabriele had taken to get them to Taormina. The bishop hugged his old friend and together they disappeared behind the sacristy door.

Father Gabriele had managed a moment before to hide the six letters he had stolen in his bedroom. Soon he would put them back in their proper place. He had been overcome with the temptation of the devil; it was he who had induced Gabriele to steal them. Soon everything would be returned and his torments would end.

As soon as Father Carlo left the cathedral, the bishop prepared himself for the solemn mass. Now was the right time to do it. Gabriele entered the sacristy and headed for the small hidden niche, where he had seen the casket the first time and opened it.

It was empty.

The casket wasn't there. He reached his hand toward the bottom of the small hollow. The young priest panicked. He heard footsteps coming from behind and quickly turned away. The bishop entered the sacristy. "Gabriele, my dear."

"Your Excellency!" Gabriele replied a little too loudly. He cleared his throat. "I saw that Father Carlo came to visit you."

"Yes. He came to retrieve the precious casket he had kept with us in Taormina."

Gabriele's blood froze. "Why, Your Excellency?"

"Sooner or later, the time would have come for me to make a trip to Rome," the bishop explained. "I believe the casket is safer within the walls of the Vatican. But for the moment, I thought to hide it in a different place. The small niche where it has been kept over the years is not safe enough. And it's better if no one knows where it is."

Gabriele felt the ground slipping from under his feet. He could no longer cleanse himself of his sin. He would live the rest of his life with remorse for his actions.

The bishop hurried toward him and clutched his arm. "Gabriele, is something wrong?"

"No, Your Excellency. I'm just a little tired."

"My son, you must rest," the bishop urged. "The Church will need much of you, and you can't afford to get sick. Your devotion is an example for all of us. I want you to take a break and I have an idea of how you might go about it."

"What is it, Your Excellency?"

"I need someone to take care of cataloging the books of the curia. No one has taken care of our library for a long time now. And it will be an opportunity for you to get away from the tiring work here in the cathedral."

NEW YORK—AUGUST 16, 2012

Marchese accepted the floor at the MI5 briefing. When he relayed the events of the evening—that he had spent it drinking wine and talking in Kathrine's apartment—the news was greeted with applause.

Dean Zona had to nod to calm down the gathering. "Marchese has made a productive step forward, but we are still far from any relevant information. The road is still long. Now he must endeavor to find out how to get to the letters—where exactly they are and when they will be moved. We must find a weak link in Graham's plan and take advantage of it, so as to take possession of them."

Marchese nodded in agreement. Kathrine had remained guarded about her work. In fact, he'd wound up giving her more information to her, rather than the other way around. Now it was his turn to turn this around and make her talk more. He didn't feel the need to mention to the group that he had slept with her, and he had remained vague on the topics they discussed. The briefing was over shortly after it had started.

Olivia approached him afterward. "I'm sorry about this morning."

Marchese shook his head, spreading a hand ardently on his chest. "It's me who must apologize for invading your private space."

"No, Francesco, you must not," she insisted. "It's just . . . you know, I found myself in a situation where—"

"There is no reason to talk about it," he said, though he did find it rather coincidental that her overnight "guest" had been singing an Italian love song.

Olivia looked at the floor. "Anyway, Congratulations. I had no doubt you could ingratiate yourself with Leed. Your progress is well deserved. And I'm sure you'll get us what we're looking for."

"Thanks, but as Zona says, the road is still long."

"By the way, what did you want to chat about this morning? Anything more than what you said during the briefing?"

Marchese waved a hand dismissively. "Nothing. I was just looking forward to telling someone how it went."

That was a lie. He had gone to Olivia's place to inform her that he had decided to share the truth with Kathrine about why he was there. He wanted to try to get her on their side. But he had realized now, based on the tone of the meeting, that neither Olivia or Zona—or any of MI5, for that matter— would approve of this tactic.

* * *

Capra lay on his bed, pondering all that he had discovered the night before. Marchese was in New York to find out more about the origins of William Shakespeare, and in doing so, he would avenge the death of his friend, Torchia.

Now he had to figure out *what* exactly he was looking for. That evening he would meet again with Olivia, and he knew it would be even easier to get her to talk to him. She had confided a great deal already. She trusted him. She had opened up. Now he needed to know every detail going forward to complete the puzzle.

As he thought of her, he discovered to his mixed annoyance and surprise that he was actually looking forward to seeing *her*. Maybe it was the sex, but then Capra wasn't exactly starved for that. That girl from the restaurant the other night —already her name escaped him—had practically dragged him to bed. Not that she had measured up to Olivia . . .

What the hell is wrong me?

Capra sat down at his laptop and made notes on what he had just discovered. Tonight, he would ask Olivia about the missing facts to definitively complete the circle.

He would invite her to dinner again. They would eat, drink, and make love, and in a moment of intimacy, he would make her open up totally. She would tell him everything he needed to know about Marchese's role, and he would have his story to take home. He'd be welcomed back to Messina as a hero and then he'd write another book, becoming even richer and more famous.

At that moment, he received a text from her: "I thought of another place for dinner, if you're free tonight."

Capra smiled. "Of course I'm free for you," he typed back. "But this time I want to choose the restaurant."

"Which one?" she answered almost immediately.

The journalist stared at the ceiling. He was trying for intimacy, and he knew exactly how to achieve it. "I'll keep you informed. Meanwhile, see if you can be ready for six-thirty."

* * *

David Graham called Kathrine into his office. His desk was a swamp of papers, and he didn't look up as she entered. "What is it, sir?"

"Sit down."

She took her seat, waiting.

"I was thinking it would be smart for you to invite our Mr. Marchese to our gala. Unless he already has another date."

Kathrine was taken aback. "Don't you think it could be counterproductive, Mr. Graham? I mean, getting him so close to you?"

"I want to see this man closely," Graham replied. "Then I will better understand how dangerous he can be for us. I'd rather keep a close eye on him that evening. Just a further safeguard. We must have everything under our control. MI5 will believe they are gaining ground with us. By inviting Marchese to the gala, they will think that we haven't unmasked them."

The proposal seemed risky to Kathrine, but at the same time, it pleased her to think of attending the otherwise tiresome the gala alongside the intriguing Marchese. In all these years now, she had never been accompanied to the Graham International Art Company Annual Gala by someone this alluring to her. "What if he refuses?"

Graham scoffed. "If I know MI5, they won't allow this opportunity to pass. I know another agent of theirs will be present. The Embassy sent us the list of attendees and we have already identified at least one of them as Security Services. They are breathing down our neck. And to have identified a second, allegedly 'clean' agent who is onto us is like icing on the cake."

Once dismissed, Kathrine went back to her desk, tense from all the mounting stress and conflicted between what she had been tasked to do and what was right—and conflicted about the directions of her feelings as she was getting to know Marchese.

It's all fake, she reminded herself. But the more she thought about it, the more she hoped it wasn't. She was certain that there was a sincerity innate in Marchese, despite some necessary darkness required by his position and his job.

* * *

Marchese reached Kathrine's building at 5:30 p.m. He had decided to wait there for her after work and take her directly to dinner without going to the gym. He hoped she would be receptive to his invitation. He had bought her a single rose and was waiting for her to appear from around the corner. He knew she always went back home first to change.

Until the night before, he had been the one who needed someone to heal his wounds. Now, faced with this vulnerable woman and feeling her long-harbored insecurity and grief, his hurts seemed to recede and his own pain became a thing of the past. Now he wanted to protect her.

He was nervous. He didn't know how it would go telling her the real reason behind their meeting. He was frightened by the reaction she might have and he was terrified to blow the operation in doing so. It was still too early to be certain he could win her to his side. Kathrine Leed didn't seem to be a woman who could be easily corrupted. But he'd realized that lying to her now, trying to extract the information from her by tricking her into it, wouldn't work; he didn't have the heart to try that route, and he knew she'd detect his uncertainty and the whole game would be over. She seemed to have the same razor-sharp intuition he had, the sixth sense that had made him such an effective police officer, and it wouldn't do to underestimate that.

But his own sixth sense told him that Kathrine was something special—and that she was beginning to have feelings for him. Feelings he was beginning to reciprocate.

He was attracted and drawn to her. Her expressions, the way she made love, the tenderness hidden behind the armor she had spent years wrapping around herself.

He couldn't use her, not with all these things considered. And after meeting her, he felt certain she would not give up any information pertinent to David Graham's dealings. She was a dedicated professional. He strongly believed it was best to tell her the truth.

* * *

Olivia had just walked into her apartment when her text tone chimed. It was Pietro. "Six-thirty at your place," he'd written. "I did some shopping and I'm going to cook for you tonight."

She melted like snow in the sun and sent him a series of hearts.

Olivia was elated by the message and thrilled that he was offering to cook. *Certainly it will be some Italian dish,* she thought.

She imagined Pietro in front of the stove in her kitchen, and it enthralled her. She was amazed at how attracted she was to him. It was the first time she had ever felt this kind of emotion, and its intensity frightened her. She didn't want to be hurt again; she had already taken her hard knocks and she could tell she really risked getting close too quickly this time. It could end in in disappointment. An Italian writer, staying in New York to complete a novel, she considered, would probably only stay a few months. It wouldn't be long term and she would eventually be devastated. She knew what it was like to feel that way. But she knew she was going to give in and run the risk.

* * *

Kathrine had been thinking all day of Marchese, of what Graham had asked her to do, and of her desire to see the detective again. Her double role. He was using her, and she was to use him.

She wasn't sure if he would show up at the gym, but she hoped he would be there.

As she walked on 5th, North along Central Park, she thought of the long walk she had taken with Marchese, of their conversations and the intensity of their lovemaking. How sad it was to get to know each other for the reason at hand! Maybe in another situation, he wouldn't even have glanced at her. Maybe she wasn't his type. Last night, she had been overcome by a strong attraction to him, and she thought she had perceived that he was experiencing the same—that it was mutual. It is not easy to feign real passion, she told herself. Might he too be developing feelings for her? She couldn't help but hope so.

At the corner of 75th, she turned right, heading for her apartment on Madison Avenue.

As she approached, she saw the silhouette of a man in front of her building.

Marchese. He stood directly in front of her door with a single rose in his hand.

She felt her heart beat faster, pounding with excitement. *He's got all the moves*, she thought with a pang of disappointment. He was everything she had wanted in a man, but he would vanish once he had accomplished his aim.

She wanted to dream, to hope, that there could be something real to all this. She cleared her throat. "Are you waiting for someone?"

Marchese turned awkwardly, the rose clutched in his right hand. "Yes! A beautiful woman. Do you know if she's already come by here?"

Kathrine smiled. "Yes, I saw a very beautiful one crossing to the other side a moment ago. If you run, maybe you can catch her."

The two laughed. He handed her the rose and kissed her gently on the cheek.

"What is that for?" she asked, smiling into his eyes.

"I would like to take you to dinner," he replied lightly. "And, by the way, I have no intention of running on the treadmill before it."

Kathrine chuckled and gestured to her doorway. "Just give me time to change. Where are you taking me?"

"To the Boathouse, in Central Park."

"I know where the Boathouse is," Kathrine retorted with a roll of her eyes.

As they turned toward the entrance of the building, Kathrine noticed two men sitting in a parked car across the street. It occurred to her that they might be spying on her, but she didn't want to make Marchese suspicious by investigating further, so she pushed the concern away.

Inside the apartment, she went to change, leaving Marchese to look out the window, admiring the view of Madison Avenue and Central Park.

She didn't make him wait long, reappearing after a just a few moments in her underwear.

She took his hand and led him to the dining table, sat down on the marble tabletop, and opened her legs, inviting him to embrace her.

"I reserved a table for six-thirty," he whispered.

She pulled him toward her and kissed him. "There's enough time."

* * *

Olivia was out of her mind with expectation as she stepped into the shower. She could hardly wait to see Pietro and wondered what dish he would cook for her.

But her thoughts also went to Francesco Marchese. Shortly, he would be meeting again with Kathrine Leed. *It must be difficult for him to relate to that cold and calculating woman,* she thought with a wince of sympathy. But he had managed to be invited up to her apartment and had enjoyed a bottle of wine with her on her sofa. He clearly was clever and Olivia was impressed by him. She believed he would succeed for them in this case, which had been going on for several years now, and she hoped that meant everything would be over soon. Maybe her superiors would send her back to London, or maybe she could ask to be transferred to Italy.

She stepped out of the shower and dried herself, thrilled by this new line of thought. Could having met Pietro be a sign of fate? They would fall in love, she would be transferred to *bel paese,* and they would live on a beach, each with their own career. Pietro would write his novels from the porch and she would protect the English Crown from threats in Italy.

She chuckled, knowing she was fantasizing too much. Just as the thought occurred to her, there was a knock on the door.

Capra was waiting outside holding two heaving shopping bags.

"Did you rob Whole Foods?" she asked, laughing.

"Let's just say they robbed me," replied Capra dryly, heading for the kitchen. "Do you know what the price of one kilo of pasta is in Italy?"

"No, but I think you're going to tell me."

"A quarter of the cost!" Capra expounded. "Same for everything else. Now I understand why Americans eat mostly hot dogs and sandwiches."

Olivia laughed, then smothered the sound with a hand over her mouth. "Americans don't just eat hot dogs and sandwiches!" she replied. "Anyway, I have been wondering all day about what you're going to prepare for dinner."

Capra turned, embracing and kissing her. "Let's start at the end. You are the dessert."

"I was hoping for that," she replied, winking. "And what about an appetizer?"

Capra grabbed her by her hips and lifted her, setting her on the kitchen countertop next to the shopping bags. She unbuckled his belt and his jeans.

"It will be a long dinner," Olivia whispered in his ear.

"Yes," Capra growled in affirmation. "Like a Calabrian wedding banquet, especially if we start like this."

* * *

The table at the Boathouse overlooked the pond. The sun was still up, but soon the sky would burst into the spectacular colors as it set over the trees of the park. The park was teeming with couples, some rowing little boats around the pond. There was even a gondola plying the tranquil water.

"I really like this place," said Marchese distantly, looking out the window.

"You are a romantic, Francesco."

"Maybe." He felt Kathrine lay her hand over his, and he turned to gaze at her. "I'm happy to have met you. In fact, let's just say I literally fell for you."

"Yeah," Kathrine chuckled, "but only physically, perhaps." She paused, peering at him. "Well, I don't think you have fallen in love with me. Not yet at least."

He held her gaze. She was joking, but real affection for her twisted in her chest. And he couldn't explain it, nor would he have been able to explain it to her. So he decided not to reply.

"You don't need to answer, Marchese," she said firmly. "I just wanted to tell you that I like you very much. The time we have spent together has been really great."

"I feel the same," he said honestly. "And I didn't answer you because this situation is a bit . . . complicated."

She flinched, and he mentally chided himself. *Complicated* didn't cover it. He was there for another reason. But behind the hurt on her face was something else—hope. It made him hopeful, too. Perhaps he had started this encounter with other purposes, but after meeting her, maybe he could be falling in love. He thrilled at the thought; he hadn't been willing to consider the possibility until now.

"What do you mean by complicated?" she asked softly.

Marchese wanted to answer, but he wanted to wait until they got back to her apartment, to talk to her about the complicated part. He had to make the right moves at the right time. Otherwise, it would spoiled everything. "It means that what I feel for you is making me question the reason why I'm in New York. The purpose of my mission and deadline."

Kathrine gave him a searching look, but he saw her eyes brighten, a mirror of the spark he felt in his chest whenever he met her gaze. Perhaps he could manipulate the entire situation so there would be a happy ending. And he was motivated at this thought.

"Francesco, I want to ask you something," she said sharply. "Answer me openly."

His heart lodged in his throat. "Sure. Ask me."

Kathrine folded her hands diplomatically. "The day after tomorrow there is a very important gala being held by my company. It's an elegant charity benefit. I would like you to be my date."

Marchese sat in stunned silence for a few moments. She had invited him into the wolf's den. He would shake hands with Graham, the instigator of the murder of the girls in Messina, the man behind the death of the bishop and, above all, the death of his best friend. He would come face to face with him. He would be struggling against a strong desire to put a bullet into Graham's forehead—impossible, he knew, but his anger would be hard to conceal.

"What are you thinking about?" Kathrine asked worriedly. "Are you not up for it? Which is not a problem. I didn't mean to spring it on you after we've been together for so little time."

Marchese smiled. *Together.* "That's not it."

"What, then?"

"I was thinking," he said coyly, folding his napkin, "that tomorrow I will have to buy a suit."

Kathrine beamed, a flush rising on her cheeks. "Perhaps we'd better order our dinner; otherwise, I'll drag you to into the bathroom to express my happiness."

"Yes, ma'am," replied Marchese, laughing into his menu.

* * *

Capra slid the baking tray of ricotta, spinach, and conchiglioni rigati into the oven.

He felt Olivia watching every movement he made from her place on the couch. "Pietro," she said at length, "I wanted to ask you something."

"Ask me," he replied, removing his kitchen gloves.

"Do you have any commitments the night after tomorrow?"

Capra pretended to think. "I do not think so. Why?"

She took a deep breath. "Because the Embassy gave me an invitation to a very important gala that a rich British man organizes each year in New York to raise funds for various charitable causes. I wanted to know if you would like come as my date."

"Nice invite. Of course!" Capra approached and kissed her. "And I'll do my best to make you look good."

He lips parted and she kissed him back passionately. "I believe I will be the envy of all the women there."

Capra grinned, straightening up to plant his hands on his hips. "OK. Twenty more minutes and then we can eat. Help me set the table."

"Sure, boss," Olivia replied, getting up from the couch.

While they set the table, Capra tried to steer the conversation to Marchese. "How are you doing with your other Italian friend?" he asked, almost disinterestedly.

"Well, he is very clever," Olivia said carefully. "His assistance is bearing fruit, but the road to go is still long."

Capra feigned a pout. "It's hard to understand what you're talking about when you can't tell me the details of your work."

Olivia turned and stared at him. "Excuse me, Pietro. Really. I do not want to—"

"Don't worry," he said hastily, raising his hands defensively. "You are bound by some professional secrecy. I don't want to get you in trouble. Unfortunately, I am a writer so I am curious by nature. Maybe too much so."

She grasped his arms and stared at him until he met her eyes. "Let me finish. I was saying that I don't want to put you at risk. I care about you more and more and my job is very delicate. I'd like to tell you everything. I've had this feeling since the day we met. I like you very much, but you have to give me time."

Capra smiled at her. He almost wanted to give her a chance. But time was not his friend, he thought as he kissed her again. "How about some wine?" the reporter asked.

"Of course!"

* * *

It was approaching 9 p.m. as Kathrine and Marchese strolled back toward her house after their romantic dinner at the Boathouse.

As they came within a few steps away of the building, Kathrine noticed again, a bit farther away this time, the same car with the two men sitting in it parked just far away enough to prevent her from making out their faces.

This can't be a coincidence, she thought nervously. *Twice in the same evening*? Did Marchese have a backup car? Or was someone following her? Maybe it was still just her paranoia. She looked up at her companion and smiled, reassured. She felt safe next to him.

They entered and took the elevator up to Kathrine's floor. Once inside, Kathrine took a bottle of rosé wine from the fridge and passed it to Marchese. "Would you open it?"

"Sure."

Kathrine went to the bedroom to change into something more comfortable. They had decided to sit on the sofa and talk.

There were many things she wanted to ask him, but she was worried about the questions he might begin to ask her. If he was there to find out about Graham and the letters, he would probably start asking broad questions before zeroing into the point. Kathrine hoped this wouldn't happen. She would prefer if they continued to talk about their lives to get to know each other better. She didn't want to think about why Marchese was really here.

She returned to the living room in a blue cami top and matching sleep shorts. Marchese was looking out of the window. He seemed to love that view, and she wondered whether he was seeing the street below or his beloved Strait or Messina. Her chest tightened painfully.

"Lost in thoughts?"

Hearing Kathrine's voice, he turned around. "Yes. A little."

Kathrine slid her arms around him. "Do you want to share them with me?"

He turned and gave her a searching look, and she saw in his eyes that he would have liked to tell her everything. Perhaps some things that didn't even concern the case. She saw the sorrow that he carried deep inside his soul, as well as a strange resignation.

He took her by the hand and led to her the couch, where she sat and accepted the "Tell me," he asked softly. "What causes that sad look I sometimes see on your face to appear?"

The question left her stunned for a moment. She first stared at him, searching his now-neutral expression for some sign of what answer he might be expecting and finding no clue. Then she stared down into her wine glass, almost hypnotized, as her personal story, which she had never really told anyone, spilled out of her mouth.

"I'm two years shy of forty. In my life I have not been very lucky with men. I have had many partners, but my last

271

relationship was so devastating that I no longer tie myself to anyone. I don't believe I might ever give myself completely to a man again. I was abused, in a way. Used and psychologically destabilized by a man who, thinking about it now, had few qualities that I really admired. Sometimes, we play games in our head. I thought it was love, but I think I confused love with need. And it's tied in with a fear of loneliness or the inability to give up, even when you know it's not right."

She looked up cautiously as Marchese laid his hand over hers on the back of the sofa. She saw sympathy on his face. And anger.

"Now you show up," she said, her voice just above a whisper. "I wasn't interested in starting anything with anyone currently. I have—or I had—my balance. I was determined I would live alone for the rest of my life. My work, in a sense, is a protection I have created for myself. I focus my day on my work to avoid thinking about what I don't have in my personal life. Of course, it's without real joy. But I am protecting a broken soul, a deep hurt. One more terrible relationship and I could really lose it. I also know . . ."

She paused, then sighed, searching for the right words to tell him how scared she was of what he represented at that moment—a real danger, given the reason why he was there. She wanted to tell him she knew he might be there to harm and use her, in the crazy hope that he would deny it, tell her it is all just a coincidence and that they were wrong about him. Or that he would confess he regretted being involved and had fallen in love with her. That now he wanted to protect her instead of destroying her and her world.

"I also know that, perhaps, you have no interest in me," she said at last. His face paled. "I mean a *true* interest. I want you to know that in these last three days you have made me experience something new. I feel alive again, in that part of me that I kept anesthetized. Turned blackout."

Her eyes stung, and she realized she was weeping. He could be a murderer, here to give her the *coup de grace* once he'd amused himself with her. Her outburst resounded like an appeal to grace before the execution. She knew that everything was at stake. They'd reached a point of no return, and now her fate going lay squarely in the hands of Marchese. Kathrine looked up at him again, her eyes full of tears. He was leaning so close she barely had to move to press her still-trembling lips to his.. She straddled him, staring into his eyes, and unbuttoned his shirt, jerking it off of him before she did the same with her pajama shirt.

"I want to make love," she whispered. "I want you to make me feel good."

* * *

Olivia got up on wobbly legs and staggered to the bathroom. They had made it through two bottles of wine—one of which had been an expensive Tuscan red a friend had brought back for her from a trip to Italy and which she'd been saving for a special occasion—and exhausted themselves on the couch again. Capra watched, feeling dizzy, and she stumbled against the bathroom doorframe. They were both drunk, but he knew that this was the moment to learn what he'd come all this way to discover.

When she returned from the bathroom, she sat between his legs. He stroked her hair.

"You make me feel good, Pietro," she said a little blearily. "Really special."

He stayed silent until he felt her go tense. "Olivia. I've been thinking about something tonight."

273

"What?" she asked nervously.

He forced a sigh. "I wanted to apologize for asking you about your job. I didn't mean to push you in a way that could get you into trouble. You don't need to share your work with me. I understand. It's just that . . . it's my first time in a situation like this and I like you so much that I just wanted to know everything about you. But I understand."

Now it was Olivia's turn to sit in pensive silence.

Capra had planted the bait. Do or die. If she resisted now, it meant that he had gotten all he was going to get. If this was the case, he would use the little information she had given him in a different way, take a different approach from here—

"Pietro, I don't work at the Embassy."

Capra's blood surged in his veins. He all but held his breath to keep from interrupting. Still lying in his lap, she stared at the ceiling as if she were attending a session with a therapist.

"I'm an MI5 agent," she said softly. "The British Security Services. I've been working for years to monitor a secret that, if revealed, could seriously hurt my country. A secret that has now fallen into the wrong hands. Much of the situation began back in your country. And my Italian friend I was telling you about came here to help us finish this. I don't know if you heard, but in Sicily, some people have died in the past few weeks, been murdered. All to steal this secret. And they succeeded. Now we know the thing we need is here in New York, in the hands of a very powerful man, a rich Englishman with no scruples and a lot of power."

Capra's heart pounded so hard it made his voice shake. "Are you an expert on ancient literary works, then?" Capra pressed, trembling, hoping she would be more precise. Piece by piece, the puzzle was coming together. Only a few more pieces and he would have it all.

"Yes, I am," Olivia replied. "And the thing we are looking for is a series of ancient letters that reveal an old secret, hidden for centuries by the English Crown and the Vatican, letters that could reveal that someone was not who we have believed he was for hundreds of years."

Chapter 19

Marchese got up from the sofa and put his clothes back on, wandering to the window and gazing at the lights of the city below him as he buttoned his shirt. Kathrine remained on the couch, looking up at him. He could see her staring in his periphery.

"I have to tell you something important."

He felt her tense, even from several feet away.

"What is it?"

"It is no coincidence we met," he said, fixing his eyes on a street lamp as if its light would anchor him. "I was sent to meet you. I had to get close to gather information that involves David Graham."

He turned and saw her staring at him, still as a statue, her face a mask of contrition and pain. The sight nearly broke his heart.

"The British Security Services brought me here," he confessed. "Five women were murdered in my city, all for the sake of the killer getting his hands on some long-lost ancient documents. In an attempt to stop the killer , my closest friend and colleague, Carlo Torchia, lost his life. MI5 thought that I might perhaps, by going through you, extract the information they needed to recover those letters. I accepted because I wanted to stop this man. I also want to avenge my friend's death, or maybe give his death some meaning so it will not be in vain. I wanted to stop the evil that's already been achieved from going even further."

Kathrine's lips began to tremble. She opened her mouth, closed it again. Then she took a shaking breath. "Francesco, I know," she whispered. "I know everything." There was finality in her tone, like she'd just played the last card in her hand.

Marchese gaped at her, bewildered. "What do you mean by *everything*?"

"I know why you're here," she explained. "I know you're here for Graham. I saw your picture in David Graham's office. They know you're here. And they know you're here to retrieve the letters."

"Then you know," he said softly, "that Graham is the one who ordered those women killed?"

Kathrine paled, but he saw resignation in her eyes, rather than shock. "I've . . . come to that conclusion, yes."

Marchese approached her, sat down on the couch beside her as his legs refused to hold him up anymore. He took her hand. "If you know, why did you let me into your life?"

Her voice trembled. "Mr. Graham asked me to find out what you had in mind and to keep you busy."

Hope surged up so fiercely it burned his throat. "Why are you telling me all this then?"

Kathrine squeezed his hand. "Because I started falling in love with you the moment you fell off that treadmill. And I hoped it wasn't true. I was hoping you were feeling something for me, too."

Her shoulders slumped as she wept. Marchese pulled her against his chest. Her arms were limp in her lap, and her tears rolled over her cheeks and spilled onto his skin.

"And you, Francesco," she murmured into his shoulder. "Why are you telling me all of this? What do you want from me?"

Marchese pressed a kiss to her brow. "I fell in love with you, too," he whispered.

Kathrine sobbed in earnest, but her arms rose and tightly encircled his waist, and Marchese found he was weeping.

* * *

Capra rose gingerly from the couch, taking care not to wake Olivia, who had fallen asleep on him. He looked down at her. Like a child, she lay on her back among the large leather cushions. She was naked, beautiful, innocent.

The journalist was out of his mind. Now he knew everything. The puzzle was complete.

Marchese was in New York to retrieve the letters containing the secret to Shakespeare's Italian origins. That he had been the reporter of the news of the deaths of the young girls of Messina. His television network had been the first one to launch the news to warn the victims, and Capra had been the first to know that the letters held the truth about William Shakespeare.

Those letters were cause of all these killings. And they could prove the true origins of the famous playwright.

Capra was already thinking ahead to the news his channel would issue: The proof that William Shakespeare was from Messina exists! And he would be the one breaking the news to the world. This time he wouldn't sell a few thousand copies of his novel, as he'd done before, but millions—millions of copies worldwide.

He had been right. His intuitions had been spot on. A rich, unscrupulous Englishman had found them. Now he had to understand what those letters really contained, what power they could truly wield in the right hands. He wanted to see and read them.

Capra was staring out the window, watching the cars pass by on West Broadway below him when Olivia screamed.

"Pietro!"

The reporter toward her. "What? what's wrong?"

"I had a terrible nightmare" she replied, hugging herself.

Capra restrained a sigh of relief and went to sit beside her, stroking her bare back. "Quiet. It's just a dream. Relax."

* * *

Kathrine had run out of tears. She rose stiffly from the couch and crossed to the window. At midnight, Central Park was more eerie than inviting, a beautiful oasis in the day that turned deadly in the darkness.

"This is a terrible mess, Francesco, a terrible mess."

She turned to find Marchese looking up at her thoughtfully. David Graham knew all about his operation and had asked her to keep the former detective busy while he solved the logistical problem with the letters, to give MI5 the run around and make them come up with no results at all.

But she had fallen in love with him instead. Now the two of them had laid their cards out.

"David Graham says he didn't know what Mark Connell was doing to retrieve the letters," she said shakily. The words rang false as she said them. "He says he didn't know about the victims and the killing. And that he would never order something like that."

Marchese's tender gaze crumpled in sympathy. "Graham knew, Kathrine," he insisted gently. "Not only did he hire someone to kill those women but, when their letters escaped his grasp, to recover the rest of them he arranged the murder of the bishop of Messina, along with his driver, a few days ago in Rome."

Her hands flew to her mouth. A new spring of tears began rolling again over her cheeks. Until then, she had understood she was working for a dishonest man, but not a murderer.

"David Graham is an unscrupulous murderer," Marchese went on, visibly restraining his anger as he spoke. She let her hands drop from her face and he took them in his. "He's had many people killed to get his hands on those letters. It's not just a matter of dirty business. Those letters represent for England a secret that the Crown wants to preserve. I don't care about that, personally. Whether Shakespeare was Sicilian or English doesn't change anything for me, but not so for England."

Kathrine firmly held Marchese's hands, as if she were holding onto a life preserver. Graham would do anything to achieve his goals. She knew he ran an illegal business in certain aspects. She was paid to be his administrator and to keep his agenda. She had not been privy to the fact that the work she did had led to the death of innocent people. She had believed the letters had been retrieved—stolen—from the Church, but that all this had brought about blood, death and sorrow at David's hands stunned her so entirely that she felt numb.

She gazed at Marchese, the man who loved her and would protect her. The happiness she had felt at first with his confession now mixed with the despair the truth about Graham.

"What shall we do now, Francesco?" she pleaded, her fear evident in her quavering voice. "What can we do?"

"Don't worry, Kathrine, I'm in this with you, now," he soothed, stroking her face and then her hair. "I won't let anything happen to you."

"I'm not afraid for me, Francesco," she replied, all the trembling suddenly gone from her voice, "but for you."

The topic of the letters—and what they represented for their future together—seemed suddenly too heavy. When morning broke and Marchese left Kathrine's apartment, she was still sitting on the sofa. They had not slept all night, nor had they talked about that ephemeral future, leaving that conversation for the coming evening during dinner in the Village and instead discussing what lay ahead and trying to work through the scenarios. Logical strategy seemed easier than hope. Kathrine was to go back to office that morning and tell Graham that nothing really new had emerged, that they had met and met again the previous evening—that everything was going as he had asked.

Just outside the building, Marchese turned toward Fifth Avenue, where he would take a taxi back to SoHo.

* * *

The sunlight streaming in through the living room curtains woke Capra, and he winced. Olivia lay beside him, her eyes closed, nestled in his arms. His head throbbed mercilessly, and he grimaced at the headache he felt sure he deserved after the drunkenness of the night before. His rising disturbed Olivia, who woke up complaining for the same reason.

She stood up and joined him in the kitchen, kissing him good morning with lips that tasted too much like the wine that was to blame for his misery. "Do you have a suit for tomorrow night?"

"No, I will buy one today," he replied, shuffling through her kitchen medicine cabinet for aspirin.

"Mmm," she purred, winking. "If I did not have to work, I'd come watch you. You in a dark suit in a dressing room?" She wriggled suggestively.

Capra's headache seemed strangely diminished at the implication. "I can wait for you, if you want!"

Olivia slumped. "No, better not. I have a busy day today. But I'm sure that, as a proper Italian, you know how to choose your own suit."

Capra chuckled, then hissed as the laughter hammered at his temples. "I'll try to make you look good tomorrow, I promise."

Olivia swallowed the two aspirin he held out to her and smiled. "Oh, I am sure of it."

* * *

When Kathrine entered Graham's office at 9:30 a.m., he motioned to her to join him in the adjoining meeting room. This happened often, but this time, she felt her heart plummet. Now Mr. Graham frightened her. She found him disgusting and felt sick at the thought that, for so many years, she had helped him in his diabolical business. She felt faint at the thought of how many times she had talked on the phone with his various henchmen, all who, in order to feed Graham's greed, had killed innocent people.

Graham took his seat at the head of the table and fixed her with an unblinking, feline stare. "Have a seat, Kathrine."

She sat down in her usual chair, wearing her usual smile, attentive to what her boss was going to tell her. As always. The difference was this time, her heart was elsewhere. She no longer saw a successful businessman in front of her, only a dirty, soulless murderer.

"How are you doing with Francesco Marchese?" Graham asked amicably.

"Good, I'd say," she replied as mildly as she could manage. "We met again last night. We had dinner. I talked about work in general. He hasn't asked me specific questions for the moment."

"Anything relevant to tell me?" Graham asked, tapping his pen on the table.

"Nothing I consider as such, Mr. Graham. He's acting like a gentleman at the moment. And as far as telling him about my work, I never went beyond the fact that I deal with the importation of works of art. No reference to the letters by either of us."

Graham nodded, folding his hands on his chest in a gesture that would have seemed like satisfaction if not for the coldness she now perceived in his eye. "Good. I can't wait to meet this fellow tomorrow night at the gala. I will be curious to see him in person."

Kathrine kept her expression carefully neutral. From what she had learned about her boss, she understood he would not hesitate to kill Marchese, or even her, if he thought his goals might be jeopardized. Her mind flashed back to the car she had seen twice the night before. What she'd chalked up to paranoia now seemed very far from it. She was almost sure Graham had ordered his men to stalk her, and a chill went up her back.

"Actually, Mr. Graham," she blurted, "there was something relevant."

Her boss sat up a little straighter. "What, Kathrine? Tell me."

"Marchese spent the night with me."

Graham's mask gave way to surprised expression. "Did you have sex?"

"No, sir," she lied. "We drank a lot at dinner and then I invited him for a last glass. He drank more than one and he fell asleep on my couch."

Graham laughed loudly, raking a manicured hand through his hair in disbelief. "Oh, God. MI5 can't find an agent that can tolerate alcohol? It's not the first time this has happened. We once found one in a bar, covered in vomit. He'd been trying to get one of my men drunk and extract information from him. In the end, my man had to call Scotland Yard to have him picked up."

Kathrine smiled slightly, sick at the thought of what unsavory things Graham might have elected to do instead.

"Very good, Kathrine," Graham crowed. "Well done."

* * *

The office door clicked loudly as Kathrine exited. The smile remained fixed on Graham's face as he grabbed the phone, dialing a number with more force on the keys than was necessary.

"I believe we must bring the matter to a close. It's getting dangerous. We need to move them."

He peered at Kathrine from behind the window that led to the office area, barely concerned with a response.

"Yes, right after the gala," he said, hanging up without so much as a "good day."

* * *

A number of MI5's team were missing from the noon meeting. As Marchese noted this with considerable unease, Dean Zona publicly announced what he had told Marchese days before: A collateral operation was being carried out.

"I can't reveal all the details yet," he clarified, "but today we must focus on the gala scheduled for tomorrow night. We were able to get an invitation from the Embassy, which we have given to Olivia."

"I was also invited," Marchese interjected.

All heads swiveled toward him.

Marchese shrugged. "Kathrine Leed asked me to accompany her."

There was a moment's silence before Zona replied, "This is an indication that she trusts you. Whether or not it's wise for you to go is another matter entirely."

For a moment, Marchese considered telling them how it really was with Kathrine. Zona might be pleased to know he had won her to their side and that she would cooperate with them. But he was no fool. He knew MI5 wasn't so secure as they wanted him to think they were; he wasn't sure anyone present in the room was entirely trustworthy.

Zona bowed his head toward the papers piled before him, clearly thinking. Marchese watched him intently. He didn't really care what Zona's preference would be. He was going to be next to Kathrine at the gala. He was going to look into David Graham's eyes. And by that evening, he was going to have a plan in place to take possession of the letters. He already planned to discuss the matter with Kathrine that evening. She would help him because they had developed a bond.

* * *

It was 3:55 p.m. when Capra left his hotel, crossed the street, and entered the Prada shop via its back door on Mercer Street.

A young man greeted him even before the door closed. As he led him to the men's department, he asked, "Looking for something special, sir?"

"I am attending a gala tomorrow night," Capra replied, fingering the cuff of a navy blazer. "I need something elegant."

"Perfect," the chipper man answered. "I'm sure we can find something suitable for the occasion. I can also arrange for a tailor for same-day adjustments."

The young man disappeared behind a staff-only door, while Capra admired the luxurious textiles. Few people milled about in the cavernous space, which had once housed the Guggenheim Museum—a Chinese businessman sporting an ornate diamond ring, a handful of eager salespeople, and a gentleman who strongly resembled the American actor Kurt Russell. Upon closer inspection, Capra decided it was likely the actor himself. "Only in New York," he whispered to himself.

The young clerk reappeared with three stunning choices. The journalist chose one among them and took it into the dressing room. From behind the curtain he heard the clerks whispering about Kurt Russell. Someday soon, the "common folk" would whisper about him. His next book, which he was already writing in his head about the secret of Shakespeare's origins, would bring him worldwide acclaim. Messina would laud him for bringing the city to the center of world's attention and for revealing the intimate truth about William Shakespeare's origins in such a well-written masterpiece.

When he stepped from the dressing room, the whispering stopped instantly. The clerk and his colleague beamed. "Dashing!" the salesman declared. "It doesn't even look in need of adjustments!"

Capra admired himself in the mirror. It looked as if the dark blue suit had been made just for him. His thoughts drifted to the evening ahead and then to Olivia and the letters. He'd taken a chance following Marchese to New York, but the opportunity it presented was beyond what he had hoped for. Feeling devious and full of himself, he turned to the clerk and said, "Everyone knows the Devil wears Prada.

* * *

Marchese strolled through the streets of SoHo. It was already after 4 p.m. and he hadn't yet found a suit. If only that were the least of his problems, he thought wryly. He stopped in front of Prada only long enough to scoff at their overstated reputation. He continued on Broadway, looking for something more to his liking.

Turning east on Prince Street, he saw Hugo Boss on the corner of Green and smiled. His phone vibrated as he was about to enter the store. It was Kathrine wanting to know his whereabouts. It had been years since someone he cared for wanted to know what he was up to, and he liked how it felt. He smiled at the sound of her silky voice.

"I'm about to buy a suit for the gala," he told her. "I'm at Hugo Boss."

"I'm sure you'll look sharp," she replied, sounding distracted.

Marchese frowned. "Is something wrong?"

"Nothing," she said hastily. "I just wanted to hear your voice."

"You'll do more than hear my voice later," he said with a chuckle. Clearly she was worried about him. He supposed the worry was warranted given his mission, and suddenly, he began to worry about her, too. "Meet me at seven at Olio e Più in the Village," he said. "I asked around, and it came highly recommended."

"I know it—and love it," Kathrine said brightly. "We can even eat outside if you'd like."

A moment later they ended the call. Their conversation had seemed so ordinary. Marchese was very simply happy, despite all that was happening. He was in love—him, the drill detective, melted like a popsicle on a sidewalk in summer by this incredible woman, who seemed even more beautiful in her soul than she was on the surface. He didn't know where this was taking him, but he knew he had to concentrate on the case first. He had to trap Graham and recover the damn letters if he was to have any chance of making that happiness last.

* * *

Olio e Più overlooked Greenwich Avenue, right on the corner of 6th Avenue in the West Village. Marchese sat at an outside table with his large Hugo Boss bag on the chair beside him.

Kathrine had told him she'd be coming from the Washington Square subway station, which was only a minute away. Marchese stood up when he saw her coming and greeted her with a kiss on each cheek. She responded with a kiss on the lips. They both laughed.

"This is a great table!" she said taking her seat. "It feels good to have a breather. I had a very busy day taking care of last-minute details for the gala."

The waiter brought a bottle of Perrier and filled their glasses. When he stepped away, Marchese's smile faded. "Did Graham ask you about our relationship?"

"He did," she said soberly. "He asked how it was going. I was vague. I told him you spent the night because you fell asleep drunk on the couch. I have a feeling his men are following me. It's why I took the subway."

That last news made him scowl, but he reached out and took her hand. "Well done."

"What are we going to do, Francesco?"

"I'm thinking it over," he replied, stroking the back of her hand with his thumb. "We must be careful. Tell me what you know about the letters."

Kathrine nodded firmly, her full lips thinning as she pressed them pensively together. "They're being stored in his safe here in New York. In a few days, he'll meet with the British ambassador, I believe to propose an exchange. He wants the queen to give him something in return for the letters. I don't know what. Only then will he transfer the letters to London."

Marchese nodded, trying to hide his disappointment. "I am aware of all this. Do you have access to the safe?"

"No. No one does." Her shoulders slumped in defeat. "It is protected by a sophisticated alarm system that only Graham can get into. It requires several complicated steps to open. I don't think it's possible to access it without him present."

There had to be a way. Marchese wracked his brain for an answer and saw by her distant expression that Kathrine was doing the same. "How do you think the letters will be moved when time comes?"

"I don't know yet," she replied, "but I think Graham may bring them to London himself, probably by his private plane."

"Too risky. I don't think he would do that."

Kathrine frowned. "Why not?"

"Graham is smart. He knows we're waiting to catch him red-handed. I believe, when the time comes, someone else will bring the letters to London by. On a different flight or on the same flight. But he won't carry them on his person."

The waiter approached and took their orders: Tagliatelle Bolognese for Marchese and Barbabietole with shrimp for Kathrine. While they waited, they spoke of Graham only a few moments more before turning the discussion to Torchia and the other tragic occurrences in Messina. Kathrine's grip on his hand tightened as he described watching Torchia being loaded into an ambulance—the last time Marchese had seen his friend alive. Then Kathrine asked the question that had been at the forefront of Marchese's mind since the night before. "What will happen to us—you and me—after all of this?"

Marchese was terrified to approach the answer, and he could see she was too, but it needed to be asked. "I do not know," he said honestly. "I just know that I feel whole when I'm with you. I want to know where all this will take us, too. I'm not afraid of the future, and I'm open to making sacrifices to be with you." He paused to gaze into her eyes. "I could make New York my home."

Kathrine took Marchese's free hand in hers, her smile reassuring him that she felt the same. But he wanted to hear her say it. "And you? What do you think?"

"I could make *you* my home," she said without hesitation.

He could have leapt to his feet, scooped her up, and sprinted toward such future right then and there. But for now, they had to make things work. He had to close this case. And he couldn't let David Graham escape. The letters wouldn't be transported to London by Graham's own hand, of that he was sure, and he had to find a way to intercept them from the safe to the carrier. Access to the safe was clearly impossible. If the letters were to be moved, it would likely occur after Graham's meeting with the ambassador. He needed to know what Garnham wanted in exchange for the letters and what kind of guarantees he would want in place before delivering them to the Crown. Marchese knew he had to scare Graham into acting sooner.

* * *

A few city blocks away, David Graham met with the most trusted members of his board of directors in Carbone, a classic Italian-American restaurant in NoHo. They sat at a small round table, and Graham cleared his throat to indicate he had an announcement to make. He noted with an inward smirk Kathrine's absence, a deliberate choice on his part.

Having had his men tail her for the past few days, he'd realized two things about his most trusted assistant: this romance with Marchese was more than an act for her, and she clearly thought her boss was far less clever than he actually was.

Just hours before, he'd stood before his safe, holding the ancient letters gingerly in his hands as if cradling the power and prestige they offered and that he could finally feel was within his grasp, and he'd come to the important decision he now voiced to all assembled.

"I have decided to transfer the letters to London on Sunday. After the gala tomorrow night, I'll be taking the necessary steps to move my treasure from my New York office to my London townhouse."

His words were met with surprise.

"You must have a compelling reason," remarked one of board members.

Graham nodded. "My instinct tells me MI5 is getting close. They are trying to distract me with this impotent Italian cop. They have something up their sleeve, and I must outmaneuver them."

"How do you plan to do it," interjected another member, "without risk of interception?"

"I won't carry the letters to London myself," Graham said coolly. "And neither will any of you. I am going to delegate the task to one of my men—one the MI5 will never suspect."

* * *

When Capra walked through Olivia's door that evening, she was standing by the stove.

"What are you doing?" he asked, coming up behind her.

She kissed him and smiled. "Tonight, I'm going to try to impress you with *my* cooking."

Capra peeked over her shoulder and grimaced. Olivia was making fish and chips.

She gave him a worried frown. "Don't you like fish and chips?"

"It's very American, but I trust you," he said, embracing her around the waist and resting his chin on her shoulder while she attended to her cooking.

"Did you find a suit?" she asked at length.

"I did—at Prada."

He felt her perk up. "Nice! I wonder the best-looking Italian man at the gala will be."

Capra's head jerked up . "What do you mean?"

"My Italian friend will also be at the gala. You can meet him."

Capra's blood ran cold. "The one who's helping you with the historical find?"

"Yes, that's him," she replied easily.

Capra stepped away from her and paced the room. This posed a problem. If Marchese attended the gala and saw him with Olivia, he would be found out.

"Are you okay?" she asked, turning from the stove with a spatula in her hand. "Are you jealous?"

"No," he said quickly. "Absolutely not. It's just that you told the Italian fellow is in law enforcement, and you work for the MI5. This is all new to me. I feel like I'm in a spy novel."

Olivia scowled at him. "You *must* forget what I told you last night. Forget that I work for MI5. I don't even know why I told you. This is a *highly* sensitive case."

Capra raised his hands in mock surrender. "You can trust me."

Her frown slipped, and she crossed the room and kissed him. "Promise me you won't mention this again."

"I promise." *Until the next bottle of wine,* Capra thought, nodding and smiling at her.

He didn't have to wait long. Within a few hours, they had finished dinner. Olivia could cook just fine, but he still loathed fish and chips. They were on to their second bottle of wine and had moved to the couch in front of the window overlooking West Broadway.

Capra pretended to sip. "Why is your Italian friend attending the gala?"

Olivia sighed, raising her eyes to the ceiling. "Again about the job," she said a little impatiently. "I told you not to mention it again."

"Shit, Olivia!" he snapped. "It's just a question about something you brought up intially, not me!" Capra rose from the couch, looking as upset as he could muster. His irritation was not entirely false; running into Marchese at the gala would expose him and mark the end of his journalistic investigation, and—he was surprised to find this thought stung—an end to him and Olivia.

He knew no one would buy that his being in New York and at this gala was a coincidence. His true identity would come out to Olivia, and she would not take it well—at all. He had to find a solution or an excuse not to go.

"Sorry, Pietro," Olivia said anxiously. "I'm just a little on edge today."

"It's nothing, I am sorry," he replied quietly, trying to look contrite. "It's just that, to me, this is all new. Dating a woman who can only talk about half her life is something I can't handle."

With that, he turned his back turned to her and stalked to the window, crossing his arms over his chest. He heard Olivia get up, and presently her arms wrapped around his waist.

"I know," she muttered into his shoulder blade. "Sorry."

The journalist did not move. He had to push his hand and find a way out of this situation. But breaking up with her seemed the only way out, and for some reason, he couldn't bring himself to do it.

"Tomorrow's gala is organized by the man we are looking for," Olivia said suddenly, her voice pitched anxiously higher. "I'm going on behalf of MI5 with an invitation from the embassy. Francesco, my Italian friend, was invited by the man's administrative assistant, who happens to be quite beautiful. It actually is s a twisted spy story." Her fingers sank into the front of Capra's shirt. "Is that better now? Are you coming to bed? I want to make love to you."

Capra's mind was made up. He could not miss the opportunity to witness everything up close—all the players under the same roof. He still didn't know how to solve the problem of encountering Marchese. If he could only ward him off . . .

Olivia's hand slid lower on his stomach. His worries completely forgotten, he turned, wrapped his arms around her narrow waist, and carried her into the bedroom.

* * *

If it was true that Kathrine was being followed, she and Marchese had to be careful. She would go home first and hope that whomever was following her would figure they were done for night. Marchese would later enter her building via a side door, as an extra safety precaution.

As predicted, when Kathrine arrived at her apartment, Paul and Frank were lurking in their car a few dozen feet from the entrance. As she entered, she cast a glance their way and saw Frank's smirking face lit up by the blue light of his phone—

texting Graham, no doubt. A shudder went through her as she boarded the elevator.

Not far up the street, Marchese peeked out from under the brim of the New York Yankees cap he had bought earlier in a souvenir shop, watching as the car started and left the spot. He knew instinctively these were the men Kathrine had told him about.

Five minutes later, in which time no other parked cars moved from their respective spots, Marchese entered the building from the side door that led to 74th Street.

Inside the apartment, he found Kathrine sitting on the sofa. She had already poured their two glasses of rosé. "Did you see anyone?"

"No one I recognized," he replied. "But I saw a car pull away not long after you walked in, so I would guess that would be the car in question."

Kathrine looked defeated. "When will all this end?"

Marchese sat down next to the woman and caressed her shoulder. "Soon, Kathrine. Very soon, I think."

"What if something happens to you?" Her voice was frantic now. "If Graham decides to have you killed?"

"Graham is not stupid," Marchese replied, by strange way of reassurance. "Killing me wouldn't be smart. It would create a fuss he doesn't need or want right now."

Kathrine wrapped her arms around him and held him tight. "Now that I've found you, it would be a tragedy to lose you."

Marchese didn't say what he was thinking: Kathrine's life was also at risk. He didn't want to scare her any more than she already was. His thoughts went to Renata for a moment, kidnapped to blackmail him and then mercilessly murdered a few years earlier during the manhunt in the Aspromonte mountains. He knew what losing the person he loved meant.

It was a pain he absolutely would not—could not—repeat under any circumstance with Kathrine.

Chapter 20

MESSINA—AUGUST 17, 1943

It had been many days since Father Gabriele had first entered the great library of the curia. His job consisted of cataloguing the thousands of books kept within, and he spent many hours at the desk he had been assigned, beside a window from which he could see Via dei Verdi. He had immediately begun his work with dedication.

He had started at six that morning and had not taken a break, except to eat a piece of bread with cheese. Book after book, Gabriele inventoried for the curia catalogue the various authors, titles, publishers, and dates of printing, along with ancient copies of the Bible and the Gospel, plus books on philosophy, history and astrology.

Messina had been bombed a few days before and since then, no one had come into the great hall of the library to consult these books. These were devastating days for the people of Messina and for all Sicilians.

Gabriele put down the book he had just catalogued and grabbed a small text published by Sansoni Editori of Florence. It was *The Tragedy of Hamlet, Prince of Denmark.*

His thoughts immediately went to the stolen letters and what he had discovered in reading them. His hand began to shake. The memory of his guilty deed ate at him every day, and his soul refused to rest. He looked around to see if anyone was watching him before he slipped the little book inside his bag. There was only one thing to do at this point. He no longer knew where the casket was kept, so he would have to deal with the letters another way.

Marchese surveyed himself in the bathroom mirror. The dark gray Hugo Boss fit him very well after a few minor adjustments, and he had paired it with a silver tie and shiny black dress shoes. He was almost ready. The limousine would pick him up shortly after it picked up Kathrine.

The evening had finally arrived when he would be face to face with David Graham. Each aware of who the other was. He reminded himself to check his anger. Graham, the instigator of the murders, of the death of Carlo Torchia, of the murder of the bishop of Messina—Marchese had to keep calm to succeed in outwitting him. He also had to keep Kathrine safe. To Marchese, that was his most important task. It would be a long night.

* * *

Across the street, Capra looked out his window toward Marchese's. He had seen the former detective meticulously preparing himself for the big event. Capra was ready, too. His stomach turned uneasily at the thought of his encounter with the Detective of Steel.

He didn't know how Marchese would react or what would happen with Olivia. How would she would react, knowing he wasn't the person she believed he was? Once she'd figured out that he knew Marchese, she would suffer on so many fronts—although, as an MI5 agent, she should know how to overcome these kinds of situations. That was what Capra kept telling himself.

He had come to New York to follow Marchese and he had a serious affair in the process. Now he wanted to have the letters in his hands, to see and read them—Shakespeare's famous "lost years" potentially explained in those lines, written by the hand of the famous playwright himself. Everyone knew that only a few pages existed as evidence of his calligraphy. Some of these were kept safe under the lock and key of the Crown.

Those letters were worth a fortune, both monetarily and historically. He absolutely had to see them.

* * *

Olivia dabbed a little more blush on the apple of her cheek and stepped back to check her face in the bathroom mirror. She had bought a reasonably priced green silk gown a few days before in a shop on Broadway. She certainly couldn't afford a Prada on her public servant's salary, but she loved her dress and knew it accentuated all her curves in just the right way.

She knew her mission came first and would be on high alert throughout the evening, but she was still excited to arrive at the gala on the arm of her Italian boyfriend. She laughed. How long had it been? Not very, she told herself. Could she really call him her boyfriend?

Despite how much she still had to learn about Pietro, she felt a real connection with him. On the surface, he was a clean, charming, and intelligent gentleman who made her feel good both in and out of bed. At the thought of the few nights they'd already spent together, a rush of warmth swept over her. She wondered how she'd keep her hands off him during the gala. Well, there was always immediately after the gala, she thought to herself with a chuckle.

* * *

Kathrine stepped gingerly into the company's black limousine. Her black mermaid gown blended with the black leather seats. She gazed out the window as the car headed south on 5th Avenue. She thought about a potential future with Marchese, wondering if their affair would continue in the coming years.

Her life had changed so drastically in a week. She had found love, had tasted terror, disappointment, passion, and uncertainty. A whirlwind that left her breathless. Nightmares always followed the passion she shared with Marchese each evening, despite how sure she felt that he'd keep her safe as long as he was near. The uncertainty of their future threatened to break her resolve, and she almost asked the driver to turn around and take her home. It was all too intense, and she wanted it to end. She wanted to hurry into that future with him and never look back.

Kathrine's limousine arrived in SoHo and pulled up in front of the Fanelli Café. Marchese was already descending the steps, and he waited barely an instant for the limo to stop before he opened the door and slid in beside her.

"You're looking handsome," Kathrine said with a glowing smile.

He kissed her gently on her cheek so as not to spoil her lipstick. "And you are looking quite stunning," he replied.

"Are you nervous, Francesco?" she asked, grasping his strong hand.

"Very much so," replied Marchese, nodding significantly toward the driver.

Her eyes darted to the front seat and she gave a tiny nod. Her free hand latched onto his arm. Marchese smiled at her as the car left for Cipriani.

David Graham rose from his desk and checked his watch as Paul and Frank marched into his office. Shortly, he would reach the party hall at Cipriani on 42nd.

"This is the briefcase you asked for," Frank said, placing a black briefcase on the table between them.

Graham ran a thumb over the chromed, designer insignia on the face of the case and smiled. An elegant but understated means to move the letters to London. The flight was already booked for the next day, and soon, secure in his country home outside the English capital, he would issue his ultimatum. Then the ambassador and the queen would have to decide what they would do. There were many possible outcomes, one of which led him straight to the dream of his life: National managerial control of all of England's museums along with a noble title. He would become the most recognized person in the art world. The artistic heritage under the control of the Crown was extensive and impressive. He would have access to the works in the catacombs of the kingdom and to all the valuable records. It was his Cibola. Just the thought of made his pulse race.

"Excellent work, gentleman," he said, adjusting the cuff of his dress shirt and straightening his silk tie. "Let's away to the circus, then, shall we?"

* * *

When Marchese and Kathrine arrived at the entrance of the historic Cipriani, they were waved right in to the gala. Kathrine had, after all, orchestrated the whole thing. As they walked deeper in, Marchese admired the high ceilings, the ornate columns, the large draped window overlooking the hall —a time capsule of New York's golden age.

Kathrine caught him gazing around and chuckled. "I'm sure you have more majestic places in Italy."

"I suppose," he conceded. "I've always been a little allergic to elaborate places like this. Not to mention neck ties." He tugged at his own and gave her a wink.

"I can see that about you," she replied with a playful smile. "No worries. You can take the tie off later."

He knew what she meant and gave her a hooded stare. When he broke his gaze away from her, Marchese's eyes locked with David Graham's from across the room.

Graham had been talking with one of the prominent guests, but he instantly excused himself and walked toward them. He had an angular jaw, and his hair was just disheveled enough that Marchese instantly knew it was deliberately so. Graham was clearly practiced at making less perceptive people feel comfortable around him. But the first thing the too-perceptive Marchese noticed were Graham's piercing eyes, which honed in on them with unwavering, almost predatory focus.

"You are simply glowing, Kathrine," he said appreciatively before turning to Marchese. "And you must be her mysterious companion. Kathrine has told me about you."

"Nice to meet you," replied the former detective, trying to flash a confident smile. "Francesco Marchese."

"A pleasure to meet you, Mr. Marchese. I hope we will have a chance to know each other better. It will be a busy evening for me, but I will try to find time for the fellow who, as I understand it, might just have won the heart of our dear Kathrine."

Marchese smiled again, despite the chill that ran through him. Was it possible Graham knew? "We're still just friends, Mr. Graham," he said, patting Kathrine's hand. "But who knows?

Maybe you'll share some secrets that I can use to conquer her heart."

Graham's smile broadened to a grin as he nodded toward Kathrine. "If we are talking about Kathrine, I will certainly do my best. What you ask is no mean feat!"

* * *

When Capra and Olivia arrived in front of the restaurant, the street was choked with limousines, the traffic almost paralyzed in front of the famous venue overlooking the Grand Central station.

Capra felt his nerves kick in as he looked out the window. He knew that Marchese was, most likely, already inside. There was no turning back now; he would have to face the situation and see it through.

"Are you impatient, Pietro?" asked Olivia, seeing him looking pensively at the crowd.

"Olivia," he blurted, "I have to tell you something important."

"What is it?" she asked, placing her hand on his thigh.

He turned and stared at her, and her eyes widened at the look on his face. "Regardless of anything that might happen between us, I want you to know that I actually like you very much. And that—" Capra halted and stared at the floor, shocked at himself.

Olivia squeezed his leg. "What's wrong, Pietro? Go on, finish."

"Nothing," he said, forcing a smile as he raised his head, "I guess I am just a little nervous."

Olivia's expression softened. "Don't be. We're going to have a fabulous time. I know I'm technically going to be working, but we will still have fun."

Capra's smile just barely held. He knew there were no words to justify what would soon happen. Her disappointment would be heavy. He had always known his ambition had a price. Capra was convinced that life was a battle, and in war, it is accepted that one must leave victims along the way. It was not the first time he had used someone to climb the stairs of success.

He already regretted the suffering that would surely come for Olivia. He would have caused this unsuspecting woman, who had opened up to him, a lot of pain and embarrassment. She had wanted only, perhaps, his sincere affection. And part of him had wanted to reciprocate.

* * *

Marchese and Kathrine were seated at a table with six others, identified by the place cards on the table as the chief of Police of New York, the managing director of a large software company, and a Republican senator, each one accompanied by his spouse.

In the distance, he saw Graham talking to a man wearing a clearly visible earpiece, perhaps a member of security. For an instant, the two looked toward their table, and Marchese had the impression they were talking about him. He knew Graham had told Kathrine to invite him to the event to gauge him and to make him believe Graham was unaware of his role at MI5; Kathrine had told him as much. Or maybe Graham was suspicious and wanted to know if there was something now between him and Kathrine—and if she was betraying him.

He felt Kathrine grab his hand in an iron grip—just as Olivia Fisher and Luigi Capra entered the hall.

The floor dropped out from under Marchese's seat, his vision blurring in shock. His mind raced. What was Luigi Capra doing in New York? What was he doing in company of Olivia Fischer, an MI5 agent?

"Francesco," Kathrine hissed. "You're hurting me."

Marchese loosened his violent grip on her hand, the anger and confusion within him reaching a boiling point. He felt his composure beginning to fray.

David Graham, Capra, Olivia, the letters, MI5. Kathrine. His mind reeled as the elegant room morphed into a lion's den in his mind. He no longer knew who his enemies and allies were.

"Sorry," he muttered, releasing her hand and rising from his chair. He pecked her on the cheek. "I need to use the men's room."

She caught him by the sleeve. "Is everything all right, Francesco? Is something wrong?"

"Everything's fine," he replied, gently patting her hand. "Nothing to worry about."

He slipped out of her reach and stalked toward the bathroom, half-dazed and furious, staring at Capra as he crossed the room. For an instant, their eyes locked and the reporter blanched. But he didn't look surprised in the least. Marchese restrained himself from slamming through the bathroom door with enough force to snap it off the hinges.

He stalked to the nearest sink and braced his hands on its porcelain lip, staring unblinking into the mirror at the door behind him.

A moment later, the door swung open again. As it closed, he whirled and seized Capra by the collar of his expensive jacket, slamming him against the tiled wall and staring murderously into his eyes. "Tell me what you're doing here," he snarled, speaking Italian for the first time in days, "and what you are doing with Olivia Fischer?!"

Capra stared back at him and flashed a nervous, utterly bewildering smile.

* * *

Graham noted Marchese's exit from his periphery.

"The Italian detective is under control and is harmless," Emanuel Tertón assured him, adjusting the clip that attached the earpiece wire to the lapel of his navy suit. "In a few hours it won't be a problem anymore."

"I trust you on this," Graham replied dismissively. "And where are we with our dear pontiff?"

"Everything is where we want with that, sir," Tertón answered smoothly. "He is too busy asking for explanations from the English Crown to care about you. I also wanted to ask you if, afterwards, we can attend to my situation that—"

Graham firmly cut him off. "Tertón, at the end of this situation, we will resolve it. You're doing well, as I hoped you would. You have done a good job. The pope's attention would have been a big problem, and your assistance will be well rewarded, my dear friend."

Tertón smiled and raised his glass in a private toast. "Thank you, Mr. Graham."

* * *

Ten minutes had passed since Marchese disappeared into the bathroom. Scanning the room, Kathrine's gaze intersected with Agent Olivia Fischer's. She also appeared to be looking for someone. *Maybe something really is wrong,* Kathrine thought, and she stood up, determinedly heading for the bathroom.

At that moment, Marchese emerged, looking considerably less tense.

"Francesco, what's going on?"

"Nothing, " he soothed. "Let's sit down. Just a small inconvenience, but trust me, I hope I took care of it."

As the couple returned to their table, Marchese saw Graham still talking to Tertón. "Kathrine, do you know the man who is talking to your boss?"

She followed his line of sight and searched her memory. "No, Francesco. He must be some outside delegate. I only recognize the local authorities or entrepreneurs with whom we have art business relations. And he's not one of them. Why?"

Marchese glanced over at Olivia and saw Capra sitting beside her. Her expression was fierce.

"I get the impression," he replied, turning his eyes back toward Graham, "that he was staring at me while he was talking to your boss."

A few tense hours passed. Marchese barely tasted his food, and he forced himself to avoid scanning the room for Capra or Graham. As the waiter circled their table again, collecting empty plates, Graham himself appeared at Marchese's side and placed a hand on the former detective's shoulder.

"So, my friends, how is the evening going? Are you enjoying yourselves?"

His smugness made Marchese want to crush his hand like an egg. That hand had indirectly pulled the trigger on too many innocent people.

"Lovely, Mr. Graham," he said mildly, clamping down on his anger. "All very refined. I imagine you will raise much money for your charity tonight."

"We'll see!" Graham replied with clearly false modesty. "That is our goal and we will know better by end of the evening."

Marchese glanced at Kathrine to see her smiling at her boss. But he felt her trembling where her knee touched his under the table. As another of the guests approached Graham, wanting his attention and he moved off, leaving them alone, she leaned in to whisper, "Francesco, do you want to leave?"

"Can you do that? I mean, don't you need to oversee the rest of the evening?" he asked, remembering she was responsible for this extraordinary display of opulence.

"No, I've assigned all the various tasks to others. I've no doubt the evening will go as well as it has these last ten years. Can we go?"

Marchese gave her a reassuring nod.

As they made their way toward the exit, pausing to retrieve Kathrine's wrap from the coat check, he saw Olivia angling toward them. She approached him nonchalantly, deliberately avoiding eye contact.

"Is something wrong?" she asked in a calm and low voice.

"There's a lot happening," he muttered, "but I can't talk to you now."

"Call me when you're alone," she ordered, reasserting her position with the Italian officer.

"I'll do that. Enjoy the rest of the evening."

As Marchese left the hall, Capra caught his eye again. The reporter sent him a nonchalant smile and raised his glass in salute, then winced, raising his other hand to rub his still-sore neck.

* * *

The limousine wound up stuck in traffic on Madison Avenue. Marchese and Kathrine stared into the night through their respective windows, their hands still loosely entwined between them.

"What went on in the men's room, Francesco?"

Marchese wanted to tell her everything. Of the shock of running into Capra and his past relationship with the slimy reporter. He was incensed at Capra's showing off with Olivia and his vulgar ambition of chasing Marchese to gain a story. But, at the moment, Kathrine already had enough to think about. They had to focus on getting the letters.

At the gala, he and Kathrine had behaved like friends. They had avoided showing affection or even holding hands visibly in front of other guests, working under the assumption that if he didn't suspect their affair, David Graham shouldn't feel threatened by their relationship. Kathrine would be risking her life otherwise; Graham would not tolerate betrayal.

"Nothing, really," he said. "The heat and situation all had a strange effect on me and I just needed to freshen up a little."

She leaned closer to whisper in his ear. "What do you think of Mr. Graham?"

"I don't care at this point, I just hope he doesn't suspect you're working with me," said Marchese, his eyes on the impassive driver. "It would make it harder to get to the letters and, above all, it would put you in danger. We need to act quickly and figure this out before the ambassador returns from London."

"What are you thinking of doing?" Kathrine asked. The look on her face suggested it was hopeless.

Marchese remained silent, thinking it over. It seemed that everything had stalled, a dead end, and this last obstacle was the most difficult. "I'm working on it" he replied, turning his eyes to her and squeezing her hand. "I'm working on it."

The limousine stopped at Kathrine's building and she got out alone. The pair had decided that Marchese would return to his apartment that evening to avoid suspicion in case whomever was spying on her was still hanging around. They had agreed to meet at 9:30 a.m. in Long Island City the next day. They would take a stroll facing the city skyline, have lunch, and discuss potential plans for that crucial week ahead.

Chapter 21

A rap at her door woke Kathrine with a start. Confused, she grabbed the alarm clock from her nightstand. Barely 8 a.m. Who could it be at that hour on Sunday morning? She scrambled out of bed, pulled on a pair of jeans and a T-shirt, and rushed to the door.

From the peephole she saw David Graham, accompanied by a man she didn't know. Her heart stopped. What did he want at her apartment, and at this hour, on a Sunday, and why had he come in person? It had happened in the past that he picked her up in his limousine, but *never* had he come to her door himself—and never on a Sunday.

Graham knocked insistently again.

Kathrine ran her hands through her hair, her mind racing and terrified. He could be there to kill her or to have her tortured. There was no valid explanation for this visit. She wished Francesco were there to deal with this. She had no doubt now that her boss was downright evil, and now no one was there to save her. Her phone was in the bedroom, and she was sure Graham would run out of patience before she could get to it and text Francesco.

She sighed deeply and opened the door.

Graham beamed at her from the hallway. "Kathrine, I hope I didn't disturb you too much on this Sunday morning. Can we come in and sit down?"

The man flanking Graham gave her a look that told her he had known she was alone and that Marchese has not spent the night. It took her a moment to place him—the limo driver from the night before.

"Certainly, Mr. Graham," she said shakily, covering her mouth as if to hide a yawn. "What has happened? To what do I owe this visit?"

Graham took a few steps into the apartment, waiting for her to close the door behind them before his smile turned into a serious and concerned look. "We have a problem and we need to move into action quickly. You are the only person I trust to help me, and it is imperative that none of the people involved to date with what I am about to share can hear from you going forward."

Kathrine's heartbeat thundered in her ears. "What's this about, sir?"

The businessman sat down in one of her plush velvet armchairs and laid a fine leather briefcase on the coffee table between them.

He stared at Kathrine. "I need you to leave immediately for London. In this briefcase there are very important documents that must arrive there tonight. I've just booked for you a first-class seat on the next flight departing from JFK. I know I am asking this without warning and preparing you ahead of time, but it is vital to the operation."

Kathrine scrambled to figure out what was going on—what was really behind what Graham was asking her to do. And what was inside the briefcase? He'd said "documents" instead of "letters." "Is it something related to the letters, Mr. Graham?"

"Yes, Kathrine, and we must act now. Don't worry about packing your suitcase. You can use your company credit card to buy whatever you need when you arrive in London. My car is waiting for you and Gregory will accompany you to the airport right away." He pointed to the man lurking in the doorway.

Kathrine's thoughts raced. Graham, asking her to follow him immediately to London? *Why me?* she thought. *Why is he choosing me?*

Maybe they would take her to an isolated place and kill her. Or maybe the briefcase actually contained the letters and he was really trusting her. If that were the case, this was the occasion that Marchese had been waiting for.

If warned, he might have the chance to intercept the briefcase. Everything could come to an end.

"Okay, Mr. Graham," she said calmly. "Just let me get my phone and my purse, and I'll be ready."

Graham's expression hardened, and a chill went up her back. "I'm sorry, Kathrine, but I think it's better if you leave your phone with me. I don't want MI5 to track it and discover your movements. We can't risk it. Once you have handed off the briefcase, you'll be free to come back or take a few days off. But until then you must avoid contacting anyone, especially with Marchese, who is *not* on our side."

She couldn't inform Francesco. She would have to carry out the operation by herself and risk her life with the letters. The room seemed to close in around her.

She sighed. "As you wish, Mr. Graham. I see this, and you are right. I had not thought about that."

She had to meet Graham's demands without arousing suspicion, maintaining the appearance of a trusted employee —a faithful collaborator.

"Thank you, Kathrine," Graham sighed. "As always, I appreciate your loyalty. Your flight leaves in less than three hours, let's go."

Rising, he passed the black briefcase into her hands.

* * *

Marchese had arrived early at their meeting place. Sitting at the LIC Corner café, he barely registered the busy street before him, absorbed with how to push Graham to transfer the letters before his meeting with the ambassador and how to position Kathrine to be able to warn him when this would occur.

MI5 could not break into his office, with or without a warrant. The risk of not finding the letters was too high. Things had to be done a certain way.

Always a political issue, Marchese thought. They had asked him for his help for just for this reason. He could get his hands dirty where they could not, and they had relied on his desire for vengeance and justice to keep him focused on their goal.

But things had become complicated. Now, Kathrine's safety was also at stake.

His phone rang and he answered. "Marchese here."

"It's Dean Zona, Mr. Marchese," the agent replied, his voice uncharacteristically tense.

The hair on the back of Marchese's neck stood on end. "What's happening?"

"I've just received a call from the Embassy," Zona said hurriedly. "It seems that two hours ago a flight was booked from New York to London on behalf of Miss Leed. Did you know anything about this?"

Marchese's hand, laid flat on the table, now curled into a fist. "For London? Leaving when?"

"In a couple of hours."

Marchese sprang to his fee, swiveling his head as if some explanation might spring out at him. "Who made the reservation?"

316

"It's an online booking," Zona replied, "paid for by credit card in the name of a company linked to David Graham's organization. We don't know anything else."

Marchese strode for the door. Kathrine was leaving for London? When they had scheduled their rendezvous at the café, she hadn't spoken at all about a trip or seemed to be hiding anything. Something was wrong.

"Let me call Kathrine and I'll get back to you soon."

He hang up without another word and called Kathrine. Her phone rang until her recorded voice asked the caller to leave a message. Then he dialed the number from which Dean Zona had called him. Zona answered on the first ring.

"She didn't answer," Marchese said sharply. "Something is happening. Send me the flight number and the terminal details. I'm going to the airport."

Zona's tone was almost patronizing. "Marchese, I've already warned a couple of our people who are already on their way to JFK. Now the matter is under our control."

"Listen, Zona," Marchese barked, trying to flag down a cab, "if Kathrine is going to London she is doing it against her will. She would have warned me."

"It is simply that the woman is faithful to her boss," Zona replied sharply. "Clearly this trip had been planned for some time and she didn't tell you. Maybe it's nothing important and has nothing to do with the letters, but that is for MI5 to decide at this point. We will keep you informed. As I told you, we have our plan B."

Furious, Marchese hung up without another word, just as a taxi pulled up before him.

"To JFK!" he ordered, scrambling into the backseat. "As quickly as possible."

"Which terminal, sir?" asked the driver.

"I'll tell you in a moment," he replied, already dialing Olivia's number. "Step on it."

Olivia picked up immediately. "Looks like you were duped, my Italian friend," she said with disappointment.

"You must believe me," he pleaded, clutching the phone, "Kathrine is not leaving of her own will. She'd have warned me. We had a rendezvous in Long Island City this morning."

"Maybe she made the appointment with you just to send you astray, to keep you busy while she left the country. You believe that's possible, don't you? Zona is convinced that's case. He says maybe your cover was blown and they played you."

Marchese pressed thumb and forefinger to the bridge of his nose. "You have to trust me. I can't explain everything to you now, but you have to believe me."

A painful pause intervened.

"What do you want me to do? My hands are tied."

"Please just give me the flight number and the terminal info. I don't need anything else."

There were a few more seconds of silence. "It's a British Airways flight. Terminal five. The flight leaves at eleven-thirty."

Marchese could have collapsed in relief. "Thanks, Olivia. You'll see that I'm right." He hung up and shouted to the driver, "Terminal 5, quickly!"

* * *

Capra frowned as Olivia turned over to face him, looking irritated.

"Your Italian friend?"

"Yes, that's right," she huffed.

Capra knew Marchese well, and whatever was going on, he knew that Marchese would be in the right. The detective's intuition was hardly ever mistaken.

"I think you should go to the airport, too," he said softly.

Olivia stared at him. "Why are you saying this?"

He reached out and tucked a strand of hair behind her ear. "From what I understand, there is an operation in progress in which you are totally invested. Would you want to be left behind and let the others get all the credit for your success?"

Olivia's face fell. "Pietro, there will be no success. My friend has been duped and will fail. It was just waste of time."

Capra fell silent for a moment. Then he got up from bed and started hunting for his clothes. "Didn't you say that your organization brought this guy from Italy because of his great investigative skills? I think your boss is underestimating him. Like all of you, actually."

Olivia flinched at this last statement, but it seemed to get through. She bit her lip pensively.

"I'll take you there, if you want," said the reporter, handing her the thong she had dropped on the floor the night before.

* * *

Dean Zona stared at his phone for a long moment after Marchese hung up, squeezing it in his hand as he'd liked to have squeezed the Italian's throat. It had been a mistake to bring him on. Zona would rely on his "plan B."

He glanced down again at the spread of photographs on the table before him, all of them portraying David Graham in compromised situations, some more sordid and graphic than the others—chained up in ambiguous positions, leashed like a dog, performing blindfolded oral sex on other men. Zona wrinkled his nose and shoved them back into the manila envelope from which they had spilled.

Zona's "Plan B" consisted of an exchange. Letters for photos. After discovering Graham's vice, MI5 had installed several cameras in the apartment at 414 Broadway. Graham's visit, sometimes as frequent as once a week, had provided them a veritable goldmine of blackmail material.

Zona smiled as he sealed the photos in the envelope, sliding it into the breast pocket of his jacket and he marched out the door. It was time to confront David Graham.

* * *

As the car merged onto the La Guardia tarmac and approached his private jet, David Graham dialed a number from memory. "Paul, where are you?"

"At the airport, boss," his henchman replied. "I've just bought a ticket to London. Same flight as Miss Leed."

Graham's grip tightened on the receiver. "Good. Keep your eyes on her. Make sure she notices your presence and that she brings the briefcase with her when she gets on the plane. Call me as soon as you have her in your sight."

"Will do."

The car stopped at the foot of the steps leading to the plane. "And once the delivery is made," he said lowly, "get rid of the weight, cleanly."

Paul paused before he replied, "Got it."

Graham exited the car and nodded to the pilot waiting for him at the top of the stairs.

"Mr. Graham," he said, smiling as his employer hurried up the steps. "I'm happy to be taking you back to London. We are leaving in five minutes."

"I'm happy too, my friend. And may God save the queen."

"God save the queen, sir."

* * *

"This is crazy, Pietro," said Olivia as they climbed into the Uber he'd ordered. It was already 9:30. "I don't even know if we'll get there in time."

"Trust me," he said, his expression neutral. "You will thank me."

A strange thought occurred to her, and she gave him a questioning look. Capra replied with a reassuring smile, and she shook her head. What she'd thought couldn't be possible.

The car turned east onto Houston. It was Sunday morning and, fortunately, the traffic was quiet. Olivia looked at her watch. She thought Marchese had two hours to figure out what was really doing down. To find out why Kathrine was embarking on a flight to London and why everything was moving so fast. The ticket was issued early that same morning. Too early to be a scheduled trip. Perhaps Marchese was right. Perhaps the woman was not aware of the flight, or maybe, as Dean Zona supposed, David Graham and the woman had outsmarted the Italian detective. Olivia's mind was crowded with puzzling possibilities.

* * *

The car carrying Kathrine took the JFK Airport exit. For the dozenth time, she considered opening the briefcase to see if the letters were inside. But with the eyes of Graham's driver watching her every chance he got, she couldn't do it in the car. She would wait until she got through security, after which she might be alone.

The driver parked in one of the pay parking stalls, and Kathrine realized with horror that the man intended to accompany her to the security gates. Sure enough, the man accompanied her to the checkpoint. As she passed through, she was directed to take the fast line reserved for VIP clients of the airline. The man didn't let her out of his sight until Kathrine was in front of the metal detector at customs.

Just as she came through the customs entrance and she began to relax, Kathrine locked eyes with Paul Morelli, seated near her boarding gate with his gaze fixed on her. It was all clear. She was under full watch and would be until she reached London.

There was no possibility of escaping with the letters—assuming they really were in the briefcase Graham had given her. Maybe it was all a ruse. Her heart raced so hard she felt her pulse fluttering in her throat.

She scanned the area and spied the women's restroom. *Paul wouldn't come in there,* she thought. She glanced at him as she entered the restrooms and saw he was raising his phone to his ear—calling Graham, no doubt. If Graham suspected she was doing anything stupid, she realized, accepted social protocol wouldn't keep Paul from storming that bathroom and putting a bullet in her head. She'd have to be quick.

Kathrine placed the briefcase on the bathroom countertop. She opened it and found a nondescript manila folder full of documents. She looked through them all. No letters. Only a contract for the purchase of some Chinese vases and a Renaissance painting.

She checked again. Nothing. But they'd rushed her here, kept her under close surveillance . . . *It's all too strange,* she thought. Rather than relief, she felt her anxiety worsen. Graham had come up with something, and it was not looking good for her.

She closed the briefcase and hurried out of the restroom. Paul was still sitting by the gate, staring at her over a newspaper. It was clear he didn't care to be communicated with; all she needed to know, as far as Graham was concerned, was that she was being watched.

She couldn't do anything. She had no letters. She would have to get on the flight for London. She thought about Marchese, waiting for her in Long Island City, in that little corner café where they had planned to meet and figure out a plan together, and her gut twisted with anguish.

Every nerve in her body told her she wouldn't be coming back from London. And Marchese would go forward in life believing she had betrayed him.

* * *

Marchese's phone began to ring as the taxi pulled up in front of Terminal 5. He checked it. It was Dean Zona. Perhaps Olivia had warned him of his Marchese's intentions. He was in no mood to argue with that English bureaucrat.

He let the phone ring and jogged to the check-in area. Kathrine was not there. He approached one of the desk attendants. The clock above her head read 10 a.m.

"My wife is taking a plane to London," he said, out of breath, "and has forgotten her cell phone. Can I see if she has already checked in or not, since I can't call her?"

The young English woman behind the counter gave him a skeptical look. "I cannot give you this information, sir. I'm sorry."

"Really, miss," he begged, white-knuckling the edge of the counter. "I just want know if she is safe at the gate and someone can deliver the phone to her or if she hasn't arrived yet."

The young clerk shook her head again. Marchese turned away from the desk, scanning the busy terminal, and then turned back to the counter. "I need a one-way ticket to London, no baggage."

The clerk cocked an eyebrow. "Which flight, sir?" she asked testily.

"The eleven thirty," he replied, recalling Olivia's earlier information.

"Your passport, please."

Mercifully, he'd thought to take it with him that morning, on the romantic notion that perhaps he and Kathrine might make good on their wish to flee together after they'd met at the café. The thought didn't seem so fanciful now as he handed the document over the counter.

She huffed and started typing on the keyboard in front of her. Several agonizing moments later, she returned it, along with a boarding pass. "The plane will start boarding in a few minutes."

"Thanks!" he called, already striding toward the security checkpoint.

Messina—August 19, 1943

Father Gabriele returned to his desk after a brief lunch at the curia's mess hall. He had spent days leafing through books, transcribing titles, and cataloguing. But today he would had another task to undertake.

In his bag, he had the sixth book to take to his room. In the past days, he had brought home with him five works by William Shakespeare. The sixth now lay in his bag, waiting to return with him to his room where, as he had done with the other five, he would peel back the inside of the cover and hide the damnable letter beneath it. Then he would glue it back again.

The letters would be hidden in the cover of these books forever—safe, but not destroyed.

There was only one letter left.

He put his hand on the bag, as if he wanted to protect that otherwise valueless book. He still burned with guilt, but in this way, he felt like he was atoning for his sin. It would be as if he had never had the letters, and no one would ever find them.

The other fourteen were safe in a secret place, of which only the bishop knew. The six he had taken from the casket would now be safe as well.

He took his register again and, still cataloguing, he began to silently pray the Rosary.

Chapter 22

Marchese stood in line at the security checkpoint, his mind crowded with harrowing thoughts. He was worried about the danger Kathrine was in. Unbidden, his mind cast up that day in Aspromonte, in Calabria. The race against time—that unsuccessful race—to save Renata. Her lifeless body.

All that should have been prevented.

He checked his watch as he exited security—10:30 a.m. Kathrine was less than a few feet away. The plane would take off shortly. He had to rush.

As soon as he cleared expedited security, Marchese jogged briskly toward the boarding gate for London, scanning the area for Kathrine, his pulse hammering in his temple. He heard his phone ring again. Dean Zona.

He groaned and accepted the call, still swinging his head around, looking desperately for her. "Marchese here."

"There's news."

"What kind?" asked Marchese, slowing his pace. The London gate came into view up ahead.

Zona huffed into the phone. "We just learned that Graham took off from La Guardia a little while ago on his own plane."

In the distance, Marchese spied Kathrine lining up. His heart soared, but he kept his voice neutral as he headed her way. "I do not understand."

"You don't understand?" Zona snapped. "It was a hoax. Miss Leed's air ticket, the ride to the JFK—all our attention on the woman, while Graham, undisturbed, was leaving New York with the letters."

Marchese was a few steps away from Kathrine when she turned and saw him. Her eyes widened, the terror in them fading as tears of relief rolled down her cheeks.

"What now?" asked Marchese.

"That's not your concern."

Zona hung up without a goodbye just as Marchese reached Kathrine. She clutched his hand in a surprisingly strong grip. "I am being watched. One of Graham's henchmen is escorting me to London."

Marchese scanned the area and knew instantly whom she was referring to; the man looked absolutely furious to see him.

"What are you to do there?" Marchese demanded, watching as the man retrieved his phone and dialed furiously.

"I don't know. I thought I had the letters with me, but I checked the content of the briefcase. These are only insignificant documents. They got me out of bed just to bring this negligible paperwork to London."

Marchese's mind raced. Kathrine had been picked up at home. She was put into a car without her cell phone, escorted to the airport, and would be watched on the flight to London by one of Graham's henchmen. It couldn't be a simple hoax.

"Did you double-check the briefcase."

"Yeah," she replied, downcast. "It's empty. Only one folder containing contracts to purchase works of art."

Marchese turned and saw the man tailing Kathrine fidgeting in the line, glancing between his phone and the two of them.

"Why didn't they let you call me?"

"I don't know," she groaned.

"This isn't a hoax," he muttered to himself.

Her brows knit. "What do you mean?"

He explained what he knew: that Graham had taken off from La Guardia a short while ago and the MI5 believed he had the letters on him and her trip was just set up as a distraction. She agreed it could be possible.

"Is this his personal briefcase?" Marchese asked.

Her expression shifted from anxious to curious. "No. It's similar but it doesn't have his initials on it."

Marchese instinctively knew that Graham would never risk carrying the letters himself. It was too risky to his career and good standing to be caught in London in possession of the stolen letters.

"Let's get out of here," Marchese said, grabbing her by her arm. "The letters *are* in the briefcase. Let's go."

The woman blanched. "What?"

Marchese pulled Kathrine off the line, and the pair started toward the exit. As they passed Graham's man, his worried expression shifted to rage. They moved away from the gate, knowing that Graham's henchman would be on their tail. Marchese glanced over his shoulder. There was still a throng of people separating them.

"Give me the briefcase, Kathrine," he said as he grabbed it out of her hands.

She didn't complain and watched from the side of her eye as he opened it and handed her the folder inside. Without breaking stride, he tore off the upper part of the inner lining. Nothing. Marchese rotated the case and tore off the other side of the lining, tore away easily, revealing the fiberboard inner body of the case. Inside lay a small plastic frame, less than a quarter-inch thick.

"Oh my God, Francesco!" Kathrine exclaimed.

"The letters are in here," he gasped.

They crossed the exit of the security checkpoint, and the corridor became more crowded. Marchese glanced back to see Graham's henchman zigzagging through the travelers, straining not to lose sight of them.

"What do we do now, Francesco?"

"I'll figure something out."

Marchese tucked the small plastic frame under his arm, took the folder from her, and stuffed it unceremoniously into the briefcase, snapping it closed.

When he raised his eyes, he found himself face to face with Olivia and Capra.

Olivia's eyes widened. "Here they are!" she said, squeezing Luigi's arm. "We've been looking for you!"

Marchese smiled only slightly. Picking up the pace, he brushed them as they passed, pressing the frame into Olivia's hands before striding on past the checkpoint.

Without a backward glance, he hurried Kathrine out to the congested sidewalk. As the din of taxi horns filled his ears, Marchese turned, waiting to see if Graham's man had taken the bait. Seconds later, the man came storming onto the sidewalk, red-faced and fuming. Marchese stared him down.

"Where do you think you're going?" he huffed.

Marchese smiled. "Home."

"Not with that little briefcase," the henchman retorted menacingly.

Kathrine, terrified, squeezed Marchese's hand.

The former detective smiled at the thug. He could not be armed; he never would have cleared security. He raised the hand holding the briefcase.

"Fair enough," he said calmly. Then he pivoted on his heel and hurled it with all his might.

The briefcase clattered onto the opposite sidewalk. The hinges snapped, flinging the contents across the pavement like fallen leaves. Paul gave a strangled yell and darted into traffic, narrowly avoiding meeting his end on the front fender of a bus, reaching the opposite sidewalk just as Marchese pulled Kathrine into the nearest shuttle bus.

"I'm with the police. Can you get us to terminal one?" Marchese asked the shuttle driver, who grunted unhappily that he could. Marchese pulled out his cell phone and added, "Quickly, please."

* * *

Olivia and Capra sat at the terminal bar, silent and shocked. Olivia's heart was still racing.

"Do you think these are the original letters?" asked Capra, eyeing the case.

"I think so, yes," Olivia said, dazed. She picked up the phone and dialed Zona's number. "We have retrieved the letters."

Zona was silent for a moment. "What do you mean by *we*?"

"Marchese recovered them. I think they were in the brief case Leed was carrying. They are safe with me now."

All skepticism melted from Zona's voice. "Where are you now, Agent Fischer?"

"At JFK airport. I'll explain later, sir."

"Get here right away," Zona ordered.

"Yes, sir." Olivia hung up and looked at Capra. "Thanks, Pietro. If you hadn't convinced me to come here—" Her voice trailed off.

Capra winked mischievously. "You can reward me on the taxi ride back to your place."

"Nice idea," she replied, "but first I need to get these to the office asap." She looked around. "Actually, first I need to use the restroom."

Capra put his hand out. "You wouldn't think of bringing those ancient documents into an airport restroom, would you?"

Oliva wrinkled her nose. He was right. She'd have to put them on a wet bathroom counter while she washed her hands. She looked into his mesmerizing eyes and, with a trusting smile, said, "Guard these with your life. I'll be two minutes."

She jogged to the closest restroom, leaving the letters in Capra's care.

* * *

Capra stepped out of the airport and immediately got on the taxi line. He cradled the small plastic frame in his arms. He was next in line. As he waited, he saw the man who'd been chasing Marchese and his lovely companion scrambling to gather the scattered documents on the street across the way. He smirked. Once gathered, the man, looking quite pale, took a place behind him in the taxi line, muttering something about being fucked and wanting to kill that Italian bastard. Capra knew just who he was talking about.

He turned to the man and insisted he take his place as first in line. The clueless henchman climbed into the next available taxi a moment later, clinging to the briefcase, and shouted, "955 Madison Avenue."

As he waited for the next taxi, which was already pulling up, Capra considered how Olivia would react and guilt wrenched at him. He knew he was hurting her and, to his surprise, he hoped he would have the chance to explain himself. Likely she would never forgive him—or herself for trusting him. This would crush her, obliterating the light that shone so sincerely from her soft eyes whenever he looked at her. What he had done was almost as bad as murder. A sword right into her heart. His grief sharpened as he climbed into the taxi.

"Where are you headed, sir?"

Capra sighed and hesitated for a moment as he started down at his phone. Then he looked up at the taxi driver and smiled.

* * *

Olivia rushed out of the restroom and back to the table where Capra had been sitting with her minutes before. There was no sign of her Italian lover. Maybe Pietro had gone to the men's room, she thought. Or perhaps one of Graham's men had forced him to go with them. A dozen possibilities entered her mind. She fumbled for her phone and called Capra's number. After a few rings, it went straight to voicemail, inviting her, in Italian, to leave a message. A tear rolled down her ashen cheek.

She hung up and dialed Zona. After several agonizing rings, his voice came in brightly on the other end: "Agent Fischer, how close are you?"

She could barely bring herself to say it. "I'm still at JFK. I lost the letters."

Rage filled Zona's voice. "What the fuck do you mean you lost the letters?"

Olivia was silent for a few seconds. All the pieces were coming together. Pietro had appeared out of nowhere, a charming Italian. Meeting her by chance, he had made her fall for him, implementing every romantic ploy she could have thought of. He had extracted all the information necessary to get to the letters. He had pushed her to go to the airport, pretending he had no apparent sense of what was going on. He had been sure that Marchese was right without knowing him—or more likely, he did know Marchese. He'd known the detective before he'd even landed in New York.

He knew everything. And he was there to fool everyone.

That realization sent a searing pain straight to her stomach, as if she'd been by shot by a rifle. Everything was false. His attraction, his seduction and smiles, the sex—it was all a sham. He'd given her pleasure and whispered beautiful words, and every breath of it had been a lie.

The teeming crowd of travelers around her spun violently in her vision, and then she vomited and the ground rushed up to meet her as her world tunneled to blackness.

* * *

Marchese and Kathrine took their seats. Within a few minutes, boarding would end and the aircraft would take off, heading for Rome.

Marchese checked his watch.

"Are you nervous?" Kathrine whispered. "Tell me it's all over."

He turned to her and smiled. For an instant, at that airport, he had thought he was losing her forever. But he was sure she had not betrayed him. He knew—he felt—how much she loved him. He'd never doubted it. And it was that certainty that had led him to the letters in the briefcase. Graham was a duplicitous man and had thought of everything. If Kathrine had brought the letters to London, it would have been impossible for MI5 to catch him. But he hadn't counted on Marchese's steadfast faith in her bringing him to that airport terminal just in time.

Whatever Zona had in mind for "Plan B" was between MI5 and Graham. In the end, Marchese had been right. But there was still a bit more to do.

"No. Kathrine," he said softly. "It's not over. There's still one last thing to do."

As he spoke, a final passenger rushed aboard the plane with just a minute to go before the flight attendant closed the door. He dropped into the seat across the aisle from them.

"Thanks for paying for my ticket," Luigi Capra said with a smirk. "It was very nice of you, Marchese."

Marchese, unsmiling, stuck out his hand.

"Can I at least read them?" Capra pleaded.

Marchese scowled. "Nope."

Capra rolled his eyes and held out the frame. "Fine. Here you are."

Kathrine gaped at the two of them. "And who is he?" she asked, bewildered.

"It's a long story," replied Marchese as he slipped the frame into the seat pocket in front of him. "I'll explain later. Now let's relax and enjoy this flight."

Capra accepted a sleep mask from a passing flight attendant and reclined his seat. "Wake me when we are in Rome," he said, the journalistic smile fading as he spoke. "I haven't slept much these days."

Chapter 23

Marchese had risked a lot. Involving Capra had been a gamble. He could have handed off the letters from the hands of a determined killer to those of an even more ambitious and unscrupulous journalist than himself. But in that restroom the night of the gala, as Marchese had squeezed Luigi's neck, the detective had realized that everything was beyond his control. Between the presence of the journalist and Olivia together and the dead end they had hit with Graham, he really needed help. Someone outside MI5 to rely on. He'd known Capra was interested in the story and how he could profit. He also mistrusted MI5, their skills, and their final purpose. The letters belonged to the Church, not to the English Crown.

Capra had agreed. He'd had to, otherwise Marchese would destroy him. If he'd revealed the plan to Olivia, there would have been no way out for him. He knew that being on Marchese's side meant backing the winning side. And he'd wanted Marchese to owe him a debt for once. No one more than Luigi Capra knew Marchese's abilities and his tenacity —that he wouldn't give up until he had the letters. And Capra had been right.

The price Marchese had extracted was that Capra had to help him recover the letters. As a reward, the journalist would be permitted to write a book—*a work of fiction*—and break the news of Shakespeare's true origins in a roundabout way. Capra was already thinking of a title. Something strong and dramatic. One in particular circled in his mind as the plane turned toward Rome . . . *Shakespeare: The Last Dilemma.*

* * *

Olivia sat across the desk from Dean Zona, her head hanging in defeat, a glass of tepid water just barely balanced in her limp hand. Her career was over. She had trusted a stranger who had deceived her and lost everything—her dignity, her job, nothing was left. Her face was still wet from the tears and streaked mascara she had tried in vain to wipe away. And now, having told Zona the whole story—she'd realized halfway through that Pietro was probably a fake name and almost laughed at herself—silence filled the office. Her chest ached, but the rest of her was numb. Her faith in people had evaporated, her heart trampled without mercy by a man who had made her fall in love with him only to destroy her. How cruel, to kill a person's soul and leave without a word, knowing they had to go on and live their life, trying to pick of the pieces of what that betrayal left behind. It would have been better to die, she thought.

At that moment, the door swung open and another agent came running in. "We have news."

Olivia raised her head.

"I hope it's good news," Zona said sourly, running his hands wearily over his face.

The agent frowned, his eyes darting between his superior and Olivia. "I don't know. But we know where Marchese is."

Zona straightened up, then rose from his chair, his expression fierce. "Where?"

"On his way to Rome. And Ms. Leed is with him."

"What the fuck is he doing?" Zona demanded.

"I don't know. But there is something even more inexplicable."

Zona planted his hands on his hips and craned his head back, glaring at the ceiling in exasperation. "What?"

"Marchese bought three tickets on the same flight. For him, Miss Leed, and a guy named Luigi Capra."

"And who the fuck is that?"

The young man took a piece of paper from the small folder in his hand and passed it over. "I did a little research. It seems that he is a Sicilian journalist and writer. He arrived in New York on the same flight as Marchese a week ago. I have a picture of him right here."

Zona grabbed the sheet, looked at it. His scowl turned grim and he passed it to Olivia.

The photo left no room for doubt. Shock smote her again.

The Pietro she knew was actually Luigi Capra. From Messina.

And he was in this with Marchese.

"We all have been tricked," Zona said, sounding almost sympathetic now. "Marchese cheated us all. Me, Agent Valton, and you. Your friend Pietro—or rather, Luigi, stole the letters and then handed them over to Marchese. And right now they're all flying to Rome. Their purpose?" He shrugged wearily. "Anyone's guess."

Olivia shook her head. Marchese could not be that kind of person. He was honest. She could not have been that wrong about him, too. Everything proved him to be an unblemished man of principle. He couldn't have done it for his own personal interest.

Olivia stared at Dean Zona and rose shakily to her feet, clutching the photo hard enough to crumple its edge. "Marchese is bringing the letters to their rightful and original owners," she said softly. "He is taking them to the Vatican."

* * *

337

Graham's private plane touched the Heathrow tarmac just before 6 p.m. As he landed, Graham turned on his cell phone. Instantly, the notifications screen flooded with over ten voicemails, all from Paul. Unfamiliar anxiety rose in his chest. Before he could listen to the first of them, the phone began to ring.

"What's up, Paul?" Graham answered. "Have you already arrived in London?"

A few seconds of silence passed. "Marchese took the letters."

It took a moment for this to fully register to Graham—and then he punched the airplane window hard enough to bruise his knuckles. "How the fuck did that happen?"

"He showed up at the airport," Paul replied hoarsely, "and met Miss Leed before she left. He tore off the padding of the briefcase and the two vanished into thin air."

"How the fuck did you lose sight of them?"

Paul cleared his throat. "I went to Miss Leeds's apartment. No trace of the two. Frank is there now watching the place in case they come back."

"Asshole!" Graham roared. "Do you think they'd ever go back there? You are an idiot! I'm surrounded by idiots!" Graham hung up the phone. "Bastard, shit cop! You've ruined everything."

He stormed down the steps to the tarmac, clutching the phone in a white-knuckled grip. But no car waited to meet him. Instead, two MI5 officers stood blocking his exit at the foot of the stairs.

"What the fuck do you two want?" he snarled.

His fury had no apparent effect on the stone-faced officers. The one on his right spoke up. "Mr. Graham, we need to talk to you. We have something to share with you."

The man sighed deeply and looked at the sky. "Do I have a choice?"

"Follow us."

The two agents escorted Graham to a small conference room in the airport hangar, where they produced an envelope full of photos and laid them in on the cheap laminate table in front of him.

David Graham stared at the photos, expressionless. He spent a few seconds observing them. "And what would you like to tell me by showing me these photos?"

"We know you don't have the letters with you," said the agent who'd greeted him. "We know it well. And we know what you did to obtain them."

"But you have no proof," Graham said haughtily, "which means you cannot arrest me. So what do you want?"

The two men exchanged glances and then stared at Graham, their faces hard. "If you don't want us to disclose these images to the press," said the second agent, "you must listen to us very carefully. We want you to leave England forever. The Crown no longer appreciates your presence in this country. We want you to forget about the letters and if we even hear of any attempt on your part to recover them again, we are authorized to do anything to stop you."

David Graham smiled and looked down at the pictures again.

"And we mean," the first agent said sharply, "that you will leave England *right now*."

Messina—August 20, 1943

When Father Gabriele rounded the corner to face the curia, the acrid smell of smoke greeted him. He barely needed to raise his head to see the flames billowing through the roof. The windows had been blown outward, and charred bits of countless tomes flitted out the windows and twirled skyward, carried on waves of blistering air. The library had become a hell, fire and smoke enveloping everything. What few tomes could be saved had been heaped onto the pavement outside, a pathetically small testament to the thousands of others that had been swallowed by the blaze inside.

The pastor clutched his hand over his mouth, trembling, and turned away, staggering back the way he had come.

He thought of his work—of all the books turning to ashes. He thought of the letters and touched his little bag. The last one of the six was still inside it. He had planned to put the book back in its place on his return. The other five remained behind him, likely engulfed in flames along with the copies of William Shakespeare's books that he'd hoped would shelter them.

All was lost. The devil was taking them with him, the outcome that fate had deemed justified for his sinful act.

He stumbled into an alley, took out the copy of *Much Ado About Nothing* he had with him, and stared at it.

"You will stay with me forever," he whispered. "You will be my cross. The cross that I will bear throughout my life to atone for my sin."

With that, he straightened up and turned his steps toward the cathedral of Messina.

Father Gabriele could never have imagined what his act would set in motion in the future. The drama, the pain and the death that, because of his sin, would come because of these letters over the years. He did not know that the five books in which he had hidden the other letters would be saved and one day come into the hands of five people who would be swept away by the curse. The curse that began the day he had stolen them from the casket.

His sin would have fall to others. His temptation would be contagious and the strength of the secret would contaminate all who sought to hold them.

Rome—August 20, 2012

Kathrine held Marchese's hand as they crossed the central nave of St. Peter's Basilica. She gazed upward, stricken by its beauty. It was the first time she had passed through that door and she had not anticipated the emotional reaction it now elicited. It took her breath away. Michelangelo's Pietà, the sculptures by Bernini, and the imposing columns of its aisles exuded a power that could move even those usually indifferent to the pleasures of art.

"I've been to museums and galleries all over the world, but this, Francesco . . . this is incredible!"

She brought her eyes back to earth and saw Marchese was distracted with other thoughts; they had to meet the pope's private secretary shortly. But he squeezed Kathrine's hand, clearly pleased that she was feeling so inspired.

Since they had landed in Rome, Kathrine had slowly calmed down. They had not planned a future; they were just living in the moment. They bought some clothing in a shop in Via del Corso just before and had changed in the hotel they had booked in Via Condotti. But she knew Marchese would not rest easy until he knew that the letters were safe in the hallowed halls of the Vatican, one of the securest places in the world. They had only caused death. Whoever touched them ended up in a spiral of violence and pain. It was time to lock them back in the casket. Like the Ark of the Covenant, that wooden box, once opened, brought bad luck, death, and perdition.

Once they arrived at the corridor leading to the pontiff's offices, they found the pope's secretary, Cordovara, waiting for him. The shook hands. "Nice to meet you, Mr. Marchese,

Ms. Leed," he said, to Kathrine's surprise, in English. "Follow me, please."

The pair followed the man past several closed doors, up a grandiose marble staircase, and around a corner into a lavishly carpeted corridor lined with Swiss Guards protecting various doors.

"For security reasons, Mr. Marchese," Cordovara said, "we need you and your companion to clear another checkpoint. Please don't be annoyed."

Marchese nodded. "Certainly."

Six Swiss Guards waited for them in the control room. Among these was a man whom Marchese and Kathrine immediately recognized.

"Let me introduce you to the Commander of the Vatican's Swiss Guards, Mr. Marchese."

Emanuel Tertón met Marchese's eyes with a glazed look. There was a few seconds of silence, in which Kathrine could hear her own pulse throbbing below her ear.

The men shook hands. Marchese's knuckles were white as he gazed into the eyes of the man who, two days earlier, had been in the company of David Graham at the gala.

As they passed the checkpoint, leaving Tertón behind, Kathrine felt the commander's eyes boring into her back.

* * *

Tertón's hands shook as he ducked into the deserted staff bathroom and opened his cell phone. "Mr. Graham. This is Tertón."

"Go on."

Tertón swallowed hard. "I am in the Vatican. I've just encountered Marchese. I believe he's recognized me. He's here to meet the pope. I think—"

342

"You think he's giving him the letters."

"I don't know if I can stop it, he's too—"

"Calm down, Tertón," Graham said amicably. The calm in his voice was more chilling than any rage would have been. "I have no more interest in the letters. There's something else I want you to do for me."

"Mr. Graham, I do not know," Tertón pleaded. "I'm in trouble if he's recognized me."

"Tertón, don't forget what I possess. Your secrets. Your vices. I have everything in my files. You'll be in trouble if you don't listen to me. I want you to kill Marchese. And if Miss Leed is with him, kill her too."

"But Mr. Graham—"

The call was interrupted. Tertón stared at the phone, seized with despair. His life had been in Graham's hands for years, ever since those three prostitutes had knocked on his door. A trap Graham had laid for him to keep Tertón under his thumb. He thought of his shame, the disgrace that would rob him of his career. Of his wife and three children, who would never forgive this. Of his parents, his family, who had invested all their resources to make him a Swiss Guard.

Graham's instructions had been clear. As he walked toward the pontiff's private office, his petrified, desperate expression gave way to nothingness, to an unfeeling void.

* * *

Capra lay on the bed in his room at the Hotel Excelsior. It was all over. Now he had to put the story together and write a bestseller. As he stared at the ceiling, his thoughts went to Olivia. The woman had opened her heart and he had filled hers with misery in return. For the first time in his life, Capra felt emptiness inside him. New York had changed and confused him. He had tried not to admit to himself all through that interminable flight to Rome, but he had felt right with that woman. She had made him feel loved and desired as never before. In Messina, women flocked to his power and fame, hoping to get a television job or a connection to him for show. Even for a simple appearance during a talk show, women would offer sexual favors, and Capra had always taken advantage of it. His bed was a bustle of women, of young brainless Barbies who gave themselves to him with the hope of visibility. That magnetism had even followed him to New York, and he found he was regretting his dalliance with Antonella, about which Olivia had had no clue. He'd never regretted such a thing before.

Olivia was different. She'd wanted him as a man, not a business transaction. She'd purely fallen in love with him, even though he had promised her nothing.

Capra got up from the bed and got dressed. "Jet lag is playing tricks on me," he whispered bitterly to himself as he left the room.

* * *

The pope held out his hand to Marchese who knelt to kiss his ring. Kathrine did the same.

"My dear Francesco," the pontiff intoned, "you bear the name of the saint who inspired me so much in my journey of faith. And you too, today, you have been an inspiration not only for me but also for many of my colleagues and brethren. Your heroic gesture has saved something very precious to our Church. And although I can't do it publicly, I thank you from the bottom of my heart. I will always pray for you so that you can always continue on the right path."

"Thank you, Your Holiness," replied Marchese, handing over the frame containing the letters.

The pope gingerly accepted the frame, glancing at it briefly as a beatific smile filled his face. "I see and appreciate that not even curiosity touches you. You don't want to read what these letters contain?"

Marchese shook his head. "Your Holiness, these letters harm everyone who has ever come into contact with them. As it should be, they must be guarded and hidden again, far away from any kind of temptation. I feel relieved to get rid of them forever, and I will be much more comforted when I know they are safe."

The pope lowered his head, staring at the frame. His thumb stroked the corner of it. "I understand very well," he said softly, even sadly. "The devil hides in everything. Around every corner. For him, even the simplest thing can become an opportunity for revenge against the Creator."

A sharp noise split the air behind them—a gunshot, and close by.

Another rang out, closer this time, and Marchese gripped Kathrine's hand tightly.

"What's happening out there?" the pope exclaimed to his secretary.

Marchese understood instantly. Tertòn was there for him and for the letters.

Before he had time to seek an exit, the door burst open and Tertón strode in, his gun already upraised and aimed straight at Marchese.

Marchese's first thought was to grab Kathrine and shield her. Tertón fired twice.

* * *

Kathrine sank to the ground, pushed there by Marchese. Blood splattered her face and hands, stained her blue dress with blood. The stench of gunpowder filled the room, and Marchese groaned, rolling off her. Kathrine screamed out, but she heard no sound come from her mouth.

What followed happened so swiftly that she could later only barely piece it together. Two more shots rang out, and Tertón collapsed in a heap onto the marble floor. Two men in Swiss Guards' uniforms rushed in and strode anxiously toward her. Two others spirited the pope away through a small doorway that had opened beside his desk while his secretary shouted orders, his voice sounding to her disoriented ears as if it were coming from the bottom of a well. Three other men began dragging Emanuel Tertón's body out of the room.

She turned her head dazedly, feeling the marble floor grind against her skull, her blurry eyes striving to find Francesco's. Her tears mixed with the blood on her face.

Francesco's blood.

She groped for him until she found his arm. He made no move to take her hand.

At that moment, the two guards reached her, grabbed her arms, and tried to move her away.

Kathrine squirmed, screaming out Francesco's name as they lifted her from the floor. Then she saw him, sprawled on the ground at her feet. His shirt was soaked with blood. His eyes were closed, his body still. Beside him, a pool of blood spread slowly across the floor, gradually encircling the small plastic frame that lay a few inches from his body.

Chapter 24

Olivia was just closing her suitcase when a knock sounded on the door. Her flight would take off for London at noon. She had been transferred to MI5 headquarters.

As she rose from her seat on the bed, she recalled what she had been through in that house, in that city, the city that never sleeps and where everything can happen. Dean Zona had saved her job, knowing that he too had been screwed. Everyone had fallen into what they now called "the Marchese trap." Nobody knew the truth about how things had really gone; Marchese had vanished along with Pietro—no, Capra.

But it didn't matter anymore. Olivia's pride and feelings had been damaged beyond repair. Zona and the whole team that had dealt with Graham's case had been moved on to other sensitive operations, but she was going to end up behind a desk on the second floor of a steel building overlooking the Thames.

David Graham had sold his company shares and moved, along with all his wealth, to the Cayman Islands. He was no longer a danger to the English Crown that had unofficially banned him from England. Kathrine Leed had disappeared as well. The only one who could have shed any light on what had really happened after that frantic encounter at the airport was Luigi Capra. At the thought of him, Olivia felt a twinge of grief in her chest.

She opened the door. The young UPS delivery guy waiting in the hall gave her an envelope, made her sign the receipt, and took his leave.

She closed the door, walked to the living room, sat down on the couch, and opened the envelope. And pulled out a one-way plane ticket to London.

Olivia frowned, her sadness pierced for the first time in days by total confusion. She already had a ticket for the same flight. She slid her hand back into the envelope and pulled out a letter. It was from Luigi Capra. Within three lines, tears spilled down her cheeks.

STRATFORD-UPON-AVON—OCTOBER 10, 2012

Marchese trailed behind Kathrine as they ascended the steps of the Holy Trinity Church. She pecked him on the cheek as he drew abreast of her.

"Am I walking too fast?"

"No, Kathrine," he replied, squeezing her hand. "It's fine."

She frowned worriedly. "How do you feel?"

"Like someone who was shot twice."

Kathrine laughed. "Even now, you can't give up your attempts at humor, can you?" she asked playfully, pressing in on Marchese's arm.

Marchese had been publicly declared dead after the shooting in the Vatican. The pope and his general secretary had decided, together with Marchese, that his life would always be in danger; the letters carried a sort of curse. They created a new identity for him and gave him a Vatican citizenship. There weren't many people asking questions about what happened in their registry offices.

He'd been shot in the right arm and shoulder. No vital organs had been damaged. Ten days in a hospital under a false name were enough for the former detective, who had then checked himself out. Kathrine had stood by him night and day.

A few days later, the pope himself had visited him in the middle of the night and offered Marchese an appointment as the head of a department of the Vatican Secret Service. Marchese would travel the world, overseeing operations aimed at recovering stolen relics or documents that could damage the Roman Catholic Church. Marchese had accepted on condition that he could always have Kathrine with him. He had come to the conclusion that there was no safer place for her than beside him.

They both had changed their names. They had become Frank and Kathy Rizzo.

Entering the small English church, they headed leisurely toward the altar. At their feet, weathered marble slabs contained the remains of the Shakespeare family. The famous poet and playwright was interred in the middle. Next to the altar, a small glass niche held an ancient document.

"Is that what I think it is, Francesco?" Kathrine asked.

Marchese smiled. "The William Shakespeare's certificate of baptism. It says he was baptized here, in this church in Stratford-Upon-Avon, on April 26, 1564."

The two looked at each other knowingly, turned, and left the small church.

Once outside, Marchese stopped to gaze out over the gravestones of the small cemetery. The thick fog of the day made it all the more macabre, like they'd been dropped into a Sherlock Holmes movies.

Kathrine shivered beside him. "Do you think that one day the truth about Shakespeare will come out, Francesco?"

Marchese pondered the question. They had not discussed this since his brush with death in the Vatican. He had never been interested in the secret itself, not even in all those weeks of death and suffering.

"I don't know. I don't believe so. No one wants this thing to be known. And I really believe nobody really cares. Everyone's satisfied believing the story they've already been told about him. And maybe it's what's best. What matters is what Shakespeare left us as a literary legacy. Nothing else, really. And maybe, who knows? Maybe even Shakespeare himself wouldn't want the truth to be known. Otherwise, he would have made it known himself, at least on his deathbed, if it mattered to him."

Their shoes crunched on the frosty gravel as they made their way toward the car. As they left the last headstone in their wake, a familiar voice echoed out through the fog. "Mr. Rizzo, there is a woman who would like to say hello to you."

Kathrine and Marchese turned to find Olivia Fischer approaching from the graveyard, hand in hand with Luigi Capra. "Hi, Francesco," she said, waving cheerfully.

Marchese looked at the sky, feigning impatience.

Capra approached and gave them his most irritating smile. "You succeeded even where Romeo and Juliet failed. I gotta hand it to you."

"Don't tell me you came all the way to England to pat me on the back, Capra!"

"No, Francesco," Olivia replied, her smile disappearing. "We're here because the work you started unfortunately isn't finished."

"Life's but a walking shadow, a poor player that struts and frets his hour upon the stage and then is heard no more: it is a tale told by an idiot, full of sound and fury, signifying nothing."
—William Shakespeare, *Macbeth, Act V*

Made in the USA
Middletown, DE
25 April 2022